Secret seductions and hidden desires...

THE PARKS EMPIRE: HANDSOME STRANGERS...

Three of your favourite authors bring you
three glamorous, satisfying romances

THE PARKS EMPIRE: HANDSOME STRANGERS...

LOIS FAYE DYER

ELISSA AMBROSE

GINA WILKINS

MILLS & BOON

THE PARKS EMPIRE: HANDSOME STRANGERS…
© Harlequin Books S.A. 2009.

First published in Great Britain 2009
Harlequin Mills & Boon Limited,
Eton House, 18-24 Paradise Road, Richmond, Surrey TW9 1SR

The publisher acknowledges the copyright holders of the individual works, which
have already been published in the UK in single, separate volumes, as follows:

The Prince's Bride © Harlequin Books S.A. 2004
The Marriage Act © Harlequin Books S.A. 2004
The Homecoming © Harlequin Books S.A. 2004

*Special thanks and acknowledgement are given to Lois Faye Dyer,
Elissa Ambrose and Gina Wilkins for their contributions to
The Parks Empire series.*

ISBN: 978 0 263 87164 7

64-1009

Printed and bound in Spain
by Litografía Rosés S.A., Barcelona

THE PRINCE'S BRIDE

BY
LOIS FAYE DYER

Lois Faye Dyer lives on Washington State's beautiful Puget Sound with her husband, their yellow Lab, Maggie Mae, and two eccentric cats. She loves to hear from readers and you can write to her c/o Paperbacks Plus, 1618 Bay Street, Port Orchard, WA 98366, USA.

For my niece Carol and her husband, Simon.
May you have a long and fruitful life together.
Be careful, strive to be happy and remember
to always be kind to one another.

Chapter One

"Brenda, do you think the newspaper stories about Father are true?" Emily Parks cradled a delicate teacup, warming her chilled fingers against the heated china. Despite the seventy-six-degree temperature outside, the kitchen of Walter Parks's San Francisco mansion was shady and cool. The windows in the dining alcove stood open and a slight breeze blew in off the Pacific, carrying the faint tang of salt and sea.

"Hard to say how much of the news reports a person can believe." The older woman's voice held doubt.

"I've always known Father was completely ruthless in business, but it's hard to believe that he'd be involved in anything criminal."

"Impossible to believe that he might do something illegal?" Brenda's eyes were shrewd behind her glasses. "Or difficult for you to accept that a member of your family might have done something outside the law."

Emily frowned, considering the question. "Maybe it's more that I simply don't want to believe that my father is capable of being involved in illegal business deals. Heaven knows he wasn't much of a father, but he's the only parent I've ever known." She glanced up at Brenda. Seated across the small walnut table, her plump, five-foot tall body encased in a soft blue uniform dress, the Parks's family housekeeper exuded concern and maternal affection. Brenda wasn't Emily's birth mother, but in all the ways that counted, she'd earned the right to be called "Mom." "If it wasn't for you, I would probably have grown up with a revolving group of nannies."

"*Hmmph.*" Brenda sniffed, her teacup clicking against the matching blue Wedgwood saucer as she lowered it with a snap. "Your father never had any sense when it came to hiring household help. How he managed to build that jewelry store of his into such a powerhouse is a constant puzzle to me."

Emily laughed. "That 'jewelry store' is San Francisco's version of New York's Tiffany's, Brenda. I'm sure Father has razor-sharp judgment when it comes to hiring employees for the business, but I've always thought the only intelligent thing he ever did for his personal life was to hire you to take care of us all those years ago."

Brenda's eyes twinkled. "Now that was a win-win situation. I was free to spoil you four children with no interference from your father. And in addition, he paid me a good salary." She patted her short gray hair and winked at Emily. "I was able to save enough to go traveling this year."

"How did you like Paris?" Emily loved hearing Brenda's tales of her travels. She longed to travel but for the moment, her growing business demanded every hour of her time.

"I loved it—the Champs Elysée, the Eiffel Tower, the Seine, the Monet paintings in the Louvre's Orangerie..." Her voice trailed off, a reminiscent smile curving her mouth. "I think I'd like to go back there for my honeymoon."

Emily's tea choked her in midswallow. She gasped and coughed, her eyes watering. It took a moment before she could speak coherently. "Honeymoon? What honeymoon? I didn't even know you were dating someone!"

"I'm not." Brenda said, her plump face serenely confident. "But I've answered a few personal ads and met some very nice men. I'm sure that I'll eventually find someone that matches my requirements for companionship.''

Emily couldn't hide her astonishment. ''I didn't know you were interested in finding a husband, Brenda. I've always thought you were married to your job.''

''I was,'' Brenda agreed. ''After my John passed away, you children were a blessing and caring for you filled every moment. I didn't have the time or the energy to lose myself in grief, thank goodness. But now that you're all out of the house and don't need me anymore, I've been thinking more and more about finding a male friend to spend the rest of my life with.''

''You're amazing.'' Emily slowly shook her head. ''It takes a certain kind of courage to look for love even once, but searching twice in one's lifetime? You deserve a medal.''

''Courage?'' Brenda looked at Emily over the rim of her glasses, a small frown creasing a line between her brows. ''Why courage?''

''Because it seems to me that being loved once in a woman's life is a rare thing.'' Emily shrugged and lifted her cup. ''The chances of it happening twice have got to be slim to none.''

''Oh, hon.'' Brenda's voice held sympathy and she covered Emily's free hand with her own atop the table. "Not all men are like your father and the men you've dated."

"Perhaps." She didn't bother to hide the skepticism she felt. She didn't need to—not with Brenda. "But if there are any nice guys in the world—with the exception of my brothers—I've never met them."

"So you've given up on finding a prince?"

"I'm afraid so."

Brenda sighed. She sipped her tea and a smile curved her mouth. "It's difficult to believe that the little girl who loved fairy tales has grown up to be a woman who doesn't believe in love. Remember how you declared that you were going to marry a prince when you grew up, just like Cinderella?"

"I remember." Emily's answering smile faded quickly. "That was a long time ago, Brenda. Unfortunately little girls grow up and have to live in the real world. Much as I would love to have a real family, with a husband who would love me and cherish our children—I've given up on finding my prince."

"I'm afraid your father has a lot to answer for." Brenda frowned, concern chasing away her smile. "He's ruined your faith in men. But all men aren't like Walter Parks. And someday, somewhere, the right man will come along and you'll have the family you've always wanted."

"I hope you're right, Brenda," Emily's voice

held a deep well of sadness. "It would be lovely to believe in fairy tales again."

"Hmmph." Brenda shook her finger at her. "Just be sure you're paying attention so you can recognize him when he arrives. Not all princes ride a white horse and wear a crown, you know."

Emily laughed. "Yes, ma'am. I know. But while I'm waiting for him to ride up to my door, I think I'll spend my time building my company, since I suspect that dream has a much better chance of coming true."

Lazhar Eban was on his way to Walter Parks's library on the first floor of the sprawling mansion. Distracted by the contract he scanned while he walked, he turned left instead of right at the foot of the stairs, moved down a hallway and found himself standing just outside the kitchen, frozen by the conversation he'd accidentally overheard. The gold framed mirror hanging on the wall opposite him reflected the kitchen interior. On the far side of the room, tucked into a bay window looking out on the kitchen garden, was a comfortable dining nook where two women sat. The older woman was the housekeeper who'd shown him to his room late the night before. Lazhar instantly recognized the stunningly beautiful younger woman. Her thick mane of glossy hair was golden-brown, her eyes a bright green, and dimples flashed beside her lush mouth when she smiled. Emily Parks, Walter Parks's daughter, was the reason Lazhar had abruptly changed his busy schedule and flown to San Francisco.

Her photo had accompanied an addendum to a business proposal from her father, received at Lazhar's office only three days before.

Walter had approached him months earlier with a business proposal that had the potential to be lucrative for his country. He'd been on the verge of signing but had had second thoughts when the San Francisco newspapers publicly accused the American gem trader of questionable business practices. When he told Walter that he was reconsidering, Walter sweetened the deal by offering his daughter, Emily, as the bride Lazhar needed. The investigative report faxed to him from his security force as he flew over the Atlantic reflected an image of a sophisticated woman from a rich family, educated in private schools, who had built a thriving wedding consultant business in the years since graduation from college. His investigator could find no indication that Emily was currently involved with anyone, nor that she had been so since a canceled engagement some three years before. Emily appeared to be focused on her career, with her social life existing only as an extension of her work.

Given the fact that she was one of the most

beautiful women Lazhar had ever seen, he found it nearly impossible to believe that she wasn't involved with someone, but it appeared that she was not.

Which was all the better for him, he'd thought with satisfaction.

But in person, Emily Parks wasn't quite what he'd expected.

The beautiful face in the photo had fascinated him with the faint vulnerability behind the cool green gaze and the hint of passion in the sulky mouth. But the fleeting expression of stark loneliness that he glimpsed on Emily's face as she spoke with Brenda struck a powerful chord within him, calling to him on a level far deeper than her surface beauty.

She wanted to believe in fairy tales again.

A woman who once believed in fairy tales is a romantic, he thought, she'll never agree to a business merger marriage. His eyes narrowed as Emily pushed her hair back from her face and smiled warmly at Brenda. Even that small, graceful gesture from her was enough to send his blood pounding a little harder.

To hell with it. He wanted her. And he was going to have her, he vowed. It was good fortune that his need for a wife coincided with finding a woman that he wanted to bed.

But after overhearing Emily and Brenda's conversation, he knew he needed a change of plan. He was convinced there was no chance that she'd meekly agree to marry where her father commanded. Lazhar turned away from the mirror's reflection of the two women in the kitchen, moved silently back down the hallway, crossed the marble floor of the entry to the library and tapped on the heavy door.

"Come in."

Walter Parks looked up as Lazhar entered, a distracted frown quickly replaced by an affable smile of welcome.

"Lazhar, come in, come in." He gestured at the leather-covered chairs facing his desk. "Have a seat."

"Thank you." Lazhar dropped into the chair, his gaze flicking to the single sheet of paper in Walter's hand. "I hope I'm not interrupting?"

"No, not at all." Walter's fingers closed, slightly crumpling the sheet of paper before he dropped it atop his desk. "What can I do for you?"

"I've changed my mind about Emily."

Walter's tanned, lined face flushed, his cold brown eyes narrowing. "Why? Has she done something to offend you? Because if she has, I'll talk to her—"

Lazhar gestured abruptly, cutting off the older man's comments. "No, she's done nothing. In fact, I haven't even been introduced to her. I've simply rethought our original plan and decided that I don't want her to know about our business arrangement. I'll introduce myself and let matters take a more natural course.''

''Ah, I see.'' Beneath his salt and pepper hair, Walter's eyebrows rose, deepening the cynical expression on his leathered face. ''I take it that you're agreeing to my proposition, then?''

''If Emily agrees to become my bride, I'll sign the contract,'' Lazhar said. Walter's swift satisfaction was easy to read. ''But not until,'' Lazhar added.

Walter's mouth twisted in displeasure before the older man nodded his agreement.

''Excellent.'' Lazhar stood. ''I want your assurance that you won't mention anything about our arrangement to your daughter.''

''You have it.'' Walter rose and held out his hand.

The two shook hands, sealing the bargain.

''I'll be staying at the Fairmont Hotel on Nob Hill and driving there immediately. Since I don't want Emily to know about our plans, I think it's best that we aren't seen together before I have a chance to speak with her.''

''Very well.''

Lazhar strode out of the office, glancing back briefly. Walter was already focused on the sheet of paper he'd been studying when Lazhar first entered the room. He wondered briefly what had so riveted the businessman's attention but quickly forgot the incident as he crossed the entryway and moved swiftly up the stairs to one of the spacious guest rooms on the second floor.

"Your Highness?" A small man, hanging a snowy-white shirt in the closet, looked around with surprise.

"We're leaving, Pierre." Lazhar crossed the room to the desk and closed the lid on his laptop.

"Very well." The unflappable valet removed the shirt from its hanger and began to fold it.

Ten minutes later, his luggage tucked into the spacious trunk and Pierre sharing the front seat with the driver, Lazhar left the Parks estate and headed for downtown San Francisco and a luxurious Tower suite waiting for him at the historic Fairmont Hotel.

Meanwhile, Emily and Brenda were finishing their tea, unaware that they'd been observed by Walter's guest.

"I wonder if Father..." The back door burst open, startling Emily into silence. She didn't recognize the uniformed security guard who halted abruptly when he saw them.

"Sorry, ladies." His gaze swept the room. "We have an intruder on the grounds. Have you seen anyone?"

"No." Emily glanced at Brenda, who shook her head. "We haven't. Is this person dangerous?"

"I doubt it, ma'am. I think it's Maddy Jones, a reporter who's been trying to get past the gates to interview Mr. Parks."

"Oh, thank goodness, Andrew." Brenda's voice held heartfelt relief. "I was afraid a criminal was on the grounds. A reporter is a nuisance, to be sure, but only an annoyance."

"Yes, ma'am. We'll find her. If you see anything suspicious, let us know." The guard touched his hand to his hat and stepped back through the doorway.

"We will," Brenda called after him.

Emily pushed back her chair and stood. "I'd better get back to work, Brenda. Thanks so much for listening to me."

"You don't need to thank me." Brenda enveloped Emily in a quick hug. "I love having you visit. I don't see enough of you now that you don't live at home."

"I know. Work keeps me so busy." Emily linked arms with Brenda and they walked out the back door and around the house to the front courtyard, where her sporty little BMW was parked. "Why don't you meet me for lunch next week? There's a new French restaurant near my office that I'm sure you'll love."

"It's a date."

Emily hugged her goodbye and drove away, feeling immeasurably comforted by Brenda's down-to-earth wisdom and unfailing affection. As always, the older woman was a stable rock of sanity in what was often a dark world surrounding her father.

While Emily was leaving, Walter was frowning at the sheet of paper he'd picked up from his desktop the moment Prince Lazhar left his office. The letter was written by his daughter, Jessica, and addressed to his estranged wife, Anna, at the Switzerland sanitarium where she'd lived for many years. Cryptic though the words were, Jessica clearly stated that her mother's suffering would soon end and that Anna would be "out of her father's clutches" very soon.

"What the hell does she mean by that?" Walter muttered to himself, glaring at the sheet. He'd read the letter over and over, but couldn't decipher precisely what Jessica could be referring to. One thing he did know, he thought grimly, was that he had enough problems without his daughter and wife stirring up more. He wanted Anna to remain in Switzerland, safely tucked away as she had been during all the years since he'd first forced her to go there.

With quick decision, he picked up the phone and punched in the phone number for Sam Fields, an investigator he'd used in the past. He'd have Jessica followed and her movements reported to him. It was the easiest way to learn what she and her mother were up to.

Emily's office was organized chaos.

"It's barely nine o'clock and I'm already behind."

Emily glanced up. Her assistant, Jane, stood in the doorway, the neon-blue pencil tucked above her ear a bright spot of color against the corkscrew blond curls that brushed her shoulders. The bright blue was repeated in the paisley scarf draped artistically over one shoulder of her simple little black dress.

"It's crazy-busy today," Emily agreed. "Did you find the lilies for the Everston wedding?"

"Yes." Jane's pixie face lit with satisfaction. "It took five calls but I finally located some in Seattle. They're being flown down this afternoon."

"Excellent." Emily sighed with relief and took a sip of her vanilla latte. "How Mrs. Everston could have forgotten to tell us until the day before the wedding that her daughter simply must have lilies at the altar is beyond me."

Jane shrugged philosophically. "That's a mother-of-the-bride for you—stressed and forgetful. I'm just thankful she didn't want something that had to be flown in from South America or China!"

"Good point." Emily saluted Jane with her logo-stamped paper cup from the espresso stand on the corner. "It could have been worse."

"Emily?" Natalie, the receptionist in Emily's three-person office, joined Jane in the doorway. Her air of suppressed excitement was palpable.

Emily eyed her with curiosity. "What is it, Natalie?"

"You'll never guess who's on the phone."

"Who?" Emily and Jane waited expectantly.

"An aide to Prince Lazhar, the Crown Prince of Daniz."

Emily's eyes widened and she exchanged a quick, surprised glance with Jane. "Prince Lazhar? Of Daniz? What does he want?"

"He wants to schedule an appointment for the prince to meet with you this afternoon."

Emily didn't need to glance at her calendar. She already knew what her day looked like. She shook her head. "I can't possibly, Natalie. Maybe tomorrow." She flipped her desk calendar open to the following day.

"Emily, you can't tell a European prince that he has to go on a waiting list," Jane said firmly. "Especially not this prince. It's all over the tabloids that he's looking for a wife. Maybe he wants you to handle the wedding."

Emily was unconvinced. "I doubt it, Jane. You're talking about a royal wedding. I've never handled anything of that magnitude…I'm sure he'll hire a bigger firm, maybe from London or Paris, perhaps New York.''

''You'll never know unless you talk to him,'' Jane urged.

Emily glanced at Natalie and received an eager nod of agreement.

''All right.'' She turned the page of her calendar to today's date and skimmed it quickly. ''This is impossible,'' she murmured, as she ran her finger-tip down the list, shaking her head. ''I really don't have any openings, but…tell his aide that I'll squeeze the prince in between the Benedict fitting and the Powell catering conference.''

''Excellent.'' Natalie grinned. ''I've always wanted to meet a real prince.'' She disappeared down the hall.

''You're squeezing a royal prince in between an Atlanta socialite and a California movie star?'' Jane lifted her eyebrows.

''That's the best I could do. Katherine Powell is always late so I'm hoping I'll have a few moments before she makes her entrance. Speaking of which.'' Emily glanced at her watch. ''I'm already behind.''

''This is where I came in. Back to work for me.'' Jane waggled her fingers at Emily and dis-appeared down the hall. A moment later, Emily heard the murmur of her voice as she spoke on the phone.

''The prince of Daniz.'' Emily said softly, staring blankly at the blinking cursor on her computer screen. The news of the king of Daniz's declining health and his wish to see his son wed had been well chronicled in the press. What reason other than business could possibly have sparked his request for an appointment? Was it possible that the prince might actually be considering hiring her to plan his wedding? The prospect of the assignment and what it would do for the future of Creative Weddings was tantalizing.

She shook her head and yanked her thoughts back to the file open on her desk. She had far too much work to do today. Daydreaming about planning a royal wedding would have to wait.

Fortunately for Emily, the Atlanta socialite had booked a late luncheon and needed to cut her appointment with Emily short. Emily ushered the young bride-to-be and her mother out the door, walked to the ladies' room to freshen her makeup, and was just slicking color onto her lips when Natalie burst into the room.

''He's here!'' Natalie's eyes sparkled with excitement. ''And he's just as gorgeous in person as he is in print!''

''Is that possible?'' Emily teased.

''Trust me.'' Natalie fanned her face with her

fingers. "In his case, it's more than possible. It's a fact."

"Now I'm even more curious about the mysterious prince," Emily commented. She gave her reflection in the mirror one last inspecting glance, smoothed her palm over the scarlet suit jacket and across the hip of her pencil-slim skirt, and satisfied that she was tidy, followed Natalie into the hallway. They reached the reception area and Natalie veered off to her desk near the entry, gesturing significantly across the room. A tall, dark-haired man stood with his back to them, looking at a collection of French Impressionist prints on the wall.

"Your Highness?"

He glanced over his shoulder as Emily approached, then turned to face her.

Oh my goodness, she thought as she met the impact of eyes so dark a brown that they appeared black. *Natalie was right, he's drop-dead gorgeous.*

His lashes narrowed, his gaze sweeping her from head to toe and leaving a trail of heat in its wake.

"Miss Parks?"

"Yes, I'm Emily Parks. And you must be Prince Lazhar." *And you,* she thought, *are a dangerous man.* Not only was he handsome, with hair as black and glossy as a crow's wing, olive skin stretched taut over the planes of high cheekbones, black lashes so long and thick that it seemed a crime to waste them on a man, and a powerful body that was six feet four inches of toned muscle and hard angles, but he fairly oozed testosterone and radiated sex appeal. She wasn't sure what protocol required when greeting a royal prince, but held out her hand and managed a polite smile.

"Please, call me Lazhar." He smiled and took her hand in his. His fingers and palm were slightly rough against her own smooth skin.

"Very well...Lazhar." Realizing that her hand was still enclosed in his warm, much larger one, she took a step back, the small, evasive movement slipping her hand from his. She gestured to the archway leading to the hall and the offices that opened off it. "Won't you come into my office?" She glanced at Natalie and found her pretending to read a file while slanting sideways, fascinated looks at the prince. "Natalie, will you bring us coffee, please."

"Right away."

Emily's skin prickled with awareness as Lazhar walking behind her out of the reception area and down the short hallway to her office. Something about him had set all of Emily's female instincts shrieking a warning. This was no tame, civilized male. Lazhar Eban threatened her feminine independence on a very basic level. It took all her composure to keep from canceling their appointment and finding an excuse to ask him to leave. Relieved that she could put some distance between them, she gestured to the two damask-covered armchairs arranged before her desk.

"Won't you have a seat." She rounded her desk and dropped into her chair, upholstered in a soft blue that echoed the damask of the armchairs, and folded her hands together atop the desk. "What can I do for you, Your Highness?"

Emily had handpicked the chairs facing her desk specifically because they were large enough to accommodate husbands-to-be and small enough not to overwhelm the more slender forms of their brides. But Lazhar made the chair he sat in seem small and his muscled, broad-shouldered body, combined with the sheer force of his presence, seemed to dominate the room.

"I'm getting married," he said, his gaze fastened on hers. "And I want you to organize the wedding."

Emily was speechless. She'd wondered whether this might be the reason for his appointment, but his statement still staggered her. She gathered her composure and nodded. "Very well." She flipped open her notebook and picked up her gold pen. "I'll need some parameters. What date have you scheduled for the wedding?" Pen poised, she looked at him, waiting.

"As soon as possible."

"You and your fiancée haven't picked a date?"

"No. Is that a problem?"

Carefully Emily placed her pen on the gleaming cherrywood desktop. "Perhaps not a 'problem,' exactly, but certainly a concern since it's impossible to begin planning without a time frame in mind. And I'm afraid our calendar is booked several months, sometimes more than a year, in advance."

"What's the earliest date that you're available?"

Emily wondered briefly if he was thinking of a small, private wedding. Surely a royal affair would be scheduled by the palace and the date set in stone? "Before I look at dates, perhaps we should discuss what sort of a wedding you wish to have. Depending on the preparations needed, we may be able to schedule your event sooner, rather than later."

Lazhar shrugged. "I'm afraid I don't have a lot of latitude in the wedding ceremony. Royal weddings in Daniz are ruled by tradition and our customs require that the celebration is a week-long affair."

Emily blinked, startled. "So," she said slowly, "you're asking me to plan a week-long celebration, including a royal ceremony, within as little time as possible?"

"The palace has event coordinators that will assist you. What I need is someone to plan, organize and delegate. And I'm willing to pay whatever is necessary to have you devote your time exclusively to the event in order to speed the process.''

Emily was stunned. A royal wedding on her résumé would open doors in Europe and the Middle East and had the potential to gain worldwide recognition for Creative Weddings. But it would mean working with the prince, and she wasn't sure that was wise. On the other hand, in her experience the groom rarely spent a great deal of time with the wedding consultant. The husbands-to-be were always more than happy to leave the details to their prospective brides. ''I assume that the wedding will be held in Daniz?''

''Yes.''

She toyed with her pen, stalling for time while she tried to absorb what he was saying. She glanced up at him through her lashes and found his dark gaze fastened on her, a slight air of tension surrounding him. ''May I ask why you chose my firm?''

''You were highly recommended by the Radissons,'' he said smoothly. ''Their daughter Angela is a good friend of my sister, who was a member of the wedding party.''

''Ah, of course.'' Emily instantly made the connection. Angela Radisson was a San Francisco society deb, several years younger than Emily, and wonderfully unspoiled. The wedding party had included several of Angela's college friends, one of whom had been a beautiful dark-haired young woman named Jenna. Gazing at Lazhar, sprawled casually across from her, she immediately saw the family resemblance. "I wasn't aware that Jenna Eban was a princess."

The grin that curved his mouth was wickedly charming. "My sister likes to shed the 'princess' title on occasion and pretend she's not royal. I'm not surprised that she didn't tell you, but I'm a little surprised that you didn't suspect."

"Why is that?" Emily absorbed the impact of the effect the smile had on his already handsome face.

"Because Jenna tends to be a magnet for the tabloids. It's good to know that they didn't spoil her fun."

"Ah. I see." Emily forced her attention back to the wedding. "Well." She picked up her pen and flipped the pages on her calendar, swiftly scanning appointments and calculating. "Depending on the expertise of your palace staff—and I assume they're accustomed to planning grand functions—?" She glanced up. Lazhar's nod of agreement reassured her. "Good. Then it may be possible to have the ceremony in six months." She frowned, shaking her head slightly. "But that's a very tight time-table. And I'll need to do an on-site inspection…" she murmured. Once again, she consulted her calendar before glancing up at Lazhar. "I'm afraid I'm fully booked for the next two weeks but I can carve out a four-day-weekend after that to fly to Daniz and meet with your people."

"That won't work."

Emily blinked. "What won't work?"

"I don't want to wait two weeks. I want you to start immediately. Preferably, this afternoon."

"I'm afraid that's impossible," she said coolly. "I have prior commitments that I can't reschedule."

For a moment he was silent, his enigmatic gaze meeting hers with an oddly assessing light. "So it's a question of your workload and timing, not of your willingness to begin the wedding preparations immediately?"

"Yes."

Emily's agreement seemed to satisfy him, for he nodded abruptly. "Very well. Then we're agreed that you will come to Daniz as soon as your calendar is cleared?"

"I believe that's mutually agreeable. I won't be able to give you a projected cost for our services until I've been to Daniz, however."

"That won't be a problem." He shot back the cuff of his shirt, frowned at his watch and stood. "I'm afraid I don't have time to discuss further details as I have another appointment this afternoon. Perhaps we can resolve the issue over dinner tonight.''

"Oh, but I—" Emily broke off. Despite her instinct to distance herself from him, she couldn't afford to miss this opportunity. It's just business, she reminded herself. "Very well, dinner would be good. Where would you like to meet?"

"I'll pick you up at seven."

"I can meet you at the restaurant—I wouldn't want to inconvenience you."

"It's not a problem." He smiled at her, a slow, wicked grin that curled her toes and shortened her ability to draw a breath. "I look forward to it."

He turned and left the room. Emily wilted in her chair and stared at the doorway where his elegantly clad, broad-shouldered body had just disappeared.

"Well?" Natalie and Jane interrupted her, their faces alive with curiosity. "What did he say?"

"He wants us to handle the arrangements for his wedding."

They shrieked; Natalie did a quick dance while Jane clapped her hands with delight.

"This is excellent, Emily. What a coup! When do we start?"

"Not for at least two weeks—that's the earliest I can fly to Daniz."

"What date is the wedding?" Jane asked.

"There isn't a date, not yet. The prince wants it

scheduled as soon as possible but I told him I doubted it could be done in less than six months.''

''Six months? That's all?'' Jane's eyes rounded behind her wire-frame glasses. ''For a royal wedding? You're joking, right?''

''No. He insisted that he wants the ceremony scheduled as soon as possible and that the palace staff will assist.''

Jane looked doubtful. Natalie fairly bounced with excitement.

''I want to apply for a promotion to Jane's assistant—even if it only lasts through the wedding. I'll never have another chance to attend a royal wedding.''

Emily smiled at the younger woman's enthusiasm. ''If we really do plan this wedding, Natalie, I promise you can go with us.''

Natalie beamed with delight.

''So,'' Jane said, ''who's the lucky woman? Who is he marrying? She'll be a princess, and someday, the queen, right?''

''I don't know who he's marrying.'' Emily suddenly realized that Lazhar hadn't offered the information and she'd failed to ask. It wasn't like her to miss such a vital piece of data. ''I'm having dinner with him tonight…I'll ask him the name of his fiancée, among other things.''

''You're having dinner with him?'' Natalie's eyes widened.

"It's strictly business, Natalie," Emily said firmly. "He had an appointment and had to cut our discussion short so I..."

"Hello? Hello, is anyone here?"

The rich, throaty tones floated into the office.

"Yikes." Natalie hurried for the doorway. "That must be Katherine Powell!"

Jane and Emily exchanged a wry glance.

"She does love celebrities, doesn't she?" Jane said.

"Yes, she does," Emily chuckled with affection. "I think that's ninety percent of the reason that she works here."

"I can't wait to hear all the details. Call me after you talk to the prince tonight, okay?"

"I will," Emily promised, then stood as Natalie ushered a stunningly beautiful woman into the room. "Good afternoon, Katherine."

Lazhar didn't have another appointment. But he wanted Emily to join him that evening and finishing their discussion seemed the easiest way to convince her. After meeting her, he was even more determined to marry her. He needed a wife; she wanted a husband and children. They'd both get what they wanted.

After talking with Emily in person, however, he was even more sure that she wouldn't marry him to further her father's business plans. Emily Parks was beautiful, with golden-brown hair, bright green eyes, smooth tanned skin that his fingers itched to touch, and dimples that flashed when she smiled. The fitted scarlet suit and high heels made the most of her slim figure and long legs and conveyed the image of an upwardly mobile businesswoman. But Lazhar saw a well-concealed vulnerability and wariness beneath her smooth, sophisticated exterior. If he hadn't overheard her conversation with the housekeeper at the Parks's estate, he might have missed it and accepted the surface image. But the yearning in her voice when she spoke with the housekeeper about a family and children made it impossible for him to see only her sleek, lovely exterior.

After meeting Emily, he was convinced she was the woman he wanted for his bride. Now, all he had to do was convince Emily.

Chapter Two

This is just a business dinner, Emily told herself that evening as she turned in front of the mirror to check the back of her dress. *There's no reason for me to be nervous.* The simple cocktail dress was a Vera Wang design, the off-the-shoulder black silk tasteful and perfect for a business dinner with royalty. Not that she'd ever had dinner with a prince before, she thought, refusing to consider that the butterflies fluttering in her midsection might be caused by Lazhar's handsome face and charming smile and not by his royal status.

She smoothed a hand over her hair, noting absentmindedly that it brushed against her shoulders; she made a mental note to call her hairdresser and schedule an appointment to have the thick fall trimmed a quarter of an inch. One last inspecting glance assured her that she was as ready as she'd ever be. She turned away from the mirror, picked up a tiny black handbag and left the bedroom.

The doorbell rang just as she entered the living room and she glanced at the antique French clock on the mantelpiece.

Seven o'clock. Not only is he royal, he's also punctual.

She pulled open the door and although she'd thought she was prepared to see him, still her breath hitched and she found herself staring helplessly at the man outside her entry. He took her breath away. In the hours since she'd seen him at the office, she'd managed to convince herself that he couldn't have been as heart-stoppingly handsome as she'd first thought. But she'd lied to herself, she realized as she met his gaze. He really was as sinfully sexy as she'd remembered.

"Good evening."

His gaze swept her from the crown of her head to her toes, making the return journey just as swiftly, his mouth curving in a smile. "Good evening. Ready to go?"

"Yes." Emily stepped across the threshold and pulled the door closed behind her.

He moved back, falling into step beside her as she walked toward the elevators.

"Do you like living here?" he asked, his tone curious as he surveyed the hallway while they waited for the lift.

"Yes, very much." Emily's gaze followed his, moving over the red and cream floral carpet, the pale green walls with their gold-framed prints, and the matching discreet name and numbers beside the six doors that opened off the short hallway. "I love living in the center of the city and though the building is older, it's well-maintained and secure."

"Ah. And security is important in San Francisco," he commented as the elevator pinged and the doors opened.

"I suppose it's important everywhere, don't you think?"

"Yes." His voice turned grim. "Very important."

He took her arm and ushered her into the lift, his body briefly brushing hers as he leaned past her to push the button for the lobby floor. The faint scent of soap and aftershave reached her, the slightly rough texture of his suit jacket teasing the bare skin of her arm. Although he was impeccably polite and made no overt moves, she felt crowded by him and too aware of his much bigger body. He was so blatantly male that he made her feel overwhelmingly feminine. She couldn't recall any other man of her acquaintance eliciting such a strong response.

"Does Daniz have a crime problem?" Emily asked, determined to conceal her reaction. She vividly remembered the photos she'd seen in a travel brochure of the small kingdom on the Mediterranean Sea. Tucked between the eastern border of Spain on one side and France's southern edge on the other, Daniz's sun-drenched beaches were adored by tourists and its fabled Jewel Market was equally revered by the gem industry. Crime didn't seem a part of that fairy tale picture.

"I suspect every country in the world has a problem with crime, some more so than others." Lazhar's deep voice sent a slow shiver up Emily's spine. "Daniz's crime rate has never been high when compared to many countries but there's always room for improvement. We've increased the police force and taken an aggressive proactive approach over the last few years and the result has been a decrease in all types of crime."

"Is this part of your plan for national security?" He raised an eyebrow in inquiry and Emily smiled. "I confess I did some online research this afternoon in an effort to learn a bit more about your country before we talked this evening. Part of what I learned is that you were appointed to lead the Daniz National Security Forces five years ago."

"Ah." His mouth quirked. "I hope you only

visited the official Daniz Web site and not the sites featuring gossip from the tabloids.''

Emily laughed. ''I did visit the Daniz government site, but I also read a few very interesting tidbits at a site called Secrets of the Royal Families of Europe.''

Lazhar groaned and shook his head. ''I'm afraid to ask what you learned there. I hope you didn't believe anything you read.''

''Most of it sounded like pure fiction. Unless—'' she looked at him with interest ''—you really did fly across the Mediterranean on a hangglider to spend the night with a harem dancer?'' The swift expression of horror that flitted across his face made her laugh. ''No?''

''Absolutely not.'' His deep voice held disgust.

''Pity.'' Emily sighed, watching him through the screen of her lashes. ''I thought perhaps she was your fiancée.''

''No, definitely not.''

The elevator reached the lobby, the doors opening with silent efficiency. Two muscular men in dark suits stood sentry at the door to the street; they snapped to attention, one of them speaking into a small two-way radio as Lazhar took Emily's arm and they exited the elevator. They crossed the black and white marble floor and one of the guards opened the door while the other fell discreetly into step behind them. Outside, another black-clad, burly man held the door of a long black limousine open wide. Emily was about to enter the limo when someone called her name.

She paused and glanced down the street. "Hello." A smile lit her face. Her brother Cade was striding toward them along the sidewalk. "What are you doing here?"

"I'm picking up Stacy—she's visiting Anabeth."

"Oh, I wish I'd known she was near, I would have stopped in for a hug." Emily adored Cade's five-year-old daughter; the precocious little girl shared Emily's love of shopping and they'd formed a mutual admiration society of two. Stacy's friend Anabeth lived in the next apartment building and the two often shared playdates.

"I'll call you the next time I bring her over, I promise." Cade nodded at Lazhar and held out his hand. "Lazhar, it's good to see you. I didn't know you were in town."

"I've just arrived—the trip wasn't on my schedule and my aides didn't have time to contact you."

Emily glanced from her brother to Lazhar. "You two know each other?"

"Yes. Of course." Cade grinned at her. "But I didn't know you and Lazhar were acquainted."

"We just met today," she said calmly. Cade was her fraternal twin and loved to tease her as if they were still twelve-year-olds. When his eyes twinkled, she knew he'd jumped to the conclusion that she was dating the handsome prince and was going to comment. ''But I'm looking forward to doing business with him,'' she said smoothly, before he could speak.

Cade blinked at her and she could almost see his brain shift gears.

''Business? What kind of business?''

''Wedding planning, of course,'' she said, leaning forward to press a kiss on his cheek. ''Give my love to Stacy and tell her I'll see her tomorrow.''

''Sure.'' Cade nodded at Lazhar as the prince handed Emily into the limousine. He bent to peer into the interior, his hazel gaze intent. ''You're in good hands with Lazhar, Emily.''

Emily barely had time to wonder what he meant by the cryptic comment before the bodyguard closed the door and the limo pulled smoothly away from the curb. She glanced back to see Cade standing on the sidewalk, watching them drive away.

''How is it that you know my brother?'' she asked Lazhar as the car eased into traffic.

''We met some months ago when he came to Daniz to visit the Jewel Market.''

''Ah,'' Emily replied. Cade was an attorney and he handled much of their father's contracts for the Parks jewelry store; he was being trained as the heir apparent to succeed when Walter retired. Not that anyone who knew Walter thought he would ever retire, in fact, it was generally agreed that he'd probably die at his desk, working on a new deal. But nevertheless, Walter considered Cade his heir and demanded that his son spend a large amount of time on Parks Empire business interests. "So you're in the gem industry, like my father?"

"Not quite like your father, I suspect," he corrected gently. "For centuries, the Daniz Jewel Market has been a center for international jewel dealers and gem trading is important to my country. Because my family rules Daniz, I'm involved by necessity with the Market, but gems aren't my sole business."

"So you're not obsessed with jewels?"

His dark eyes were grave. "No, Emily, I'm not obsessed with jewels. I have neither the time nor the inclination. I'm deeply committed to the people of Daniz and to my family and I find they require all my attention." He shrugged. "I suppose some might call the depth of that commitment obsessive, but I choose to believe otherwise."

"I find it admirable that you choose people over business interests," Emily commented, unable to look away from his warm gaze. "In my experience, such a choice is very unusual. My father's primary commitment is to his business…he's driven by the next negotiation and making each new contract bigger than the last, with more money, more perfect gems, higher profile clients. The men in his circle that I've met, no matter how old or young, all seem to feel the same. It's refreshing to meet someone who's involved in the gem industry but whose life is apparently not owned by it.''

Lazhar laughed, white teeth flashing against tanned skin, his dark eyes amused. ''I confess that I've met traders at the Jewel Market who were willing to sell their soul for the price of a rare diamond, ruby, or sapphire. But I'm not one of them.''

''I'd love to visit the Jewel Market,'' Emily said. ''I've heard it's a fascinating place.''

''I think so,'' Lazhar agreed. ''We've preserved the building and the interior much as it was when it was first built, three hundred years ago, by the King of Daniz and the Prince of Persia. The mosaic tiles on the floors and walls, the handmade carpets and wall hangings, the gold minarets…all are well worth seeing.'' He smiled at Emily. ''I'll give you a tour when you visit my country.''

''I'd like that very much.'' He really is charming, Emily thought. The limousine slowed and she realized that she'd been engrossed in their conversation and hadn't noticed their route. She glanced out the window and then back at the prince, puzzled. ''This looks like the airport.''

''It is.'' He agreed.

"Wc'rc having dinner at the airport?" She wasn't aware of a five-star restaurant located at the San Francisco International Airport. Certainly not a restaurant that a man of Lazhar's caliber would choose, she thought.

"Not at the airport."

The car slowed and parked beside a sleek jet. The bodyguard seated next to the driver leapt out and opened the door for Lazhar. He exited, turning to hold out a hand to Emily, and she followed him out onto the tarmac. The evening was warm and balmy; a slight breeze lifted her hair, skeining it across her face. She brushed it back, tucking it behind her ear.

They were standing a few feet from the steps leading up to the main cabin of a private jet. The logo on the tail spelled out Daniz in vivid blue and gold. Beside her, Lazhar spoke to one of the bodyguards in what Emily thought was French. Finished, the man nodded, bowed and reentered the car, which pulled away.

"This is your plane?" Curious, she glanced from the jet to Lazhar.

"Yes." He tucked her hand through the crook of his arm and led her toward the steps. "I think you'll find it comfortable."

Emily abruptly stopped walking, her movement halting Lazhar as well. "I'm sure I would," she said carefully. "If I were traveling on it, but I'm not."

"Actually we are." Lazhar's smile flashed, his dark eyes teasing. "And our destination is a surprise. I think you'll find the food well worth the trip."

"We're flying out of town for dinner?"

"Yes."

Uncertain, Emily hesitated. She didn't know Lazhar well enough to get aboard a plane with him headed for an unknown destination. On the other hand, Cade *did* know him well and had assured her that he was trustworthy. Her brother's recommendation overcame her innate wariness and she gave in.

"Very well—if you promise the food is worth the flight."

"I promise." Lazhar led her up the steps to the cabin.

"Good evening, Your Highness." The white-coated steward greeted them with a bow.

"Good evening, Carlos." Lazhar seated Emily in one of the high-backed, upholstered seats next to the window with a small table between them. Both chairs and table were bolted securely to the floor and the chairs had seat belts. Behind him, the steward closed the outer door as the powerful jet engines rumbled to life, vibrating the cabin floor beneath Emily's feet.

"I need to talk to the captain for a moment, please make yourself comfortable, I won't be long."

Emily murmured an assent, her gaze following Lazhar until he disappeared through the door at the end of the cabin. The summerweight, pale gray suit he wore was beautifully made and clearly custom tailored to fit his long legs and broad shoulders.

She sighed and shook her head at her own foolishness. Lazhar Eban was engaged to be married—already taken and off-limits. And even if he were available, he wasn't her type of man at all. He was much too high profile, too powerful and too rich—all qualities that her father also possessed. Emily had intimate knowledge of just how difficult it could be to live with such a man.

On the other hand, Lazhar Eban was quite possibly the handsomest, sexiest man she'd ever met.

"If you'll fasten your seat belt, ma'am, we're about to take off." The steward advised.

"Of course."

He nodded his thanks when Emily clipped the latch and tugged the belt snugly across her abdomen. He left the cabin, Emily assumed to take his own seat elsewhere, and in moments, the sleek jet taxied down a runway and lifted smoothly into the air. She glanced out the window to see the Golden Gate Bridge appear off the wingtip before fluffy white clouds obscured her view.

Lazhar must have had to remain in the cockpit with a seat belt on, until we're airborne, she thought as she gazed curiously around the luxurious cabin. The interior of the Daniz royal family's jet was unlike any private plane she'd ever been on. There wasn't a utilitarian piece of furniture in sight, even the sturdy chair she sat in was upholstered in a glorious deep blue fabric that felt like rough silk. Her feet rested on a thick carpet with jewel tones of scarlet-red, cobalt-blue, antique-gold and pearl-white that complemented the cabin fittings. The walls were a discreet, smooth pearly-white, the wooden doors a deep mahogany set into arched doorjambs that reminded her of Spanish architecture. A collection of small French Impressionist paintings were clustered on one wall, their muted colors glowing against gold frames. Emily's gaze lingered on the unique furnishings that made the plane's interior as comfortable as a lavish hotel suite, and she was reminded that Daniz bordered Spain, France and the Mediterranean. Clearly the royal family enjoyed the best of all their cultures.

The plane climbed steeply and it wasn't until it finally leveled out that Lazhar rejoined her, the steward following closely on his heels with a tray holding a chilled bottle of wine and two stemmed glasses.

Lazhar took the two filled glasses from Carlos's

tray and handed one to Emily. "To your health—
and to our successful business enterprise."

"To a beautifully organized wedding ceremony," Emily responded, tilting her glass in salute
before tasting the wine. "Mmm, delicious."

"It's a Spanish vintage from the Penedes region." Lazhar dropped into the chair next to her
and lifted his glass to eye the golden liquid. "And
a favorite of my father's."

"And of yours?"

"And of mine," he agreed.

"Would you like to have it served at your wedding?" Emily set the exquisitely cut wineglass on
the parquet table that separated her chair from Lazhar's and took a small notebook and gold pen
from her bag.

Lazhar shrugged. "Yes, of course. If you think
it's appropriate."

"I think it's an excellent choice. I'll make a note
to request that the caterer use it. What is it called?"
He told her, his deep voice smoothly switching to
Spanish. She wrote down the name, vintage and
year, then closed her notebook and placed it on the
table, her pen next to it, before picking up her
wineglass once more. She took a sip and observed
him over the rim of her glass. "Are you going to
tell me where we're going for dinner and if the
menu will be Spanish to match the wine? Or must
I wait until we get there."

"We're having dinner aboard the plane."

"Aboard the plane?" Confused, Emily stared at him.

"But tomorrow," he continued, "we'll have lunch in Daniz. I'll have the palace chef uncork another favorite vintage for you to taste."

"I beg your pardon?" Emily was certain she'd misunderstood him. Daniz was at least a ten-hour flight away from San Francisco.

"By lunchtime tomorrow, we'll be in Daniz."

Emily was speechless. His gaze didn't flinch from hers, he seemed to be waiting for her to react to his blunt statement. Her surprise quickly gave way to anger and she returned her wineglass to the table with a snap.

"Are you telling me that this plane is flying to Daniz?"

"Yes."

"With me on it?"

"Yes."

"Without your asking me if I were willing to go to Daniz?"

"You told me this afternoon that you're willing to go to Daniz. It was only a question of the timing."

"I also told you that it would take at least two weeks to clear my calendar."

"Which is why I discussed the situation with your assistant, Jane, and why the staff from my embassy in San Francisco will be reporting to your office tomorrow. They'll do whatever your assistant requires of them until you return. They'll also install the necessary equipment to link your office to the palace media room so you can be in touch with your staff at any hour of the day or night, whenever you feel it necessary.''

Emily was furious. ''How kind of you. But that doesn't change the fact that you failed to ask for my permission to do any of those things. Nor did you bother telling me about your plans when you lured me aboard this plane.''

''I can only apologize. When I spoke with Jane she assured me that she would be happy to take your appointments over the next couple of weeks. She also told me that the chance to combine a holiday in Daniz with work was something that she firmly believed would be good for you.'' Lazhar paused, eyeing her. ''She seemed quite taken with the idea, in fact, she volunteered to go to your apartment to pack your bag and get your passport this evening.''

''Jane helped you with this conspiracy?''

''She assisted with the arrangements, yes.''

Emily fumed, silently wondering what on earth Jane could have been thinking.

''I know you might not like my method of getting you to come to Daniz, Emily, but I'm sincere about the limited time frame. I don't know how familiar you are with Daniz politics, but the news reports about my father's health are true. He's not well. We don't know how much time he has left and he wants to see me married as soon as possible. I want your firm to handle the wedding plans but I can't wait two weeks—not because I'm being difficult and high-handed, but because I don't know how long my father will be with us. And I'll do whatever is necessary to give him what he wants," he added grimly.

His words defused Emily's anger as little else could. She didn't have a good relationship with her own father, but she could understand a son's wish to please a dying father. "Very well," she said. "When you put it that way, there's little I can say. However," she added when she saw relief ease the tense lines of his face, "I want to talk to Jane about the office arrangements before I agree."

"I thought you might." He lifted the tabletop between them, revealing a telephone in the cabinet beneath. "While you're talking with her, I'll check with the pilot about our flight time."

Her temper still simmering, Emily pointedly waited until the door closed behind him before lifting the receiver and dialing, tapping her nails impatiently against the arm of her chair while she waited for Jane to pick up.

"Hello?"

"I'm going to fire you for this, Jane."

"Hi, Emily." Jane's voice held a smile, despite Emily's grim tones.

"I can't believe you did this—what were you thinking?"

"I was thinking that a) You've got a genuine shot at planning a royal wedding that would send Creative Wedding's status through the roof; b) You're so conscientious that you would never want the Benedicts or Katherine Powell, or any of your other clients, to feel that you gave royal wedding arrangements priority over theirs; and c) You can't miss this opportunity. It's just too good."

"I know all of this, Jane. I took it into consideration when I told Prince Lazhar that I could fly to Daniz in two weeks, after I cleared my calendar."

"But the prince made it very clear that he can't wait two weeks," Jane said. "And although I know you want to be there for each and every detail for your clients, Emily, I looked at your schedule for the next two weeks and I really can handle your appointments till you come home."

"What about your own work?"

"Most of what I've booked as priority for the next few weeks is glorified errand-running and double-checking details for the Andersen and Heaton weddings next month."

"Hmm." Emily sighed, still not totally convinced.

"Emily," Jane's voice coaxed. "We've known each other since high school. Have I ever lied to you?"

"No."

"Then trust me, going to Daniz is the best opportunity you've ever had to build your business. It's like found money. This could make Creative Weddings the most important bridal consultant firm in the U.S. Not to mention," Jane added persuasively. "That you're going to spend a week or more in one of the most beautiful countries on the Mediterranean. And you'll be staying in the palace. You haven't had a vacation since we left high school—this is the perfect chance."

"You're sure you won't be buried under at the office?"

"Positive. Besides, your prince said he's sending over staff from the Daniz Embassy. They're accustomed to dealing with diplomatic receptions and galas and they can do all the errand-running on my calendar while I'm free to deal with your appointments."

"All right," Emily said reluctantly. "You've convinced me. But I'm still not happy with the fact that neither you nor the prince asked me if I was willing."

"Hon, you would have refused," Jane said with an affectionate chuckle. "I can hardly get you to go out to dinner on a weekend because you're working. Getting you to agree to anything that takes you away from the office is difficult. You really need this break.''

Emily sighed. ''Brenda told me last week that she was worried that I was working too many hours.''

''Brenda's right,'' Jane said promptly.

''I'll expect you to stay in touch, daily,'' Emily said.

''Absolutely,'' Jane replied.

They discussed a few items on the morning's schedule before they rang off, after Jane promised to check in with Emily each day while she was in Daniz.

The receiver had barely settled onto the phone base when the cockpit door opened and Lazhar strode into the room.

Emily waited until he sat down next to her before she spoke, answering the unvoiced question in his eyes. ''Jane will handle my schedule while I'm in Daniz but she'll be in contact every day, and if something comes up that needs my attention, I'll fly home immediately.''

Relief mingled with satisfaction on his face and he nodded. ''This jet is at your disposal, should an emergency arise. And if all goes well, I'll fly you home when you've had time to tour my country, visit the palace, meet the people of Daniz and feel you have enough information to plan the wedding.''

Emily picked up her notepad and pen. ''I suppose that's reasonable,'' she said reluctantly. ''How long do you think that will take?''

''A week, perhaps two. It depends on when you feel you've seen enough to feel comfortable planning a wedding that fits within our culture.''

''I'll pencil in a week.'' Emily gave him a cool look. She'd always secretly longed for travel and adventure but her single-minded focus on building her company had taken up all her time. Of necessity, she'd put that dream on the back burner. Lazhar was unwittingly fulfilling one of her childhood wishes but she was still annoyed at his high-handed method of gaining her cooperation.

''A week,'' he repeated with a nod. Emily read satisfaction in his eyes before his gaze left hers. He pushed one of the buttons located in a key pad on the chair's armrest, then picked up the wine and refilled their glasses. As he was returning the bottle to the tabletop, the cabin door opened and the steward entered.

''Ah, Carlos,'' Lazhar greeted the man. ''We're ready for dinner.''

''Very well, Your Highness.'' Carlos bowed and disappeared through the doorway, only to return promptly with a wheeled cart. He worked efficiently and quietly, whisking a linen tablecloth and napkins from the cart to cover a mahogany table near the back of the cabin. He took silverware from one of the cart's compartments, china and stemware from another, and in moments, the table was set, food steaming on the plates.

He bowed and pushed the cart out of the cabin, closing the door behind him.

Emily, who had watched the steward's transformation of game table to dinner table, glanced at Lazhar. "Is Carlos a genie in his off-hours? Because that was quite a trick."

Lazhar returned her smile. "He's very good at his job." He stood and held out his hand. "Shall we?" Emily took his hand and let him draw her to her feet. "He's worked for my father, and now me, for over twenty years. I followed him around as a child when our family traveled, trying to uncover his secret for producing food at the precise moment my parents wanted it, but I never did. The only thing I ever managed to learn was that he's amazingly organized."

Lazhar pulled out a chair and seated her before taking his own seat across from her.

"This looks wonderful." Determined to maintain a polite, professional distance between them, Emily picked up her fork and took a bite. The grilled fish was crisp on the outside, perfectly cooked on the inside. She sampled the paella as well, the flavors of saffron, red and green peppers blending with shrimp and mussels in a mouthwatering combination. "It tastes even better than it looks."

"I'm glad you're pleased. I'll pass your comments on to Carlos."

They chatted easily during dinner. Lazhar seemed more than willing to answer her questions about his country and the customs that would impact the royal wedding. He had a wry sense of humor that had her laughing and his insightful comments about the differing economic stratas in his country made her realize that he wasn't a prince who isolated himself in a luxurious castle. He must spend a lot of time working alongside the residents of Daniz, she thought as he related a story about attending a rural wedding of a distant cousin. The wedding celebration continued for a week and during that time, the male guests helped erect a small house for the newlyweds. It was clear that Lazhar relished the physical activity of pounding nails and raising walls.

Their dinner long finished, their dessert plates empty and the bottle of wine drained, they remained at the table, Emily listening with fascination to his stories about life in Daniz. I could care too much for this man, she realized as she gazed at him, his features animated when he described how the guests had carried his cousin and his bride around the house on their shoulders before leaving them inside the finished structure.

"We'll drive out to the country and visit my cousin and his wife while you're in Daniz," Lazhar commented, glancing at his watch and lifting an eyebrow in surprise. "It's late. I'm afraid I've been boring you with family stories."

"No, not at all." Emily glanced at her own small diamond-studded watch and was shocked to find that it was after midnight. "I had no idea it was this late."

"You should try to get some sleep." He stood and once again, held out his hand. "The bag Jane packed for you is in the bedroom."

Emily put her hand in his, palm against palm, her fingers sliding against his rougher, larger ones. She was getting accustomed to having him take her hand, she realized, and for some reason, didn't mind it. There was something about him that found its way past her defenses and instilled confidence, generating acceptance.

He showed her to a beautifully decorated bedroom off the main cabin and left her with a polite good-night. A wave of weariness hit Emily as she closed and locked the door, her gaze searching the room. Her suitcase sat atop a luggage rack next to the bed and she pulled out her pajamas and toiletry bag, quickly preparing for bed. She was so tired she barely noted the opulent fittings of the bath and bedroom before she turned out the light and slipped between the silk sheets. Within seconds, she was sound asleep.

Their landing and transfer from the plane to the black Mercedes limousine waiting for them the next morning was smooth and effortless. The driver left the airport by a private gate, nosing the big car into busy morning traffic along a wide avenue. Seated next to Lazhar in the back, Emily was entranced by glimpses of the azure sea as they passed narrow side streets leading from the vehicle-choked avenue down to the Daniz Harbor. The limousine made a sharp turn and she caught her breath as they plunged down one such street, so narrow that oncoming vehicles nearly brushed door handles.

"Don't worry," Lazhar said, his deep voice amused. "Antonio has driven this route a thousand times and never so much as scratched the paint."

Emily's gaze left the colorful scene outside her window and glanced at him to find him watching her, an understanding smile curving his lips. A reluctant smile lifted the corner of her mouth in response. "I thought I was accustomed to narrow streets and steep hills," she commented, gesturing at the window beside him. "But San Francisco didn't prepare me for this."

He chuckled. "This part of Daniz City is built

on a series of hills that march up from the harbor and since it's been here for centuries, the streets weren't built to accommodate automobiles. I'm accustomed to it since I've lived here all my life, but I warn visitors that they should think twice before hiring a car and driving here.'' He paused, his gaze intent on her face. ''What do you think of my city?''

''It's beautiful.'' Her voice sounded as enchanted as she felt. Their car stopped at an intersection, waiting for a crowd of strolling pedestrians to cross the street in front of them, and Emily leaned closer to Lazhar, the better to see out the side window. A carpet with a pattern worked in deep burgundies and rose-reds hung outside the shop on the corner, its lush colors vibrant against the pink-tinged stones of the building behind it. The shop door set into the heavy medieval archway stood open and Emily caught a glimpse of an Aladdin's cave of brilliant color before the car moved forward, leaving the shop behind.

They drove past an open-air market, flowers and fruit making brilliant splashes of color against the ancient stone walls laced with black ironwork balconies above.

''You're sincere about finding my city beautiful.''

It was a statement, not a question, and when Emily drew her gaze from the view outside the window to look at Lazhar, his expression held a quiet pride and satisfaction.

"Yes, it's absolutely fascinating."

They shared a spontaneous smile of accord and for one brief moment, she felt as if she'd known him forever, that he understood exactly how much she enjoyed this glimpse of his city, so very different from her native San Francisco despite both being built on steep hills. Then he glanced away from her and out the window, pointing out the fountain in the center of the square they were currently circling, and the moment was gone.

Emily's first view of the Daniz Royal Palace left her speechless. The castle sat atop a hill, with breathtaking views from all sides. The rose-tinted stone building had medieval square towers with crenellated tops standing guard at each end, the walls connecting the towers lined with high, arched windows on the top two stories, the lower story having only small, square openings covered with glass. It looked like a fortress, which indeed, it had been during its early years.

The limousine smoothly negotiated the winding avenue, lined with Italian poplars and centuries-old buildings housing apartments above and shops at street level. Then they passed through impressive wrought-iron gates manned by uniformed guards to enter the palace grounds. Lush green lawns dotted with huge, century-old trees edged the driveway leading to the palace itself; the car swept to a stop on the cobblestone circular driveway before an imposing door.

The driver and bodyguard immediately exited and held open the door for Lazhar, who handed out Emily, turning away for a moment to converse in low tones with the guard.

Emily's fascinated gaze swept the castle facade, drinking in the sight of stone sculptures carved above each of the many windows and what seemed to be a hanging garden halfway down the building's length, one floor up where a stone balustrade topped the first level.

"Sorry to keep you waiting," Lazhar took her arm and they walked toward the doorway.

Emily barely had time to note the coat of arms carved into the stone above the arched doorway, the two snarling panthers holding crossed swords over a crown. Then they were inside, crossing an entryway tiled with a blue and gold mosaic pattern; the room was easily large enough to hold several hundred people.

"Antonio is taking your bag to your room," Lazhar told her as they ascended one side of the curving staircase to the second floor. "My mother and sister always need to rest after flying home from the States due to the jet lag. When you're ready, your maid will tell you where to find me and we'll discuss the itinerary for your stay."

"Very well," Emily murmured. She caught glimpses into rooms off the hallway that were decorated in a mix of Mediterranean architecture, Persian carpets, Italian glass, French furniture, and Moroccan pillows. She was charmed by the beautiful building with it's jewel-box rooms; somehow the interiors she saw managed to combine palatial elegance with the warmth of a real home.

"Here we are." Lazhar pushed open a door and halted. "If there's anything you want or need that you don't find, please don't hesitate to ask."

"Thank you." Emily stepped into the room, her gaze quickly sweeping the lovely furnishings before she turned to look at him, her fingers closing over the door handle. "You're very kind."

"Not at all." He shrugged, his lashes narrowing as he assessed her. "You look ready to fall asleep standing there. Get some sleep," he said abruptly. "We'll talk after you've rested." And he reached out and caught the edge of the door, gently moving it out of her grasp, closing it between them.

Left alone, Emily surveyed her room and realized that it was actually a suite of rooms. The ruby-and-cream Persian carpet was thick and plush beneath her feet as she walked across the airy sitting room to peek through an open door. Here, the drapes were partially drawn across floor-to-ceiling windows, barring the hot sunlight from the interior. The wide bed was draped in sheer white panels, the pale lemon sheet and green silk coverlet turned back invitingly below the embroidered pillows. Despite the effects of jet lag that had her yawning, Emily walked to the archway and stepped out into a lovely garden. Walled on three sides for privacy with bougainvillea spilling hot pink flowers over the sand-colored stones, the garden was a riot of white and pink roses, fragrant lavender, sage, rosemary and silvery artemisia. One wall was only waist-high and the view of Daniz Harbor and the Mediterranean Sea beyond was breathtaking. Emily drew a deep breath. The tang of salt carried by a faint breeze from the harbor mingled with the sweet scent of the garden's floribunda roses. The breath turned into a yawn and she reluctantly turned away from the spellbinding view of sea and garden to reenter the bedroom. She showered, pulled on a nightgown, and climbed into bed.

She fell asleep the moment her head hit the pillow.

When she woke, the midafternoon sun was slanting through the half-open drapes. Disoriented, she stared at the ceiling for a long moment, wondering why it was a pale rose instead of the eggshell-white she normally saw when waking in her bed in San Francisco.

Because I'm not home in San Francisco. She sat up, pushed her hair out of her eyes, and stared around her. The airy, shaded room was exotic and

opulent, a mix of architecture that reflected the
countries and cultures that bordered Daniz. The
Spanish archway leading to the sitting room was
edged with Greek tiles in green and gold and the
French influence was apparent in the delicate Louis
XIV chair placed in one corner near her bed. An
exquisite Italian vase of handblown glass stood on
the dresser, its shade of deep green a perfect foil
for the white roses and trailing greenery it held.
And the high ceilings and airy hangings tied back
on the bed, that matched the sheer white draperies
at the windows, reminded Emily that Morocco was
just across the Mediterranean Sea.

It was so lovely and so exotically different from
her apartment in San Francisco that she felt transported into another world.

It is another world, she reminded herself. *The
royal palace in a foreign country is definitely light
years away from my apartment in San Francisco.*

She tossed back the silky sheet and light coverlet
and rose, wondering what time it was and how
long she'd slept. She picked up her watch from the
nightstand.

"Two o'clock? How could I have slept so
long?" she murmured, dismayed that the day was
half gone. She hurried into the bathroom where she
found herself pausing once again to stare with
pleasure at the effect of green and cream tiles, thick
cream-colored turkish towels, and pale jade marble

tub and sink. It wasn't that she was unaccustomed to the beauty and comfort that money could provide. She'd grown up in her father's opulent mansion; her playmates and friends all lived in similar wealthy homes. But there was something subtly different about Lazhar's home. The deep jewel tones of the carpets were softly muted as if they had covered the teak and marble floors for years. The paintings of ladies and gentleman that hung on the walls bore a resemblance to one another and Emily suspected that they were Lazhar's ancestors. The furnishings spoke of centuries of wealth and history yet conveyed a welcoming warmth that she'd never felt in her father's oddly sterile mansion.

Emily shook herself out of her reverie and turned on the shower faucets, stripping quickly and stepping into the tiled surround.

A half hour later, showered, hair blown dry, makeup applied, wearing only a towel she walked back into the bedroom and halted abruptly. A maid dressed in a soft royal-blue uniform edged in gold, was just setting a tray with teapot and scones atop the small table near the window.

''Good afternoon.'' Her soft voice was friendly and polite, the English words faintly accented with a musical lilt.

''Hello.'' Emily glanced at the very English teapot with its pink tea rose pattern. *Yet another country heard from,* she thought.

The maid opened a door to a walk-in closet. "I unpacked your bag this morning and hung your dresses in here." She pulled open a drawer. "And I folded your lingerie into the drawers." She looked expectantly at Emily. "Would you like me to help you dress, ma'am?"

"I think I can manage but thank you for unpacking my things."

"You're very welcome," the young woman murmured. "When you're dressed, I'll show you to the breakfast room."

"Thank you."

The maid smiled and left the room.

Emily waited until the door closed behind her before walking into the closet. She recognized only three of the many dresses and suits that hung on the long rod suspended along one wall. The closet was filled with gowns and casual wear, shoes on racks against the end wall, lingerie tucked into the drawers fitted against the opposite wall from the dress rack. She flipped through a row of dresses, noting the designer labels, before pulling open the drawers to glance at the filmy lingerie, all in her size. The clothing and underpinnings were gorgeous but Emily was torn between appreciation for the beautiful clothing and sheer annoyance that Lazhar obviously knew her measurements, right down to her bra and panties.

Was it possible that he'd ordered an entire wardrobe just for her? *No,* she thought, discounting the idea. That was a grand gesture that a very rich man might make for a potential lover, not for a business associate.

Still, he'd clearly noticed some things about her since he'd guessed her measurements perfectly.

Unless Jane told him, she thought. Emily resolved to have another serious talk with Jane about her role in aiding Lazhar's high-handed methods when she returned to San Francisco.

Chapter Three

Emily followed the maid through unfamiliar halls until the young woman halted, pulled open a door and bowed.

"Prince Lazhar is here, madam."

"Thank you," Emily murmured, and was rewarded with a warm smile from the maid before she stepped across the threshold and the door closed silently behind her.

Lazhar sat at a round table, documents spread across the snowy cloth next to his coffee cup. He looked up as she entered the small dining room, a swift smile curving his mouth, his gaze heating as it flicked over her from head to toe and back again. "Good afternoon, Emily, did you sleep well?"

"Yes, very well, thank you." Emily sat down in the chair held by a white-coated male servant and murmured a thank you when he poured coffee from a carafe into her cup.

"And your room is satisfactory?"

"More than satisfactory." She smiled at him. "The view of the harbor is amazing, as is the garden off the bedroom. Do all the rooms have walled gardens?"

"Many of them, yes." Lazhar dropped the document he was holding and lounged in his chair, nodding at the servant who immediately filled his coffee cup. "The palace gardens are my mother's pride and joy. She'll be pleased you're enjoying her babies."

"Her babies?" Emily looked up from the ruby-red marmalade she was spreading on her toast.

"That's what my mother calls the gardens. She told my sister and me that since we haven't given her grandchildren, she's making do with plants as a substitute for babies." His smile flashed, white against tanned skin, his eyes warming with quick affection. "She's as anxious as my father to see us happily married and starting our own families."

"And do you and your sister agree with her?" Emily asked, curious.

He shrugged. "I can understand our parents'

wish to see us happily settled—especially since my father's health is uncertain. Jenna, however…'' He shook his head, amused. ''My sister is adamant that she won't be nudged into marrying before she's ready.''

''So there's no fiancé waiting in the wings for your sister?''

''No. But it's not for lack of trying by my father.''

Emily couldn't help but smile with sympathy. ''It hadn't occurred to me before, but I suppose I should be grateful that while my father tries to control my life in other ways, he's never nagged me about getting married—'' She broke off, leaning back to let the silent servant place a plate with salmon quiche on the table before her and didn't see the fleeting expression of regret on Lazhar's face. The quiche was every bit as delicious as the sweet cantaloupe and honeydew melon cubes in a small bowl next to her plate. She wondered idly if the family chef would be preparing the wedding food before she remembered that she needed to speak to Lazhar about the designer wardrobe hanging in her bedroom. ''Speaking of being grateful…'' She glanced up at him to find him watching her, his dark eyes enigmatic. ''I noticed that the closet in my room is filled with clothing,'' she said carefully.

''I asked Mother to have her assistant stock the

closet for you—it seemed only fair since I didn't give you time to pack your own things before we left San Francisco,'' he said smoothly.

How clever of him, she thought, her gaze never leaving his as she slowly sipped water from a chilled Waterford crystal glass. *If I object, then I've insulted his mother. Very clever, indeed.* She returned the glass to the table. ''Please convey my thanks to your mother,'' she said, her voice purposely neutral. ''That was very kind of her.''

''I'll be happy to,'' he replied.

His words were as carefully polite as hers had been, but the amused glint in his dark eyes told her that he knew very well that she was uncomfortable with the situation. The clothing and lingerie were all the right size and that he had guessed so accurately made her painfully aware that he was far too familiar with the female body in general and hers in particular. The undercurrent of sexual tension that stretched between them stole her breath. *He's getting married soon,* she told herself, unable to look away from the heat in his eyes. *It's crazy to feel so attracted to him.* Lecturing herself didn't make her heart stop pounding against her ribcage, nor did it cool the warmth moving slowly through her veins.

''Your Highness?''

Lazhar's gaze left hers, moving past her to the doorway. ''Yes?''

"King Abbar would like you and Miss Parks to join him in his garden this afternoon."

"Very well. Tell him we'll be with him shortly." The servant bowed and left the room and Lazhar once again focused his attention on Emily. "I hope you don't mind postponing our discussion of your itinerary until later. My father mentioned earlier that he wanted to meet you and since he must spend much of his time resting, we all tend to adjust our schedules to fit his."

"That's perfectly understandable—I'd be delighted to meet the king." Emily glanced at her plate and realized that while she'd struggled to cope with the sexual tension between them, she'd mindlessly continued to fork food into her mouth and her plate was empty. She barely remembered chewing and swallowing. Annoyed that Lazhar had distracted her to such an extent, she blotted her lips with her napkin and placed the linen square neatly beside her plate. "I'm ready."

Lazhar didn't comment but again she caught the gleam of amusement in his eyes as he stood and held her chair.

They left the dining room and by the time they made a right and then a left turn down wide hallways, Emily was completely confused.

"Has a guest ever gotten lost in the palace?" she asked as they passed an open doorway and she caught a quick glimpse of a sitting room, tastefully decorated in feminine rose and pink shades.

"Often, but never for long. See the gold corded ropes hanging next to every third door?"

"Yes." Emily hadn't noticed them before.

"They're bell-pulls connected to the main housekeeping office. If you're ever lost, just tug on one of them and a speaker hidden in the wall above the door will allow you to ask directions from one of the staff."

"That's very ingenious."

"Mother thought of it. I wanted to tie the speakers into the security system with the cameras but she thought it was too intrusive. She didn't want guests reminded that they're being watched, particularly here in our family quarters." Lazhar paused outside mahogany double doors carved with the Daniz coat-of-arms. The two palace guards flanking the doors snapped to attention, saluted, and pulled open the heavy doors.

They crossed the threshold and Emily's eyes widened as her gaze swept the expansive apartment. The white marble floor was partially covered by scattered Persian carpets in the royal colors of deep blue and gold. The room seemed more Eastern than European with its low blue sofas, mahogany tables, and large blue and gold silk pillows piled on the floor. One whole wall was glass with transparent white panels of silk drawn over half the length to deflect the brilliant, hot sunshine pouring into the high-ceilinged space. Emily caught her breath as they crossed the room and stepped through open doors into the garden beyond. The walled garden was bigger, more lush than the one outside her suite of rooms but it was the view beyond the waist-high stone balustrade that halted her. Not only were the harbor and the city's red-tiled roofs visible but also the pine and cypress covered hills above Daniz City's narrow streets. The king's garden boasted a one-hundred-and-eighty-degree view of mountains, harbor, sea and city that was so impressive that for a moment, Emily didn't notice that she and Lazhar weren't alone in the garden.

"Ah, Lazhar, is this lovely young woman our guest from San Francisco?"

"Yes, Father, this is Emily."

Startled from her absorption, Emily realized that Lazhar had been standing silently, waiting for her attention, and that an older man sat on a cushioned chaise lounge at the far end of the garden, shaded by the wide, leafy branches of an acacia tree. "I'm so sorry," she apologized, embarrassment heating her cheeks. "I'm being terribly rude, please forgive me." She gestured at the panoramic view. "You have such an amazing view."

Lazhar cupped her elbow and escorted her the length of the garden to the small semicircle of chairs arranged beneath the spreading branches of the tree.

"Emily, I'd like you to meet my father, King Abbar."

"It's a pleasure to meet you, sir." Emily wasn't sure if she should curtsy but before she could decide, the king gestured at the wrought-iron cushioned chairs next to his lounge.

"Please, join me."

Emily felt the king's shrewd gaze assessing her as Lazhar seated her next to his father and took the chair beside her.

"I'm pleased you find my country interesting," the king continued.

"What I've seen so far has been fascinating," Emily confided, charmed by the friendly warmth in the king's dark eyes. Despite the sun, his skin had the pallor of ill health and his thin body seemed fragile; nevertheless the family connection between father and son was readily apparent. This is what Lazhar will look like when he's older, she thought, taking in the bone structure and keen nearly black eyes, the boyish grin that curved his mouth as he nodded with approval at her comment, his assessing gaze developing a distinct twinkle. Like his son, he had an air of masculine elegance, though his white jacket, shirt and pale-gray slacks were much more casual than Lazhar's gray suit.

"You must take her to the Jewel Market, Lazhar.'' King Abbar's gaze turned thoughtful as he glanced from his son to Emily. ''Or perhaps you have already seen the Market, Emily? I understand that your father has been involved in gem trading for many years.''

''Since before I was born,'' Emily confirmed. ''He and my brother have visited the Market here in Daniz, but I haven't had the pleasure.''

''Your father didn't take the family with him on business trips?'' the king asked, waving a servant closer to pour coffee for his guests.

''No. He doesn't believe in mixing business with family matters.'' Emily smiled her thanks as she took a delicate cup and saucer from the young man serving her. She didn't see the questioning glance King Abbar gave Lazhar, nor the slight shake of his son's head in response. ''We didn't travel with him at all. In fact, I've never been out of the States until last night.''

''Never?'' Lazhar's surprise was evident.

''Never—except for short trips across the U.S. border into Mexico and Canada and I don't count those since they're our neighboring countries.'' She sipped her coffee, the sweet, strong brew foreign to her tongue. ''Not that I didn't want to travel,'' she said hastily as she glanced up to find the king's dark gaze assessing her. ''I planned to take a year off and tour Europe after college, but then I had the opportunity to start Creative Weddings and I decided to postpone a European tour until later. Since then, I've focused on building the business and any traveling I managed to squeeze in has been to visit clients in the U.S. I can't seem to get away from the office for longer than a day or two.''

''Then we're fortunate that you've taken this time to spend with us,'' the king said. ''I understand that you've agreed to plan Lazhar's wedding.''

''I'm very interested in the possibility,'' Emily said carefully. ''As I told your son, however, I won't be able to put together a comprehensive proposal until I've seen the facilities, talked to your staff, and have a bit more input from him, his fiancée, and your family.''

The king waved away her concerns. ''I'm certain that your proposal will be acceptable. My son has chosen you and I have complete confidence in his judgment in this matter. Even more so now that I've met you.'' His eyes twinkled.

''Thank you, Father,'' Lazhar said wryly.

This is how it should be between a father and son, Emily thought, as the two exchanged a look of complete understanding. Seeing Lazhar with his father made Emily realize why he had spirited her out of San Francisco and what made him willing to do whatever it took to make his father's wish a reality. He clearly loved his father and even Emily, who had never felt that mutual affection between herself and her father, couldn't help but recognize the depth of the connection between the two.

"I told Emily that she needs to tour the country and meet our people in order to understand more about Danizian culture before creating a wedding plan," Lazhar continued.

"An excellent idea." The king nodded in agreement. "And you'll be her guide, of course—where will you begin?"

"I thought we'd dine at the palace this evening, with mother and Jenna. Emily can sample traditional Daniz recipes and the work of the chef who will be preparing the food for the reception and wedding banquet. After dinner, we'll tour the casino." He looked at Emily. "Unless there's something else you'd prefer to do this evening?"

Emily shook her head. "Not at all, it sounds like an excellent plan."

The king glanced at his watch. "I'm sure you'll enjoy both our chef's dinner and the casino, Emily. And now, I'm afraid I must say good afternoon. I have another appointment that I must keep."

Emily rose, waiting while Lazhar helped his father to his feet before the king took the arm of a burly manservant. The white clad servant had appeared so silently that Emily was unaware he was near until he stepped forward to hold out his arm for the king to lean on.

"Good afternoon, Emily." The king held out his free hand. "I'm very glad you've come to stay with us."

"Thank you." Emily took his hand in hers, surprised by the strength in the thin fingers. Although he was as tall as his son, King Abbar seemed almost frail in comparison to Lazhar and the stocky servant. An indomitable spirit and will blazed from his eyes but it was clear that the king was ill.

"We will talk again tomorrow."

"I look forward to it."

The king smiled with approval and turned to his son. "Come to my rooms before you go down to dinner, Lazhar. There is something I wish to discuss with you."

"Of course, Father."

Emily stood silently beside Lazhar, watching the king's labored steps as he left the garden with his aide and disappeared through a door at the far end of the patio.

"Your father is a very charming man," Emily commented as Lazhar walked beside her to reenter the high-ceilinged living room. "The two of you seem very close."

"We're father and son," Lazhar said simply, opening the door to the hall. Again, the guards snapped to attention.

"So are Cade and my father, but I've never thought of their relationship as anything but...

distant.'' ''Difficult,'' or even ''adversarial'' might better describe the association between her brother and Walter, she thought, but years of listening to her father's commands forbidding any discussions about the family with outsiders made her choose a milder word.

''That's unfortunate.'' Lazhar paused outside a door and Emily realized that he'd returned her to her suite. ''My father and I have grown closer since I became an adult and took over our national security. But even when I was a child and he was busy with the grueling job of running the country, with a thousand daily demands on his time, he always insisted that we share meals together as a family and each evening, he and mother tucked us in bed.'' A fond smile quirked his mouth. ''They're both very hands-on parents. How about you, Emily?'' he asked softly, his gaze focused intently on hers. ''Do you want children? Do you see yourself as a mother who insists on tucking them in each night? Or would you leave them to nannies and governesses?''

''No governesses.'' Emily shook her head. ''And no nannies.''

''You say that with great conviction,'' he commented.

''I was raised by my father's housekeeper. Brenda is a wonderful woman and we were very lucky to have her, but children should have their parents involved in their lives.'' Realizing that she may have revealed more than she intended, Emily shrugged and tried for a careless tone. ''But I probably won't have children, so it's a nonissue for me.''

He lifted an eyebrow, folded his arms across his chest and leaned his shoulder against the wall. ''You don't plan to have children? You don't look forward to marrying?''

He looked as if he had all the time in the world to discuss her marital status, or lack of one. Emily almost groaned out loud. Why had she been so adamant about methods of parenting children? Granted, she felt very strongly about the issue, but she needed to keep Lazhar at arm's length. His affection and care for his father had already melted some of the barriers she'd erected around her emotions. She didn't want to discuss her feelings about children with him. What if he were understanding and kind? *Excellent qualities if I were his fiancée because they would make me love him more,* she thought, *but since I'm only the wedding planner and a business associate, not so good for me to know.*

''I have a company to run,'' she said lightly. ''I don't have time to think about children, certainly not for the foreseeable future.''

''But someday, you plan to marry and have children,'' he prodded.

"I doubt it." Something about him compelled her to be truthful when she'd planned to be evasive. She couldn't bring herself to lie outright to him.

"That would be a terrible waste," he said quietly. His gaze left hers and stroked over her face, lightly grazing her lips with an almost tangible touch. He brushed a strand of hair from her cheek and tucked it behind her ear. "You'll have beautiful children, Emily, and you'll make a wonderful mother. You have a soft heart and good instincts."

His deep voice thrummed along Emily's veins, making her blood move more swiftly. His dark gaze held hers and Emily felt her bones melting, her body swaying toward his where he leaned against the wall.

The murmur of voices, growing louder as they moved nearer down the hall, snapped Emily back to awareness. She flushed. Lazhar's fingers trailed across her hot cheek before his hand fell away and he pushed away from the wall to open the door behind her.

"Dinner's at eight. I'll be back to take you to the dining room. I wouldn't want you getting lost."

Emily murmured a thank-you and stepped inside, closing the door and sagging against it for support because her legs felt like rubber.

Lazhar Eban is a dangerous man. She moved

away from the door. *I bet every woman he meets falls in love with him. But not me—I can't afford to care about him. I'm only here to plan his wedding.* She shook her head at her reflection in the wall-to-wall mirror over the bathroom vanity. Her cheeks were flushed, her eyes dark, and to her dismay, her nipples were clearly visible, pushing against the white silk blouse she wore under the jacket of her yellow linen suit.

Damn. She groaned and turned away from the woman in the mirror. Lazhar would have noticed, he'd been standing too close, his attention too focused on her, and he was too male to have missed the obvious signs of arousal.

She stripped off her clothes and turned the shower jets on, determined to have a better grip on her emotions during dinner and the planned visit to the Daniz Casino.

Lazhar knocked at his father's open bedroom door later that evening.

''Come in.''

King Abbar was in bed. The huge mahogany bedstead had blue silk hangings, tied back with gold cord against the four heavy posts at each corner. The headboard was carved with the royal crest and a dozen fat white pillows cushioned the king's back against the wood. The pillow shams, sheets, blankets and bedskirt were all white. The king preferred plain over opulent and while he'd left the rest of the palace's historical decorations intact, he'd stripped his own bedchamber of all gilt and velvet the moment he ascended to the throne. The result was a room that was supremely comfortable and reflected the king's masculine practicality.

"Good evening, Father. How are you feeling?"

"I'm well, all things considered."

Lazhar acknowledged the king's dry comment with a half smile as he walked across the room. Despite his father's constant reassurances, he knew that each day was a struggle. He searched the lined face and saw the weariness in the droop of eyelids and the slump of thin shoulders once military straight. "Are you sure you want to talk? I can come back in the morning after you're rested."

"I'm tired, but that's nothing new. Don't fuss, Lazhar, I get enough of that from your mother. Sit, sit." Abbar gestured at the chair next to the bed, but didn't wait for Lazhar to drop into it before he continued. "I like your Emily. I confess I had doubts when you told me that you'd chosen Walter Parks's daughter as your bride, but I was most pleasantly surprised when I met her today. She's nothing like her father. In fact, I quite liked her."

Tension that Lazhar hadn't realized existed eased at his father's words. Relieved, he crossed one ankle over the opposite knee, leaned back in the chair, and chuckled. "I thought you would. And no, she's definitely nothing like her father."

"The connection with Walter Parks may turn out to be more of a problem than an asset. Are you sure you want to be involved in business dealings with him? He has a reputation for ruthlessness among the gem traders."

"I can handle him."

"What about the rumors that he's been involved in illegal activity? I read the newspaper articles you faxed me from San Francisco and I have to wonder whether Parks is a company we should associate ourselves with."

"What I learned about Parks while I was in San Francisco leads me to believe that the company is strong, but that Walter Parks may have reached the end of what could be a dirty career path. I had the impression that what was printed in the newspaper might be just the tip of the iceberg."

The king pursed his lips, his gaze shrewd. "And in spite of those problems, you don't think a business association between Daniz and his company will tarnish our reputation?"

"No. The deal is airtight and I've had every aspect of the contract details checked. Walter Parks's personal life may self-destruct, but the Parks company won't, certainly not in the mining venture that we'll be involved in."

"Very well. Does Emily know about the connection between you and her father?"

"No, and I don't want her to until I'm ready to tell her."

"And when will that be?"

"I don't know yet."

The king shook his head. "She doesn't appear to be the kind of woman who will easily forgive being lied to."

"I'm not lying to her. I've never told her I *didn't* know her father."

"*Hmph.* Perhaps not. But you're lying by omission when you purposely keep silent because you know that the acquaintance would affect how she feels about you."

"You're probably right," Lazhar admitted reluctantly. "I plan to tell her, but not until we know each other better. If I tell her now that I'm considering joining her father in a gem mining operation, she'll write me off as just another of her father's business associates obsessed with jewels. I need time."

"Then you'd better hope that she doesn't learn the truth before you tell her." Abbar considered his son for a moment. "What made you choose Emily over all the other women you know? You hadn't met her before this week, had you?"

"No. I've been to San Francisco on business more than once but our paths never crossed at any of the gem market functions and after hearing her comments about how she views the industry, I'm not surprised. I doubt she attended very many jewel conferences.''

''So you literally had never seen her until Walter Parks sent her photo to you?''

''No, I'd never seen her.''

''What was it about her picture that was so intriguing?'' King Abbar's voice was mildly curious.

Lazhar shrugged. ''She's a very beautiful woman.''

''True,'' the king agreed. ''But there are many beautiful women in the world. And if gossip can be believed, you've dated several hundred.''

Lazhar's gaze sharpened, scanning his father's face. ''Gossip? Who's been telling you tales?''

Abbar waved a hand dismissingly. ''No one important. Don't worry, Lazhar, I'm aware that you've been very circumspect about the women you've associated with since college. But that doesn't mean I don't know their names, or that I haven't seen them, either in photos or in person.''

Lazhar shook his head, a slight smile tugging the corners of his mouth upward. ''You have eyes and ears everywhere.''

''Yes,'' Abbar said mildly. ''I'm the king, it's my job to know these things. And since I'm well aware of the long list of women friends you have,

I'm even more curious as to why, out of all the women you know, you chose Emily Parks?''

"Besides the fact that she's beautiful, well-educated and socially adept so she can cope with the responsibilities of being part of our family, Walter made marriage to her part of his business proposal.''

"Marrying solely to gain an edge in a business deal doesn't sound wise, Lazhar.'' A frown wrinkled Abbar's forehead.

"That's not the only reason,'' Lazhar said dryly. "I suppose I should admit that I took one look at her picture and wanted to bed her. That didn't change once I'd met her, in fact, it's grown stronger.''

"Ah.'' The two exchanged a very male look of understanding. "Perhaps not the single best reason for marrying, but certainly important.'' Abbar's shrewd gaze studied Lazhar. "Did you reach any other conclusions about your Emily when you met her face-to-face that convinced you she was the woman you wanted to marry?''

Lazhar had an instant memory of Emily and Walter's housekeeper talking about her yearning for a family. "Yes.'' His gaze met Abbar's. "She wants to marry and have children, but seems to have given up on the possibility. I can give her what she wants and needs, in return, I'll get what I want and need. It's a good bargain.''

"But you haven't told her any of this?"

"Not yet."

"Ah." King Abbar shifted against the pillows. "I think you should find a way to tell her your plans as soon as possible. Women can be unreasonable if they get the misguided impression that we're not consulting their wishes."

Lazhar mentally winced. His father was right, he thought, and Emily already had good cause to be displeased with him after he'd whisked her away from San Francisco without consulting her.

"You're right, Father. I'll tell her as soon as I can think of a way to bring up the subject without causing her to run straight back to San Francisco."

"I think you have your work cut out for you, son," Abbar said with a smile of commiseration.

Lazhar read the growing signs of weariness on his father's face and in the greater slump of his shoulders. He glanced at his watch and stood. "I promised Emily I'd collect her for dinner. I don't want her to get lost." He bent and kissed King Abbar's forehead. "Good night. I'll see you at breakfast."

"Good night, my son."

Emily planned to wear the Vera Wang cocktail dress that evening, the one she'd first donned for dinner with Lazhar in San Francisco. But when she walked into her closet to look for the little black dress, she gave in to temptation and slipped into a sinfully sexy, ankle-length, emerald-green evening gown. The lace-covered bodice was cut straight across the upper curve of her breasts and the short sleeves cupped her shoulders, leaving the long line of her throat and creamy shoulders bare. The dress was a slim, straight tube of emerald lace over satin, slit up the side to her thigh. Emily stared at her reflection in the mirror. She'd owned designer gowns since she was in her teens but she'd never had a dress that made her feel so alive. The color made her eyes glow a deeper, more mysterious green; her hair gleamed with golden highlights under the dressing room lights; her skin smooth and lightly tan against the delicate emerald lace.

I shouldn't, she thought, torn with indecision. *But on the other hand, will the queen be offended if I don't wear the clothes she ordered for me?*

Her conscience was still arguing with her love of pretty clothes when a light rap sounded at the door. The clock on the mantel read seven forty-five.

''You're early,'' she said as she opened the door for Lazhar and turned to collect her Palm Pilot from the delicate French table just inside the doorway.

''I know,'' Lazhar acknowledged as she stepped into the hall and he closed the door. ''What's this?''

"This?" Emily held up the small electronic day-planner.

"Yes, that."

"It's my planner."

"I know what an electronic day-planner is, Emily, I use one myself. What I don't know is why you're taking it to dinner."

"It's easier to carry than a notepad and pen. If your mother or sister discuss any details they think should be included in your wedding, I can jot down notes so I won't forget."

"Emily," Lazhar halted her by the simple method of closing his hand around her arm. "This is just a casual family dinner. You don't need to take notes."

"But...."

"No buts." He slipped the Palm Pilot out of her hand and tucked it into his jacket pocket. "You can take all the notes you like tomorrow, but for tonight, forget about work, okay? My mother is looking forward to meeting you, and Jenna to seeing you once again."

Emily sighed and gave in. "All right. But if you really want this wedding to take place in six months, then I must start the preliminary work tomorrow. And I need to contact my office first thing in the morning to check with my assistant and verify that she isn't having any problems with clients that I need to resolve since I left without talking to anyone. Early tomorrow, I must get back to work," she said firmly as he tucked her hand through his arm and resumed their walk down the corridor.

"Of course," he assured her.

But the amused glint in his eyes and the grin he gave her made Emily shake her head. "Just remember, you're the one who said he wanted a wedding celebration put together in a very short time," she said.

"I know. I promise I'll let you take all the notes you want tomorrow."

An hour later, Emily was thoroughly charmed by the queen, who insisted that Emily call her Caroline, and she was reminded again how much she'd liked Jenna Eban when they'd met at her friend's San Francisco wedding.

"Have you seen Angela since her wedding?" Emily asked over dessert.

"Twice," Jenna nodded. "She was in Paris with her husband three months ago and I met them there for the weekend. And I flew to San Francisco six months before that to stay with her for a week."

"And both times she brought home a plane load full of new clothes," Lazhar commented, a smile tilting his lips as he sipped his wine.

Jenna shrugged. "We shopped," she admitted. Her dark eyes were bright with mischief. "It was

Paris and San Francisco, after all, how could we *not* shop?''

''Easily,'' her brother said. ''Your closets were already full. What did you do with all the clothes you must have thrown out to make room for the new ones?''

''I donated them to charity,'' Jenna replied. ''Mother and I packed two boxes and took them to the Sisters of Mercy Hospital for their annual fund-raiser. The nuns were delighted to get them.''

''I'm sure they were. I wouldn't be surprised if some of them had never been worn.''

''Not true!'' Jenna shook her head. ''Absolutely not true. I didn't give away anything that I hadn't worn several times.''

Caroline smiled at Emily. ''Lazhar always teases us about the number of gowns we buy, but we're often photographed and the press has an amazing ability to remember if we wear an outfit more than two or three times.'' She sighed. ''It's a shame, really, because I've had to give up some gowns and suits that I truly loved.''

''Except for her Chanel suits.'' Jenna put in. ''She can't bear to part with them.''

''They're classics,'' Caroline said firmly. ''And I have to draw the line somewhere. Besides, I really adore those suits.''

''It's not easy being a queen,'' Lazhar said to

Emily, his deep voice filled with affectionate teasing as he grinned at his mother.

"That's true," Caroline said promptly. "Your family is well-known in San Francisco, Emily, and I'm sure the society photographers follow you. Do you have this problem?"

"Very rarely. Now that I'm an adult and no longer live at home, I seldom attend functions with my father. But when he requires the family's appearance at one of the charity dinners or fund-raisers that the Parks company supports, I try to make sure I never wear the same dress twice."

"How do you do that?" Jenna asked.

"I taped a list to the inside of my closet door and write down dates, events and what I wear to each one."

"Emily likes to make lists," Lazhar commented.

"I like to be organized," she corrected him calmly, determined to ignore the shiver of attraction she felt each time he smiled at her.

"Mother and I make lists, too," Jenna added. "Except my maid keeps track of what I wore where and when. Mother's secretary keeps a running total for her."

"I have a staff of two terrific women at the office that keep track of my business appointments," Emily commented. "I'd be lost without them."

"It's the same for Jenna and I, as well as Lazhar

and his father. Our commitments to appear at functions on behalf of the crown are a part of our family business,'' Caroline said. ''Without staff to assist us, we'd be hopelessly lost in no time.''

''Do royal functions take up all of your time?'' Emily asked, curious.

''A great deal of it,'' Caroline responded. ''I always make time to spend with the family, of course. And Jenna has cut back on some of her volunteer work because she's become more involved with the day-to-day running of the palace stables since my husband asked Lazhar to take over as head of Daniz security.''

''Mother also spends one day a week at the Sisters of Mercy Hospital,'' Lazhar said. ''Volunteering in the children's ward.''

''I trained as a pediatrics nurse before marrying Abbar,'' Caroline explained to Emily. ''And although my other duties make it impossible to have a full-time career outside the palace, I like to keep my hand in at the hospital.''

''And she gets to hold the babies.'' Jenna winked at Emily, a mischievous smile lighting her face. ''I think that's the real reason she never misses her time at the hospital.''

''Until you and your brother give me grandchildren, I have every intention of cooing at babies in the maternity ward every chance I get.''

Jenna rolled her eyes, Lazhar chuckled, and their

mother serenely sipped her coffee, ignoring them both.

Just like an ordinary family, teasing each other over dinner, Emily thought. *Only this family lives in a royal palace and their husband and father is the king.* She found it amazing that they were so warm and approachable. Lazhar was relaxed and open, teasing his younger sister, affectionately attentive to his mother. The cool businessman she'd first met in her San Francisco office was absent, replaced in this private setting by a son and brother who clearly loved his family.

She was having trouble keeping her perspective. It was increasingly difficult to think of Lazhar as a client when everything about him seemed to have been tailor-made to fit her private dream of the perfect man.

He's not perfect, she told herself firmly. *This is the guy that tricked you into boarding a plane and then flew you to a foreign country without first asking your permission.*

A small voice reminded her that Lazhar had an understandable reason for doing so, but she ignored it. She needed reasons to convince her foolish heart that Lazhar wasn't a perfect prince. She'd take what she could get.

Emily was still contemplating the unwise attraction she felt for Lazhar when they left the palace for the Daniz casino. They'd said good-night to

Jenna and Caroline after dessert—Caroline leaving to look in on her husband and Jenna off to join friends at a small birthday party. Emily had hoped Lazhar's sister would join them to provide a buffer between herself and the prince, but Jenna waved goodbye with a promise to see them the next morning.

Fortunately for Emily's peace of mind, Lazhar seemed intent on playing tour guide as the black Mercedes limousine wound through the narrow streets. The city seemed even more exotic and foreign to Emily under cover of night, the narrow streets sometimes shadowed, sometimes brightly lit.

''The casino provides employment for many of our citizens as well as generating income for the monarchy,'' Lazhar said as they turned a corner onto a wide avenue.

A short block away, the avenue ended in the circular driveway facing the casino.

''It looks like photos I've seen of the Opera House in Paris. Is there a connection?'' Enchanted, Emily smiled with delight and looked at Lazhar for confirmation.

''The architect was Charles Garnier, who also designed the Paris Opera House and the Monte Carlo Casino in Monaco.'' Lazhar leaned closer and his fingertip brushed her cheek, just to the left of the corner of her mouth. ''When you smile, you have dimples.'' His voice was distracted, his gaze intent.

Emily forgot to breathe. Warmth lingered where the tip of his finger had touched her. ''I know. You haven't noticed them before?''

''I noticed. But they aren't always there.''

A tiny frown of confusion pleated her brow. ''They aren't?''

''No. Only when you really smile, like you did just now, do they appear.'' His voice was deeper, the smooth tones roughened and faintly uneven.

''I didn't know,'' she murmured, held by the heat in his eyes and the slow, repeated brush of his fingers against the spot near the corner of her mouth. He bent nearer, his big hand cupping her chin, his fingertips gently covering the frantically beating pulse in her throat. He was going to kiss her. Emily desperately wanted him to; her lashes lowered, her gaze fastened on his mouth as he drew closer.

The car stopped moving.

Despite the opaque glass that separated them from the driver and bodyguard in front, Lazhar heard the passenger door open and knew that he had only seconds. He forced his fingers to leave Emily's silky, warm skin and eased away from her. Her lashes lifted and she stared at him, clearly disoriented.

''We're at the casino,'' he murmured, watching

her. The bemusement cleared from her eyes and she glanced over his shoulder just as the door opened behind him.

''So we are.'' Her cheeks were flushed but her voice was calm, composed.

Lazhar wished he were as cool but frustration tightened his muscles and he had to quell the urge to pull the door shut, take her in his arms and to hell with the crowd gathering outside. Instead, he slid out of the car and turned to hold out his hand to Emily.

The thigh-high slit in her gown's skirt allowed a tantalizing glimpse of shapely leg, ankle and strappy heeled sandals as she took his hand and let him draw her out of the limo. The casino security staff stood in a semicircle, creating an oasis among the elegantly dressed crowd of onlookers.

Someone called to Lazhar and he lifted a hand, smiling with cool ease before tucking Emily's hand through his arm and bending closer. ''The security staff will escort us into the casino. Don't worry, just keep walking and smile and wave.''

Lightbulbs flashed, excited Danizians and tourists called hellos as they moved quickly across the forecourt and through the wide bronze doors into the casino's huge foyer.

The security staff, each holding a walkie-talkie in their hand and wearing headpieces that allowed them to hear, escorted them across the marble floor to a series of arched doorways.

Emily's eyes widened as they paused at the top of the shallow stairs just past one of the rococo-carved doorways. Before them stretched the main floor of the casino. Carpeted in plush red, with enormous Waterford crystal chandeliers suspended from the domed ceiling, the gaming tables a mix of turn-of-the-century mahogany and state-of-the-art machines, the Daniz Casino was awash in a glittering, shifting crowd of tuxedo-clad men and designer-gowned women.

The air hummed with excitement and tension.

"Oh, this is marvelous. What fun." She turned to Lazhar, smiling with anticipation. "I love it."

"I'm glad you approve." He nearly groaned with frustration. He wondered how long she'd want to play? How long till they would once again be in the dark privacy of the limo and he could touch her again, taste her as he wanted to? "What do you prefer? Cards? Roulette? Dice?"

"I have no idea." She smiled at him again before her fascinated gaze drifted over the scene be fore them. "I've only been to Las Vegas a couple of times and I tried my hand at blackjack, but only because the friend I was with played."

"Friend?" The swift stab of dark jealousy took Lazhar by surprise.

Chapter Four

"Yes, my friend Jane and I were there for a wedding convention last year." She looked up at him. "You remember Jane, don't you."

Relief washed over him. "Yes, I remember Jane."

"Lazhar?"

The casino manager, his tall lean body elegant in a black tuxedo and a welcoming grin on his swarthy face, strode quickly up the steps from the gambling floor. The guards stepped aside, allowing him to enter the small oasis of space their circle created around the prince and Emily.

"Esteban." Lazhar held out his hand. "How's business this evening?"

The manager's handshake was brief but firm. "The house is doing well, as usual."

"Good to hear. Emily, this is Esteban Garcia, the man who controls the casino. Esteban, this is Emily Parks." Emily was friendly but no more than polite as Esteban bowed over her hand and returned her smile with a glint of male appreciation. She glanced at Lazhar. When she lifted a brow in inquiry, he realized that his jaw was set, his fingers curled into fists and he had the distinct urge to punch Esteban for smiling at her and holding her hand for seconds longer than he thought was necessary.

What the hell is wrong with me? He'd wanted many women, but he'd never before felt this combination of possessiveness and lust.

He flexed his fingers, purposely relaxing tense muscles. "Emily would like to play," he said, his voice bland. "Perhaps the roulette wheel?"

"Certainly." Esteban took one of the handheld walkie-talkies from a guard and spoke into it, his fluent Spanish liquid and musical. He handed the small transmitter back to the guard. "It's arranged. Would you like to play in a private room upstairs or down on the floor?"

Lazhar looked at Emily. She was half-turned away from them, her face animated as she drank in the sight of the colorful crowd shifting under the glittering lights, her gaze following the activity on the casino floor with obvious interest. "Downstairs—I think Emily will enjoy the excitement of the crowd."

"Very good." Esteban gave a quiet command and the guards moved down the shallow, carpeted steps. "If you and Miss Parks will come with me, Lazhar..."

A ripple of excited whispers followed in their wake as the three crossed the huge room, the guards clearing a path in front of them with Lazhar's personal bodyguard following behind.

Lazhar was accustomed to celebrity status and the attention his presence always received. He accepted it as part of the downside of being born into the royal family. But tonight, he was more aware of being the focus of all eyes because of Emily. Would the attention worry her? Annoy her? Scare her? How would she handle it?

He needn't have worried, he realized a few moments later. Emily dealt with the attention with calm serenity. Most of the casino guests were intent on their own gambling, but a small crowd of onlookers gathered around the roulette table where Esteban himself manned the wheel. Lazhar seated Emily on one of the tall, low-backed stools upholstered in red leather and took the seat beside her.

There were four other people at the table, three

men and one woman. The men nodded briefly in greeting, while the woman's gaze flicked assessingly over Emily and lingered for a moment on Lazhar before returning to the wheel on the table in front of them.

"Roulette is easy to learn." Lazhar rested his arm on the back of Emily's chair and leaned close to her, his lips brushing the delicate shell of her ear. "Esteban will give you chips." He gestured at the stack of playing chips on the table in front of each player. "You notice that everyone has different colored chips so the dealer can quickly identify the bets." He nodded at Esteban and the dealer deftly counted and then slid two handfuls of blue chips across the table to Emily. "Now you place your chips on the numbered squares on the table, wherever you'd like."

Emily looked up at him. "How do I know which numbers to choose?"

"Some players have lucky numbers they always play. Some believe in intuition and playing their hunches for the night."

"I don't have a lucky number and my intuition is silent. So how do I pick a number?"

"Tell me the first number that comes into your mind—quick, don't think about it."

"Seven," she said promptly.

"Now another number."

"Twenty-two."

"Okay. Now pick any combination of those numbers between one and thirty-six—add, subtract, whatever—and put chips on those numbers."

She stared at him for a moment, a small smile curving her lips. "Does that work? Will I win?"

He shrugged. "I have no idea. It was my grandfather's system and he swore that it worked for him."

"That's good enough for me." She looked at the table with interest and carefully placed chips on seven, twenty-two, and twenty-nine. Then she paused, studying the table, half-turning to murmur. "Why are some of the chips sitting directly on top of the numbers, and some placed at the corners?"

"The ones on the corners are 'corner bets'—the bet covers the four numbers that join at the corner where the chip sits." He nodded at the black and red squares numbered from one to thirty-six and her blue chip resting squarely in the center of number twenty-two. "Your bet on number twenty-two is called a 'straight bet'—the ball has to stop on the wheel at twenty-two in order for you to win."

"Hmmm," Emily tapped the tip of her forefinger against her chin and considered the table. "Which bet has the best odds?"

"The straight bet—the odds are thirty-five to one."

"Then I'll stay with that." She smiled at him, the elusive dimple at the corner of her mouth appearing and disappearing in a flash. "If I win, I win big."

"True." Amused at the risk-taker attitude in Emily when he'd mostly seen her exhibit cool, calm control up until now, Lazhar nodded at Esteban.

The dealer acknowledged him with a barely perceptible nod in return. "Bets down, ladies and gentlemen." The other players around the table nodded and Esteban spun the wheel in one direction and the small silver ball in the other. The ball left the track, rolling onto the spinning wheel. "No more bets!"

The ball bounced and moved, coming to rest in a black compartment of the wheel.

"Black twenty-nine." Esteban called out.

Emily clapped her hands with glee. "I won!" She looked up at Lazhar. "I did win, didn't I?"

"Yes, you definitely won," he said dryly, exchanging an amused glance with Esteban as the dealer stacked a large pile of chips in front of her.

Emily's eyes rounded. "I won all that?"

"The odds were thirty-five to one." He grinned at her. "You wanted to win big, remember?"

"I remember." She flashed him a wide smile. "This is fun." She watched the other gamblers at the table as Esteban either deftly swept away their lost chips, or paid out their wins. Each of them instantly returned chips to the table.

"Should I pick the same numbers, or different ones?"

"Your choice. What do you want to do?"

"I think I'll use the same numbers." Emily put chips on the numbers she'd chosen for the first round. Then she took three chips from her winnings, stacked them neatly on top of the original pile that Esteban had given her, and moved them aside.

"What are you doing?"

"I'm playing with the money I won and leaving the original chips alone. That way," Emily explained, "when I lose the chips I've won, I'll know it's time to stop playing. If I mix the two piles together, I'm afraid I won't remember what the original investment was."

Surprised, Lazhar searched her earnest expression.

"What?" A tiny frown pleated her forehead between her brows and he smoothed it away with his fingertip. Faint pink color bloomed on her cheeks and throat.

"I'm impressed," he said softly, his gaze holding hers as Esteban set the wheel and ball in motion and announced no more bets.

"Why?"

"Because very few people are wise enough to play with the house's money and not theirs. Especially not when they're new to gambling—they usually get swept up in the excitement and lose track of the amount of money they're investing.''

Emily glanced at the stack of blue chips. ''How much money am I investing?'' she asked, curious.

''Red seven,'' Esteban announced.

''This is a hundred-dollar table,'' Lazhar said casually.

''A hundred dollars?'' Her gaze flicked from him to the table, where Esteban was once again collecting from the losers and paying the winners. He deposited a stack of chips in front of Emily and she looked at Lazhar. ''Are you telling me that each of the chips I'm playing with is worth a hundred dollars?''

''Yes.''

''That means I've won—'' she quickly calculated ''—seven thousand dollars?''

''That sounds right.'' He chuckled at her stunned expression.

''But what if I'd lost?''

He shrugged. ''You wouldn't have seven thousand dollars.''

''But I would have lost six hundred dollars.''

''True, but since you're my guest, and this is by way of a business meeting…''

She shot him a look of complete disbelief.

''…and since you're really 'working' tonight, soaking up the atmosphere of Daniz, the house would have forgiven your debt.''

Emily was skeptical. "Why would they do that?"

"Because my family owns the controlling interest in the casino."

"Ah." Understanding smoothed the slight frown from her brow. "I see."

They stayed at the roulette table for several more spins of the wheel before leaving it to try a game of blackjack. For the next hour and a half, Emily sampled the games beneath the gilt dome. Lazhar strolled beside her, answering her questions about the games, showing her how to roll the dice at the craps table, and keeping her champagne flute filled. When she'd had enough of playing, they toured the other rooms on the casino's lower level. The central gambling space was huge and wings to the right and left of the domed area housed two five-star restaurants connected by a wide marbled passageway lined with exclusive designer shops. They browsed, window-shopping but not entering any of the exotic shops before they returned to the central room and climbed the sweeping staircase to look into several of the private gambling rooms on the second level.

Her curiosity satisfied, Emily paused on the wide balcony that circled the casino floor. With Lazhar leaning casually beside her, she rested her hands on the polished mahogany railing, her gaze sweeping the crowded floor below.

"It's a fascinating place," Emily commented. "The air nearly vibrates with anticipation and I can almost taste the excitement."

Below them and to their right, a young woman dressed in a white evening gown, diamonds glittering at her ears, wrists, and around her throat, shrieked with delight and jumped up and down, hugging her silver-haired companion.

"I think she won," Lazhar said dryly.

Emily laughed, her bright green eyes sparkling with amusement. "I'm sure you're right." She glanced at the scene below before she asked. "You said that your family owns the casino?"

"A controlling interest," he corrected her.

"Ah." She turned her back to the balcony and fixed her gaze on him, clearly curious. "Did you spend much time here when you were growing up?"

"A fair amount," he admitted. "My grandfather loved to gamble and he'd tell my mother that he was taking me out for ice cream, then we'd come here. He taught me to play roulette before I was six and poker before I was eight."

"Did your parents object that he was teaching you to gamble instead of buying you ice cream?"

"At first," he conceded. Lazhar never talked about his grandfather to anyone outside the family circle, but something about the genuine interest in Emily's green eyes made him want to confide in her. "My mother lost her temper when she found out but after my grandfather told her that I'd learned to do math far beyond my schoolmates, she calmed down."

Emily laughed. "Did you win often?"

"Not at first. But after a while, yes."

"What did you do with all the money?"

"Put it in the poorbox at St. Catherine's."

Her eyes widened and Lazhar could have kicked himself. He'd never told anyone else what he and his grandfather had done with their earnings. The truth had slipped out, seduced from him by the warm interest in Emily's green eyes.

"That's wonderful," she said softly. "You weren't tempted to spend it on candy and toys when you were six?"

"I was," he said ruefully. "But my grandfather wisely discussed all the possible things we could do with the money, then took me to visit the nursery school at St. Catherine's. Afterward, he told me that I could decide whether I wanted to keep the money or share it with the children at the church. Of course, I chose the church."

"That must have been a difficult choice for a six-year-old to make."

Lazhar remembered very well how he'd felt when his grandfather first asked him if he really wanted to spend his winnings on candy. A reminiscent smile curved his mouth. "At first, yes. But my grandfather was a very wise man. He didn't tell me I had to give the money to St. Catherine's. He talked about how fortunate I was to live in a palace and to be able to play cards in the casino; then we walked through Daniz, in and out of the shops, through the residential districts, both affluent and poor areas. By the time we finished, I'd learned an important lesson about the responsibilities that came with the benefits of being born into the royal family.''

"And the responsibility of being royal is what made you decide to give the money to St. Catherine's?"

"Partly. But mostly I did it because I loved my grandfather. If he thought I should give the money to St. Catherine's, that was a good enough reason for me.''

"He sounds like a wonderful man."

"He was." A flashbulb went off below them and Lazhar realized that they'd been standing in full view of the throng on the floor below for too long. The paparazzi had clearly found them. He turned his back to the railing and held out his arm, elbow bent. "Are you ready to move on to the next stop on our tour of Daniz nightlife? Or do you want to chance your luck at another table here in the casino?"

"I'm ready to continue the tour." She took his arm and they moved down the sweeping staircase.

They said good-night to Esteban and left the casino. Lazhar's car waited on the paved forecourt, the driver holding the door open. A small crowd of photographers began snapping photos the moment they left the building.

"Just smile and wave," Lazhar advised Emily, keeping her moving forward at a smooth pace. Moments later, they were in the car, doors closed, and the limo was purring smoothly away from the brightly lit building.

"Goodness, is it always like that?" Emily asked.

"Not always. The local media has a long-standing arrangement with my family—they respect our privacy and in exchange, we have a publicist that arranges photo ops and information releases on a regular schedule."

"So photographers don't usually follow you when you're out for the evening?"

"No, but ever since the tabloids publicized my father's wish to see Jenna and I married, the international media has flooded Daniz with reporters and photographers. They're not so willing to stick to the schedule set up by the palace office." He shifted, his wrist grazing against the bulk of the roll of bills forgotten in his jacket pocket. "I nearly forgot about this." He shoved his hand in his pocket and took out the bundle of money, holding it out to her. "What do you plan to do with your winnings?'' he asked, setting the thick roll on her lap.

''I have no idea. It's a lot of money.'' She glanced at him, the streetlights flickering light and shadow over her features. ''I know.'' Her dimples flashed as she laughed. ''Let's drop it into St. Catherine's poorbox.''

Arrested, he stared at her for a moment before his mouth quirked. ''You're sure you want to do that?'' His voice held amusement. ''You could buy a lot of candy with that much money.''

''I'm sure.''

''Whatever you say.'' He leaned forward. ''Nico, stop at St. Catherine's.''

Moments later, the limo eased to the curb and Lazhar handed Emily out. He caught her hand and led her up the flight of stone steps and into the dim church. Not five minutes later, they hurried back down the steps and reentered the car.

''I wonder what the Sisters will think when they empty the box this week.''

''They'll probably think an angel visited them in answer to prayer.'' Lazhar raised their linked hands to his lips and brushed a lazy kiss against her knuckles. ''And they'd be right.''

Emily couldn't catch her breath to respond. His warm mouth barely grazed her fingers, but she felt the impact down to her toes. And the heat simmering in his eyes made her heart stutter in reaction.

The car slowed and braked to a stop. She tugged her fingers from his, glancing out the side window to see a small sign swinging over an arched doorway, the soft rose-colored neon spelling out Pilar's.

"Where are we?"

"At a friend's club." The bodyguard pulled open the door and Lazhar exited, turning to hand out Emily.

Emily stepped out beside Lazhar and waited while he spoke in Spanish with the bodyguard. They were joined by three men from the black sedan that pulled up and parked behind the Mercedes limousine. Emily hid an amused smile. She hoped they weren't planning to fade into the background, because the four tall, burly men would never be mistaken for anything other than what they were— men whose duty it was to guard the prince of Daniz.

The liquid, musical Spanish conversation flowed around her but she didn't understand a word of the discussion. While she waited for them to finish, she glanced with curiosity first up, then down, the cobbled avenue. The city street they stood on was narrow and winding, lined on each side with stone buildings five-stories high, each festooned with wrought-iron balconies dripping with trailing flowers and greenery. The sweet scent of climbing roses mingled with lavender and spicy carnation to drench the night air with perfume.

Lazhar might claim this evening was strictly business, she thought, but for her, it was a dream come true. Daniz seemed very exotic and foreign to her and the sights and smells of the principality were seducing her senses.

And then there was Lazhar himself. The handsome prince was proving to be much more than a charming face with royal connections. If she wasn't careful, she thought, she'd find herself falling in love with the man beneath the royal trappings.

And that would be a disaster. He would soon be marrying someone else, a woman with a pedigree to match his lineage and the training to become the queen of Daniz. Loving him would guarantee her a broken heart.

The car door slammed, the sound drawing her attention back to Lazhar just as he finished speaking with the burly bodyguards.

"Sorry to keep you waiting," he murmured. He took her arm, his fingers warm, the calluses faintly rough against her skin.

"Is everything all right?" She glanced over his shoulder at the two men following close behind them.

"Everything's fine." His hand left her arm to rest on her waist and he moved her ahead of him through the door held open by one of the body-guards. ''They wanted to leave two men outside to watch the entrance in case the photographers followed us. I convinced them to come inside and enjoy the music and food.''

A wave of sound greeted them. The unmistakable strum of twelve-string guitars accompanied the staccato rap of boot heels against bare wood floors, nearly drowning out the murmur of voices, muted laughter and click of glassware.

''Lazhar! Welcome, my friend.''

Emily stepped back as a big bear of a man wrapped Lazhar in a hug and planted a kiss on each cheek.

''Joaquin,'' Lazhar laughed and returned the hard hug.

''I haven't seen you for at least two weeks. Where have you been?'' the man demanded.

''Out of town. I've just returned, and I brought someone to meet you and to see Pilar dance.'' Lazhar caught Emily's hand and drew her forward. ''Emily, I'd like you to meet Joaquin. He owns the club.''

''I'm very pleased to meet you,'' she said politely. Joaquin had black eyes and a strong nose above a curved black bandido mustache that drooped over his upper lip, giving him a ferocious look. Given his size and the rest of his demeanor, she would have found him intimidating if not for Lazhar's warm endorsement.

"It's a pleasure to meet any friend of Lazhar's, especially a friend as pretty as you are." He winked at her.

"I hoped we'd be able to see Pilar dance," Lazhar said. "Is she here?"

"Yes, she is, but…" Joaquin shrugged one massive shoulder. "A new costume isn't working and she's temperamental tonight. Who knows what her performance will hold."

"Pilar only dances better when she's upset," Lazhar said with amusement. "And temperamental is Pilar's normal mood."

"*Si.*" Joaquin grinned, his teeth flashing whitely against his coal-black mustache. "My Pilar is a woman of strong emotions, not a woman of calm and serenity—which only makes the flamenco more passionate, eh?" Without waiting for a response, he gestured at a waiter. When the young man quickly approached, Joaquin issued orders in a spate of Spanish and the waiter bustled off. "Now," Joaquin continued, giving them his full attention once more, "your usual table is being prepared. If you'll come with me?"

He led them through an archway at the end of the entry hall and into a large, low-ceilinged room. They wound between crowded tables arranged in a semicircle around an open space of bare hardwood floor.

Lazhar was greeted with familiarity by more than one person as they crossed the room and each time, he acknowledged them with a smile and a greeting that included their name.

Emily wondered if Lazhar was a regular visitor at the club for his arrival didn't cause the speculation and exclamations from the crowd that she'd seen at the casino.

"Do you have time to join us for a drink?" Lazhar asked Joaquin as he seated Emily at a horseshoe-shaped booth, upholstered in burgundy leather, on the far side of the room.

"Let me check on the kitchen staff and if all is well, I'll be back to catch Pilar's performance with you," he promised, taking Emily's hand in his. He bent and kissed her fingers with an old world courtesy that was entirely natural. "It is a pleasure to have met you, Emily." He released her and grinned at Lazhar. "Emily will make a beautiful bride."

"Yes, she will."

Startled, Emily couldn't gather her wits to ask Joaquin what he meant by his parting comment until he was gone. Before she could call him back, he was intercepted by a waiter. Their brief conversation ended with the young man nodding and hurrying away. Joaquin had gone barely three steps more before a customer caught his attention and he paused to chat with the two couples seated at the table.

"I don't think he's going to make it to the kitchen very quickly," she commented.

"Not likely," Lazhar agreed. "He treats every customer as if they're a family friend and they love him for it."

"What did he mean by saying that I'd make a beautiful bride?" she asked Lazhar, half-turning to face him on the leather seat. He sat beside her, one arm resting along the top of the booth, his fingers within touching distance of her nape. A candle flickered in the center of their table, adding its faint glow to the dimly lit room, but still, his face seemed shadowed, his gaze enigmatic.

"I think he was stating the obvious," he said smoothly. "You're a beautiful woman. It follows that you'll make a beautiful bride when you marry." He glanced away from her at Joaquin, who was now three-quarters of the way across the room, still chatting with customers. "Joaquin is part-Spanish, part-Danizian, and he tends to assume that all young, beautiful women will marry someday."

"And you think that's all he meant?" Emily was distracted by Lazhar's matter-of-fact, almost casual observation that he thought her beautiful, but she remained uncertain about Joaquin. Still, she couldn't imagine what other meaning could be attached to the club owner's parting comment.

"What else could he have meant?" Lazhar's dark gaze returned to her, sweeping over her hair and face before lingering on her mouth. He lifted his wineglass and gestured at hers. "This is another Spanish wine that I wanted you to try."

Emily allowed herself to be diverted by the abrupt change of subject and lifted her glass to her lips. The cool, slightly tart white wine was delicious. "It's very good," she agreed, wondering how much of it she dared drink since she'd already indulged in two glasses of champagne at the casino.

The soft thrum of guitars suddenly crescendoed and the crowd burst into applause.

"Ah, this will be Pilar." Lazhar bent closer to make himself heard over the crowd noise, his lips brushing her ear. "Have you seen flamenco dancing before?"

His deep voice shivered up her spine. She told herself to ignore the sensual pull he effortlessly exerted, but it was a losing battle and she knew it. The most she could hope was that she could remain outwardly unaffected so that he didn't know what his slightest touch and the sound of his voice did to her.

"No." She shook her head. "Jane had tickets to the touring company of the Madrid Dance Ensemble's performance at the San Francisco Playhouse last summer, but I had to cancel at the last minute. A section of the program was to be flamenco...I was very disappointed to have missed it.''

"The Madrid Ensemble has performed here in Daniz. I thought they were quite good," Lazhar said. "But Pilar is a star in her own right. I think you'll enjoy this." He looked up as the guitars strummed faster, louder. "Here she is."

The woman who swirled onto the spotlit wooden floor between the guitarists and audience made an instant impact. The crowd cheered and whistles echoed through the room as she spun slowly, heels rapping the floor in a counterpoint to the guitars' beat. She was tiny, with exotic features topped by braided ebony hair pinned in a heavy, intricately wound knot at her nape. A single, perfectly shaped red rose nestled against her black hair, echoing the scarlet of her classic Spanish dress. She whisked her skirts above her knees and the ruffled underskirt framed shapely legs clad in sheer black stockings. Her small feet were encased in black leather heels with a strap that accentuated the delicate bones of her ankles. She was a visual feast, beautiful and exotic. Energy poured from her, charging the air with electricity, crackling throughout the room as her passion for the dance infected the audience.

She whirled and dipped, her feet stamping out the rhythm with blurred speed, her castanets clicking as the guitars increased their tempo, luring her ever faster.

Emily couldn't take her eyes off the dancer and when the music crashed to a halt and she struck a pose, the entire audience burst into spontaneous applause, including Emily.

Before she had time to catch her breath and analyze the performance, however, Pilar was joined by a man. Dressed all in black, he was much taller than the petite Pilar and he radiated the same intensity and emotion. Once again the music began and Emily quickly realized that Pilar and her partner were acting out a classic male-female courtship with their dance, advancing, retreating in a pattern that stirred her and had her breathless.

"Flamenco is all sex and emotion—primal and haunting." Lazhar murmured in her ear. Emily tore her gaze away from the pair dancing in the spotlight, her gaze meeting his. Sexual attraction pulsed between them, stealing what was left of her breath. She couldn't pull her gaze from his and the need to lean forward, to cross the short space separating them and taste his mouth, was nearly overwhelming. She was hardly aware that the dance ended, the guitars going silent. The crowd roared their approval.

''You liked it.'' Lazhar's voice held quiet satisfaction.

Emily licked her lips, her throat gone dry. ''Yes, very much,'' she murmured, barely able to think. She struggled to find a safe, innocuous conversational subject. The heat in his eyes told her that he knew what she was feeling and Emily's heart raced faster, the room much too warm. ''She's wonderful. Is she a local woman, someone you and Joaquin grew up with?''

''No, she's Spanish.'' His voice was deeper, rougher than normal. ''Her agent booked her into the club about five years ago and Joaquin took one look at her and fell in love. When it was time to go, the rest of the troupe left but Pilar stayed. They were married within a few months and she's been dancing here ever since. She tours Europe for two or three months out of the year but hates to leave home and Joaquin for longer.''

''She's so tiny and he's so big, they must make an interesting looking couple.'' Emily was grateful that Lazhar had followed her lead but despite their carefully polite conversation, tension and heightened awareness crackled between them.

Lazhar grinned, his eyes crinkling at the corners, the lines of his face softening with amusement. ''He can pick her up with one hand, but trust me, Pilar may be tiny, but Joaquin has to fight for his share of influence in their family.''

The guitarists began a set of mellow music. Lazhar glanced at the polished dance floor, quickly filling with couples moving to the music.

"Dance with me." He caught Emily's hand, drawing her with him out of the booth.

Chapter Five

It was a mistake. He knew it the moment she turned into his arms and lifted her hand to his shoulder. He'd been taking advantage of any excuse to touch her all evening with a guiding hand on her arm or her waist. All of the contact was socially acceptable between a man and a woman spending an evening together.

But even that small physical connection had been enough to set his blood simmering. He'd forced himself to rein in the growing urge to thread his fingers through her thick sweep of golden-brown hair, slick his tongue over the plush fullness of her lower lip and taste her.

Now only inches separated her from him but holding her loosely within the circle of his arms wasn't enough, not nearly enough. The music pulsed around them, the dance floor growing more and more crowded until another couple jostled them, bumping Emily off-stride. Lazhar caught her closer, supporting her weight against his.

''Sorry,'' she murmured.

''Don't be.'' He welcomed the excuse to wrap her tighter, her slim body resting against him, her thighs aligned with his, the soft curves of her breasts against his chest, her temple touching his jaw, her silky hair brushing his throat and chin. Having his arms around her wasn't enough but he knew that they were being observed by too many eyes, friendly though they probably were. If he gave in to the urge to kiss her in this very public place, the press would pursue them more than ever. And he didn't want Emily hounded by paparazzi.

So they stayed on the dance floor, slowly swaying to the throb of the passionate guitars, until the musicians took a break. Lazhar knew he'd reached his limit; he couldn't sit next to Emily and carry on polite conversation when all he could think about was making love to her. Reluctantly he released her, stepping back only slightly, his hand resting on her waist, and nodded briefly at the two bodyguards seated at a table on the edge of the dance floor.

The two men moved quickly and by the time Lazhar and Emily stepped out onto the sidewalk, the Mercedes was waiting for them, engine running, the back door held wide.

Lazhar couldn't bring himself to release her hand and let her move away from him. Emily didn't protest so they sat silently, pressed thigh-to-thigh, as the car purred along the winding road that climbed to the palace. He could have raised the privacy window, shutting them away from the chauffeur and guard in the front seat. But though he trusted the two men implicitly, he didn't want the faintest hint of gossip to touch Emily. He'd always been scrupulously careful about keeping his personal life private and he felt even more strongly about protecting Emily. If all went as he'd planned, she would be his wife; he wouldn't give anyone cause to question her actions.

So he held on to control by his fingertips and fought back the need to pull her into his arms.

He smoothed his thumb over the back of her hand, then the silky skin at her wrist, and felt the frantic pound of her pulse beneath his fingertips. Impatient to reach privacy, he dismissed his driver and then the guard as soon as they arrived at the palace, leaving him alone to walk Emily to her suite.

Aware that security cameras scanned the corridors at regular intervals, he opened the door to her suite and followed her inside.

The room was shadowy, dimly lit only by the faint light from a bedside lamp left burning in the adjoining room.

"Lazhar, I don't think…" Emily began, her normally clear tones husky with emotion.

"Shh." He silenced her with a fingertip against her lips. "Don't think."

He backed her against the door panels, lifted her hands to place them around his neck, and lowered his head to cover her mouth with his.

And was instantly lost in the hot, honeyed taste of her mouth that opened willingly beneath his, the press of her body that curved so perfectly against his own, the scent of her skin and hair that stirred his senses with every breath he drew.

He was drunk on the taste, scent and feel of her. He sank his fingers deep into the heavy thickness of her hair and tilted her face up to his. She murmured incoherently, her arms tightening around his neck to hold him closer as the kiss turned hotter, the press of their bodies more urgent in the thick silence of the darkened room.

Lazhar wanted her. Emily clearly wanted him. And the bedroom was only steps away. But when he drew back, intending to obey the urging of his body, pick her up and carry her the few feet to her bed, sanity intruded.

"Damn," he muttered, resting his forehead against hers while he struggled for control.

"What?" Emily murmured, opening heavy-lidded green eyes to look up at him, confusion vying with arousal on her expressive features.

"We can't do this."

"Why?" Awareness chased away the drowsy, passionate cast of her face. Still flushed, she stiffened and pulled out of his arms. "Of course we can't." Her voice was equally stiff. "I think you should leave now, Your Highness. Thank you for a lovely evening."

Lazhar was painfully aroused but he couldn't help smiling ruefully at the contrast between the vibrant, passionate Emily he'd held a moment before and this prim, annoyed and obviously uncomfortable Emily who faced him now.

"It was my pleasure." He caught her shoulders and bent to take her mouth in a brief, possessive kiss. "Especially this." She glared at him, speechless, and he smiled, delighted with her. "I'll see you tomorrow."

She didn't answer and he stepped outside, pulling the door shut behind him. He clearly heard the sharp thud as something hit the panels. It was probably her purse, or maybe a shoe, he thought as he moved quickly down the corridor, whistling softly, his hands shoved into his pockets.

* * *

Emily woke to the sound of birds warbling and chirping outside her room, where the early-morning sunshine flooded the garden. Despite the early hour and the late night before, she rose, showered, dressed in a bright yellow sundress she found hanging in the closet, slipped her feet into matching leather sandals, and within the hour was ready to search for the breakfast room.

She stepped out into the hall, pulling the door closed behind her, and paused, trying to remember if the maid had led her to the right or the left the prior morning.

"I think we went to the right," she murmured. She set off down the thick carpet that ran down the center of the wide hallway, leaving black-veined grey marble floor visible along both sides.

She hadn't gone far when a man wearing the blue and gold uniform of a house servant entered the hall from a side passage and walked toward her.

"Miss Parks?"

"Yes."

"His Highness, King Abbar, asks that you join him for breakfast in his garden. I'm to take you to him, should you choose to accept his invitation."

Emily smiled with delight. "I would be more than happy to join the king."

The man bowed. "If you'll follow me, please. This way." He gestured down the hallway he'd

just traversed and set off, Emily walking behind him.

Once again, she quickly lost her bearings as they
turned into yet another hallway and then another.
At last, however, they reached the familiar door
where the soldiers stood guard and her guide led
her through the king's spacious sitting room and
out into the sunshine.

"Good morning, Emily," King Abbar's lined
face lit with a smile.

"Good morning, Your Highness." Emily let the
servant pull out a chair and seat her. "How lovely
of you to invite me to share breakfast with you."

"And how gracious of you to accept." The
king's eyes twinkled. He gestured at the waiter,
who leapt into action, deftly pouring equal streams
of coffee and hot milk into the Limoges china cup
next to Emily's plate. "What would you like to eat
this morning? My chef will make anything you
want, from American pancakes to British kippers
to a Danizian omelet."

"I think I'd like an omelet."

"Excellent." He waved his hand and the servant
bowed and withdrew. "That is my choice as well,
together with fruit and our own Danizian version
of coffee, which is a bit of a cross between Turkish
coffee and Italian espresso. You must taste it and
tell me what you think."

Emily obediently lifted the cup to her lips and

sipped. The rich flavor of strong coffee blended with the vanilla-flavored milk, creating a smooth, succulent drink.

"Mmm." Emily gave a small hum of appreciation, her eyes closing briefly. "This is almost sinfully delicious," she told him. "I have a favorite coffee shop in San Francisco, not far from my office, and I'd love to take this recipe home with me so I can ask the owner to make it for me. Is that possible?"

"I will have my assistant write it down for you," he smiled approvingly. "I'm pleased that you like it. How are you enjoying other things about my country? Are you having a pleasant visit?"

"I'm having a wonderful time," she said promptly. "Last night we visited the casino and a club named Pilar's where we saw flamenco dancing."

"Ah, yes, I believe that Pilar's is one of my son's favorite nightspots." King Abbar's gaze was veiled and he looked away, lifting his own cup to drink. "What did you think of our casino?"

"I was fascinated." Emily leaned forward, the heady rush of excitement she'd felt when she'd won last night returning in a gust of memory. "And I actually won at roulette."

"Did you?" The king's eyebrows winged upward in surprise. ''Are you often lucky at games of chance?''

''I have no idea. Last night was the first time I've ever played roulette. Lazhar explained the system his grandfather used and when I tried it, I won. A lot,'' she added, still faintly incredulous at the ease with which she'd gained such a large sum.

His gaze sharpened and he watched her closely over the rim of his cup. ''Lazhar told you about the gambling system his grandfather used?''

''Yes.'' Emily lowered her voice. ''He told me that his grandfather taught him to play blackjack and roulette when he was only six years old, is that true?''

The swift grin that curved the king's mouth was as mischievous as a boy's. ''Yes, I'm afraid it *is* true. My father—Lazhar's grandfather—thought Lazhar should have a chance to experience life out from under the watchful eye of palace protocol. So he took my son to many places that in retrospect, perhaps he shouldn't have, and taught him things that might have been better learned when he was older.''

''But Lazhar loved him very much and treasures those memories of his grandfather,'' Emily said with a soft smile.

''Yes, he does.'' The king eyed her consideringly. ''Did Lazhar tell you that?''

''He told me that he gave his winnings to St.

Catherine's because his grandfather thought he should and he loved his grandfather,'' Emily said. ''I gathered from Lazhar's words and his tone that he treasured the time he spent with his grandfather.''

''Yes, we all did.'' He sighed heavily, his expression sad.

''I assume that Lazhar's grandfather is no longer with you?'' Emily asked tentatively.

''He passed away just before Lazhar's eighteenth birthday.'' King Abbar was silent for a long moment, apparently lost in memories. Then he roused himself, visibly shaking off the brief melancholy. ''What did you do with your winnings from last night? Are you thinking of visiting the Jewel Market to search for the perfect diamond or ruby later on this morning?''

Emily laughed. ''No, not at all.'' She glanced around, saw that they were completely alone as the servants had disappeared into the king's suite. ''I did what Lazhar and his grandfather did.''

He eyed her. ''And what was that?''

''I stuffed the money into an envelope and dropped it into the poorbox at St. Catherine's.''

His thick white eyebrows lifted in surprise. Then he chuckled, the deep sound of amusement startling birds from the tree in the corner of the garden. ''How much was it?''

''About ten thousand.'' Emily frowned. ''I

think. I won seven thousand at roulette, but then I lost at the dice table and won several hands of blackjack, so I can't be sure of the exact sum, but I think it must have been around ten thousand dollars.''

''That's a tidy sum,'' he commented. ''I'm sure the sisters at St. Catherine's will put it to good use.''

Their breakfast arrived and the conversation turned to more general subjects. King Abbar answered her questions about his beloved Daniz and in turn, Emily willingly shared details about her life in San Francisco. When breakfast was finished, a last cup of coffee shared, and he reluctantly left her for his doctor-ordered morning rest, she gladly agreed to return for a game of chess before dinner that evening.

The same servant who had escorted her from her bedroom suite to the king's rooms, guided her to a sun-filled morning room where the queen and Jenna were sharing morning coffee and croissants.

''Good morning, Emily,'' Caroline greeted her. ''Did you sleep well?''

''Very well, thank you.'' Emily took the chair drawn out by a house servant, murmuring her thanks as she sat.

''I understand that you've already had breakfast with Abbar this morning,'' Caroline said. ''But perhaps you'd like another cup of coffee?''

"Coffee would be lovely." Emily waited until the servant poured the mix of rich coffee and milk into her cup. "I confess, I'm hoping to take the recipe home with me."

Jenna laughed and her mother chuckled.

"We love it, too. I used to steal sips from Papa's cup when I was tiny," Jenna said. "I think I was fifteen before he gave in and agreed to let me have coffee with breakfast."

"I didn't want you drinking coffee at all before you were sixteen and I strongly suspect that your father purposely pretended not to see you stealing sips from his cup when you were a little girl." Caroline's gaze rested fondly on her daughter and they exchanged a look of warm understanding.

Emily caught an underlying current of sadness from the two women. Beneath the queen's graciousness and Jenna's impish humor there was a thread of pathos when they talked about the king. She suspected that the emotion was due to his ill health and her heart went out to them.

"What are your plans for the day, Emily?" Caroline asked.

"I need to check in with my office staff back home, and then I'm hoping to begin preliminary work on the plans for Lazhar's wedding."

"Ooh, fun." Jenna's face lit with enthusiasm. "What will you do first?"

"I'd like to look at the venue for the event—I

assume the ceremony will be held in a church in the city and the reception here at the palace?''

''Yes, that's the traditional method,'' Caroline confirmed. ''The church is St. Catherine's and the largest ballroom would be best for the reception.'' A soft smile curved her mouth. ''That's where Abbar and I were married.'' She sighed before visibly collecting herself. ''The palace chef will cater the reception, which is always preceded by a sit-down luncheon for four to five hundred people.''

Emily made mental notes while fervently wishing she'd brought her Palm Pilot or at least a pencil and notepad with her.

''Mother, Emily should jot this down,'' Jenna said firmly, holding up a hand. ''Otherwise, we'll have to schedule a meeting to go over this again in your office and it's much more pleasant doing it here over coffee and croissants. Right, Emily?'' She paused, looking expectantly at Emily.

''Yes, much more comfortable,'' Emily agreed. ''If that's acceptable to you, Your Highness?''

''Please, call me Caroline. We'll be spending many hours together planning this wedding and we may as well be comfortable together. And that's an excellent idea, Jenna.'' She lifted a tiny silver bell from its place beside her crystal water glass and shook it. The tinkling sound was immediately followed by the appearance of a young girl wearing the palace uniform. ''Ah, there you are, Sofia.

Please bring a pen and pad of paper for Miss Parks.''

Emily barely had time to say thank you to the queen before the girl was back, handing her a gold-capped fountain pen and a leather-bound notebook.

"Thank you, Sofia. Now, where were we? Ah, yes, the ceremony is held at St. Catherine's, the reception here at the palace, and there will be four to five hundred people at a sit-down luncheon. There will probably be a thousand or so invited to the reception,'' Caroline continued. "You'll want to discuss menus and timing with our chef, of course. And the protocol of invitations, seating, etc., will need to be coordinated by the palace diplomatic office. The most difficult seating arrangements will be those for our relatives. Our family is related through a tangle of marriages and descendants to most of the royal families in Europe, all of whom will think they should have a front-row seat.'' Caroline sighed. "And I never can keep track of who's not talking to who at any given moment.''

"Which is why you have Maria, Mother,'' Jenna said. "That's Mother's secretary,'' she explained to Emily as she spread jam on an airy croissant. "The woman is amazing—she never forgets a thing.''

"True,'' Caroline agreed. "I don't know what

I'd do without her. Now,'' she said briskly. ''What else do we need to talk about before you begin?''

''How big will the wedding party be? I'm assuming that there will be bridesmaids, flower girl, ring bearer. How many bridesmaids and grooms-men?'' There was no immediate answer. Emily glanced up from her notes to find both Caroline and Jenna looking at her with arrested expressions. ''Is that a problem? The bride hasn't discussed that with you yet? If she hasn't, I can inquire when I speak with her.'' Emily was instantly reminded that she still didn't have the bride's name. ''Will she be available later today, perhaps this afternoon?'' Caroline and Jenna exchanged a swift look, but neither responded. *What's going on here?* Emily wondered, baffled by their silence.

''That, um, that may be a problem,'' Jenna said at last.

''Is she not here in Daniz?'' Emily thought a moment. ''I usually meet with the bride in person in this preliminary stage, but if she's out of the country, we can always set up a conference call to get the necessary input.''

''Unfortunately,'' Caroline said carefully, ''that won't be possible, either.''

''No?'' *This is more and more curious,* Emily thought. Where was the elusive bride?

''No.'' Jenna shook her head, opened her mouth

as if to speak, then closed it again and looked helplessly at her mother.

Emily's gaze followed Jenna's. Caroline looked from one to the other and visibly collected herself.

"You must promise, Emily, that what I am about to tell you will not go beyond this room," she said.

Startled, Emily stared at her for a silent moment before replying. "Yes, of course."

"There is no bride."

"I beg your pardon?" Surely she'd misunderstood, Emily thought.

"There is no bride," Caroline repeated. "Lazhar isn't engaged. He has no fiancée."

"But…" Emily floundered. "But he told me he wanted to hire my firm to plan his wedding."

"Yes, I know."

"So…he *doesn't* want me to plan his wedding?" Emily was beyond confused.

"No, no, he *does* want you to plan his wedding," Caroline said quickly. "But he doesn't have a bride yet."

"Yet?"

Caroline sighed and massaged her temple with her fingertips. "I'm doing a very poor job of explaining this. Since the tabloids have announced it to the world and made it common knowledge, I'm sure you're aware that it's Abbar's dearest wish to see Lazhar married. His health is delicate and he feels a need for haste. Lazhar would move mountains to give his father whatever he wants at this stage, we all would. But in this instance, I think my son is wrong.'' Caroline paused to sip from her cup, clearly fortifying herself before continuing. ''When he told me a month ago that he meant to schedule the ceremony and choose a bride sometime between then and the wedding date, I was appalled. I told him that a person can't pick a wife the same way one negotiates a business deal but he wouldn't listen to me. So—'' she spread her hands in a gesture of helpless acceptance ''—here we are. Planning the wedding of my eldest child without a bride to make decisions with us.''

Emily was speechless. Underneath her shock, joy bubbled irrepressibly. *He isn't engaged. He's not in love with another woman.*

But he will be. The knowledge that he would choose a bride sometime in the next few months deflated the exuberant bubbles.

''Well,'' she said carefully, meeting first Caroline's, then Jenna's gaze. ''Are you two willing to make decisions that the bride normally makes?''

''You mean like the color of bridesmaids dresses, how many attendants, etc.?'' Jenna asked.

''Yes, those and others.''

''Sure,'' she said airily. ''We three can pick out colors and decide on cake flavors, can't we, Mom?''

"Of course," Caroline agreed.

"Well, then." Emily drew a deep breath. "It's certainly unorthodox and I've never planned a wedding without a bride's input before, but I don't see why we can't do it." A thought occurred to her and she shot a narrow-eyed glance at the queen. "I'm assuming that if Lazhar decides on a wife at the last moment, she won't be allowed to change all the arrangements at that point?"

"Absolutely not," Caroline said firmly. "That would make the entire project impossible."

"Then it appears to be doable."

"Excellent!" Jenna clapped her hands. "This will be fun—sort of a practice session for the wedding I might have some day."

"Do you have a groom in mind?" Caroline's voice was hopeful.

"No."

"Oh."

Emily coughed to hide an amused chuckle. Caroline was the picture of a mother hoping that her daughter would wed; Jenna equally typical of a young woman refusing to be nudged. They may be queen and princess, Emily thought, but they were no different than thousands of other mothers and daughters in this age-old tug-of-war.

"What did you think of the casino?" Jenna asked, abruptly changing the subject.

"It was fabulous," Emily replied. "I loved it."

"Did you go anywhere else?" Caroline asked.

"Lazhar took me to a nightclub called Pilar's and we watched flamenco dancers. I was fascinated. I've never had the opportunity to see flamenco before but after watching the floor show, I definitely plan to find a club in San Francisco where I can see more."

The door from the hallway opened and Lazhar strolled into the room.

"Good morning, Mother." He bent and kissed Caroline's cheek, straightening to look at Emily. His gaze flicked over the bare little sundress and he smiled at her. "Good morning, Emily. Sleep well?"

"Yes, thank you." Emily refused to acknowledge the sudden race of her heart. He was wearing faded jeans this morning, with a short-sleeved T-shirt tucked into the waistband and polished black cowboy boots on his feet. Gone was the European prince. This Lazhar could have been any American male, dressed for a casual morning at home.

Except that the watch on his wrist was a Rolex and very few men of Emily's acquaintances wore faded Levi's with quite that air of elegance.

Face it, Emily, she thought. *You're hopelessly hooked on the guy.*

"I'm on my way to the stables and I thought you might want to come with me, Emily, if you're finished with breakfast."

"First she needs to call her office, Lazhar," Jenna put in. "And she has a list of other places to visit as well. Oh, and we told her," she added offhandedly. "So you don't need to worry about letting it slip out."

Lazhar eyed his sister quizzically. "Let what slip out? What is it you told her?"

"About the bride. That you don't have one."

Lazhar's dark gaze was hooded as he met Emily's. "Really. You told her."

It wasn't a question. Indeed his tone was so neutral that Emily couldn't tell if he was pleased that she knew, or that he disapproved of his mother and sister sharing that family secret.

"I've promised not to tell anyone," she said calmly. "And they've assured me that the lack of a bride to help plan the ceremony won't impact the organizing of the event, since they'll make the necessary decisions that your fiancée, if you had one, would normally make."

He raised an eyebrow, his eyes unreadable as his mouth quirked in a half smile. "Really," he murmured. "That's efficient."

Unsure what he meant and unable to tell from his expression whether he was pleased or unhappy with their arrangements, Emily was relieved when Jenna glanced at her watch and broke in.

"Drat. I was due at the stable office ten minutes ago." She pushed back her chair and stood, round-ing the table to drop a kiss on her mother's cheek. "I'll see you two there after you've made your calls, Emily."

And with a quick wave and a cheeky grin, she was gone.

"I think that's our cue to head for the media room," Lazhar said to Emily.

"Please keep the notebook and pen, Emily," Caroline said as Emily was about to remove the pages with her notes. "You'll be making lots more notes today, I'm sure."

"Thank you." Emily rose and left the room, Lazhar right beside her. Neither of them mentioned last night's kiss, and Emily decided to chalk it up to the combination of champagne and wine they'd both drank.

She refused to let him shake her composure, regardless of the fact that she was more aware of him than ever.

Chapter Six

Emily had forgotten about the time difference between Daniz and San Francisco, and when she dialed her office number, the answering machine picked up. She left a message telling Jane that she'd call back that evening, which equaled morning in California's time zone, and followed Lazhar outside.

They left the palace and took a shortcut through a lush garden, exiting through a wrought-iron gate that let them out into a wide, paved lane. Farther down the lane to their left were the stable buildings. Directly across from them stretched a paddock where horses grazed and sprinklers turned lazily under the hot sun, creating small rainbows as they watered the already lush green grass.

Lazhar crossed the lane to the paddock fence and whistled. The dozen or more horses grazing within the enclosure looked up, ears pricking with interest. On the far side of the pasture, a white mare whinnied and trotted toward them, a long-legged filly at her side.

"How beautiful," Emily murmured, so riveted by the horse that she was barely aware she spoke aloud. Head up, small ears pricked forward, her tail a banner held high, the mare's fluid gait was pure poetry. Beside her, the little white filly shadowed each movement her mother made as if attached to her by an invisible cord.

The mare slowed to a walk as she approached the fence, coming closer until she could bump her nose against Lazhar's chest. He laughed and took a lump of sugar out of his pocket, holding it on the flat of his palm. The mare daintily lipped the cube from his hand, her strong teeth crunching the little square.

"This is Sheba," Lazhar told Emily, straightening the white forelock between the horse's intelligent brown eyes before stroking his palm down her nose. "And her baby, Elizabeth."

"Elizabeth?" Surprised, Emily looked at the purebred Arabian baby. The little filly's wide-spaced dark eyes, dish face, beautiful conformation, and delicate-boned long legs made her a miniature copy of her mother.

"Jenna named her—Elizabeth was born the day after my sister watched the BBC production of *Pride and Prejudice* for the first time."

"So she's named after a Jane Austen heroine?" Emily laughed. Lazhar looked pained but resigned.

"Her long registered name includes Shalimar, which is what I'd hoped to use as her common name. But after Jenna began calling her Elizabeth, everyone else followed suit, and now she answers to that name only." He sighed and shook his head. "A royal Danizian filly answering to an English name. Where's the sense in that?"

"Oh, I don't know. I kind of like it." Emily stretched her arm over the top rail of the white wooden fence and waggled her fingers invitingly. "Come here, pretty baby. Hello, Elizabeth."

The inquisitive filly pricked her ears, clearly listening as Emily crooned. Tentatively she stretched her neck toward the fence, her nose not quite touching Emily's fingertips, and blew a gust of warm air against her palm. Then she jumped back to race off, jolting to a stop several feet away before spinning to run back to her mother. The little horse stopped on the far side of the mare and peered around her mama's chest at the humans.

Charmed, Emily laughed aloud. "She's darling."

"She's pretty cute," he agreed with a half grin.

"Will she stay here when she grows up?" Emily asked, looking around at the idyllic pastoral setting. It seemed the perfect place for a horse.

"Yes." Lazhar gave the mare one last pat and stepped back from the fence. "We're a breeding farm, so many of the fillies and colts born here are sold away from the stables, but Elizabeth won't be. Her mother belongs to me, not to the palace, and I bred her to a stallion owned by the king of Saudi Arabia. She has impeccable bloodlines and she'll live her life out here at the farm where hopefully she'll give birth to many colts and fillies as valuable as she."

"And just as cute?" Emily asked, turning to look over her shoulder for one last glimpse of the little filly. Sheba stood at the fence, watching Lazhar walk away, but Elizabeth was already caught up in other things, nosing at a leaf on the ground.

"Probably every bit as cute."

They reached the stables; the doors stood open and they turned down the wide corridor that ran from one end of the huge barn to the other. Box stalls lined both sides of the alleyway and horses shifted in the occupied stalls, coming to peer out over the top of the gates to watch Lazhar and Emily go by.

Lazhar greeted them by name, stopping to introduce Emily to the individual mares and tell her a little about them.

"Back in San Francisco, when I researched you and your family on the Internet," Emily said as they strolled on after he'd fed a mare a sugar cube from what seemed to be an inexhaustible supply. "I read an article that said the palace stables are world-famous and that your family has been breeding Arabian horses for generations."

"That's true," Lazhar confirmed as they walked out of the shaded alleyway between the stalls, redolent with the scent of hay, saddle leather and horses. The cobbled courtyard beyond was surrounded by stone buildings and the narrow alleys between them led to grassy pastures. They passed grooms leading mares, Arabians with proud small heads and dainty ears, lush tails that nearly brushed the ground behind their back heels, and glossy coats. Several of them were heavily pregnant, their bellies round with foals. "The son of the first king of Daniz married a Saudi princess and part of her dowry was a stallion and mare from her father's herd. That pair was the beginning of the Daniz Stud."

"You have quite a family history," Emily remarked as they strolled across a cobbled forecourt, through a stone archway, and reached a low building with Office printed on a small brass sign beside the heavy door.

"A great deal of tradition is tied to that history," Lazhar agreed. "But unlike my ancestors, I can waive the dowry for my wife. She doesn't need to be rich—my family has all the money it needs. I can marry where I want—and if I choose, I can wed her even if all she has in the world are the clothes on her back."

Before Emily could react to his flat statement, he pulled open the door and motioned her inside. The office, cool after the heat outside, was empty.

"Jenna?" Lazhar crossed the room and disappeared down a short hallway. In seconds he was back. "She must be out in the stables somewhere." He glanced at his watch. "We don't have time to hunt for her if we're going to visit the Jewel Market this morning."

They left the office and retraced their steps to the palace, Lazhar leaving Emily at her door. A half hour later, after freshening her makeup and collecting her purse, she sat beside him in a gleaming silver Porsche as he negotiated the curving road leading into the city.

"This is St. Catherine's." Lazhar gestured to their right as they slowed for a turn.

"It looks a bit different in the daylight," she said, gazing at the soaring arches and towers of the church. She and Lazhar had climbed the stairs and entered the quiet church after leaving the casino the night before in order to drop her winnings in the poorbox. The tower lights had glowed against the night sky and the interior had been softly lit with minimal lighting. Today, the soft rose-colored stone had a patina of age, the graceful church an elegant grande dame of buildings among her century-old neighbors. "I believe your mother said that, according to tradition, royal weddings are held at St. Catherine's?"

He nodded, glancing at her as he downshifted to climb a hill. "St. Catherine's for the wedding ceremony and the palace for the reception." The breeze ruffled his hair, his eyes concealed behind sunglasses. "Remind me to introduce you to Antoine Escobar—he's the chief of protocol for the family and can give you all the details about which wedding traditions are set in stone and what you can change if you wish."

"Perhaps I can talk to him this afternoon?"

"If we return to the palace early enough, certainly."

Emily made a mental note to remember the protocol chief's name as Lazhar swung the car to the curb and turned off the engine. "We'll leave the car here." He leaned toward her to point out her window and down the side street. "The Jewel Market is just down the street, the large building with the pillars and dome. I thought you might want to walk from here and browse in some of the shops on our way.''

"I'd love to, thank you."

Emily stepped out onto the sidewalk just as Lazhar's bodyguards, parked in a dark sedan behind them, exited the car, exchanging nods with Lazhar.

"I didn't realize the guards were following us," she commented.

"They go everywhere with us since the paparazzi invaded Daniz," Lazhar confirmed. "After the wedding, I'm sure life will settle down once again and the reporters will get bored and leave us to chase another story. In the meantime, I've doubled the guards for family members. Jenna and I can no longer move about as freely as we once did."

"Does it bother you, being the focus of so much attention?" Emily asked.

He shrugged. "No, I can't say it bothers me, exactly, but it does make life a bit more inconvenient."

They paused outside a spice shop. Narrow wooden carts edged the wall on each side of the doorway and held small bins filled with a display of spices. Emily closed her eyes, breathing deeply to draw in the heady scents of coriander, cinnamon, nutmeg, lemons and so many other intriguing flavors that she couldn't identify them all.

"Want to go inside?"

She opened her eyes to find Lazhar watching her, his face amused. "It smells heavenly." She gestured at the bright colors on the carts. "And it looks gorgeous."

They stepped over the stone doorsill and entered the small shop, Lazhar loitering at her side as Emily browsed the scented shop, fascinated. She paused to watch the shop owner scoop nutmeg into a paper cone, then twist the top closed. He repeated the action with several other spices before the woman handed over her coins, tucked her purchases into her shopping bag, already bulging with fruit, and left the store.

They followed her outside and moved on down the street, pausing to gaze into shops. Emily purchased a cut-crystal glass vase for Brenda at a china shop and a bottle of Spanish wine at a vintner's for her brother, Cade. Lazhar handed her packages to one of the bodyguards to carry and they strolled on. They reached the end of the street that led to the Jewel Market and paused, waiting for traffic on the busy main street to slow before they crossed. The small crowd waiting on the curb allowed them privacy, although they smiled and nodded, some bowing with respectful deference. Emily assumed they were native Danizians and perhaps accustomed to seeing members of the royal family on the streets.

Lazhar turned to speak to one of the bodyguards,

his attention distracted, and in that brief moment, a small child, no more than two or three years old, wiggled free of her mother's grasp and darted into the street.

Emily didn't pause to consider her actions. Without a thought for her own safety, she ran after the little girl, sweeping her up into her arms just as a car bore down on them. Horns blared and the driver slammed on his brakes, the tires squealing in protest. The edge of the car's bumper grazed her skirt as she leapt to safety on the curb and was grabbed by Lazhar, held safe in his arms.

"What the hell are you doing?" he roared, his arms tight bands around both Emily and the little girl.

Shaking from the adrenaline still coursing through her veins, Emily lifted her head to answer him but was silenced by his grim expression. Behind the dark lenses of his sunglasses, she thought she glimpsed fear in his eyes, but couldn't be sure.

The child, silent until now, whimpered. Emily looked down at her and managed a smile. "Hey, sweetie," she crooned softly. "It's all right. Don't be scared. You're fine."

The crowd around them, shocked into silence by the speed with which the life-and-death rescue had occurred, began to stir.

Emily wiggled, trying to loosen Lazhar's bruising grip. At first, he just stared at her, but then he seemed to realize that she wanted to be set free and his arms abruptly released her. But his hands settled possessively on her waist, his heavier male body a solid wall behind her.

She looked around for the child's parent just as a woman, sobbing hysterically, pushed her way through the crowd to reach them.

"Mama!" The tiny girl held out her arms and Emily let her go, surrendering the sturdy little body to her frantic mother.

She was instantly aware that her legs were wobbly, her hands trembling in the aftermath. Lazhar's hands tightened on her waist, easing her back slightly until she rested against him, his much broader bulk supporting her smaller frame.

"How can I thank you, miss?" the mother said, her daughter clutched tightly in her arms. "One moment she was next to me, the next moment she was gone. If you hadn't been so quick to run after her…" Fresh tears trembled on the young woman's eyelids, spilling over to trickle down her cheeks.

Impulsively Emily reached out to comfort the distraught mother, her hand closing with sympathy on the woman's bare forearm. "But she's safe now." She smiled warmly at the woman, clad in a clean but faded dress and the black-haired, dark-eyed little girl in a worn, too-small red jumper.

"And I bet you won't let go of your mother's hand again, will you? Streets can be very dangerous."

The little girl nodded solemnly, her gaze fixed on Emily's face, before she turned to pat her mother's cheek. "Streets are dane-ja-rus, Mama. I have to hold your hand."

"Yes, baby." The woman smiled through her tears, exchanging a look of female amusement with Emily. Her gaze moved past Emily and her eyes rounded, evidently unaware until then of the identity of Emily's companion. "Your Highness." She bowed, executing a graceful semicurtsy.

Around them, the crowd followed her example as the women curtsied, the men bowed.

Lazhar exchanged greetings with them, taking time to speak quietly to mother and child. Emily was instantly reminded of his position as the prince of Daniz and the respect and affection the residents felt for him. What she didn't realize was that those same Danizians were smiling approvingly at her, nodding knowingly at each other as she and Lazhar said goodbye and crossed the street to reach the Jewel Market.

"Are you sure you want to do this?" Lazhar asked as they entered the stone building. His hand cupped her elbow as they walked through the metal detector and then halted, waiting for the body-guards to circle the detectors, flash their badges, and be waved on by the inspectors. Lazhar drew her into the relative privacy of an alcove, his back to the entryway, sheltering her from the view of passersby.

"What? Visit the Market?"

"Yes. We can leave it till another day."

His voice was clipped, his big body tense.

"Would you like to skip our tour today and come back later?" she asked, uncertain why he was so edgy.

"Not if you feel up to touring the Market. Are you sure you wouldn't like to go back to the palace and rest?"

"Why would I need to rest?" She was having difficulty defining what his problem was, did he think the car's bumper had hit her when it had actually only grazed her skirt?

"You could have been killed back there. Don't you feel the need to recover?" His voice was carefully even, a direct contrast to the tension that gripped him.

"No. My legs were a little rubbery after it was over and we were back on the curb, safe and sound. And my hands were shaking. But I'm over that now." The muscle ticking in Lazhar's jaw didn't ease. Emily tried again. "I'm fine, Lazhar, just fine. But I'd be happy to go back to my room and rest, if you're still concerned. Would you like to return to the palace?"

"What I'd like is for you to stop jumping in front of moving cars," he ground out.

"I don't make a habit of jumping into traffic. In fact, I've never done so before." She tilted her chin and faced him, narrowing her eyes at his stormy features. "What is your problem?"

"My 'problem' is that you seem to take your safety too lightly," he said through clenched teeth.

"I do not," she said promptly. "I'm normally very cautious. Although," she admitted reluctantly, "I usually think carefully before I act and I confess I didn't think just now. When I saw the little girl running into traffic, I didn't consider what might happen. I just ran to catch her—it was purely instinct, no planning."

Lazhar's hot black gaze scorched her for a long moment. Then the tension in his big body eased, his eyes softening. "You have the instincts of a lioness with her cubs, Emily." His face solemn, he brushed the backs of his fingers down her cheek in a slow caress. "Will you protect your own children so fiercely?"

The stroke of his warm fingers against her suddenly hot cheek mesmerized Emily. What was it about him, she wondered, that made all her resolve to keep her distance fly out the window?

By the end of a very busy week, filled with tours of Daniz in which Lazhar showed her the best of his beloved country, comfortable breakfasts and luncheons with Caroline and Jenna while they went over lists for the wedding-with-no-bride, and long afternoons visiting with King Abbar, Emily felt as if she'd known the family forever. She'd long since fallen completely in love with Daniz's flower-scented nights, friendly people, narrow winding streets, and golden sandy beaches lapped by the Mediterranean.

Unfortunately she was afraid that she was equally in danger of falling head-over-heels in love with Lazhar. Each hour spent in his company made her admire him more. She knew it was unwise to risk her heart, but found it impossible to avoid him entirely. Not that she tried very hard, she thought, as she sat across a low game table from King Abbar, her elbow propped on the table, her chin resting on her palm while she contemplated her next chess move.

"Is the board that sad?"

King Abbar's mild voice interrupted her thoughts and Emily looked up to find him watching her with a half smile. "What? Sad?"

"Yes, sad—you sighed. And you're frowning rather fiercely at your rook and my knight," he pointed out, nodding at the carved jade chess pieces.

"Oh." Emily sat up straighter, folding her hands in her lap. "I'm sorry, I was thinking of something else when I should have been focused on the game.''

Abbar waved a thin hand in dismissal. "No need to be sorry. The game will wait until this afternoon. Where is my son taking you this morning?"

"I think he mentioned shopping at the bazaar."

"Ah." The king's smile widened. "You'll enjoy that, I'm sure. Caroline loved to visit the bazaar to buy little trinkets and household goods when we first married. The palace storage rooms were filled with every conceivable thing she may have wanted, but she said we should have our own, bought just for us and our family.'' His voice lowered and he leaned forward to whisper. "I suspect the underlying reason was that my wife simply loves to shop.''

Emily laughed. "Many women do," she whispered back. "I know I do."

"You do what?"

Lazhar's lazy inquiry startled Emily. She hadn't heard him enter his father's sitting room. She glanced over her shoulder, her heart doing its accustomed little skip as he walked toward the table where she sat with Abbar.

"Love to shop." She was pleased that her voice was calm and didn't betray her increased heart rate and faster breathing. "Your father was just telling me that the queen enjoyed shopping in the bazaar as a young bride."

"She still enjoys the bazaar," Lazhar said dryly. "She and Jenna can spend hours picking out fresh fruit and vegetables for dinner. And even more hours if the linen maker has a new shipment of lace from Italy."

The king chuckled, his eyes twinkling as he nodded his agreement. "That's my Caroline. She barely notices fine diamonds and rubies, but mention handmade lace and she can't reach the shop quickly enough."

Emily's interest was piqued. "Will we visit the shop that carries handmade Italian lace this afternoon?"

"If you'd like."

"I'd like," she answered promptly. She moved her knight to a new square, removing one of Abbar's pawns from the board. "Can we continue our game this afternoon, Your Highness?"

"Mmm-hmm," he murmured, pondering her move and analyzing his possible answering moves. "Take her to the bazaar, Lazhar, and when you return, Emily, we'll finish our game."

"Excellent."

Lazhar held her chair and Emily rose. King Abbar leaned back in his chair, weariness in every line of his thin body but a smile of genuine pleasure on his face as he looked at the two of them standing together. "Enjoy yourselves."

They crossed the room and were on the threshold when Abbar spoke. "I'm delighted with your choice of a bride, Lazhar. You have my blessing."

Emily froze, her startled, disbelieving gaze flying to Lazhar, but he was looking at his father and she couldn't see his eyes.

"Thank you, Father."

Before Emily could speak, Lazhar's grip tightened on her arm and he hustled her through the door, past the guards and down the hallway. He threw open the first door across the hall from the suite they'd just left and urged Emily inside, releasing her to close the door and lock it behind them.

Emily spun to face him. "What did he mean by that? He approves of me as a bride? We have his blessing?"

"My father believes that you're the woman I'm marrying."

The blunt statement stunned Emily. She stared at him blankly, trying to assimilate what he'd just told her.

"How did that happen? What made him think we're getting married?"

"He likes you. You heard him, we have his blessing," he said obliquely.

"I'm the wedding planner, not the bride." She thrust her fingers through her hair in agitation. "How could this have happened?" She took three quick steps away from him and spun to stalk back. ''You have to tell him. Now.''

''I can't.''

''Of course you can! You have to.''

''I can't. He liked you the first time he met you and every day since you arrived, he's grown more attached to you and to the idea that you'll be part of his family. I don't have the heart to tell him you're not the one.''

''But you'll have to tell him sooner or later,'' she argued, nonplussed at the situation. ''He's going to notice when you say 'I do' and the woman standing beside you isn't me!''

''Yes, he would,'' Lazhar said grimly. ''If he lives long enough to attend the wedding.''

Emily was shocked into silence. ''I had no idea he was…'' She paused, a lump in her throat. She swallowed thickly. The lump moved lower, settling under her breastbone. In the short week she'd been in Daniz, she'd developed a genuine fondness for the king. ''How long?''

''The doctors can't, or won't, give us a date. But not long.'' He voice was bleak.

''I'm so sorry, Lazhar.'' Needing to comfort him and be consoled in return, Emily stepped closer and laid her hand on his arm.

He instantly covered her fingers with his own, his warm hand trapping hers against his hair-roughened, muscled forearm. ''I don't want to disappoint him, Emily. He's grown very attached to you this week and it would devastate him if he learned that you're not going to be his daughter-in-law.'' His fingers tightened over hers. ''Which is why I have to ask for your help.''

''My help? With what?''

''My father's greatest wish, perhaps his dying wish, is that I marry. I can't wait six months to find a bride. I need one now. He already loves you, Emily, and wants you as part of our family.'' Lazhar paused, then looked into her eyes. ''Marry me.''

Chapter Seven

His blunt words struck Emily speechless. She stared at him, thinking for a moment that she'd misheard him. But his face was set, his expression grim and determined; she couldn't doubt he meant what he said.

Marry me. Under different circumstances, she would have been overjoyed if he'd said those two words. But he wanted to marry for his father's sake. He didn't love her. How could she want to say ''yes'' and ''no'' all at the same time? she thought wildly.

Her usual cool composure was destroyed and her

panic must have shown on her face because his gaze softened, the hard lines of his face easing.

"I can see I've shocked you."

She pulled her fingers from beneath his, turning to pace away several steps before facing him again. "That's an understatement." She thrust her fingers through her hair, thoroughly unsettled. "It's noble of you to want to move heaven and earth to make your father happy, but marriage seems like a drastic step."

He shoved his hands into his pockets, his face inscrutable. "The marriage can be annulled, after—" He stopped speaking.

Emily's heart hurt at the unspoken acknowledgment that his father's time with the family was limited. In the short week she'd been in Daniz and observed Lazhar with his father, she'd realized that the father-son bond between them was undeniably powerful. And even though her acquaintance with the king was of short duration, she, too, felt a deep affection for him.

"How long…" She paused as her voice wavered, tears clogging her throat. "How long do the doctors think he has?"

Lazhar's answer shocked her.

Should she do this? *Could* she do this—marry a man for a few weeks in name only?

Emily had a quick mental image of King Abbar smiling at her as they played chess, heard again his words of praise and gentle pride in her when Lazhar told him about the child in the street, remembered the love on Caroline's and Jenna's faces when they spoke of him.

The slight headache she'd woke with that morning grew a little stronger and she rubbed her aching temples with her fingertips.

"Isn't there someone else that can be your pretend-bride?" She gave up trying to ease the headache. "I'm sure I read somewhere that royal families pick out fiancées for their children the day they're born. Don't you have one of those?"

"No, I don't." He shook his head, a bemused smile lifting the corner of his mouth. "Where did you read that?"

"Probably somewhere on the Internet," Emily said, refusing to be distracted.

"And even if I did have a childhood fiancée," Lazhar continued. "It wouldn't change the fact that you're the one my father wants. You're the only person that can do this, Emily."

"You're sure? You're absolutely positive that there's no alternative solution?"

"I'm sure."

"I'd have to talk to Jane about the schedule at the office." She frowned at the swift satisfaction that flashed in his eyes and was just as quickly banked. "I'm not promising that I'll do this," she warned him. "But I want to help. I've grown attached to your father in the time I've been here and if it's at all possible for me to be away from the office for a couple more weeks, I'll go along with your scheme. But I can't destroy my business in the process.''

''Understood.'' He nodded. ''And thank you, Emily, you won't be sorry.''

She thrust her fingers through her hair again, ruffling it even more. ''I hope not.'' She wasn't convinced, but was willing to try to work out a solution.

''Your firm won't be hurt financially,'' he assured her. ''And it's probable that the cachet of planning a royal wedding will enhance your business portfolio, so in the long run, Creative Weddings may be a stronger company.''

''True.'' Emily agreed. She looked away from him, considering the possible complications her agreement to pose as his fiancée might cause. ''What about the publicity factor?''

''What about it?''

''I'm assuming that the reporters will find out about our pretend engagement, whether you tell them or not. How will you explain a marriage that only lasts for a few weeks?''

''I'll deal with that when the time comes. Since that won't happen until my father is gone, I'll have bigger issues to cope with and the gossip about my short marriage probably won't seem that important."

"No. I suppose it won't." Suddenly the details of how a pseudoengagement and marriage would work didn't seem important to Emily, either. They were small indeed, compared to the loss of a man who was a beloved father, husband and ruler over a country whose residents adored him and would deeply mourn his passing. "All right," she said with sudden decision. "I'll do it."

"Excellent." The fine tension that held him dissipated, his voice filled with relief.

"We have to tell your mother and Jenna the truth."

"No." Lazhar was adamant. "My mother can't keep a secret from my father. He'll know she's hiding something and when he asks, she'll spill everything. And Jenna's the same with my mother. Neither of them can lie to each other or to my father."

"Which means that I have to lie to them." Emily narrowed her eyes at him. "I don't lie."

The corners of his mouth quirked, his eyes amused. "You never lie?"

"Not purposely." She lifted an eyebrow at his patent disbelief. "Lies create only losing situations and they can destroy lives."

"True." He eyed her consideringly for a moment. "I agree with you, Emily, but in this instance, telling my mother or Jenna is tantamount to telling my father. And if he knows our marriage isn't real, then none of this will work.''

She wasn't happy. And when she wasn't happy, her bottom lip plumped out in a very un-Emily-like—and sexy—pout. Lazhar badly wanted to haul her into his arms and kiss her senseless but he kept a tight rein on the urge. He'd been struggling to control the instinct to claim her ever since she'd agreed to their marriage and elation had roared through him.

He knew she was attracted to him. He also knew she was fighting it. She was skittish around him, holding him at arm's length with polite conversation, but when they were body to body, his mouth on hers, she melted like hot wax.

He'd crossed his fingers inside his pockets when he'd told her that their marriage could be annulled. He was gambling that before they reached that point, she'd admit that the marriage worked. It was true he wanted her to marry him because his father had quickly become attached to her, but with each day that he spent with her, he increasingly wanted her for himself.

He didn't just want her, he craved her.

And that had never happened with any other woman.

Lazhar refused to think about what that might mean beyond the fact that the sexual attraction between them was hotter, more compelling, than anything he'd ever felt before.

"There has to be a way to do this without lying to everybody," she insisted.

"Not that I can think of." He shook his head. "My father is still the king and the ruler of Daniz, despite his poor health. He has contacts and sources that even I'm unaware of—if we tell anyone that our engagement and wedding aren't real, he'll find out."

Clearly unhappy, Emily frowned and gave in. "All right," she said reluctantly. "But I still think it's wrong."

"So do I," he agreed. "But I can't come up with an alternative. We can't tell anyone, and we have to go through the traditional courtship phases, otherwise, Father will never believe us."

"Traditional courtship? What does that entail…exactly?"

Lazhar managed not to smile. Despite his casual words, she had immediately honed in on the courtship reference and she was eyeing him with suspicion. "Probably pretty much what makes up an American courtship—spending time together, meeting the parents, receiving an engagement ring, a presentation ball, instruction by the protocol officer as to the duties of a princess and future queen." He shrugged. "Just the usual stuff."

"Just the usual stuff," she repeated. "Protocol

lessons on how to act when the bride is a princess and future queen, and a presentation ball? Trust me, Lazhar, those are *not* part of an everyday, normal American courtship.''

''Perhaps not, but the rest is perfectly ordinary. Given your background as the daughter of wealthy parents and your business experience in navigating society weddings, you're uniquely prepared to cope with the palace rules that govern my family's public life.''

''I hope you're right,'' she muttered. ''Okay.'' She drew a deep breath. ''We'll tell them tonight?''

''Yes—unless you'd like to tell Jenna and Mother now. The sooner the better as far as I'm concerned, but the timing is up to you.''

Emily glanced down at herself, her lashes lowering and shielding her eyes from him. His gaze followed hers, skimming the curves beneath the simple rose-pink sundress she wore. Strappy leather sandals left her feet nearly bare, her toenails painted with a rose enamel that matched the dress.

''I'm not dressed for an important occasion— and telling your mother that I'm going to be your wife is very important.''

Lazhar thought she looked good enough to eat, but if she felt the need for a less casual outfit, he was amenable. ''Then let's go to the bazaar as we originally planned, and while we're out, we'll stop at a jeweler's and pick out a ring.''

A flash of panic moved over her face, quickly replaced by resolution. She visibly straightened and tilted her chin slightly.

''That sounds like a good plan. Perhaps we can tell your parents and Jenna at dinner tonight?''

''If that's what you'd like to do.''

''I would.''

The trip to the bazaar, followed by a visit to an exclusive jewelry store near the Jewel Market, marked the beginning of a whirlwind day for Emily. She worried all afternoon about the prospect of telling Lazhar's family that she would be his bride, but after the initial surprise, both Caroline and Jenna were elated. King Abbar was equally pleased, though he believed that they were merely formally telling him something he already knew.

Now that they knew that Emily was to be the bride, Caroline and Jenna threw themselves wholeheartedly into the preparations for the wedding. They agreed with Lazhar that the ceremony should take place as soon as possible and together, they decided to set the date for a Saturday, two weeks away.

Given the army of assistants available to the royal family, Emily thought pulling off a wedding this big in two weeks might be possible, but just barely. She'd organized several hundred weddings over the last few years, but this time, she knew she would not only have to coordinate all the details of the gala event, but she would also have to handle all of the things that only a bride could do— like standing perfectly still for an hour while the designer bridal gown was fitted.

She desperately needed Jane.

Before Lazhar left the family gathering to escort his father back to his room, Emily told him her plan to enlist Jane's help. Then she pleaded exhaustion from the eventful day and returned to her suite. She kicked off her shoes, grabbed the phone and dialed Jane's home number in San Francisco.

Jane picked up on the second ring.

"Hello?"

"Jane, thank goodness I caught you in."

"Emily? Is that you? Where are you?"

"I'm in Daniz, and yes, it's me. I think." Emily padded into the bedroom and sank onto the comfortable bed. The linens were turned back invitingly, the lemon-yellow silk sheets subtly rich against the leaf-green of the coverlet.

"You think?" Jane's voice sharpened with concern. "Is everything okay?"

"Yes and no." Emily tucked her feet under her to sit cross-legged, her apricot skirt a pool of lush color against the bed covering. "The good news is, Creative Weddings is definitely going to plan the Daniz royal family wedding…''

Jane's crow of delight interrupted her.

"…the bad news,'' Emily continued when Jane calmed. "Is that I'm the bride.''

"What?"

"I know,'' Emily acknowledged, easily picturing the disbelief and confusion that must be visible on her friend's pixie face. "It's a long story, Jane, and I'll explain everything, I promise. But first, I need to know how quickly you can get here. What's the schedule like at the office?''

"Actually it's not too bad. Once the clients knew that you were in Daniz to consult with the prince about his wedding, they were so delighted that they might be sharing *their* wedding consultant with a royal family that they've all been amazingly cooperative. Also, the staff from the Daniz Embassy has been incredible. One of the women, Trina, is a natural and Katherine Powell adores her. In fact, I think she's trying to talk her into going back to Hollywood to work as her personal assistant.''

"Really?'' Emily laughed. "I hope Trina has a lot of patience.''

"That's what I told her. Katherine is definitely high maintenance—which of course, is probably one of the issues that you're concerned about in the office. But you can stop worrying, all is well.''

"That's a huge relief," Emily admitted. "Do you think you'll be able to clear your calendar and fly to Daniz? I can't do this without you."

"I think so." Jane's voice turned serious. "Emily, are you happy? I have to tell you, when you left here with the prince, it never occurred to me that you were the bride he was searching for."

"It never occurred to me, either," Emily assured her. "But, now I am. It's complicated, Jane, and not something I can explain over the phone. But I'll tell you everything when you get here, I promise."

Jane's sigh came clearly over the phone line. "All right, Emily, but curiosity is killing me. Be prepared to be grilled the moment I get there."

"I'll explain it all, I promise, as soon as possible. Now, tell me about the Benedict wedding, did you find the Irish lace that Mrs. Benedict wanted for the gown?"

By the time Jane rang off, after bringing Emily up-to-date on the details of her clients' plans, Emily was confident that Creative Weddings was functioning smoothly despite her absence.

She returned the portable phone to its base and realized, as a wave of weariness washed over her, that the long day had sapped her energy. She was exhausted. Within a half hour, she'd stripped off the peach-tinted silk gown and hung it away in the closet, showered, pulled on a thigh-length white chemise nightgown, and slipped into bed.

The following morning, Emily had breakfast from a tray in her room while she used her laptop to make lists for the many details of the wedding. At nine-thirty, a servant knocked on her door to deliver an invitation to join the queen for early-morning tea. It wasn't until she entered Caroline's sitting room, however, that she realized that she was the queen's only guest, neither Jenna, Lazhar, nor the king were present. The queen sat alone at the round, linen-covered table tucked into an alcove looking out on her beloved garden. Filmy draperies let the light in through the floor-to-ceiling windows but kept out the sun's glare. A delicate English bone china tea service sat in front of her and the table held only two place settings.

Uh-oh. Emily took one look at Caroline's face and nearly panicked. *She knows we lied to her.*

"Good morning, Emily." Caroline's grave expression lightened with a fleeting smile. "Won't you join me."

"Thank you." Emily sat in one of the dainty, silk-covered rose chairs, shaking out and smoothing her napkin over her lap.

"That will be all, Theresa, I'll ring if I need you."

The serving girl nodded, bowed and quit the room.

With the ease of long practice, Caroline poured tea into two fragile teacups, passing one to Emily. ''Do try the almond cookies,'' she commented as she followed the steaming tea with a small serving plate loaded with pastries and cakes. ''They're one of my favorites and the chef always includes them with my morning and afternoon tea. Although,'' she added wryly as she stirred honey into her cup, ''I'm sure they're responsible for that last stubborn five pounds that I just can't seem to budge, no matter how much I diet.''

''I think we all struggle with 'the last five pounds,''' Emily said.

''Some of us more than others.'' Caroline's smile faded. ''I wanted to talk with you privately about the wedding, Emily.''

Emily managed not to wince, but just barely.

''I know my son can be very persuasive and difficult to refuse when he wants something,'' Caroline continued, ''but if he's pressured you, in any way, to convince you to marry quickly, you must tell me and I'll talk to him. A woman's wedding day is very important and you should have the day you've always dreamed of—you shouldn't be so rushed that your big moment is spoiled.''

Emily had braced herself to hear the queen demand an explanation of the lies she and Lazhar had told her about their pretend engagement and marriage. She was so surprised by the queen's offer to intercede on her behalf, that she was at a loss for words. "I don't know what to say," she managed finally.

"Just tell me what's in your heart," Caroline said encouragingly.

Emily remained silent, frantically trying to think of a way to explain without telling further lies.

When she didn't speak, Caroline lifted her cup and sipped, eyeing Emily over the rim. "Marrying into the royal family can be an overwhelming prospect. Believe me, I had concerns before I said yes to Abbar, and they didn't all go away before the wedding, nor even immediately after," she added, returning the delicate cup to its saucer. "Let me be frank, Emily. I know my son well and I have no concerns about his desire for this marriage. However, I have the feeling that you may be having second thoughts about the wedding."

"No." Emily didn't have to lie about this—all of the reasons she'd agreed to marry Lazhar were still valid. She understood his driving need to grant what may well turn out to be his father's last wish.

"Then you do love my son?" Caroline asked gently.

She should immediately say "yes." She knew she should. Not only was it what Caroline needed to hear, but it was also the first truth in all the lies she'd been mouthing since she'd agreed to cooperate with Lazhar's plan.

But for her heart's sake, Emily knew she should say no. She should deny loving Lazhar, both to Caroline, and to the prince himself.

He's going to break my heart, she thought, acknowledging the fear that had subconsciously tormented her ever since she'd agreed to marry him.

Falling in love with a royal prince who only wanted a temporary wife was emotional suicide. How could she have let this happen, she thought wildly. Now that the date was set and they were publicly committed to the wedding, she realized that she desperately wanted a real marriage with Lazhar. And there was absolutely no hope of that ever happening.

"Emily?" Caroline's concerned voice drew Emily out of her thoughts and she realized that the queen was watching her, concern written on her patrician features.

"I'm sorry." She managed a small smile of apology. "I was distracted." Her gaze met Caroline's. "I love Lazhar more than I ever thought it was possible to love someone."

Her voice rang with conviction and her sincerity brought an instant smile of relief and delight to Caroline's face.

"Well, that answers that," she said. "And you're positive you don't feel pressured to marry sooner than you would like?"

"No, not at all." And it was true. Emily didn't

mind having the wedding quickly. The sooner begun, the sooner done, she thought. If she focused
on the practical aspects of what she was doing,
then perhaps she could forget that this wasn't to
be a normal marriage, but a marriage in name only.

''Very well.'' Caroline nodded decisively.
''Then it's settled. We can proceed with the arrangements.'' She opened a folder lying to the left
of her teacup, scanning the top sheet before handing it to Emily. ''This is your schedule for the day.
A rather full one, I'm afraid, but we've much to
accomplish if you're to be married in less than two
weeks.''

Emily nodded. The list divided the day into fifteen-minute increments and was booked so completely that she would have little time to spend
with Lazhar, and virtually no time to be alone with
him. Given the scorching kisses they'd shared, the
lack of privacy between them was a good thing,
Emily thought, because she wasn't at all sure she
could resist him. And the more physical intimacy
between them, the harder it would be to leave him
when she had to go back to San Francisco alone.

But as determined as Emily was to keep distance
between them, Lazhar was equally determined to
have her as close as possible.

He joined Emily, Jenna and Caroline for lunch,
only to have his mother whisk Emily away to a
meeting with the palace staff, followed by a fitting

for her wedding gown. Frustrated, Lazhar bided his time. Before dinner, he leaned against the wall outside the door to her suite, waiting.

His patience was rewarded when Emily opened the door and stepped into the hall, closing it behind her before she turned and saw him. She gasped, her hand flying to the black lace bodice of her gown, to press just over her heart. "Lazhar! You startled me."

"Sorry." He threaded his fingers through hers and tucked her arm beneath his, keeping her close as they walked down the hall. "I didn't mean to frighten you. I wanted a few moments alone with you to ask how you're coping with my family and the wedding plans."

Emily's fingers tightened on his. "Your mother asked some very pointed questions at breakfast but I think my answers satisfied her."

"What did she want to know?"

"She was concerned that rushing the marriage wouldn't give me the wedding I may have dreamed of having. She was very sweet, actually." Emily glanced sideways, her gaze meeting his for a moment before her lashes lowered and she looked away, facing forward so that he saw her profile and couldn't read her eyes. "She volunteered to talk to you and stop the wedding, if I wanted."

Lazhar tensed. "And what did you tell her?"

''I assured her you hadn't pressed me to choose an early wedding date.''

''But I did, didn't I.'' Regret flooded him. ''I was so focused on marrying you that I didn't give enough thought to what this might do to your dream of the perfect wedding.'' He bit off a curse, impatient with himself for having been so dense. He'd been thinking of their days together as man and wife, and that he could give her the children and home she'd told Brenda she wanted. He'd totally forgotten that the wedding itself might be Emily's first concern. He should have known better; Jenna had been planning her wedding since she was a little girl. ''I'll do whatever it takes to make the ceremony as close as possible to your dream. Tell me what you want, and I'll get it for you, Emily. I didn't mean for you not to have—''

''Lazhar.'' She broke in. ''There isn't anything about this wedding that doesn't exceed all my hopes or expectations.'' A smile curved her mouth, her eyes sparkling with laughter when he continued to frown at her. ''It's a royal wedding, for goodness' sake. What girl doesn't dream of having a royal wedding?''

''There isn't some detail you want changed— flowers, the dress, something?'' She shook her head in response but he wasn't convinced. ''You're sure?''

''I'm positive.''

Lazhar's muscles relaxed. "Good. What else did you and my mother discuss?"

"The details of the wedding, mostly we talked about the schedule for the next few days. It's going to be crazy."

They reached the closed door to the family dining room. Emily stopped, turning to look up at him. Her green eyes were dark with concern. "I really don't like lying to your family. I wish we could tell your mother and Jenna the truth."

"We can't. I regret it as much as you do, and I respect your wish to tell them what we're doing, but none of this will work if my father learns the truth. We can't take that chance."

She sighed heavily, the fabric of her gown tightening over the swell of her breasts. Lazhar determinedly kept his gaze on her face.

"All right," she conceded.

Unable to resist, he bent and pressed a quick kiss against her soft mouth. "It will be fine, Emily," he promised. He pulled open the door. "Have you talked to your family? Are they coming to Daniz for the wedding?"

"I called Brenda—she's very excited and says she wouldn't miss it. I couldn't reach my father but I left a message with his secretary, and I'm waiting to hear from my sister and brothers."

He nodded, silently acknowledging her comment, mentally making a note to make sure that as many of her family members as possible were present for the occasion.

"By the way," he said as he opened the door. "The family jet is picking up your friend Jane in San Francisco. She'll be here late tomorrow evening."

Her eyes widened, her fingers tightening on his. "Thank you so much." Delight mixed with relief in her voice.

"No problem. I know you want her help with the wedding details. If there's anything you need, Emily, you only have to ask."

They crossed the threshold, entering the dining room to join his family for dinner.

Emily kept reminding herself that her engagement to Lazhar was a sham and their marriage would be solely because of the king's ill health and Lazhar's love for him. Nevertheless, with each considerate, thoughtful thing Lazhar did, and with each additional hour spent in his company, she fell more deeply in love with him. Providing his jet to fly Jane to Daniz was such a sweet thing to do, she thought as she donned her pajamas later that evening.

Jane arrived late the next evening and knocked on Emily's door before eight the next morning. Still in her pajamas, Emily was so glad to see her familiar face beneath her blond curls that she could have cried.

When they were seated comfortably on Emily's bed, steaming teacups in hand and a plate of the queen's favorite almond cookies between them, Jane fixed her with a commanding stare.

"All right, tell me everything."

"Oh, Jane…where should I start…" Emily pushed her tousled hair back from her face.

"Start at the beginning," Jane said promptly.

"Very well. As you know, the original plan was to spend a week or so here in Daniz, gathering information to put together a proposal for Creative Weddings to handle Lazhar's wedding."

Jane nodded, her eyes gleaming with interest behind her wire-frame glasses.

"Somehow, the king misunderstood. Instead of seeing me as a consultant who perhaps might be hired to plan his son's wedding, he decided that I was the woman Lazhar had chosen for a bride. And before I could untangle the confusion and explain to him who I really was, Lazhar convinced me to go through with the wedding."

"Did he seduce you? Threaten you?" Jane bristled.

"No, of course not," Emily said hastily. "The media reports about the king being ill and wanting to see Lazhar married before he dies are true, Jane. He's very, very ill. He's also one of the sweetest, kindest, most wonderful men I've ever met.'' She stared into her teacup without really seeing the amber liquid. ''I'm not sure how it happened, but I've grown so attached to him in the short time I've been here that I couldn't bring myself to hurt him by telling him I wasn't marrying Lazhar.''

Jane's face was troubled, her brown eyes filled with concern. ''But Emily, how can you marry the prince just to make his father happy? What chance will your marriage have if you start out on such shaky ground?''

Emily trusted Jane completely and she badly needed to tell someone the truth. She leaned forward so her whispered words would only reach Jane's ears. ''It isn't a real marriage, Jane. His physicians have told the family the king has very little time left and after he's gone, the marriage will be annulled.''

Shocked, Jane's eyes widened. ''You're kidding?''

''No, I'm absolutely serious.''

''So, your marriage to the gorgeous prince is a complete fake? The big wedding, the title of princess—it's all only for a few days, or weeks, and then it's over?''

''Yes.''

''And when it's over, what then? Do you come back to San Francisco and go back to running Creative Weddings as if nothing happened?''

"That's the plan." *Except I doubt that my life will ever be the same again,* Emily thought.

"Wow." Jane shook her head in astonishment, visibly trying to absorb the impact of what Emily had just confided to her. "This is wild." Her eyes narrowed. "You can't let the press know," she said firmly. "They'd rip you to shreds. Heaven knows what kind of spin they'd put on your story, but it wouldn't be kind."

"I know," Emily agreed. "You're the only person, besides Lazhar and myself, who knows this isn't a real engagement. He won't even let me tell his mother and sister, because he swears they can't keep anything from his father and we don't want him to know the truth, of course."

"What are you getting out of this, Emily? I mean—" Jane shook her head, her gaze shrewd "—it's easy to see what Lazhar gets, but what about you?"

"I get exactly what I hoped to get when I came here—I'll plan a royal wedding. The cachet of that connection for Creative Weddings will be invaluable and my business will expand from the States to Europe."

"But if you're divorced shortly after you marry, you'll be notorious. The tabloids will go crazy."

"True." Emily shrugged. "But I doubt that will harm the business. In fact, the attraction of having an ex-princess as their wedding planner might pull in more clients.''

"You're probably right,'' Jane said dryly. "Americans love celebrities. What about your fee for all this?''

"You mean for planning the wedding?''

"Yes.'' Jane nodded. "And for posing as the bride. Is he doubling the usual fee for your services?''

"No. In fact, I insisted that Lazhar have his attorneys draw up a prenup agreement that dealt with all the financial issues. I'm sure the palace would have done it anyway, but I wanted to be sure it covered our particular circumstances. He assured me he would find a way to word the agreement so no one knows we plan to separate quickly.''

Jane's eyes darkened, her expression worried, a tiny frown veeing her eyebrows as her lips pursed.

"What?'' Emily waited, sure that Jane had something important to say.

"Are you sure you can do this and survive with your heart in one piece, Emily?''

Emily had never managed to conceal her emotions from her best friend. She couldn't lie to her. It was so like Jane to cut to the heart of the matter. "No, I'm not sure. But I'm sure I want to do this.'' Jane looked unconvinced and Emily knew she couldn't explain the connection she felt to King Abbar. "I know this probably doesn't make sense to you, but I'm positive that I want to do it. I've only known the king a very short time but I felt an instant affinity with him—almost as if he were the father I always wanted.''

''And never had,'' Jane put in, her tone leaving Emily in no doubt of the dislike she felt for Walter Parks.

''No, my father isn't anyone's idea of the perfect parent,'' Emily conceded. ''But that doesn't mean I can't appreciate a man who's clearly adored by his family. If taking a few weeks of my life to play the role of princess will make him die happy, then I'm willing to do so.'' She waved a hand at the room where they sat. ''And it's not as if I'm in during any hardships to do it, Jane. Not only is my business gaining stature, but I'm living in a palace, visiting exotic locales, meeting fascinating people. All very good stuff.''

Jane shook her head, her blond hair brushing her shoulders. ''I can't argue with any of the benefits of this arrangement you've agreed to. But, you're the last person in the world I'd expect to be involved in something like this, Emily.''

''What do you mean?''

Jane spread her hands, tea sloshing dangerously close to the rim of the delicate cup in her hand as she gestured. ''You never lie. I don't think I've even heard you utter a half-truth to anyone. Oh, sure, you're diplomatic and sometimes you don't tell the stark truth. Like the time Mrs. DiAngelo asked you if an avocado-green dress was perfect for her as mother-of-the-bride, and you managed to convince her that the pale pink evening suit was more flattering to her complexion. If you'd told her the real truth,'' Jane said darkly, ''you would have told her that she has excruciatingly bad taste in clothes and the green dress was unspeakably ugly. Which is exactly what I wanted to tell her.''

Laughter surprised Emily, lightening her mood. ''Thank goodness you didn't tell her that, Jane.''

''I wanted to.'' Jane sipped her tea and lifted an eyebrow, surprised. ''Yum, this is wonderful.''

''The queen has it mixed specially for her. It's delicious, isn't it?''

''Yes. I know you love tea, Emily, but it's never been my favorite. However, I could be convinced to drink this every morning. And these cookies are incredible.'' She took one from the plate and ate it in two small bites.

''Those are the queen's favorites, too. The palace chef makes them specially for her and since she knows I love them, she asked him to always serve them with my tea tray, just as he does for her.''

Jane heaved a theatrical sigh. ''Are you sure there's no way this marriage can't be permanent? Because I have to tell you, Emily, living in the palace has definite perks, not to mention the fact that Prince Lazhar is absolutely gorgeous.''

Emily smiled and shook her head. ''No, I'm afraid not. But for the moment—'' she lifted a cookie from the plate and saluted Jane with it ''—we can indulge in all the perks we want.'' She popped the dainty cookie in her mouth, chewed and swallowed. ''Or as many as we can fit in between the endless list of things to accomplish before the wedding day.''

Jane rolled her eyes, set her cup aside and dusted off her fingers. ''Where's the list? And do you really think we can pull off a royal wedding in less than two weeks? I thought you originally said that six months was going to be an extremely tight schedule.''

''Six months would have been difficult, and two weeks would be impossible if the family hadn't agreed to an abbreviated version of the traditional royal wedding.'' She slipped off the bed, walked into the sitting room to collect her notebook from the table where she'd left it late the night before, and returned to rejoin Jane. ''Here's the schedule for today,'' she handed Jane the sheet prepared by the queen's secretary.

Jane silently scanned the schedule before looking back up at Emily. ''You're booked in fifteen-minute increments, Emily.'' She glanced at her watch. "Starting in forty minutes. What can I take care of on this list for you today?"

"I thought you could take my notes and check in with the palace protocol officer—he's coordinating the church and reception invitations and seating. Then the palace florist needs some personal attention—I'm confident that they know exactly what I want, but I don't want to ignore them. It's important that everyone feels they're a vital part of the team."

"Of course." Jane glanced at her watch again. "You'd better finish getting dressed. You only have thirty-eight minutes left before your first appointment."

"Right." Emily slipped off the bed and moved quickly to the bathroom. She paused at the door to look back. "Jane, I'm *so* glad you're here to help me. I can't tell you how much I appreciate your flying in at such short notice."

"Are you kidding? I'd have been furious if you hadn't called me." Jane's face lit with a grin and she winked at Emily. "This is going to be great fun. Now get dressed."

Feeling immeasurably relieved and cheered by Jane's practical approach, Emily disappeared into the bathroom.

Chapter Eight

The wedding was spectacular.

The hot Mediterranean sun poured golden light over Lazhar and Emily as they exited the church, pausing at the top of the stone steps to wave at the crowds filling the streets around St. Catherine's. The people of Daniz cheered and tossed flowers in the air, covering the church steps with roses. They were clearly delighted with their prince's choice of a bride.

''They love you,'' Lazhar whispered in Emily's ear as they waved to the noisy crowd.

Emily nodded, continuing to wave and smile as

they moved down the flight of stone steps to the limousine waiting at the bottom. She was still dazed by the kiss he'd given her after they'd taken their vows. When he'd lifted her white lace veil and took her in his arms, she'd expected a brief touch of his lips on hers to satisfy tradition. No matter how brief or polite, however, she knew any kiss from Lazhar would be electric and she'd mentally braced herself to remain calm and composed. But the kiss began with such tenderness that it shook her preconceived notions and ended with a carnality that left her feeling he'd physically and publicly claimed her as his.

For a groom that supposedly wanted a temporary marriage, Lazhar was acting amazingly like a future lover.

Emily didn't know how she felt about that. And she had little time to consider it as the car whisked them back to the palace for the first of the festivities, a late-afternoon brunch for five hundred of their closest friends and important dignitaries. The brunch was followed by the wedding reception that took up the evening.

It was nearly midnight before Emily and Lazhar could bid their guests farewell and escape to his private residence in the southern wing of the palace.

Emily was unfamiliar with this section, but she easily recognized the uniforms of the guards who were posted at the entrance to the wing. The reception gaiety continued unabated far below them on the first floor, on the other side of the palace, but here all was quiet, the hallway empty except for the two of them and the guards at the entrance behind them.

The hall was decorated much as the other areas of the palace and had a lovely Persian carpet runner, its colors glowing beneath the light from the gold-and-crystal sconces installed at regular intervals on the walls. Oil paintings hung between the sconces, the stunning seascapes and florals interspersed with family portraits.

''This carpet feels so good after standing on marble floors all day,'' she remarked, relishing the cushioning beneath her aching feet. She was tempted to stop, lift her skirt and slip off the white satin, narrow-heeled pumps. She loved the way the shoes looked, but they were killing her feet.

Lazhar paused outside a door, turned the knob and pushed it open. Then without warning, he bent and swung Emily into his arms.

She gasped and clutched at his shoulders. ''What are you doing?''

''Carrying my bride over the threshold. I understand it's an American custom.'' He smiled down at her, turning sideways to maneuver the long train of her white lace wedding gown through the door.

He nudged the door closed with his heel before striding across the room.

Emily gained a quick impression of a sitting room that equaled the beauty of the other rooms she'd seen in the palace and then they were in the bedroom. Lazhar halted, lowering her to the bed where the voluminous skirt of her gown pooled around her, the satin and lace startlingly white against the deep blue of the silk spread.

He caught the hem of her skirt and pulled it above her knees. Emily's heart stuttered but before she could speak, he slipped off her shoes and tossed them over his shoulder onto the floor. Then he swung her legs sideways so he could sit beside her on the edge of the bed, rested her aching feet on his hard thighs, and rubbed her instep with his thumbs.

"Ohhhhh," she groaned. This was certainly not what she'd expected when he lifted her dress, but it was sheer heaven after the long, endless day spent standing in reception lines.

"Feel good?" He lifted an eyebrow, his dark gaze assessing her face, a smile curving his mouth.

"Wonderful." Emily closed her eyes as he worked out a knot in the muscles and eased the stressed tendons. "If you ever need a second career, you could always be a masseuse," she said with a soft moan.

"I'll keep that in mind," he said with amusement.

"I thought the wedding went well, didn't you?" she asked absently.

"Very."

"I didn't realize that there would be so many Americans there, except for my family of course."

"We do a lot of business with American companies," he explained. "And quite a few of the Americans at the brunch were friends of mine from Harvard. We've kept in touch over the years."

Intrigued, Emily opened her eyes and looked at him. The room was shadowy but the lamp on the bedside table threw a pool of light over the bed where they sat. Lazhar's hair gleamed with blue-black highlights, his lashes lowered over dark eyes as he focused on her foot. She wore skin-toned, thigh-high stockings and her foot in the pale hose seemed small and very feminine enclosed in his tanned hands, the other resting on the black tuxedo slacks covering his thigh.

He lifted his lashes and his gaze met hers. Emily was instantly reminded that they were alone together in his bedroom, this was their wedding night, and the kiss he'd given her at the church had been far from platonic.

Emily wasn't a virgin, but her experience was limited to the man she'd been engaged to after college. Their physical relationship had been pleasant, but not earthshaking. Their engagement had ended badly when she learned that his interest in her was generated by his burning desire to advance his career in her father's company. Disillusioned, she'd thrown herself into building Creative Weddings and hadn't taken time to pursue a connection with another man since.

Still, she'd experienced the mechanics of sex and understood what the heat in Lazhar's eyes meant.

"I didn't know you went to Harvard," she commented, struggling to keep her tone light. "Tell me about it."

The slight lift of the corners of his mouth told her that he recognized her ploy, but still, he answered her. "I attended public school here in Daniz as a child but after graduating at sixteen, I wanted to go farther afield. I convinced my father to send me to the States for college and he picked Harvard."

"He picked Harvard?" Emily was diverted despite herself by his choice of words. "Don't you mean Harvard accepted your application? Or does a prince automatically have his choice of any school?"

"I suspect most college-level schools would seriously consider a prince," he admitted with a shrug. "But in my case, I had the necessary grades to be offered admittance at several schools, and my father picked Harvard.''

''Did you *want* to go to Harvard?''

''Yes.'' He smiled at her. ''I chose Harvard, but the king had to approve the choice.''

''I see. So it was a royal-protocol-thing?''

''Yes. Although I don't think it's uncommon for parents to give final approval for their children's college choice.''

''You're probably right. And you were sixteen when you entered Harvard? In the States, college freshman are normally eighteen years old—did you feel out of place with your classmates being two years older than you?''

''No, it didn't bother me.''

''Somehow, I can't picture you living in a dorm room and riding a bike to class,'' she mused, narrowing her eyes in thought.

''I didn't ride a bike to class, but I did live in a dorm room,'' he said.

''Did you enjoy the whole college experience— being away from home and family, all on your own?''

''I wasn't exactly on my own…my bodyguards had the room next door.''

Emily stared at him in shock. ''You're kidding?''

''No, I'm not.''

''It never occurred to me that you would need

guards at school.'' She shook her head. ''Especially not in the States.''

''Hmm,'' he murmured. While they'd been talking, his fingers had left her toes and instep and move upward to her ankle. Now they moved higher, finding the tired muscles in the back of her calf and kneading.

''*Ohhh,* that's…'' Indescribable, she thought. Her eyes drifted closed with sheer pleasure and she leaned back on her elbows.

He moved to her other foot, her ankle, then her calf. Emily stopped talking, lulled by the warm stroke of his palms on her skin and the firm press of hard fingers as they worked the tired muscles and eased away the aches.

Unfortunately for Emily, having his hands on her ankles and calves led to thoughts of having them on other parts of her body. Her heartbeat pounded faster, harder, surging in a rhythm directly connected to the stroke of his hands against her skin.

''Hey.'' His deep voice was as warm as the last caress of his palms against her calf when he released her and stood. ''Don't go to sleep—you won't be comfortable in that dress.''

She was relieved that he'd assumed her eyes were closed because she was tired. She didn't want him to know that his hands on her had aroused her to the point where she doubted she would be able to fall asleep at all.

He took her hands and drew her to her feet, his palms cupping her shoulders to turn her away from him. She caught her breath as he freed the button at her nape, then moved to the next one. There were thirty-two buttons from her nape to just below her waist. She knew the exact number because the seamstress had teased her about how much her husband would enjoy unbuttoning them. At the time, her only concern had been how she would manage to get out of the dress by herself, since she didn't anticipate Lazhar helping her. Now, she didn't know how she'd survive having him slip loose those thirty-two buttons.

Breathe, she told herself, determined to get through this without revealing how his touch affected her.

But with each button he freed, the back of his fingers brushed her bare skin beneath the dress. Wearing a bra hadn't been an option since it would have spoiled the line of the bodice, so the designer had incorporated a foundation garment into the gown itself.

Emily knew the moment Lazhar realized that she wasn't wearing anything under the bodice for his fingers stilled. The tip of his forefinger traced the line of her spine from her nape to just below her shoulder blades.

''You're not wearing anything under this?'' His voice was an octave lower than normal, husky with arousal.

''Not under the bodice.'' She could only manage the barest of information. The sound of his voice weakened her knees, already seriously threatened by the slow brush of that fingertip down her spine. She didn't breathe again until he moved to the next button.

He reached the fastening at her waist and moved lower to undo the final button. Then he slipped his hands beneath the open edges of the gown and stroked upward, widening the gap between the edges of the gown from below her waist to her nape. The loosened bodice sagged and Emily caught the pearl-edged lace and satin neckline, holding it against her breasts with both hands.

''Lazhar,'' she said, struggling for control as he bent his head, his mouth hot, damp against the sensitive skin at her nape. Her lashes drifted lower as he nipped her, instantly soothing the tiny sting with his tongue. ''I...we shouldn't do this.''

''Why not?'' he murmured, his hands closing over the narrow sleeves of her gown and tugging the bodice lower.

''Because making love isn't part of our plan.''

''Making love to you has always been part of my plan, Emily. I've wanted you since the first moment I saw you.''

His blunt statement shocked her. She twisted in his arms, looking over her shoulder. The hard planes of his face were taut with arousal, desire streaking dusky color over his cheekbones.

"But you said the marriage would be annulled. We never planned for this to be a real marriage—sleeping together will only complicate things."

"It doesn't need to be complicated. I want you. You want me. That's about as simple as it gets between a man and a woman." His arms slipped around her waist and he pressed her against him. "You touch me and I burn."

His arms encircled her, her naked back tight against the white linen shirt covering his chest. Emily felt the heat that poured off him, sending her own temperature higher, and the slam of his heartbeat that echoed the frantic race of her own.

His hand stroked her throat, moving upward to cup her face as he turned her in his arms. "We're married, Emily. And this marriage can be as real as we decide to make it."

"But when our few weeks together are over, what then?" Emily's palms rested on his white silk shirt. His heart pounded beneath her hands and she curled her fingers, pushing against his chest.

He let her shift away from him, but didn't release her, their bodies still touching from waist to thigh while the fingers of one hand still cupped her cheek.

She searched his face. "I'm sure the sex would be wildly satisfying, Lazhar, but I don't want an affair. And that's what we'd have."

"No." His thumb grazed her bottom lip. "Not an affair. We're good together, Emily. We make a good match. And we'd have beautiful children," he added, his hand dropping to smooth over her flat midriff.

Emily caught her breath. "Not fair." Her voice was husky with emotion. "You know I don't plan to have children."

"I also know you'll make a wonderful mother, Emily." His voice roughened, deepening. "Stay, Emily, share my bed."

"Beyond tomorrow?" Her voice sounded drugged, her body throbbing with the need to give in.

"Forever, if you'll stay." His eyes were heavy-lidded with passion, his fingers smoothing compulsively over the bare skin of her back where her dress gaped open. His hand slipped beneath hers, tugging the edge of her neckline from her grip and easing it downward.

Emily stiffened, struggling to hold back the wave of pleasure that washed over her. "We agreed to marry for only a few weeks. That's not forever," she argued. But her words lacked conviction, her protest at odds with her body's need to give in.

The bodice slipped to her waist, kept from falling farther by the tight press of their hips, leaving her bare from the waist to the crown of her head. His gaze left hers, black lashes lowering as he looked down—and his big body shuddered.

His fingers tightened on the soft skin of her back and midriff, his body straining against hers, held in check by the force of his will.

"If you're going to say no, do it now." His voice was guttural. "You've got about two seconds before it'll be too late."

And in that instant Emily knew she was going to take the biggest gamble of all.

"Yes." She slipped her arms around his neck, her breasts lifting against the warm linen of his shirt. "I want you, Lazhar."

"Thank God," he muttered. One big hand cradled her head and he bent, taking her mouth with a kiss that seared her. Then his mouth left hers and closed without preamble over the swollen, sensitive tip of her breast.

Emily moaned. Lazhar's mouth left her breast and took hers.

The white wedding dress pooled around her feet when he lifted her and swung her into his arms. Focused on the shuddering pleasure of his mouth on hers, Emily was barely aware of him carrying her to the bed. The silk spread felt cool beneath her bare back and thighs when he laid her down, lifting himself away from her to strip the brief white lace bikini panties down her legs. He tossed them over his shoulder, his eyes hot and intent on her body as he stood to shrug off his own clothes.

Burning with need, Emily watched impatiently while he shed his jacket and shirt, then unbuckled his belt and unzipped his slacks. He shoved the slacks and silk boxers down his legs in one swift movement and knelt on the bed. Emily shivered. His eyes were predatory, his broad, muscled body heated and aroused, totally focused on her. For one brief moment she felt threatened by the power inherent in his much bigger body, but then he slid his arm under her and lifted her, cradling her upper body against him while his mouth took hers, their legs tangling as he pressed against her from mouth to toes. His weight bore her back on the bed and she wrapped her arms and legs around him, binding him closer.

"Please," she murmured when his mouth left hers to take her breast once more. She twisted frantically when he stroked a hand over her hip and rocked against her. "Please…"

He growled something unintelligible and surged against her, demanding entrance.

Emily stiffened, struggling to accept him.

"Relax, honey." His voice was gravelly, taut with restraint, his muscles trembling with the effort needed to give her time to adjust.

"I'm trying." She stiffened, pinned beneath his weight, breathless, her hands clutching his biceps. "You're too big."

His hand brushed between them, finding her and stroking in small, seductive circles.

"Ohhh." Emily forgot to try to relax, totally focused now on the incredible pleasure of his touch. Lazhar flexed his hips and she cried out as he surged inside, sending her over the edge in a blinding climax. He followed her in a swift, passionate drive that left them both sated and exhausted.

She lost track of how many times they made love. Sometime during the hours before dawn, he carried her into the shower and then back to bed, where he tucked her bare body against his and she fell asleep, exhausted.

Morning sunshine filtered through the light draperies covering the tall windows and reached their bed, waking Emily. Her lashes lifted and she lay perfectly still, adjusting to the fact that she wasn't alone. Lazhar's arm was a warm, possessive weight at her waist. Her body was curved, spoon-like, against him with his powerful, hair-roughened thighs against the back of hers and her bottom tucked into the cradle of his hips. He was still asleep, she thought, reassured by the slow, gentle rise of his chest against her back and shoulder blades as he breathed.

His forearm, deeply tanned and lightly dusted with fine black hair, lay under hers. She covered the back of his hand with hers, struck by the marked difference between his much larger hand and strong, square-tipped fingers with their neatly trimmed nails and her own much smaller hand, the slender fingers tipped with pink-enameled nails. The bones of her narrow wrist seemed even more delicate next to the sturdy width of his.

She'd never thought of herself as a small woman, but Lazhar was a big man, his bones thicker than hers, his body heavily muscled, his legs longer, the reach of his arms greater. Yet despite the passionate abandon of the night before, he'd unfailingly harnessed that strength to give them both only pleasure.

What she'd shared with Lazhar wasn't the lukewarm emotion her ex-fiancé had elicited. In fact, she thought, bemused, there wasn't anything about Lazhar that was remotely like any other man she'd ever known.

''Good morning.'' The deep voice was raspy with sleep.

Emily had been so absorbed in her thoughts she hadn't noticed the change in the tenor of his breathing. She looked over her shoulder. His dark hair was tousled, his jaw shadowed with black beard. His gaze was heavy-lidded, growing more so as his hand left her waist and cupped her breast.

''Good morning.'' Her voice was throaty as well, but not from sleepiness. The caressing movements of his fingers against her breast were stealing her breath, making her bones melt like hot wax.

''Come here.'' He tugged her onto her back, slipped his arms under her and rolled until she lay on top of him.

Emily shivered with the abrupt sensual stroke of her body against his. Sprawled along his broad, hot length, her hips pressed to his, she was well aware of his growing arousal.

The abrupt rap of knuckles against the outer sitting-room door broke the sensual tension that bound them. Startled, Emily's eyes widened and she instinctively shifted to move away. His arms tightened, refusing to let her leave him.

''Ignore it. Whoever it is will go away. We're on our honeymoon.'' He lifted his head and caught her mouth with his, luring her deeper into a kiss that made her forget the sound. He wrapped his arms around her and rolled once more, reversing their positions so her soft, bare body was pinned under the harder angles of his.

But the knocking didn't stop.

''What the hell...'' His voice exasperated, Lazhar reluctantly lifted away from her, bending back down to press one more hard kiss against her faintly swollen lips. ''Don't move.'' He rolled off the bed and stalked naked across the room, grabbed his black slacks from the floor where he'd tossed them the night before, stepped into them and zipped them as he left the bedroom.

Emily lay sprawled where he left her, a faintly bemused smile curving her mouth. She shifted, stretching, and realized that she ached in places she'd never noticed before.

Her husband was an amazing lover. She knew now why she hadn't missed the physical side of their relationship when she'd split with her ex-fiancé. He hadn't touched her, not really, not in any of the ways that Lazhar had. Lazhar had stripped away all her defenses, refusing to let her hold anything back from him and the result was that she felt linked to him, branded somehow.

Mated, she thought, realizing that's what had happened between them during the long night.

The murmur of voices ceased, the outer door to the sitting room closed, and she sat up, tucking the sheet under her arms and over her breasts, to look expectantly at the bedroom door, waiting for Lazhar to appear.

When he did, he carried a breakfast tray, loaded with covered dishes, a carafe of orange juice, and another carafe that Emily hoped held coffee.

''My father had the chef send up a tray,'' Lazhar said with a grin. ''Evidently he thought you didn't eat enough last night at the reception and since it's nearly lunchtime, decided to feed us.''

"How sweet of him," Emily exclaimed, touched by her new father-in-law's thoughtfulness. "I didn't realize it until now, but I'm starving."

Lazhar set the heavy tray down atop the rumpled sheets and plumped the pillows, tucking them behind her and nearer the center of the bed. "Slide over and lean back."

Emily moved to the middle of the bed where she sat cross-legged, the plump pillows cushioning her bare back against the carved headboard, the silk sheet tucked around her.

Lazhar picked up the tray and moved it to the middle of the bed, joining her with the food between them.

He lifted the covers from two plates. "Omelets and crisp bacon." Lazhar handed one of the plates to Emily. "I'm sure this American breakfast is in honor of you, Emily—the chef and his staff want to make you feel at home."

"It worked." Emily smiled at him, setting the warm plate on her lap so she could pour coffee into two delicate Wedgwood cups. "And if they've sent us Daniz salsa for the eggs, then it's a perfect breakfast."

"Salsa?" Lazhar lifted the lids from several little pots, uncovering jam, marmalade and honey, before he found Emily's spicy red sauce. "Here we are."

They ate in companionable silence. Plates

empty, Lazhar refilled their coffee cups, handing a cup and saucer to Emily. ''What would you like to do today? We can drive inland and sightsee, play tourist, if you like.''

''That might be fun, I'd love to see more of—''

The phone rang, interrupting her. Lazhar leaned across her to catch up the receiver of the phone sitting on the nightstand.

''Hello?''

Emily felt his body tense and he shot her a quick glance.

''Hold on.'' He handed the receiver to Emily. ''It's a business call. I'll take it in the other room. Will you hang up the receiver for me after I pick up in there?''

''Of course.''

His gaze held hers for a moment. Then he caught the back of her head in one hand and held her still for a kiss.

''I'll be right back.''

She nodded, bemused and breathless from the sudden heat that always bloomed when he touched her. *Maybe we should cancel the trip into the countryside and just stay in our room all day.*

''You can hang up now, Emily.'' Lazhar called from the other room.

His voice startled her and she realized she'd been sitting motionless, smiling at the door where he'd disappeared, totally distracted by thoughts of him.

"All right," she responded. She stretched to reach the phone but the breakfast tray tipped precariously. She caught it, sliding it toward the end of the bed, then twisted to return the phone.

"...she went through with the wedding. I thought we'd take care of signing the contracts today."

Emily paused, frowning at the receiver, still in her hand. That voice was unmistakable: it was her father. Why was Walter Parks calling Lazhar? Without giving a thought to the fact that she was eavesdropping, something she would never ordinarily do, she lifted the phone to her ear.

"I signed the documents yesterday...they'll be delivered to your office by courier sometime tomorrow," Lazhar said.

"Excellent." Walter's satisfaction came clearly over the line. "You won't be sorry, Your Highness. We'll both make a great deal of money from this enterprise. And I'm sure my daughter will make you a good wife. All in all, the best kind of merger, with both of us getting what we want."

"If you ever tell her, the deal is canceled." Lazhar's voice was cold, lethal.

"No, no, of course I won't," Walter said hastily. "Emily isn't likely to approve of my offering her to you as part of a gem deal, despite the fact that you needed a wife and she always dreamed of being a princess.''

Emily's heart stopped, pain shafting through her. Her father had offered her to Lazhar as part of one of his high-stakes deals? And Lazhar had accepted?

''Just so you understand that this subject is never to be mentioned. Not to anyone.''

''I understand.''

And he's lying. He knows how I feel about telling lies.

Her hand trembling, Emily carefully eased the receiver onto the phone base. Outraged and heartsick, she sat perfectly still, her dreams of a future with Lazhar lying shattered in pieces around her.

Betrayal was an ugly word. And that's what Lazhar had done to her, she thought. Nausea shook her and she swallowed thickly, refusing to give in to the devastating heartbreak.

The unexpected sound of someone knocking once again on the sitting-room door startled her and she jumped, rattling the cups in their saucers on the tray. She heard the outer door opening, then Lazhar's deep tones alternated with another male voice before the door clicked closed.

She braced herself, trying to prepare for the confrontation that she knew must happen immediately. Staring at the doorway, she clasped her hands tightly together, waiting for Lazhar to appear.

When he did, his expression was so somber that she knew instantly something was very wrong, something not connected to the phone call from her father.

''What is it?''

''Father—he's had another heart attack.''

''Oh, no.'' Emily clutched the sheet tighter over her breasts, fear for the king searing her. ''Is he…?''

''He's alive. But his doctor doesn't know how much damage has been done. They're taking him by ambulance to the hospital.''

He pulled open the closet door, disappearing inside and Emily slipped out of bed, quickly donning her silk robe. She joined him, gathering underwear from a drawer and snatching a pair of white slacks and coordinating white-and-blue knit top from their hangers. She raced into the bathroom, performing her usual morning routine in record-breaking time. When she returned to the bedroom moments later, she found Lazhar dressed in jeans and a long-sleeved white shirt, sitting on the edge of the bed to pull on socks and boots. While he used the bathroom, she slipped into sandals and collected her purse from the closet.

When he left the bathroom, unshaven, his hair damp, she was ready and they left the suite, moving quickly down the hallway. Lazhar's chauffeur had the car waiting, engine purring, and a guard opened the rear passenger door the moment they exited the palace.

The drive to the hospital was nearly silent. Despite the shock of the overheard conversation, Emily didn't object when Lazhar threaded their fingers together, resting their clasped hands on his thigh. She knew a confrontation between them was inevitable, but it would have to wait. For now, they were joined by their mutual worry over the king's health.

Fortunately the press apparently hadn't yet learned of the king's medical emergency, for there was no crowd of reporters and photographers waiting outside the hospital. Nevertheless, their driver took them around the back to a little-used entrance that assured them privacy.

Escorted by his bodyguards, Lazhar and Emily rode the elevator to the fourth floor. Here, royal guards stood sentry at intervals along the halls, the entire floor cordoned off. They moved quickly, their footsteps loud in the nearly empty hallway.

"Your mother and sister are in here, Your Highness." A guard held open the door to a private waiting room.

They stepped inside, the door closing quietly behind them.

Caroline, standing near the window, looked over her shoulder and saw them. Her face crumpled, tears welling in her eyes. "Lazhar."

''Mother.'' Lazhar's long strides erased the distance between them and he folded her close.

Emily held back her own tears as Jenna joined them and Lazhar hugged her as well, murmuring comfortingly to the two women. Emily looked away, struggling to hold back the flood of emotion that threatened to destroy her composure. A small kitchenette unit took up one corner of the waiting room and she crossed to the short counter, occupying herself with pouring coffee into two of the foam cups stacked next to the machine.

''Emily?''

She glanced up to see Lazhar gesturing her near and carrying the two steaming cups, she joined the trio. Lazhar took the cup she handed him, sipping without comment while she exchanged hugs with Caroline and Jenna. Both women reflected the strain, their faces tearstained.

''Have you talked to the doctors?'' Emily asked.

''Just briefly,'' Caroline said. ''They told us they had to run tests and would be back to tell us the results as soon as they were available.''

''But Dr. Schaefer was certain that Father had a heart attack at the palace?'' Lazhar asked.

''Yes. Abbar didn't feel well last night but we thought it was indigestion and perhaps he'd overexerted himself at the wedding festivities. He stayed in bed this morning, resting, and he was sleeping when I left to deal with morning mail and some other things that I couldn't postpone.'' Caroline's voice faltered. ''It wasn't an hour later when Maria came in to tell me Dr. Schaefer was with your father. I ran to his room and arrived just as the doctor was calling for the palace ambulance to transfer him to the hospital.''

''Maria came to my room and told me right after she saw Mom,'' Jenna put in. ''I sent Ari to tell you and Emily, then ran straight to Papa's room, but they were just wheeling him out on a gurney. We rode here in the ambulance with him.'' Her voice trembled and she pressed her fingertips to her lips, her eyes filling with tears once again.

''Shh,'' Caroline murmured, slipping an arm around Jenna's shoulders. ''Your father has the best doctors available in Europe. He's going to make it through this.'' Her last sentence was a fierce, whispered promise.

''Your Highness?''

All four of them turned toward the doorway and the man dressed in surgical scrubs who entered. Each face held varying degrees of hope and dread.

''Dr. Schaefer.'' Lazhar held out his hand and the doctor shook it briefly as he joined their group. ''How is my father?''

''He's holding his own,'' Dr. Schaefer said gravely. ''The good news is that this latest heart attack didn't damage the heart muscle. But he has blockage in two arteries that we have to deal with immediately.''

Oh, no. Emily caught her breath. *Does this mean open-heart surgery? Is he strong enough to survive that?* The memory of the king's thin hand, resting on the game pieces as they chatted between chess moves, and how frail his body seemed, filled her with dread.

Beside her, Caroline's indrawn breath was a sharp, audible gasp and Jenna clasped her mother's hand.

''We've known about the blockages for some time and the potential need for surgery, but were waiting for the king to grow stronger. We no longer have time to wait. We have to deal with them now, rather than later. However,'' he continued, his gaze meeting Lazhar's and then Caroline's, ''we have an option for treatment.''

''What is it?'' Lazhar's voice was calm, but the empty foam cup slowly crumpled in his grip.

''Instead of performing open-heart surgery, which the king may or may not survive, we can do a coronary balloon angioplasty. It's a minimally invasive procedure that will clear the blockages. Then we'll install stents in the artery to support the weakened area and prevent the blockage from recurring.''

''What do you mean by minimally invasive?'' Caroline asked, her voice strained.

"We don't have to make an incision in the chest wall," the doctor explained. "We place a catheter into the femoral artery, then insert a balloon to clear the blockage before we put in a stent."

"A stent?" Caroline asked. "What is that?"

"It's a latticed, metal scaffold, very tiny, that's placed within the coronary artery where the blockage was to keep the vessel open."

"My father talked to me a month or so ago about this procedure," Lazhar said. "And he said he'd decided not to go through with it."

"Yes, that's true," Dr. Schaeffer agreed. "But he didn't want to choose any of the possible surgical or procedural options such as angioplasty at the time. He opted to try dietary changes and alternative medicine first."

"But those options didn't work." Jenna's comment wasn't a question.

"No, they did not," Dr. Schaeffer concurred, his voice somber. "And now it's imperative that we take measures to correct the problem and a coronary balloon angioplasty is the least invasive option open to us. He was lucky this time. As far as we can tell, there was no damage to the heart. But if we don't deal with the artery blockages, there's no guarantee that he'll be this lucky the next time."

"He'll have another heart attack?" Caroline asked, her voice tense.

''Yes.''

Lazhar's dark gaze met Emily's before moving on to Caroline and Jenna. Emily caught the subtle, slight nod that first Caroline, then, more reluctantly, Jenna, gave him.

''Very well.'' Lazhar nodded abruptly at the doctor. ''How quickly can you do it?''

''The staff is prepping the operating room now.''

Chapter Nine

T ime inched slowly past as they waited for Dr. Schaeffer to return with a report on the procedure. A half hour into their vigil, a hospital official knocked on the door to tell them that the press had gathered in front of the hospital and Lazhar left to speak with them. Emily looked out the window, watching the surge of reporters as Lazhar stepped out of the building, four floors below.

Behind her, Jenna flicked on the television set and found a news channel. The live feed showed Lazhar nearly surrounded by the crowd of reporters and photographers, two uniformed guards at his back. His face was impassive, his voice calm as he gave a brief update on the king's condition before he was barraged by questions from the reporters.

"How does he do that?" Emily murmured, watching Lazhar respond to a reporter while several others clamored to be heard.

"He's had lots of practice," Jenna said, her gaze on the television screen. "After Lazhar came home from university in the States, Papa slowly turned more and more of his duties over to him."

Emily nodded in acknowledgment of Jenna's comment. "He seems so calm, so in control."

"He's been that way ever since the kidnapping."

Startled, Emily's gaze left the screen and fastened on Jenna. "Kidnapping? What kidnapping?"

"He didn't tell you?"

Emily shook her head.

"Lazhar was kidnapped while he was at Harvard. I think it must have happened during his second year there because he was seventeen at the time. The people that took him were radicals who wanted to rid Daniz of the monarchy. They also wanted a ton of money," Jenna added. "They held Lazhar for five days before a combination of Daniz and American security forces got him back."

Anger surged through Emily, her hands clenching into fists. "Did they harm him?"

"He had a few bruises, but no serious injuries.

It changed Lazhar, though. He seemed older after that—more serious, and that's when he took up martial arts and switched the focus of his classes to defense and military training.'' Jenna turned to Caroline, who was pacing between the bank of windows and the open door, where she paused to search the hallway before returning to the windows. ''Don't you think Lazhar changed after the kidnapping, Mother?'' Caroline continued to stare out the window and didn't respond. ''Mother?''

Caroline jerked, looking around. ''Yes?''

''I asked if you agreed that Lazhar changed after the kidnapping when he was at Harvard.''

''Yes.'' The queen pushed her hair off her forehead, distracted. ''Yes, he seemed to go from being a teenager to a man overnight.'' She frowned, her gaze focusing on Emily. ''Horrible business. He didn't tell you about it?''

''No.'' Emily shook her head.

''He probably hasn't had time,'' Jenna commented. ''What with your whirlwind courtship and now this…'' She trailed off, waving her hand to indicate the hospital room.

''Yes, that's probably it,'' Emily agreed, knowing it was more likely Lazhar hadn't told her about this traumatic event in his life because theirs was a marriage arranged for convenience, not for sharing their lives and confiding the details of the youthful experiences that had formed them. After all, she hadn't shared the private moments of her teenage years with him, either, she thought. And it was unlikely she ever would, she reflected bleakly, for as soon as she knew the king was on the mend, she would be returning to San Francisco to resume her life. Her real life. Not the fairy tale dream of marrying a prince that for one unforgettable night, she'd believed had become reality.

On the television screen before her, she saw the press briefing breakup, Lazhar reentering the hospital's wide glass doors with the two guards.

Moments later, they heard the sound of the elevator, then footfalls in the hallway, and Lazhar appeared in the doorway. His gaze swept the room, finding Emily.

"Any news?"

"Not yet." She turned away, busying herself with pouring water into the coffeemaker and measuring coffee into the basket.

He crossed the room and slipped his arms around her waist. "Are you all right?"

His voice was a low-pitched murmur, his breath feathering across her cheek, shivering her nerves.

"Yes. I'm fine," she managed to say. "Or as fine as any of us can be at the moment."

His lips brushed her throat just below her ear and Emily closed her eyes, the moment bittersweet. Then his mother called his name and his arms tightened briefly before he released her. Emily tried to breathe past the pain lodged in her chest, just over her heart, and forced her hands to finish the task of switching on the coffeepot, brushing the few spilled grounds from the counter and dropping them into the trash basket next to the cabinet.

She managed to avoid having any meaningful conversations with Lazhar as they waited. Confined as they were to the waiting room with Caroline and Jenna and sometimes members of the palace staff, it was surprisingly easy to do. Everyone was worried and distracted by the threat to the king's health.

At last, Dr. Schaeffer joined them, his green scrubs wrinkled, his face weary but smiling. ''The procedure was a success,'' he told them.

Caroline dropped her face into her hands and sobbed. Jenna threw her arms around her mother, tears rolling down her cheeks. Emily felt her own cheeks grow damp and brushed away tears with her fingertips. Lazhar slipped his arm around her shoulders and hugged her close, tucking her face against the warm column of his throat, his grim face lit with relief.

''What happens now?'' he asked. ''How long will he be hospitalized?''

''At least three days and probably longer. I want to be very sure that he's completely stable before he goes home and I'd like to see him gain a few pounds.''

"So would I," Caroline said, her sense of humor resurfacing through her tears.

The doctor smiled at her and Jenna gave a watery chuckle.

Lazhar reached out to shake the doctor's hand and Emily used the opportunity to slip out of his arms.

"Can we see him?" Caroline asked.

"Yes, just as soon as he's out of recovery and in his room. I'll ask the nurse to let you know the moment they've settled him in," the doctor assured her. "The staff will need some time to get everything set up, monitors attached, etc. and make him comfortable."

"Thank you, Doctor."

"Just doing my job. I'm glad I had good news to tell you. If you have further questions, don't hesitate to ask for me at anytime. I'll be staying here at the hospital until the king goes home so the staff can always reach me."

He left them, his rubber-soled shoes squeaking slightly on the waxed tile floors as his tall lanky body disappeared through the door.

The six days following the king's heart attack passed swiftly. Between the long hours Emily and Lazhar spent at Abbar's bedside at the hospital and the additional duties Lazhar assumed for his father, Emily managed to avoid being alone with him almost completely. He came to bed long after she did and the few times that she was awake, she pretended to be asleep. She didn't resist when he slipped his arms around her and eased her against him, a part of her cherishing those few moments when she could allow herself to be close to him.

She knew their time was limited, however, for she'd decided to confront Lazhar and tell him she'd overhead his conversation with her father and knew they'd used her as a bargaining chip. She would tell Lazhar and return to San Francisco as soon as the king was home from the hospital and out of medical danger.

A phone call from Brenda reminding her that the date of her father's gem smuggling trial was near only increased her determination to leave Daniz.

She went with the family to the hospital on the day the king was to be released, a part of the group as the king waved to the crowds of adoring citizens. But as soon as they reached the palace and King Abbar was settled into his rooms, the family occupied with the pleasure of having him with them once again, she gave him a last hug and kiss and slipped away to the suite she shared with Lazhar.

She was packing, her bag open on the bed, when Lazhar entered the suite. He reached the bedroom door and halted abruptly.

"What are you doing?"

She glanced at him, then back at the soft silk robe in her hands, continuing to fold it. "I'm leaving this evening, flying home to San Francisco." She carefully laid the robe in the suitcase and looked at him. "I know the real reason you married me, Lazhar. I overheard you talking to my father the morning King Abbar had the heart attack."

He looked as if she'd slapped him. "Emily." He started toward her. "You were never meant to know."

"I understand." She held up her hand and took a step back her voice shaking with pent-up anger. "Please. Don't come any closer. I'd like to end this without a big scene."

His eyebrows winged upward in surprise before veeing down in a scowl. "Well, that's not likely to happen. And you *don't* understand."

"Yes, I do," she said evenly, determined not to lose her temper. "Your conversation with my father was very clear. He offered me to you as a bride in return for concessions in a gem deal. You agreed. Oh," she added. "You also told him never to tell me."

"Because I didn't want you hurt. I knew if you ever found out about the deal Walter thought he made with me, you'd never believe that I didn't marry you because of it."

"You were right," she said coolly. "I don't."

He cursed and dragged a hand through his hair. "Dammit, Emily, you've got to let me explain."

"No, I don't." Despite her best efforts to control her anger and hurt, her voice rose. "No amount of explaining will erase the fact that you purposely married me to get a better deal from my father. It's outrageous."

"I agree. It would be. If it were true, but it's not."

"Stop. Just stop!" Emily felt her temper slip beyond her rigidly held control. "I agreed to marry you because of your father. Now that he's past the crisis, the need for this sham of a marriage is over. I'm leaving." She grabbed a handful of lingerie from atop the bedspread and threw it into the suitcase. "How I could have been so stupid as to fall in love with a man who has a business machine for a heart is more than I can understand. You're just like my father," she fumed, glaring at him.

Lazhar's eyes narrowed, shock quickly replaced by triumph. "You love me."

"I do *not* love you." Annoyed that he'd managed to ignore all her comments except the one she wished she'd left unsaid, her voice rose another level, but she was beyond caring if she could be heard outside the room. "I hate you. Didn't you listen to anything I said? You're just like my father. I want the annulment you promised and I want it now. The sooner the better."

"We can't have the marriage annulled," he said reasonably. "We consummated our vows, remember?"

"All right, then divorce me." Emily planted her hands on her hips and glared at him. She was so angry she could nearly feel steam coming out of her ears and he appeared totally unaffected. In fact, he looked amused, his arms crossed over his chest, his body relaxed, the corners of his mouth quirked in a half smile. When he didn't answer, she grabbed the last item from the bed, the black Vera Wang evening gown, and tossed it on top of the stack of clothes. Then she slammed the lid closed, zipping it with quick, angry movements.

She swung it off the bed but before she could move, Lazhar intercepted her.

"Honey, please. Put the bag down and listen to me."

She tried to step around him, but he shifted, blocking her.

Irritated, she stopped, staring at him, impatiently tapping her foot.

"I didn't marry you because of a business deal."

She lifted an eyebrow in disbelief, but remained silent.

"It's true that I was looking for a bride because of my father's health and his wish to see me married. It's also true that Walter sent me your picture along with a suggestion that I consider you as a wife as part of the deal we were working on.'' Despite the withering glance she gave him, he kept talking. ''But what Walter didn't know is that I took one look at the photo of you and ordered the plane readied to fly to San Francisco.''

Her eyebrows shot up in disbelief.

''It's true.'' He laid his hand on the blue linen shirt, just over his heart. ''I swear. Why else do you think I moved heaven and earth to get you to come back to Daniz with me?''

''Because my father asked you to and you wanted his signature on a contract.'' She shot back without hesitation.

''Emily, Walter's the one who was anxious to close the deal. Not me. I was having second thoughts about doing business with him when he sent your picture. He needed me far more than I needed him.''

''So you're saying that you *won't* make money from the contract with my father?'' Her voice was loaded with skepticism.

''Oh, I'll make money,'' he conceded. ''But I would have passed on the proposal if it hadn't been for you. The Parks business is solid, but your father is in serious trouble and were it not for meeting you, I wouldn't have linked Daniz's reputation with him.''

For a moment, Emily wavered. He seemed sincere, his voice filled with conviction. Then she remembered his cold voice as he told her father that he must never tell her about their deal, and her resolution firmed. "All of that is immaterial. I want an annulment, and if we can't get one, then a divorce."

"Even if you divorce me, Emily, I won't give you up."

"If we're divorced, you'll have to."

"No, I won't. If it takes a year of courting you, I won't give you up. I'll camp outside your door in San Francisco, send you flowers every hour, show up at your office every day—"

"That sounds suspiciously like stalking," she interrupted.

"It isn't stalking when the woman loves you. Then it's called courting."

Emily threw her hands up. "For heaven's sake, Lazhar. Why are you being so stubborn? You *don't* love me. I just happened to be available when you needed a wife and I slotted nicely into place between a gem deal and keeping your father happy."

Lazhar winced. "It sounds pretty bad when you put it so bluntly."

"Can you deny that's the reason you brought me to Daniz?" she demanded, her eyes narrowing.

"No," he admitted. "But I can certainly deny that's the reason I asked you to marry me." A muscle flexed in his jaw, all amusement erased from his features, his previously relaxed stance suddenly tense. "I know now that I fell in love with you the day I met you, Emily. Anything else became irrelevant after I'd spent less than two days with you." His forefinger lifted to brush gently against a spot near her mouth before stroking down her throat. "I love your sense of humor and the way your dimples flash when you really laugh. I love the way you genuinely care about the people around you. I love your bravery, though you damn near scared me to death when you jumped in front of the car to grab that little girl." His voice deepened, roughening. "I love the way you turn to fire in my arms when we make love. In fact—" his fingers left her throat and lifted to gently tuck a strand of hair behind her ear "—I love everything about you."

"Lazhar, I don't think…" Emily's voice trembled. She badly wanted to believe him, but she was torn.

He stopped her words by touching his fingertips to her lips. "I love you, Emily, and I want to spend the rest of my life with you. I want babies and family Christmases and everything else that goes with being married to you. Please don't throw away all we can have because I've been an idiot."

Emily could no longer deny the sincerity that was written on his features and rang in his voice.

Tears welled, spilling over to trickle down her cheeks.

"Hey," he murmured, brushing the dampness from her cheeks with his fingers. "I didn't mean to make you cry. If you can't believe me and still feel you have to go home, I swear I'll let you go. But don't ask me not to follow you. I can't let you go without trying to make you love me again."

"I haven't stopped loving you." Emily's fingers covered his, cradling them against her cheek. "But when I knew that I was part of a business deal, I couldn't believe you meant it when you told me that our marriage could be real."

"It can," he said, his deep voice husky with emotion. "If we want it to be. Do you want it, Emily? Do you want me?"

She did, she thought, the surge of love she felt for this man burning away the anger, hurt feelings, and sadness that had tormented her for the last six days.

"Yes," she whispered. "I do."

"Thank God." He bent his head, brushing open-mouthed kisses over her forehead and cheeks. Her lashes drifted closed and his lips were butterfly-light against her eyelids. Then his mouth found hers and the cherishing, reverent kisses turned hot.

Her arms locked around his neck, her hands spearing into the thick silk of his hair. He tugged her blouse loose from her waistband, his hand slipping beneath to cup her breast over the thin lace of her bra. Emily moaned and lifted heavy lashes to look up at him when his mouth left hers.

"We've been married for six days and spent only one night making love," he muttered as he stripped her blouse away and ripped open the zipper on her skirt. He shoved it down over her hips and it pooled around her feet. "I must be eligible for sainthood."

Emily smiled at him. There was something very appealing about a frustrated male tearing a woman's clothes off. Especially when the male was Lazhar.

"I know exactly how you feel," she murmured, her fingers busily unbuttoning his shirt. She reached the button just above the waistband of his jeans and tugged. When the shirt didn't easily pull free, she abandoned it and unbuckled his belt.

His arms wrapped around her while he unhooked her bra, Lazhar froze when she eased down the zipper of his slacks and slid her hands beneath the opening to wrap around him. Totally absorbed, her fingers testing the hot silk over steel length of him, Emily slowly became aware of the tension that held him motionless.

She glanced up. His eyes were closed, his face tortured with pleasure. He dropped his forehead to rest against hers and his chest rose and fell, faster and faster as he breathed deeper, visibly reaching for control.

"That's enough." His voice was guttural, strained, and he stripped the loosened bra down her arms and dropped it. His hands closed over hers, his body surging briefly against her palms before he gently removed them from his skin. "One more minute and I'd have lost it," he told her, picking her up to lay her on the bed. He stripped off the rest of his clothes and joined her, nudging her thighs apart and crawling between them. "And I don't want to do that until I'm inside you."

His mouth covered hers at the same time she felt the blunt tip of his arousal nudging for entrance. Then he slid home, joining them irrevocably; they both shuddered with relief at the surge of hot passion that ripped through them.

Two weeks later, Lazhar handed Emily out of a long black limousine in front of an upscale seafood restaurant on San Francisco's Fisherman's Wharf. Beyond the Wharf, the scenic Bay was a wide expanse of gray water, capped with the occasional white curl of foam atop waves. The breeze that blew in off the sea was tangy with salt and held the brisk chill of mid-October, teasing their hair and nipping at their faces.

Lazhar pressed a warm kiss into Emily's palm before tucking her hand through the crook of his arm, his hand covering hers against the light wool of his coat sleeve. "Are you sure you feel up to going to a party tonight?"

She smiled up at him. "Absolutely. I'm looking forward to seeing my family and a party given by Cade and Sara is a perfect way to introduce you to the Parks family members who couldn't make it to Daniz for our wedding."

"I suppose so." Lazhar looked unconvinced. "But if you get tired, tell me and I'll take you back to the hotel immediately."

Emily leaned closer to whisper in his ear. "You just want to get me alone in our hotel room."

Lazhar laughed, a deep chuckle that warmed her. "You're right. If I had my way, I'd lock the doors, order room service and keep you there for the next week." He nodded his thanks to the doorman who pulled open the heavy glass door to the trendy restaurant.

She squeezed his arm in sympathy as they crossed the threshold. "I know exactly how you feel," she confided. "But humor me tonight, okay?"

"Whatever you want, sweetheart." He dropped a light kiss on the tip of her nose. The easy, loving gesture warmed Emily.

"Check your coats, sir?"

Lazhar and Emily stopped just inside the lobby, its warmth welcome after the chilly October evening outside. "Yes, thank you." He waited for Emily to unbutton her ankle-length, light wool coat, then slipped it off her shoulders and handed it to the uniformed coat-check girl. Beneath the red coat, Emily wore a scarlet cocktail dress, the sleek little bodice held up by narrow shoulder straps, the skirt a sassy swathe of silk and lace. Below the skirt, her long, shapely legs ended in dainty feet and strappy red sandals.

Lazhar shrugged out of his topcoat, handed it to the girl, took the claim ticket she gave him, and turned back to Emily. His gaze flicked over her from the gleaming fall of shiny gold-brown hair to the tips of her toes and his dark eyes heated, gleaming with approval.

"You were wearing a red suit when I met you," he murmured as he took her arm and started toward the private banquet rooms. "I don't know how I managed to keep my hands off you that day and I have no idea how I'm going to accomplish it tonight."

"You won't have to wait all night, just until we get back to the hotel," she said, teasing.

He groaned in mock pain and she laughed. "Oh, look." She pointed at a sign on the wall behind him. The nautical letters read Poseidon Patio, and a sign pointed down the hallway before them. "I think that's where we're supposed to go."

Lazhar and Emily made their way down the hallway. The walls were ornately patterned with shiny shells and conches that reflected the sea theme in the outer lobby. The doors to the patio banquet room stood open, the sound of laughter and voices reaching them easily. They paused on the threshold, hands linked, searching the crowd for Cade and Sara.

"Emily!" Brenda greeted them with delight, leaving a small group of chatting guests to bustle forward and enfold Emily in a warm hug.

Emily laughed and returned the hug with enthusiasm.

Brenda released her and stepped back, holding Emily's hands in hers as she shrewdly assessed her. "You look absolutely wonderful, hon," she said, bestowing a brilliant smile on Lazhar. "You've clearly made my girl very happy, Your Highness. Bless you."

Lazhar grinned at the diminutive Brenda, his gaze moving possessively over Emily at his side. "Thank you."

Brenda's gaze sharpened, a tiny, inquisitive frown pulling her eyebrows into a vee over her nose. "There's something about you...you're almost glowing. Is there any chance..." Her eyes widened at Emily's smile and her gaze flew to Lazhar. "Are you? Can you be...?"

Emily glanced questioningly at Lazhar, who nodded.

"You're the first person outside the royal family to know, Brenda." She leaned closer to whisper in Brenda's ear. "I'm pregnant."

Brenda beamed. "Oh, Emily, my dear child. I'm so happy. So very happy for you." She squeezed Emily's hands tightly, tears glistening in her eyes behind the lenses of her glasses.

"Thank you, Brenda." Emily glanced at her husband, her eyes twinkling. "Just the day before I met you, Lazhar, Brenda warned me to pay attention so I didn't fail to recognize my 'Prince Charming' when he finally appeared."

"Did she?" Lazhar said lazily, smiling at the gray-haired woman his wife adored. "Then I have to thank you, Brenda, for giving my Emily such sound advice."

Brenda chuckled and slipped her arm through Emily's. "Let's find Cade and Sara and tell them the good news."

"Is my father here?" Emily asked, scanning the crowd as they wound their way across the room.

"No. Cade told me they invited Walter, but I haven't seen him yet."

"Jessica!" Emily halted their progress to throw her arms around her sister, interrupting her conversation with a fiftyish, black haired man, graying at the temples. Blond and curvy, Jessica shared Emily's dimples, a legacy from their mother.

"Emily!" Jessica left her conversation in mid-sentence to greet her sister. "How are you? I'm so glad you made it tonight." Smiling, she glanced at Lazhar. "Thanks for bringing her, Lazhar. I admit I was a little worried when you took her so far away, but now that I know you'll fly her back to visit us, I'm not so concerned."

"Emily can return to visit anytime she wants, in fact," Lazhar commented as he met Emily's eyes. "She'll be in San Francisco at least quarterly every year to check in with her manager at Creative Weddings."

"Is Jane taking over the San Francisco branch?" Jessica inquired.

"Yes, and she's very excited about it," Emily replied. "We'll work very closely, of course, which will be easy to do since Lazhar has the most amazing telecommunications facility. And she'll also be involved in the smaller European branch that I'm planning in Daniz."

"Wonderful."

Jessica would have said more, but just then, Cade called to Emily. She looked over her shoulder to see her brother, his arm slung around Sara's shoulders, beckoning to her.

"I have to go. I'll talk to you later," Emily promised.

"Okay." Jessica watched Emily, Lazhar and Brenda move off through the crowd, a small smile curving her lips.

"Both you and your sister have your mother's dimples."

"Yes." Jessica glanced behind her at Derek Moss. "I'm sorry, I should have introduced you. That was very rude of me."

He shrugged. "Not at all, you were excited to see each other." He nodded across the room where Emily, Lazhar and Brenda had joined Cade and Sara. "Does Emily keep in touch with your mother?"

"I don't know." Jessica's smile disappeared. "We never talk about her."

"That's too bad," Derek said gently. "Perhaps those of us who once knew and loved your mother should have tried harder to keep in touch. I think I'll write her a letter this very evening, renew old ties."

"That's a lovely idea." Jessica's smile returned. "I've been corresponding with her for some time and plan to fly to Switzerland soon to visit her in person. My father would be furious if he ever found out, but this is something I have to do."

Neither Jessica nor Derek were aware that they were being observed. Private Investigator Sam Fields, hired by Walter Parks to follow Jessica, leaned against the wall across the room, holding an untouched glass of whiskey.

If Jessica could have foreseen the impact that Sam would have on her life in the coming weeks, she might have paid more attention to the odd fore-boding that shivered up her spine. Instead she merely hugged herself, wondering at the sudden chill before it eased and she forgot about the incident, caught up in the excitement as Cade lifted his voice above the crowd noise.

"Attention, attention everyone."

The group quieted, turning expectantly.

"We have more great news tonight. Emily and Lazhar just told me they're expecting a little prince or princess in about eight months."

The room burst into cheers, applause, and shouts of congratulations. Emily flushed, laughing at some of the racier comments. Lazhar, his arm around her waist, smiled down at her and bent to press a kiss against her temple.

Cade glanced at his watch. "It's getting late. Dinner should be ready soon. Is everyone here?"

"I think so." Sara's gaze moved over the crowd, trying to count guests. "Hmm. We may still be short one or two people."

"I think I'll visit the ladies' room before we sit down to dinner," Emily said to Sara.

"It's just off the hallway outside the main door to the banquet room," Sara explained.

"I'll be right back," Emily murmured to La-zhar, who was discussing the Jewel Market with Cade. He nodded; Emily could feel his gaze following her as she made her way through the crowded room and out into the hall.

An hour later, after dessert and coffee, Lazhar and Emily joined the other guests on the dance floor.

Emily snuggled into her husband's arms, her fingers threaded into the thick hair at his nape, her body nestled against his.

"Um," she sighed happily. "I had a lovely time tonight, didn't you?"

"Yes, and now that I'm finally getting to hold you, it's even better," he said dryly. He tipped his head back to look down at her, his gaze searching her face. "How are you doing? Not too tired?"

"No, not at all. I feel wonderful. Oh, that reminds me!" She smiled, dimples flashing. "You'll never guess what happened when I was in the ladies' room before dinner. My brother Rowans' wife, Louanne, told me she's pregnant. And Sara confided that Linda Mailer, my father's accountant, is also pregnant. I swear, the baby-fairy must be waving her wand over the Parks family." She chuckled. "Brenda will be over the moon with excitement. We're going from having only Cade's little girl to three more babies in the family."

Lazhar's gaze heated and his arms tightened. He whirled her smoothly through the half-open balcony doors and out into the cool night air. He stopped in the shelter of the overhang that blocked the Pacific breeze, backing Emily up against a support column.

"I'm eternally grateful to whatever fairy or angel waved her magic wand to bring you into my life, Emily. You and our baby," he pressed his palm to her still-flat midriff, his big hand warm and possessive on her belly. Then he took her mouth in a hot kiss that melted her bones and stole her breath.

Brenda was right, Emily thought, dazed by the force of emotion that shook her. Despite her once-cynical attitude toward love, she'd found her very own prince.

* * * * *

THE MARRIAGE ACT

BY
ELISSA AMBROSE

Originally from Montreal, Canada, **Elissa Ambrose** now resides in Arizona with her husband, her smart but surly cat and her sweet but silly cockatoo. She's the proud mother of two daughters, who, though they have flown the coop, still manage to keep her on her toes. She started out as a computer programmer and now serves as the fiction editor at *Anthology* magazine, a literary journal published in Mesa, Arizona. When she's not writing or editing or just hanging out with her husband, she can be found at the indoor ice arena, trying out a new spin or jump.

Prologue

He removed the heavy gold chain from around his neck. "I want to give you something. You might say it's the closest thing to my heart. I know it sounds crazy, but I feel as if I've known you forever.

He fastened the chain around her neck, and the medallion fell between her breasts. "Beautiful," he whispered, but then his face clouded over.

"What is it?" she asked, tracing the line of his jaw with her fingers.

"There's something I have to tell you. I'm not who you think I am."

"Shh," she said, replacing her fingers with her lips. "We're exactly who we need to be."

Chapter One

Linda Mailer was late.

She hurried up the walkway that led to the upscale seafood restaurant, the smell of broiled fish and grilled shrimp mingling with the salty sea air. Waves slapped against the pier below, while behind her the sun slowly descended into the cliffs beyond the Bay.

She glanced at her watch, wondering why she had bothered to show up at all. She didn't belong here. She wasn't sure she belonged anywhere. At first, she had refused Sara and Cade's invitation, but when Cade's sister Emily had insisted she come, she'd caved in.

How could she say no to a princess? Albeit, Emily was a princess by marriage, but she was a princess nonetheless.

Emily Parks—correction, Emily Eban, Princess of Daniz—had told her she was practically family. Nonsense! The only person Linda was close to in that family was Walter, her employer and Emily's father, and he wouldn't even be here tonight. Besides, if she were practically family, wouldn't that make her practically a princess? Her mouth curved down in self-deprecation. A princess was the last thing she felt like.

In the lobby of the trendy seafood restaurant, Linda tried to ignore her queasiness and checked her coat with the attendant. She looked down at her dress, a shapeless frock that hung loosely on her frame and fell to her ankles. When she'd first seen it on the clearance rack in the department store, she'd known it would be perfect. A dark gray-green, it would allow her to blend into the background.

Gazing around at the decor, she headed toward the Poseidon Patio, where the party was being held. Ornately patterned with shells and conches, the walls had been painted to reflect the depths of the sea. She more than blended in. She could virtually disappear into the backdrop.

She had something to hide, and the dress she was wearing would do the job.

Not that she was showing yet. But she knew she couldn't take any chances. At the office, she sat all day immersed in ledgers, hardly ever raising her head, but here she would be on display. People would be looking.

And if they looked closely, they might guess her little secret.

Her little secret, as she preferred to call it, was the reason she was late getting to the party. Morning sickness—now that was an interesting euphemism. Sure, she was queasy in the morning, but the feeling persisted all day and night, not even subsiding when she was asleep. Last night, she'd dreamed she was on a cruise in the midst of a storm. The ship was rocking and she was reeling.

Mercy, not here, she thought now, as nausea overcame her. Queasiness was one thing; this was something else. It was as if the restaurant's decor had sprung to life, as large ocean waves seemed to roll off the walls, threatening to swallow her up.

That decided it. She wouldn't stay. She had no intention of spending her Saturday evening either trying to avoid small talk with people she hardly knew or hiding in the bathroom, bending over the porcelain throne. After the nausea had somewhat subsided, she headed back to the coat check.

"Linda, hurry! We're just about to start dinner."

Linda cast a rueful glance at Sara Carlton, Emily's sister-in-law. Correction, Sara Parks, now that she was married to Cade. Lately, it seemed as if everyone Linda knew was getting married, and although she was happy for them, sometimes she couldn't help but feel annoyed. It had nothing to do with her not-married-and-never-had-been status; on the contrary, matrimony was not one of her life's priorities. Simply, newly married couples always seemed to probe into what they considered her sad-single state, and now that Sara had spotted her, it was too late for a getaway.

Smiling brightly, Sara approached her. Chic in a three-quarter-length silk dress, she didn't merely walk; she floated, as though some of her sister-in-law's new royal status had flowed into her through osmosis.

"Come, I'll show you to your table," she said, "but first, I want you to meet my twin brothers."

Actually, half brothers. The office had been buzzing for weeks about Tyler and Conrad Carlton, the "surprise" sons of Walter Parks. The identical twins and Sara had shared the same mother, but what made the situation even more complex was that Cade Parks, Sara's husband, was also a half brother to the twins, through Walter.

Illegitimate, Linda said to herself, recalling the gossip. Such an outdated term, yet apparently it was still used. She shuddered. It was such an ugly word. Would people use it to describe *her* child?

Her thoughts returned to Walter and his family. Even though the DNA testing had confirmed his paternity, he refused to acknowledge his two grown sons. Linda felt a wave of guilt. Like Walter, she should have refused to come to the party, which was being given by Sara and Cade to welcome the twins into the family. Shouldn't her loyalty lie with Walter? Although she had to admit Cade and Emily—his *legitimate* children—always treated her well, making sure to include her in every family function. As much as she hated social gatherings, it would have been rude of her to refuse this invitation, just as she had never been able to refuse any of the others.

Strangely, even Walter had insisted that she go. It was as if he wanted to attend the party but was sending her in his place. The notion, of course, was preposterous. He wanted nothing to do with that side of his family. He'd made that clear—to her, to his family, even to the press.

Sara led the way to the ornate banquet room, toward

her handsome new husband. When Linda's gaze turned to the man next to Cade, her heart stopped beating.

Standing next to Cade was Thomas McMann.

The man she'd run from two months ago.

Sara's face was beaming. "Linda, I'd like you to meet my brother, Conrad Carlton. Conrad, this is Linda Mailer, the woman I've been telling you about. I've placed you at the same table, since you two have so much in common."

This couldn't be. There had to be an explanation. A lot of men looked alike. When they'd met two months ago, she hadn't been wearing her glasses, and the bar had been dim. *They're all the same when the lights go out,* her mother used to say.

She studied him surreptitiously. He looked like a lot like Thomas, but something was different. Something she couldn't name. The longer she studied him, the more obvious it became that he wasn't the man she'd spent the night with.

She collected her breath, then looked back at Sara. Like every other newlywed Linda had ever known, Sara wanted to play matchmaker. But even if Linda were interested in meeting someone, which she emphatically was not, Conrad was the last man she'd choose. So much in common, Sara had said. Not in this lifetime, Linda thought. According to the gossip in the office, Conrad was wild and carefree, always up for a party. She, on the other hand, was as exciting as a potato. Her idea of a challenge was balancing a checkbook.

No, Conrad Carlton, alias Party Animal, alias Ladies' Man, wasn't her type.

Then again, she wasn't sure she had a type.

Say something, she ordered herself. Make small talk. Smoothing a wrinkle in the fabric of her dress, she mumbled, "Uh, I hear you're a rancher."

He looked at her through cold, green eyes, as though she had materialized from nowhere. "And I hear you're an accountant. I'm sure you get this all the time, but I have to ask. Why would someone with your looks choose such a staid profession?"

She regarded him warily. Someone with her looks? Was he nuts? Was he *flirting?*

"I like figures," she said, then looked down at the floor. Good grief, how could she have said something so moronic?

Apparently he was deaf, because he looked at her as though she'd uttered the most interesting tidbit he'd heard in years. "So, done any personal audits lately?" he asked.

Sara and Cade stood by quietly, watching the exchange. From the expression on their faces, Linda could tell they were pleased. She'd hoped that now that she was thirty, the pressure from others to follow in their matrimonial footsteps would slack off, but so far it hadn't. Why did newly married couples always feel the need to spread their happiness? She was referring to those well-meaning yet nosy people who for some altruistic reason—or sadistic, depending on what view you took—were eager for her to experience the same bliss they claimed to be experiencing. So what if half those blissful couples ended up in divorce court?

She looked back up at Conrad's face. The way his eyes were assessing her body seemed to suggest that he wouldn't mind doing a personal audit of *her*.

She flinched under his gaze. It was unnerving how much he looked like Thomas. Something else unnerved her, as well. Conrad had a twin brother…an identical twin brother…

No. I hadn't been wearing my glasses that night, she reminded herself, and then cast her unsettling thought aside.

She was sure that Sara had asked him to be attentive. Why else would he be flirting with her? Her cheeks grew warm. Just what she needed—a pity date. He was obviously waiting for her to reply, but she felt as tongue-tied as a competitor in a peanut-butter-eating contest. If she couldn't get through one minute of small talk, she didn't have a chance of making it through dinner.

He wasn't flirting, she decided. He was mocking her. It wouldn't be the first time someone had made her profession the target of a joke. Not that she cared. Maybe to some people accounting seemed boring, but the truth was, if she had to confess to one passion in life, it would be numbers. She loved the feeling she got when preparing a spreadsheet, or when all her bank statements reconciled, or when she was off by a mere cent and, after methodical and careful backtracking, could pinpoint the error. There was truth in numbers. Working with them gave her a sense of order.

Her gaze shot to the doorway. Maybe after everyone was seated, she could make her escape. Maybe no one would notice.

"Excuse me," he said abruptly. "I think my date has arrived." He turned away, and a moment later he was talking to a sultry blonde in a short black cocktail dress that seemed to have more material in back than it did in front.

Sara's mouth dropped open in shock, and her cheeks went pink with embarrassment. "I'm sorry, Linda. I had no idea he'd invited someone to the party. I was sure the two of you would hit it off. You're a very basic sort of person, and so is he. Like I said, the two of you have a lot in common." When Linda didn't respond, Sara continued, "No, really. How much more basic does it get than living off the land? Underneath all that bravado, he's really a down-to-earth, practical person. Like you. Oh, I know he has a bit of an attitude, but that's just a veneer. He's having a hard time accepting everything that's happened."

Linda frowned. Conrad might have issues, but the notion that he had anything in common with her was preposterous. Furthermore, going through a rough patch didn't give a person a license to be rude.

But maybe he couldn't help himself. Maybe he didn't even know he was being rude. She seemed to have that effect on men.

She realized it had a lot to do with the way she dressed, the way she carried herself. She'd learned that people paid a price for enjoying themselves, and now she went out of her way to show the world—specifically the male portion—that she wasn't interested.

"It can't be easy for him," she said charitably. "Or his brother," she added, thinking about what Sara had told her about Tyler Carlton. Moody, she'd described him. Linda couldn't decide which trait was less desirable, moodiness or rudeness. Evidently, each brother wore his scars differently.

"Speaking of brothers," Sara said, waving at someone across the noisy room, "do you realize how remarkable this whole thing is? Not only are the twins my brothers, they're also my brothers-in-law! Complicated, isn't it?"

A man across the room waved back. "Uh, yes, complicated," Linda agreed, peering through her glasses to get a better look at him. Weaving his way through the crowd, he slowly approached them, and for the second time that evening her heart came to a halt.

Was this déjà vu or had she simply lost her mind? How could she make the same mistake twice in one evening?

But this time she wasn't mistaken. This time it was him.

Thomas McMann. The man she'd slept with on the night of her thirtieth birthday.

The memory of that warm August night came back in a rush. How her best friend and roommate, Sadie Heath, had convinced her to have a makeover for her birthday. How they'd gone to the piano lounge in that fashionable hotel on Nob Hill. How Linda had met a man at a table by the bar.

How his lips had felt against her neck as the elevator made its slow ascent to the third floor, where he'd rented a room.

She remembered how she'd felt the next morning when she'd spotted the gun on the bureau.

Sheer, cold terror.

Suddenly, the events of the past few weeks fell into place. The thugs coming in and out of Walter's office. The strange document she'd found in his home. The stories circulating about his embezzling.

Walter had enemies.

Thomas must have known who she was right from the start, before they'd even met at that bar. He'd been tailing her to get to Walter. Had even gone as far as seducing her. All part of a day's work.

On one level she knew that what she was thinking didn't make sense. Walter wasn't even here. But when it came to guns, all logic evaded her. Terror pervaded her body, just as it had that morning two months ago when she'd fled from the hotel.

She had to warn them. Had to warn them all, but the words wouldn't come. Why did she always get so tongue-tied? She prayed for the scream to erupt, but her whole body felt paralyzed.

He was getting closer. Five feet…four feet…

Panic rose in her throat.

He undid the button to his jacket, reached inside…

And that was all she remembered, before blacking out.

He'd thought she looked familiar, and now, seeing her up close, he knew why. The woman lying on the blue tufted carpet was Lyla.

For the past two months he'd combed the entire city, looking for her without success. In his relatively short career as a law officer, he'd put countless felons behind bars, but he hadn't been able to locate the one person he'd been desperately seeking.

He didn't like to ask himself why he'd been so desperate to find her. It wasn't as if she'd gotten under his skin. No, nothing like that. He just wasn't used to women running out on him, and he deserved an explanation.

At least, that was what he'd told himself.

Lyla. Hoping to run into her, he'd become a regular at the lounge in that swanky hotel on Nob Hill. He'd figured a girl like her needed action, that sooner or later she'd return to the scene of the crime, so to speak. Return in search of a bigger pot of gold.

Lyla. A looker like her would have no trouble reeling in dates. She could have any man she wanted, and so he'd figured she'd show up at the lounge. She could probably smell the money, from the bottom of the Hill. Which was probably why she'd pulled a disappearing act in the morning. She'd figured out that he was no Donald Trump.

Lyla. Since that night he'd searched every bar in every hotel, asking endless questions—just so he could find her and tell her a thing or two. So he'd tried to convince himself.

"Someone call an ambulance!"

Sara's voice jolted him out of his shock, and his instincts took over. He leaned over and felt for a pulse. Then, after satisfying himself that she hadn't been injured in the fall, he scooped her up in his arms. "She'll be all right," he said to the small crowd that had gathered. "Please move aside. Give her some air. Where can I take her that's quiet?" he asked Sara. He tried to sound detached and professional, but he knew he was failing miserably.

Which irritated him. He had no feelings for this woman. None whatsoever.

"There's a lounge in the ladies' room," Sara answered, looking at him quizzically.

He hurried out of the banquet room, Lyla nestled in his arms, Sara following closely behind. He kicked open the door to the ladies' room. An elderly woman in an old-fashioned beehive hairdo took one look at him and screeched.

"'Scuse me, ma'am," he said, pushing past her. Clutching her purse, the woman sprinted down the hallway.

A teenage girl entered the lounge, stopping in her tracks when she saw Tyler. "Oops, sorry, I guess I have the wrong—" Her gaze fell on Lyla. "Uh, I'll come back later," she said, backing out the door.

Under the curious gawk of two other women, he gently deposited Lyla onto the couch. "Must be those house martinis," the taller woman said. "Can we do anything?"

"Everyone, out!" he barked, then immediately regretted his tone. The stranger was only trying to be helpful. She was probably right. Lyla wasn't sick; she was just drunk.

Nevertheless, he was still concerned. Which puzzled him. What did he care? She was nothing to him.

Agitated, he ran his fingers through his hair. Maybe he'd been mistaken. Maybe the woman on the couch wasn't the same mysterious creature he'd made love to only weeks before. The woman he'd met in August had been exciting and lusty, with wild red curls tumbling down her neck. This woman's hair was tied straight back in a ponytail, her dark inviting eyes—her dark now-closed eyes—hiding behind thick-framed glasses. And that thing she was wearing looked more like a sack than a dress, the way it concealed her body from her chin to her ankles.

The night he'd met her she'd been wearing a tight

leather miniskirt and a skimpy halter top. He'd seen right from the get-go that she was dressed to advertise. The woman he'd met would never be caught in a tent like this.

Or would she? He had to admit he didn't really know her. Except, of course, in the biblical sense.

At the sink, Sara began soaking a handful of paper towels. "You'd better wait outside," she said over her shoulder. "I'll take care of Linda."

"Who?" Didn't she mean Lyla?

"Linda Mailer. Walter's accountant."

He felt as if he'd been punched in the stomach. *My father's* accountant, he said to himself. Not that he or anyone else needed to be reminded that Walter Parks was his father. News of the paternity had been splattered across every newspaper in the state. Fortunately, however, not one photo of him or Conrad had been printed. The best way to get information, Tyler knew, was to remain undercover. Wanting to remain anonymous for as long as possible, he'd been careful to avoid reporters and had asked his twin brother to do the same. He'd even slipped by Walter's secretary when he'd visited the office, demanding answers from the notorious gem dealer.

My father. Even unspoken, the words left a sour taste on his tongue. But even stronger than the bitterness he felt was his need for vengeance. Walter was the reason he'd relocated to San Francisco. Although Tyler hadn't been officially assigned to his father's case, he continued to work with the prosecution. He knew he wouldn't be satisfied until he saw Walter tried, convicted and locked away for life.

Sara sat on the couch, applying the damp paper towels to Linda's forehead. "I'm going to have a talk with Walter," she said, gently stroking Linda's brow. "It's obvious he's been working this girl too hard… Oh, good, I think she's coming around. You'd better go, Tyler. The first person she sees when she wakes up should be someone she knows."

So. Lyla Sinclair was Linda Mailer, and she worked for Walter. Except she wasn't just his accountant, she was his spy. Walter knew about the ongoing investigation, but he had no idea what or how much the D.A. had on him. He wanted information and was probably paying Lyla—Linda—a bonus for her extracurricular activities.

It made sense. Hiring a private investigator to look into D.A. matters would have been too risky. Why should Walter trust an outsider when he had other options?

Why, that little tramp… She'd deliberately sought him out. Followed him that night to the hotel. He felt a small smile pull at his lips. Apparently, she'd had no qualms about mixing business with pleasure. He didn't know if spending the night with him had been planned from the start, but one thing he was sure of—she'd wanted him.

He tried to recollect how much he might have disclosed that night. Funny how he could remember what she wore, how she smelled, how her skin felt under his touch. But no words came to mind.

And then it all came back. He cringed inwardly, but his reaction had nothing to do with the case. When he recalled what he'd done, the sappy things he'd said…

He forced himself back to the present. This was the

first time he'd ever been in a ladies' room, and he was more than a little uncomfortable. Nevertheless, wild horses couldn't drag him away. He had to get to the bottom of this. "I'm not going anywhere."

There was no doubt in his mind that Sara found his behavior bizarre. "Then wait over there," she said, pointing to the alcove behind the couch near the doorway. "She doesn't know you. I don't want her to be frightened." As if on cue, Linda moaned, and Tyler reluctantly moved across the room.

Sara turned her attention back to Linda. "Open your eyes," she gently coaxed. "Are you all right?"

Why is that the first thing people ask when someone who has fainted awakens? Tyler wondered. Jeez, did she look all right? He knew she couldn't see him from her reclining position, but he could see her over the back of the couch. Even from where he stood, he could see she was paler than the moon in daylight.

His eyes roamed across her body, which seemed lost in that awful sack she was wearing. Hard to believe she was the same woman who had enticed him, the same woman who had led him by the hand to the registrar's desk and then watched eagerly as he signed them in.

Mr. and Mrs. John Smith.

Alias Lyla and Thomas.

"Thomas," she said, her voice barely a gasp.

He made a move to approach her, but Sara shot him a warning glance.

He was tired of playing the waiting game. He'd been patient far too long about a lot of things, but all that was about to change. It was payback time.

She'd played him for a fool, but this was just the first

round. This was a game she had no chance of winning. After all, who was the pro here? True, she'd managed to deceive him and then he hadn't been able to find her, but hell, he hadn't been made a detective for no good reason. At only twenty-four, he'd been the youngest cop in Colorado to get his gold shield.

Oh, yeah, things were about to change. Before he was through with her, he'd have all the information he needed to have Walter locked away.

When Linda tried to sit up, the room swirled around her. She fell back against the couch. "Wh-where am I?"

"Don't try to move," Sara said. "Wait until the dizziness subsides."

"You don't understand. Gun... have to warn them..."

"Gun?" Sara repeated. "Linda, what are you talking about?"

"That man—he was coming in our direction. He's here to kill Walter!"

Sara sighed with what seemed to be relief. "Sweetie, no one's going to kill Walter. Walter's not even here."

Linda took a deep breath. "The killer doesn't know that! He's got a gun, I tell you. I saw him go for it! He's a hired killer! What if he just starts shooting? You've got to call the police!"

"Listen to what you're saying, sweetheart. Hired killers don't just go around shooting at random. You're just a little confused. The man who was coming over to us is Tyler, Conrad's brother. He's not a criminal, he's a cop." Sara looked up and shook her head, as though gesturing to someone, then turned back to Linda. "He wasn't going for his gun, he was undoing his jacket. It was too warm in there. It must have been the heat that caused you to faint. I was feeling a little woozy myself. Believe me, I intend to speak to the management about this. Just because it's October doesn't mean they have to pump up the heat. With so many people here at the party, it's like a furnace in that room."

Linda's head was whirling. A cop? Thomas was a cop?

Thomas was Tyler?

No wonder she had mistaken Conrad for Thomas. Tall and muscular, both twins had the same dark hair, the same green eyes, the same cocky smile. Yet though they were identical twins, there was something different about Tyler. It was something unique, something that had attracted her the night they'd met.

"No gun?" she asked in a weak voice.

"No gun. Not an illegal gun, that is. Tyler is a detective with the San Francisco Police Department."

Linda groaned. "I feel so stupid."

"No, you mustn't feel that way. You're not well. People often get confused when they're sick."

"I'm not sick. I—" Linda bit down on her lip.

"What is it?" When Linda didn't answer, Sara gently prodded, "I'd like to think we're friends, Linda. You can talk to me about anything."

Why not? Linda thought. Her little secret wasn't one she could keep for long. Aside from Sadie, no one else knew. She might as well let the cat out of the bag, and this was as good a time as any.

"I'm two months pregnant," she blurted.

At first, Sara looked stunned. Then, once again she raised her head and glanced behind the couch. She made a dismissive gesture with her hand, then smiled brightly at Linda. "My, you're full of surprises! I didn't even know you were seeing anyone! I have to say, this party is turning into quite a night. It was originally intended as a welcoming party for Tyler and Conrad. Then, just before you arrived, Emily and Lazhar announced that they were expecting. And now you say you're expecting, too. Wouldn't it be something if you and Emily shared the same due date?"

Linda couldn't reply. The lump in her throat felt as large as a golf ball.

"Oh," Sara said flatly. "Me and my big mouth. You're not happy about this." She took Linda's hand. "Listen to me. I want you to know you're not alone. You're going to have to make some decisions, but remember, whatever you decide, you have friends, and we'll help in any way we can."

"I'm not going to have an abortion, if that's what you mean," Linda snapped.

"I was talking about your life in general," Sara said softly.

Her mouth trembling, Linda fought back tears. "I'm sorry. I didn't mean to snarl at you. I just don't know how this could have happened. I don't usually...I never..." She let her voice trail off.

Contrary to what Sara might think, Linda didn't have many friends. But Sara was right about one thing. Linda had some decisions to make, and soon. Though not about having the baby. She intended to have this baby, and she intended to raise it alone. She was more concerned with the practical issues. She earned a decent salary working for Walter, but San

Francisco was an expensive place to live. She could support herself just fine, but could she support a child? Yet she didn't want to leave the city. Here, she'd finally found some peace of mind. Here, she'd begun to heal.

Here, she had Walter, whom she trusted and respected, and here, she had Sadie, whom she had known since the third grade. These days, Sadie was understandably preoccupied with her upcoming wedding, but Linda knew that even after Sadie was married, they would always be friends.

Aside from the financial aspect, something else worried her, as well. What about Tyler? Would he demand a say in his child's life? She didn't want him as a role model for her child. Maybe the man she'd slept with wasn't a cold-blooded killer, but he was still a liar and a sleaze. Everyone knew why he had moved to San Francisco. It was no secret. He was trying to gather enough evidence to have Walter indicted. She was sure he'd sought her out only to obtain information. Why else would he have given her the time of day? Why else had he lied to her about his identity? If she never laid eyes on him again, it would be too soon.

Of course, her lying to him about her own identity was an entirely different matter.

"What about the father?" Sara asked, as though reading Linda's mind. She didn't ask who he was, but Linda could tell she was curious.

Sara continued to make strange gestures at something—or someone—behind the couch. "What on earth is going on?" Linda asked. She sat up and looked behind her. Once again she was overcome with dizziness, but this time it had nothing to do with the pregnancy. Tyler had overheard everything she'd said.

Over the buzzing in her ears, she heard Sara say, "I'm so sorry, Linda. I tried to get him to leave, but he wouldn't budge. But don't worry. He's family. You can trust him."

Linda was afraid that the look on Tyler's face would give him away. It didn't take more than a second. Sara had learned the answer to the question she'd held back. The astonishment in her eyes confirmed it.

Chapter Two

Just what kind of game was she playing? He rounded the couch and reached for her arm. "Get your purse, *Lyla*. We're leaving."

"Tyler, stop it!" Sara said, grabbing his wrist. "What's the matter with you? Can't you see she's not feeling well? Settle down, take a breather. Then we'll discuss this like adults. You two need to talk, but in a calm, rational way."

"You got that right," he growled. "'You two' meaning me and my father's sneaky accountant. Leave us alone, Sara."

She looked at Linda's drawn face. "I'm not going anywhere," she said with the same resolution Tyler had shown only minutes ago.

"In that case, we are." He bent low and, as he'd done earlier in the banquet room, gathered Linda in his arms.

"I'm taking her out of here. Make our apologies to the guests."

"I'm pregnant, not helpless," Linda piped up in a small voice. "I'd appreciate it if you'd put me down. Please."

She'd appreciate it? Please? Her Pollyanna act didn't fool him for a minute. For one thing, Pollyanna didn't have a body like hers. That dress she had on might be shapeless and oversize, but the fabric was thin. He could feel almost every curve underneath, and what he couldn't feel, his memory supplied.

Damn straight she wasn't helpless. She knew exactly what she was doing. She pressed her body against his, all the while looking up at him with those big, brown eyes.

She knew the effect she had on him. It was the same effect she'd had on him that night at the hotel, when he'd first seen her with her friend at a table by the bar. Two months ago, she'd played him for a sucker, but it was a role he had no intention of repeating. He was sure she was up to something. She was no more pregnant than he was.

"I'm a little cold now," she said in a pouting voice. "Did someone turn down the heat? If we're going out, I'll need to get my coat. I can't possibly leave without it." She wriggled against him, her breasts pushing against his arm.

In spite of himself, desire kicked in as though on automatic pilot. She thought someone had turned down the heat? To him, the ladies' lounge was fast becoming a steam room.

But she was right about one thing. She'd need her

coat. The coastal night air would be chilly. Reluctantly, he set her down, worried that she would bolt. He remembered how he'd felt the morning after they'd made love, when he'd awakened and discovered she was gone.

"You can get your coat from Sara later," he said, removing his sports jacket. "This should keep you warm." He slid his jacket over her shoulders, accidentally brushing his hand against her cheek. He pulled back quickly, as though he'd received an electric shock.

"The paramedics are probably on the way," Sara said to Linda. "You should let them look you over. You're still shaky."

"I'll be fine," Linda said, pulling the jacket closed. She smiled weakly at Sara. "Don't worry. I want to go with him, really."

Cupping Linda's elbow, Tyler led her through the parking lot. He unlocked his car with his remote, then walked to the passenger side and opened the door.

She didn't move. "I've changed my mind. I'm not going anywhere with you. I'm going home."

"You're in no condition to drive. What if you get dizzy?" When she didn't answer, he let out an exasperated breath. "What do you think is going to happen? Sara saw us leave together. She's a witness. Now get in before I pick you up again and dump you inside."

"What about my car? I'm parked on the other side of the lot."

"Forget about your car. We'll get it later. For Chrissake, get in."

"I would appreciate it if you didn't swear."

"Dammit, Linda—"

She stood next to the car, hands on hips, the look on her face warning him that she meant business. "I'm only getting in if you promise to tone down your language."

First, she practically accuses him of being a kidnapper, and then, she reproaches him for his language? The woman was nuts. Or maybe not. Maybe this was part of her act. Maybe she'd even staged her fainting spell. After all, she was a liar. Lyla, she'd said her name was. Lyla from Wisconsin.

"You wouldn't know a promise if it hit you in the face," he said, growing impatient. "Keeping a promise takes integrity, and you're the last person who should be talking about integrity."

"What about you, Mr. Thomas McMann?"

He had no intention of discussing ethics standing in a parking lot. "Look, are you getting in or not?"

She cast him a stony look, then climbed into the car. "Fine. But I'm only going with you because Sara was right. We need to talk."

He pulled out of the lot, the tires of his car screeching in protest. He and Linda needed to talk, all right. In a calm, rational way, Sara had said. Except what he was feeling was neither calm nor rational. How was he supposed to remain calm when the woman sitting next him was claiming she was carrying his baby? As far as being rational, what about the way his breathing had become tight and painful just because he was near her? He could feel her eyes on him as they drove off. Dark liquid eyes that could turn a man to oatmeal.

Get a grip, he ordered himself. The woman you made love to doesn't exist.

"Can you slow down, please?" she asked sweetly. "I wouldn't want you to have an accident."

He glanced at her with disdain. On the surface she was all sugar; on the inside she was cyanide. She was the type who made a show of how she preferred to see a half-empty glass as half-full. The type who was careful not to say a bad word about anyone. The type who stuck a knife in you as soon as you turned your back.

He pressed down on the accelerator, swearing under his breath.

She turned her head and stared out the window.

Moments later, he pulled off the road. He turned off the ignition, then came around to her side and opened her door. "We're here. Get out."

"Where's here?" she asked in a timorous voice.

He had to hand it to her, she was good. For a moment he almost believed she was afraid. "Baker Beach. We're going for a walk."

She looked around furtively, like a fawn searching for its mother, and then rested her eyes on his face. "I don't think this is a good idea. It's nighttime. It's so…dark."

Aw, hell. How could he stay angry when she kept looking at him that way? If he had any brains, he'd arrest her on the spot. Eyes like those were lethal. "It's not that dark," he said gruffly, taking her hand. "There's a full moon, and look at those stars. This has become one of my favorite spots. I come here whenever I have something to mull over." Something meaning his vendetta against the man who buttered her bread, but this he didn't mention. The last thing he wanted to do was discuss Walter. "Look over on your left. The view of the Golden Gate Bridge is spectacular."

"True, it is pretty here. But is it safe?"

Soft and small, her hand felt just as he remembered. Her hand in his as he'd led her from the table, into the lobby of the hotel…

"I'm a cop, remember? I won't let anything happen."

That seemed to do it, because she got out of the car. She crouched low to remove her shoes, her dress lifting well above her knees. Her hands weren't all he remembered with clarity. Those legs, long and willowy, wrapped around his waist…

"There now," she said, springing upright. "We wouldn't want to ruin our shoes, now would we? What about you, Tyler?"

His gaze traveled past the bridge, where the rugged rocky cliffs wound across the terrain. "I'm fine," he mumbled. But he wasn't fine, and it wasn't his feet he was worried about. Focus, he ordered himself. Find out what she's after.

"Listen to that roar," she said when they'd reached the shoreline. "The undertow must be pretty strong."

"You sound as if you know this beach. Not that I'm surprised. This is the nude area."

She assumed her hands-on-hips, schoolmarm pose. "Tyler, stop it right now. Why must you be so vituperative?"

Vituperative? Hell, he didn't even know what it meant. She must have read his confusion, because she clarified, "There's no call to be insulting. Anyway, you're supposed to be the moody twin, not the rude one. Although," she added, her mouth in a pout, "I can understand why you're upset. You regret spending the night with someone like me."

Something in her tone arrested him. Or maybe it was the way the moonlight played with the many shades of red in her hair, or the way the beating of his heart drummed out the roar of the ocean. "Let's get something straight. I don't regret that night. What makes you think I'm sorry?"

Shoot, why had he gone and said that? He was full of regrets, all right. The woman spelled trouble, and woman trouble was the last thing he needed. He had to remain focused, clear. He couldn't allow anything to interfere with his plans.

His mission, he called it. Yet he knew it was more than that. Somewhere along the way, he'd turned his mother's deathbed wish for revenge into a personal crusade.

"Let's face it, I'm not exactly your type," Linda said, picking at an imaginary thread on her dress.

Good thing they were at a beach. If she wanted to fish, this was the place. "Yeah? What type is that?"

"You're right, it's beautiful out here," she answered, evading his question.

Maybe she was trying to tell him that he wasn't *her* type.

She raised her head, and he could swear he saw that look in her eyes. It was the look she'd given him the night they'd met. The look that said she knew he wanted her, and that the feeling was mutual. Before he realized what he was doing, he pulled her to him, crushing her against his chest, enveloping her in his arms. She let out a breathless gasp, which he quickly silenced when he pressed his lips to hers.

Her knees must have buckled, or maybe he was the one to buckle, he wasn't quite sure. It was as if a force stronger than gravity was pulling them down, and in the next instant they were on the sand, arms and legs tangled, their bodies locked together. His lips never left hers. He pushed his tongue in deeper, eager to rediscover what he'd been fantasizing about these past two months, eager to reclaim what he'd believed he'd lost.

She didn't try to stop him. Didn't try to break the kiss.

And then her body went limp.

She turned her head away.

Well, that answered *that*. Apparently, he wasn't her type, after all. His thoughts returned to the night they'd made love, only this time the memory left him feeling cold. Obviously, she hadn't been as swept away as she'd led him to believe. So much with her mixing business with pleasure. It had all been an act.

They pulled to a sitting position. "I'm sorry," she mumbled, adjusting her glasses. "You're angry, I can tell. I don't blame you. It's just that…I can't…" She lowered her gaze.

He was the one who'd been out of line, and she was apologizing? Enough, he told himself. She was up to something, and he aimed to find out what it was. "Let's get out of here," he said sourly, rising to his feet. He extended his hand. "Take it," he growled when she just sat there. "I wouldn't want you to fall and hurt the baby. If there *is* a baby."

"What's that supposed to mean?"

"Oh, come on. I don't know what you think you're doing, but trust me, I'll figure it out. You work for Walter. That itself is proof you're up to no good."

She scrambled to her feet, dusting the sand from her dress. "He's just trying to run a business. Why is it whenever someone is successful, the rest of the world feels it's their moral duty to bring him down? Maybe if you'd take the time to get to know him, you'd realize he's a decent, caring man."

"Get to know him!" Tyler spat. "He won't even acknowledge that I'm alive. Simple, you call him. That's a laugh. Devious would be a more apt description. Did you say decent? Now that's more than a laugh. It's a bad joke. A bad joke that needs to be put to rest once and for all."

"And you'll do anything it takes, including sleeping with his accountant to get information." She picked up her shoes and, pushing past him, headed back to where they were parked.

"Let's get one thing straight," he said, scrambling after her. "I didn't know who you were that night in the lounge. I was there on official business, on a case that had nothing to do with Walter. I was about to call it a night and go home, when you approached me. You were the one who sought *me* out."

"Sought you out! Why you egotistical, self-centered boor! Tell me something, Mr. First-Class Detective, why on earth would I do that?"

"You tell me. You're the one working for Parks. From what I hear, the two of you are pretty tight. What else do you do for him?"

"Why you—" She raised her hand to slap him, then abruptly dropped it. "That question doesn't deserve a response. And I don't believe in violence."

"Glad to know it. I wouldn't want you to get physical. But I was talking about spying, darlin', nothing else. How much is the old man paying you to do his dirty work? Well, you can tell him to save his money. In fact, you can tell him we've almost got enough evidence to make an arrest, and what we have is solid."

"Almost? Now that's the key word, isn't it? But almost won't cut it. It's like the lottery. Either you win or you don't. Almost won't pay the bills. You're never going to indict him, and do you know why? You don't have any real proof. All the evidence is circumstantial. It's not concrete, or you would have arrested him by now. No, you're the spy here. You're the one who went on the prowl, looking for me. You're…oh, no, not again."

"What?" he asked.

"Morning…sickness," she sputtered. "I think…I'm going…to be sick."

He couldn't decide what was worse, a woman feeling nothing or getting nauseous after he had kissed her.

Morning sickness, she'd said. As in pregnant. Something didn't add up. What did her spying on him have to do with her claiming to be pregnant?

Instinctively, he shifted into investigative mode. The results of the paternity suit against Walter had been made public last month. What if, after learning that Walter was his father, she'd thought she'd seen a way to get a piece of the Parks fortune? She'd already slept with Walter's son; the timing would be right.

Seemed like paternity claims were in style these days, he thought wryly. Except that unlike his, hers was phony. Not only that, apparently she hadn't thought the whole thing through. How would she explain her situation seven months from now? Unless she wasn't planning to. Unless she intended to leave town long before then, with a heavy chunk of payoff cash in her suitcase. But his theory still had holes. Wouldn't she know he'd insist she see a doctor to confirm her allegation?

"Come on," he said roughly. "I'm taking you back to your car."

By the water, her face had appeared even paler than it had in the restaurant, but as they approached the car, in the dim light from the street lamp she looked almost green.

Immediately, he felt chastened. She really *was* sick. Maybe her fainting in the restaurant hadn't been an act. For the first time that evening, the possibility that she really might be pregnant entered his head.

Two questions assailed him at once. What if the baby was his? What if it wasn't?

The thought of her with another man made him crazy. Which made him even crazier. What did he care? It wasn't as if there was anything between them.

She began to sway, and instantly he was jarred from his musing. "Lean against me," he said. "Take deep, slow breaths. There you go. That's it. Slowly. You'll be okay."

She did as he said, not resisting when he wrapped his arm around her shoulder. A moment later, she looked up at him and said, "Thank you, Tyler. I feel much better." She gave him a weak smile. "You know, you're not as hard-boiled as you make yourself out to be. Underneath that rough exterior, there's a nice guy. You should let him out more often."

"And you should get some rest. I'll take you to your car tomorrow. Right now, I'm driving you home. You live in Noe Valley, right?"

She stared at him. "How did you know?"

He knew a lot more than that. Robert Jackson, the prosecutor assigned to the case, had done his homework. A file existed for anyone who had ever been associated with Walter.

"I guess Sara must have told you," she said before he could reply, and he didn't correct her. "But I'm fine, really. Take me back to the restaurant. I can drive myself home."

She didn't look fine. "No arguments. You have to think of the baby." He helped her into the car and then went around to the driver's side. The baby, he repeated to himself. But whose baby? It suddenly dawned on him that she hadn't actually said he was the father.

"I still can't believe that Thomas is you," she said as he pulled onto the road. "You realize what this means, don't you? Walter is the baby's grandfather. I can't imagine anything more wonderful."

So. She was saying that Tyler *was* the father. He suppressed a derisive laugh. It was almost ironic. He might not have inherited his father's name, but if what she was saying was true, he'd inherited one of Walter's traits. One of Walter's less admirable traits, he thought with self-loathing. Like his father, Tyler, it seemed, had a penchant for creating bastards.

But what if she was lying? She'd lied to him the night they met; why should he believe anything she told him now? He eyed her critically. That smock she had on was deceptive. Two months, she'd said. Maybe she was a little more pregnant than she claimed.

Maybe now that she knew who Tyler was, she thought she could cash in. Maybe she figured she could do a lot worse than marrying the head honcho's son. Why settle for kiss-off money when you thought you could get your hands on the whole enchilada?

She prattled on with her nauseating tribute. "I know you two don't get along, but I feel confident that in time you'll come to some sort of understanding. Once you get to know him, I'm sure you'll realize what a good man he really is."

Tyler wished he'd worn boots. He was wading in something, and it wasn't Bay water.

But what if the baby *was* his? Walter might be the paternal grandfather, but Tyler would see him in hell before he allowed him into his child's life.

This can't be happening, he thought, his head pounding. He'd never wanted a family, and since discovering the truth about who he was, his resolve had been reinforced. Any child he fathered would be descended from that monster. "I want you to have a blood test."

A silence moved through the air, as thick as the fog that was now swirling past the car windows. "They're not always accurate," she finally answered, her tone icy. "Why not do DNA testing instead? You seem to have *that* science down to an art."

"Now wait a minute," he said, striving to keep his voice steady. "I did what I had to do. I never doubted my mother's story for a minute, but I had to have legal proof that Walter is my father. I need all the evidence I can get to put him away."

Damn. He said he wasn't going to go there. Wasn't going to get into a discussion about Walter. But she had a way about her. He couldn't put his finger on it, but something about her made him want to explain himself. Made him want to seek her approval.

"Do you realize the embarrassment you've caused?" she hurled at him. "What does his paternity have anything to do with the embezzling charge? Eventually the charges against him will be dropped, but people will remember the scandal forever. Did you have to go public?"

"Hey, I wasn't the one who released the story to the papers. Not that this is the sort of thing that can be kept quiet for long."

Why was he defending himself? He wasn't the one under investigation. He wasn't the one who would be arrested for fraud and embezzlement.

He wasn't the one who would be tried and convicted for the murder of Jeremy Carlton.

In spite of his resolve to remain calm, he felt his anger rising. "Do you really believe I give a rat's tail about Walter's embarrassment? He cheated the man I believed was my father. He destroyed everything. The business, the family, my *mother*—" He stopped abruptly. Granted, his accusations were no longer a secret, but he had to watch what he said. Even if she hadn't sought him out that night to obtain information, even if their meeting had been an act of fate, she worked for Walter. Moreover, it was clear that the relationship went beyond the office. Her approval be damned; he couldn't risk revealing something Walter didn't know. "So you're saying you refuse to have the baby tested?" he asked.

"What I'm saying is that it makes no difference whether or not you're the father."

Once again he was filled with jealousy. "Are you saying I'm not?"

"You're not listening, Tyler. I'm saying it's irrelevant, since I intend to raise this baby by myself."

Was this her angle? Some sort of reverse psychology? Was this where he was supposed to get down on his knees and beg her to marry him? Well, he wasn't falling for it. If she thought she could marry her way into Walter's fortune, she had another think coming. Even if the courts ruled that Tyler was entitled to a share of the Parks fortune, he wouldn't go within an inch of that money. As far as he was concerned, it was dirty money, tainted by Walter's greedy hands.

"Walter's money has nothing to do with me," he said. "If I agreed to marry you, you wouldn't see a dime."

She let out a scornful laugh. "What makes you think I'd consider marrying you? It can't be the sex. I have news for you, it wasn't that good."

Spoken like the ice queen she was. He felt as if he'd been slapped.

And she'd accused *him* of being vituperative.

She unlocked the front door to her building, angry tears escaping down her cheeks. Stop it, she ordered herself. He can't touch you now.

If she agreed to marry him? Who did he think he was? And then to imply that she was after the Parks fortune! What gall. She could still hear his words, as though he were right there, standing beside her.

She could still feel his body crushing against hers as they tumbled to the sand…

She listened to the roar of the engine as he sped off

into the night, then quickly glanced inside the building. Good. All clear. No one was in the entranceway. No one to notice if she let go and cried.

No one lurking in the shadows, ready to pounce.

She hoped Sadie was home. She hated coming back to an empty apartment. Since becoming engaged, Sadie spent most nights at her fiancé's apartment. Next week, the situation would become permanent.

Although Linda was sorry that Sadie was leaving, she was genuinely happy for her friend. Sadie had known she wanted to be Frank's wife the first time she'd laid eyes on him, two years ago at a party. But now Linda had a problem. She'd been looking for a new roommate for weeks, to no avail. You're too picky, Sadie had accused. How can you tell what someone's like after just one meeting?

Linda knew that if she didn't find someone soon, she would have to move. Together, she and Sadie could afford the rent on the two-bedroom apartment, but on one income, it would be impossible. Then there was the baby. Raising a child in a two-parent household was expensive enough; she couldn't even imagine how she would manage doing it on her own.

Nevertheless, she didn't want to move. She liked living here. Where else would she find an apartment as perfect?

Situated in the trendy Noe Valley, the large two-story Victorian structure had been converted into a four-unit apartment complex in the early 1970s. Centrally located on a lovely tree-lined street, the building was just a short distance from 24th Street with its many shops and cafés. But this, for Linda, wasn't its main attraction.

Living here, amidst an old-world charm, she felt a kind of peace, as though she could shut out all the evil in the world just by closing her door.

She looked up at the video camera suspended from the ceiling. She knew that if there was any kind of commotion, or if the camera went dead, a police car would arrive within minutes. This added security was another reason she'd let Sadie talk her into taking the apartment in spite of the high rent.

She had to find a roommate fast, and not just because she needed someone to share expenses. She hated living alone.

Almost there now, she thought as she scurried upstairs. She felt herself relax.

But then Tyler's face rose in her mind, and her pulse skittered erratically. She didn't want to dwell on what had happened on the beach, but she couldn't stop the images from forming in her head. For one brief moment when he'd kissed her, she'd lost herself in his arms. Just as she'd done that night two months ago, she'd allowed herself to *feel*. She couldn't let that happen again. She couldn't allow herself to lose control.

When you lose control, someone gets hurt.

She couldn't believe the things she'd said to him. Usually when confronted, she became tongue-tied. But not this time. This time, she'd lashed back. She pictured the look on his face when, after he'd accused her of going after the Parks fortune, she'd attacked his masculinity. No man wanted to hear that he was a dud in bed. She hadn't said it in quite those words, but the meaning had been clear. Clear but not true, she thought, recalling that night in August. She felt her cheeks grow hot. Oh, so not true.

At first, after she'd spoken the words, he'd looked startled, even angry, but then his expression changed. Something in his eyes told her it was more than his pride she'd wounded. She'd recognized in his eyes a vulnerability that she often felt herself.

Wouldn't you know it, she thought, dismayed. The one time I speak up, I say the wrong thing. True, she'd wanted to lash out, but she hadn't wanted to hurt him. She didn't want to hurt anyone.

When she opened the door to her apartment, the noise from the TV in the living room assaulted her. She sighed with relief. Sadie was home.

Chapter Three

"That scumbag! I wondered why you were home so early."

Sadie poured herself a cup of coffee and joined Linda at the table. The tiny but cheerful kitchen was where they liked to talk things over, sometimes laughing, other times solemn, but always fortified with a plate of cookies. Linda was the first to admit she didn't like cooking, but baking was another matter. She loved the smell of fresh-baked goods, especially chocolate chip cookies. It reminded her of the kind of home she'd always dreamed of.

"It was just awful. I can't believe the things he said." Or the things I said, Linda thought, heat stealing into her cheeks.

"What about the drive home? That couldn't have been pleasant."

"Oh, he tried to make small talk—you know how much I love that—but I couldn't even look at him. Then he put in a CD and that was the end of it."

But that hadn't been the end of it. She'd wanted to yell, cry, throw something, but she'd just sat there, feeling claustrophobic next to him in the car. Tyler was already under the impression she was a little off-kilter. What would he have thought if she'd had a full-blown anxiety attack?

The events of the evening replayed in her head, causing her to groan inwardly. First, she saw him approaching in the restaurant, and then she fainted dead away. Later, she agreed to talk with him and then rebuked him for his language. And let's not leave out what happened on the beach, she reminded herself. As if she could forget. After she let him kiss her, she pushed him away. No, not pushed him. She'd just lain there on the sand, as limp as a wet noodle.

A little off-kilter? He probably thought she was certifiable.

"Drink up," Sadie said, motioning to Linda's glass. "It's good for the baby, and it'll calm your nerves."

"Yuck. I hate milk, especially warm milk. But I suppose I'll have to give up the good stuff now that I'm pregnant."

"As if you were ever a drinker." Sadie's brow creased. "I would never have left you that night if I'd thought you'd had too much to drink. You know that, don't you?"

"I told you, I only had one glass of wine," Linda reassured her, wishing it hadn't been the case. If she'd had too much to drink, she might have had an excuse for what she'd done. Not a good excuse, but an excuse nonetheless. "Besides," she said, eyeing her friend's cup, "I was talking about coffee just now. That's 'the good stuff.' Not that I'd call what you're drinking 'good.' I never did understand the reason for decaf."

"And I was talking about friendship." Sadie's face was wrenched with guilt. "This is all my fault. Some friend I was, leaving you alone in a bar."

"I wasn't alone, remember?"

"My point exactly. We should have driven home together that night, just as we'd planned."

Linda regarded her with exasperation. "Will you please lose that pained expression? You're not to blame. How could you know that I'd leave with someone I'd just met? *I* didn't even know. Sleeping with strangers isn't exactly a habit of mine." That was an understatement. Even dating wasn't on her list of preferred things to do.

She pictured Tyler's face, the way his gaze had swept over her with frank appreciation. For one brief night she'd been able to forget that she was Linda Mailer. She'd even believed him when he told her she was beautiful. All he'd had to do was whisper that he wanted her, and the next instant she'd found herself in his arms, riding the elevator up to a room.

"I shouldn't have let Frank come pick me up," Sadie pressed on. "When he called me on my cell to tell me his flight had been canceled, I should have told him I'd see him in the morning. I swear, that man lives out of a suitcase. I must be demented, marrying a pilot."

"You're all talk, Sadie Heath. You know you love him more than anything in the world."

"Oh, I'm demented all right. I should have realized right away that Thomas would bring grief. I should never have left you alone with that scumbag."

"Tyler. His name is Tyler, remember? And will you please stop calling him a scumbag? I hate that word."

Sadie gave her a sideways glance. "If I didn't know better, I'd say you have a thing for this guy. Now listen up, honey. The man lied to you, and in my book, any man who lies is a scumbag. You can't imagine how many times I hear stories like this at the salon. Sometimes the men in these sad tales are married. Sometimes they're just plain mean. But the one thing they all have in common is that they're liars, every one of them."

"He's a detective on the force. He probably wanted to be sure of me before revealing his identity."

There's something I have to tell you, Linda recalled him saying the night they'd met. Would he have told her if she hadn't stopped him? Would she have revealed her own identity?

Sadie narrowed her eyes. "Are you saying you're good enough to share his bed but not good enough to know who he is? Sorry, I don't buy his I'm-a-detective excuse for a minute. You're not a suspect in one of his cases. What sort of man acts like that?"

"A man who's been hurt," Linda answered. "A man with a grudge. Tyler's made Walter his scapegoat. He blames him for all the Carltons' troubles."

"It's more than a grudge," Sadie insisted. "It's blood-thirsty vengeance. You read the newspapers. And your office must be buzzing with gossip. Tyler won't give up until he sees Walter in prison, and he's the type who'll stop at nothing to get what he wants." She snorted. "Once a liar, always a liar."

Linda's patience was quickly vanishing. "You seem to forget I lied that night, too. Remember Lyla, *Sandra?*"

Sadie scowled at that. "You told me that the only way you'd come out with me was if we both used fake names. Not only did I lie, I felt like a thief in the night. I had to run off the moment I saw Frank in the doorway, because I was afraid he would spill the beans."

"All I'm saying is that sometimes people have to hide the truth. Sometimes they have a reason. Even you went along with it."

"Just because I went along with it doesn't make it right. I never understood why you wanted to lie in the first place."

"Don't you see? It wasn't really me that night," Linda persisted. "You turned me into someone else, and I needed a name to go with my new persona. It was all a fantasy." But the fantasy had developed into something real. Her pregnancy was a testament to that.

Sadie shrugged. "I thought a change would be good for you. I'm not just talking about the clothes and the makeup. I'm talking about the way you feel about yourself. I thought that getting all dolled up would give you a shot of confidence." She rested her gaze on Linda's dress. "While we're on the subject of clothes, where on earth did you find that smock?"

Linda sighed. "This is me. This is how I dress. I'm not you, Sadie."

"And thank the Lord for that. Somehow I don't think big blond hair would suit you," Sadie joked.

One thing about Sadie, she could lighten any mood. At the moment, however, Linda was in no mood for humor. "We don't even want the same things in life. Like marriage, for instance. I'm overjoyed for you, but it's not something I want for myself."

"We might want different things, but we both want to be happy. And you won't find happiness until you stop hiding."

"The pop psychologist speaks. Okay, I'll bite. How am I hiding?"

"For one thing, you're a beautiful woman, but you go out of your way to make yourself look dowdy." Sadie leaned in close and picked up a strand of Linda's hair. "You could use a trim. Maybe add a few highlights. Make that red really shine. And will you look at those nails!" she said as Linda reached for another cookie. "Your cuticles are out of control. Why don't you come by the salon next week? I'll give you the royal treatment. Facial, manicure, the whole works. I'll have Katrina do your hair. She's new, but you'll like her. She doesn't talk much."

Sadie was like a steamroller. Nothing stopped her. Even though sometimes Linda found it annoying, she had to admit that it was one of the qualities she admired most about her friend. It was this very persistence that had helped make *La Belle Coupe,* the beauty salon that Sadie owned and operated, the success it was. It was also this very persistence that had helped keep Linda from succumbing to depression after the accident.

"You never give up," Linda said, pushing the memory aside. The period after her sister had died was not something she liked to dwell on. "You're still trying to make me over. Can't you understand? I'm happy the way I am."

"Are you? Honey, my customers talk to me at the salon. No matter what I'm doing, whether I'm shampooing, coloring or blow-drying, if there's one thing I can spot, it's an unhappy woman. Usually she's unhappy because of something that happened a long time ago. Something in her past. But you've got to move on, I always say. You've got to get over it."

"Sadie…" Linda warned. They were heading into dangerous territory.

"Oh, I know. You want to leave the past buried. But that's just the problem. You're covering it up, like camouflage. I see this kind of thing all the time. Women come into the salon expecting me to perform miracles. I can cut their hair, dye it or perm it, but it always grows back the same. I can paint their nails or paint their faces, but it's only temporary. It doesn't last."

"Like a makeover," Linda said wryly. "Or a royal treatment at the salon."

Sadie wagged a finger. "There's nothing wrong with making yourself more attractive. If I believed there was, do you think I'd be in this business? You're not listening. I'm saying that if you've got problems, you've got to treat them, not just cover them up. Like dry hair. That's why we have conditioner. Or acne. You can't just hide it under a glob of foundation. You've got to treat it from within. Good nourishment and vitamins, that sort of thing."

"Is there a point to this?" Linda asked.

"You know what I'm going to say. I've said it to you before, and I'll keep saying it until it sinks in. Before you can put your demons to rest, before you can move on, you've got to confront them once and for all. You can't treat the soul until you acknowledge that it's ailing."

"That has to be the most convoluted reasoning I've ever heard," Linda scoffed. One thing, however, was clear. Sadie was worried about her. "I know you're just being a friend, and I appreciate it. If it hadn't been for you, I don't know how I would have survived after my sister died. But I'm okay now, and I've been okay for a long time."

Was she? Just less than an hour ago, sitting next to Tyler, she'd been worried about having an anxiety attack, even though she hadn't had one in years. But it had nothing to do with the past, as Sadie had suggested. It had been triggered by Tyler's despicable insinuations.

"I wasn't referring to the car accident," Sadie said softly. "I was referring to your mother."

Linda felt the color drain from her face. "You know what I think? I think you should save your pop psychology for your clients. I don't have to listen to this drivel."

She regretted her harsh tone the minute the words escaped her mouth. What was wrong with her? She wasn't the type who hurled insults. Normally she was the I-should-have-said type who thought of the exact thing to say after the fact, when she was alone, rehashing what had happened. But lately, she'd been throwing slurs like darts. She'd always believed that a snarky comeback would make her feel empowered, but she'd been wrong. All she felt was terrible. "I'm sorry, Sadie. I shouldn't have spoken to you that way. I know you're only trying to be helpful. You've always had my best interest at heart."

It was the truth. In the past, Sadie had been more than just helpful; she'd been a lifesaver. After Karen was killed in the car crash, Sadie had invited Linda to come out to California, where she'd lived since graduating from high school. Montana has too many bad memories, she'd said. You need a fresh start.

A fresh start, Linda repeated to herself. But now, according to Sadie, she needed to revisit the past. According to Sadie, Linda's spirit was far from healed.

"Oh, pooh," Sadie said. "If you can't throw a tantrum in front of your best friend, then she's not your best friend. Anyway, it's time I learned to keep my big mouth shut. 'Course I'd probably lose a lot of business. Those women don't come to me because they think I'm Vidal Sassoon. Not that I'm not as good," she added, a twinkle in her eye, "but to them I'm like a therapist. Only I cost a lot less, and they get a new look to boot." She took Linda's hands. "Seriously, honey, I know I've been busy with the wedding, but I want you to know you can come to me any time, with any problem. That's not going to change after I'm married. And I promise, no more world-according-to-Sadie lectures. The next time I stick my nose where it doesn't belong, you have my permission to stick my head under the dryer. In the meantime, if there's anything I can do, you just holler."

Linda rose from the table and carried her glass to the sink. "There *is* something you can do. Take me to the restaurant in the morning so I can get my car. Tyler said he'd take me, but I'm hoping he'll call first so I can tell him not to. I don't intend to see him again. This is *my* baby, and I don't want a man in my life telling me what to do." Not only were men controlling, they were undependable. She knew this for a fact. Her mother had told her, time and time again.

"Uh-huh," Sadie said in an infuriating way. "I think the lady doth protest too much. Seems to me— Oops, there I go again. Where's that hair dryer?"

Linda shook her head. "You're hopeless. Go ahead, say it. I know you're dying to. Something's on your mind, I can tell."

"Okay, since you asked. What about the jacket?"

"What jacket?"

"That snazzy blue sports jacket you hid in the closet the moment you entered the apartment. If you really didn't intend to see him again, you would have returned it before you left the car."

Linda rolled her eyes. "The pop psychologist speaks again. Are you saying I kept it on purpose so I could have an excuse to see him? What is this, high school? Well, you're wrong. I've told you over and over, I don't want a relationship. I'll never let a man get close to me."

Sadie chuckled. "Uh-huh. Honey, unless a star suddenly rises in the east, I'd say it's a little late."

Although it was only nine-thirty, Mike McGarret's, the popular sports bar where the precinct liked to hang out, was already bustling with activity. After greeting a few off-duty patrolmen at one of the jam-packed tables, Tyler threaded his way toward the bar. On the overhead big-screen TV, the Giants had just scored a run, and a loud cheer erupted.

"I didn't expect to see you here," Nick shouted over the clamor. "I take it that Parks showed up at the party."

Tyler slid onto a bar stool next to his friend at the

long mahogany bar. "That lowlife wouldn't dare show his mug," he grumbled after the noise had subsided. "Considerate of him, don't you think? Garbage like him would have stunk up the whole place."

Nick shot him a twisted smile. "Hey, if I'd known you'd be this much fun, I wouldn't have brought a date."

"You didn't," Tyler replied.

"The night is still young. It's Saturday, I'm off duty and I aim to please."

"Anyone in particular, or are you being hypothetical again?"

Joking around, watching the game, talking about women—this was what Tyler looked forward to at the end of a day. Later, he'd go home to his one-bedroom apartment where he could block out everything—job, friends, family, even his crusade against Walter. Mike McGarret's was where he unwound; his apartment was where he found refuge.

"A guy can dream," Nick said, raising his bottle in a mock salute to the leggy blonde at the end of the bar. He put down the bottle. "So what's eating you, Carlton? Aside from life, the universe and Parks. My guess is that the party was too rich for your taste. I'm not talking cuisine. I'm talking about the guest list."

Tyler signaled to the bartender and ordered a beer, then turned to Nick with amusement. "So now you're a mind reader?"

Nick tapped himself on the head. "Antennae, bud. It's what keeps us employed. A little intuition goes a long way in our line of work."

"Like I said, Walter wasn't there. Ergo, I had no qualms about the guest list. Emily, Lazhar, Cade…a person couldn't have better relatives even if he got to choose them himself." Too bad we don't get to choose our parents, he thought, but didn't say it. Some things didn't need to be spelled out. Between friends, some things were understood.

Not only was Nick Banning his partner, he was Tyler's best friend. It was no mystery why they'd clicked right off the bat when Tyler had joined the SFPD. When Nick was nine, his parents had been brutally killed. For years, he and his older brother, Mark, had been shuffled from one foster home to another. Like Nick, Tyler was a man with a troubled childhood. Feeling like an outcast was something they had in common.

"If it isn't the family that has you wound up, then what is it?" Nick asked. "Spill it, Carlton. Who is she?"

Either his partner's radar was in full operation, or Tyler was as transparent as the tape he used to lift fingerprints. "Linda Mailer," he replied. The bartender returned with a beer, and Tyler took a swallow. "Aka Lyla Sinclair." He debated mentioning the baby, but decided against it, at least until he'd figured out a plan of action.

"The woman from the hotel is Parks' accountant?" Nick let out a slow whistle. "Now that's convenient. She could be the answer to all your troubles."

Tyler knew what Nick meant. Get close to Linda, get close to Walter. Which was what he'd planned to do when he'd learned who she was. But he couldn't go through with it. He didn't use women to get what he wanted, information or otherwise. Not that spying hadn't crossed *her* mind.

He still wasn't convinced that she hadn't set out to milk him for information two months ago. The jury was still out on that one. Nevertheless, where Walter was concerned, one thing he was certain of. He and Linda were on opposite teams.

Opposites attract, he thought wryly. Maybe that was why he'd been drawn to her in the first place. "She's not the answer to all my troubles," he said. "She *is* trouble."

"Who, the virgin princess?"

Tyler stared at his friend. "I think you have the wrong fairy tale, pal. Aren't you forgetting one small detail? I spent the night with her."

Nick shook his head. "Which I find incredible. What's your secret, Carlton? You know what they call her down at the precinct. A cold fish. Everyone we questioned regarding the case says the same thing. All the guys she works with have asked her out, but she won't let any of them come within sneezing distance."

The ice queen, Tyler had thought earlier. His jaw clenched. "Just because a woman says no doesn't mean she's cold. If you have anything else to say about her that's not related to the case, I'd appreciate it if you kept it to yourself."

Nick raised his hands as though warding off a blow. "Hey, it didn't come from me. Besides, what do you care? It's not like you have a thing for her." When Tyler didn't answer, Nick grinned. "Oh, boy. The plot thickens. So that's why you've been searching for her. Here I thought you were looking for a lead in that gambling case, which is why you went to the hotel in the first place."

"You're nuts," Tyler said. "The woman means nothing to me."

"Right. Where have I heard that before? Every time

you start with someone new, it's the same old story. No, I take that back. You say it just before you're ready to call it quits."

"You're one to talk. I don't see you rushing to the altar."

"I'm working on it." He motioned to the end of the bar. "See that blonde? Who knows, she might be the future mother of my children. Mark my words, one of these days some woman is going to turn me into an honest man."

"I'll believe it when I see it," Tyler said, and took a swig of his beer. "Although you know my feelings on that particular subject."

"Yeah, I remember. In the line of fire, could get killed, not fair to our families…yada yada yada. I've heard it before. Here's a news flash. A meteor could fall out of the sky and wipe us out in the blink of an eye, but that doesn't mean I'm going to stop living. In fact, it supports what I've been saying all along. You have to live for today. And speaking of living," he said, tossing a five-dollar bill on the bar, "unlike someone else at this bar, I think I have a date. See you later, bud. Destiny awaits."

"Don't do anything I would," Tyler joked as Nick walked off. His partner was an enigma. On the one hand, he liked to stick to himself; on the other hand, he was a magnet for women.

Tyler finished his beer. He tried to watch the game on the screen, but he couldn't concentrate. He kept thinking about what Nick had said about living for today. But most people didn't make their living dealing with crime and danger. Most people planned for the future.

When Tyler had chosen to become a cop, he'd made the decision not to have kids. What if he were killed? He wouldn't want his children to grow up the way he had, without a father. He felt the same about marriage. He knew what loneliness could do to a woman. He had only to recall his mother's face.

But it was Elana's face, not his mother's, he pictured now. She'd once accused him of using his work as an excuse to avoid commitment. She'd even suggested that he'd chosen to become a cop to create this excuse. It wasn't true. As corny as it sounded, he'd always believed that good triumphed over evil and that justice must prevail. Elana had wanted marriage and kids, but he'd believed that the course he'd chosen excluded this. Eventually, they'd gone their separate ways.

Just as Nick had done earlier, Tyler raised his bottle in a silent salute. He hadn't thought about his high school sweetheart in a long time. After they'd split up, Tyler decided that relationships just weren't worth it. Too many expectations got shattered, too many hopes sucked down the drain. As for Elana, he'd heard she was married to a doctor, her third baby on the way.

Baby.

Dammit, the last thing he should be thinking of was a baby. As in family. As in marriage.

A baby deserved to have a father.

His mother used to talk about Jeremy in glowing terms, as though she could construct a father for her children out of mere words. To some extent it had worked. He wasn't the twins' biological father, and although he had existed only in their minds, he was the only father they had known.

But imagination was no substitute for the real thing. Tyler recalled the loneliness he'd felt while growing up, the acute sadness that had engulfed him whenever his friends went off with their dads. Hiking, bowling, fishing—the activity wasn't important. All he knew was that he was missing out.

If only he had one memory, one that was entirely his own. His mother had meant well, but Tyler knew that if given the opportunity, he'd trade all the hours he'd spent feeding his fantasy for one brief moment with the real thing.

His child deserved no less. And Tyler was convinced that the baby was his. He didn't know why he felt this way; it made no sense. Linda had lied the night they'd met, and she was nothing like the woman she'd pretended to be.

Maybe he believed it because of the way she'd reacted when he'd suggested she have a blood test. Indignant. Angry. Sure, it could have been an act, but how could she know he wouldn't insist? If the baby wasn't his, she had to know that he'd find out the truth.

Maybe it was because of male pride. Nick's words rang in his ears. The virgin princess, he'd called her. Cold. Those were labels bestowed by men who'd been turned down, labels men gave women who didn't sleep around. Maybe Linda was particular. Maybe she'd regarded Tyler as special.

Or maybe it was just his gut feeling. Antennae, Nick called it. It went a long way, on the job and off.

Suddenly Tyler didn't give a damn whether or not she was after the Parks fortune. All he cared about was the baby. He wanted his child to have a flesh-and-blood father, not some phantom built from dreams. Tyler could die in the line of duty, but any amount of time spent with his child, no matter how small, would be infinitely better than no time at all.

Maybe Nick was right. Maybe living for today was all anyone could expect.

Tyler considered ordering another beer. After the night he'd had, he figured he was entitled to some serious alcohol therapy. But drinking to forget his problems wasn't his style, and one drink was his limit when he knew he'd be driving. He didn't want to leave his car and take a taxi, since he planned on driving to Linda's place first thing in the morning. He had something to say to her, or more aptly, something to propose.

But there would be no ring, no kneeling, no imaginary violins playing in the background. He intended to present his offer like a business deal. She worked for Walter. She'd relate to that.

Of course, he didn't have to be unfriendly. A marriage of convenience didn't mean they couldn't enjoy a few fringe benefits. Her lovely lush lips appeared before him, the scent of her hair lingering in the air as though she were standing next to him.

He recalled the way her body had curled into his after they'd made love. With his arms around her in a protective embrace and her soft, silky hair sprayed across his pillow, they'd remained motionless, as though afraid to break the spell. After she'd fallen asleep, he'd lain beside her, still basking in the afterglow until he, too, drifted off to sleep, lulled by the gentle cadence of her breathing.

A heaviness centered in his chest. Going home to his empty apartment had suddenly lost its appeal.

Chapter Four

"Who in his right mind shows up unannounced at eight o'clock on a Sunday morning? Tell him I'm not home. No, don't. He'll never believe it. Tell him I'm still sleeping."

Sadie gawked at the face on the monitor. "You want me to send *that* away? Did getting pregnant make you blind? He's even more gorgeous than I remember. At least hear what he has to say before feeding him to the dogs."

Linda stared at her friend with amazement. "Are you sure you're the same person who called him a scumbag?"

"Let's just say I'm a forgiving person," Sadie answered, her eyes still glued to the screen. "But if you want him to leave, it's your call. Only tell him yourself. I'm not going to lie for you anymore."

"Traitor." But Linda knew that Sadie was right. It was time the lies stopped. "All right, I'll buzz him up.

It was optimistic of me, anyway, thinking I wouldn't have to face him. I'll give him his jacket, then tell him to leave. I have no desire to talk to him."

"Uh-huh," Sadie said, smiling in a knowing way.

A moment later, Tyler stood in the doorway of the apartment, looking casually handsome in a crewneck sweater and jeans. "Great security system," he said, glancing at the screen in the wall. "I'm impressed."

"Lots of little nooks in these old houses," Sadie said, openly appraising him. "You know, dark hallways, small rooms. You never know who might be lurking in the shadows."

"Somehow I suspect you're the real danger here," he said smoothly. "No red-blooded male would have a chance against two stunning women like you. Sandra, right?"

"Sadie," she corrected. "Nice to see you again, *Thomas*."

Tyler looked as if he wanted to say something, but then he burst into laughter. Linda stared at them both. Just like that, they were willing to forget about the deception? From the way Sadie was beaming at him, Linda knew what she was thinking. Husband material. Tyler was good-looking, he was charming and it didn't hurt the cause that he was the baby's father. Sadie could no more give up her campaign to get Linda married than she could resist doling out advice.

"Tyler, how about some coffee?" Sadie asked. "When a man calls a woman stunning, he deserves to be rewarded. But I have to warn you, my brew is the stuff legends are made of. Rumor has it, it could grow hair on a bowling ball."

"For heaven's sake, it's just decaf," Linda said curtly, pulling his jacket from the hall closet. She thrust it into his arms. "Besides, he didn't come for coffee. He came for this."

"Actually, I'd forgotten all about the jacket, but thanks." He took the garment and frowned. "I hate these things. Sports jackets, suits, ties…especially those penguin suits they make you wear at weddings. They make a man feel confined."

"Weddings or cummerbunds?" Sadie asked slyly.

The woman wouldn't give up. Linda shot her a warning glance.

Tyler laughed again. "I'd better watch what I say. I remember you telling me that you were engaged." He smiled at Linda. "But you're right. I didn't come for coffee. I came to take you out for breakfast. I figure since I said I'd take you to your car, why not make a full morning of it?"

His smile revealed the most adorable dimple in his right cheek. Why hadn't she noticed that before? Stop staring, she ordered herself. She tried to think of a snappy refusal, but nothing came to mind. Apparently, her newfound talent for quick retorts had suddenly vanished, taking her tongue with it.

"But you might want to put on some clothes before we go out," he said, looking at her with raised eyebrows.

With horror, she realized she was still in her bathrobe. Here she was, standing next to him, practically naked. Instinctively her hands went to the opening of her robe, and she tightened the sash around her waist. Okay, so maybe practically naked wasn't quite accurate.

The thick terry cloth robe covered most of her body, but still, what could he be thinking of her? What sort of woman answered the door wearing only a bathrobe?

And why oh why was her mind a blank? "Um...I can't go with you to breakfast. I've already eaten." So there, she thought absurdly.

Sadie waved her hand dismissively. "You call one measly piece of toast breakfast? Go on and get dressed. I'll keep your friend company." She put her arm through Tyler's. "Come on into the kitchen and I'll fix you that coffee."

There was no way Linda would leave Sadie alone with Tyler. Before Sadie was finished with him, she'd probably have him dressed as a penguin, waddling down the aisle.

Then again, maybe not. Tyler didn't seem like someone who let others make his decisions. Nevertheless, recalling the embarrassing things Sadie had once said to Frank, Linda wanted her friend out of the apartment. "A great cook...handy with a needle and thread...a talented decorator..." For someone who detested lying, Sadie did her share of embellishing the truth. Linda, a great cook? Sure, if cooking meant popping a carton into the microwave. Handy with a needle and thread meant she could replace a button. And decorating? Didn't she recently hang a Picasso print on her bedroom wall?

"Sadie, remember that sweatshirt you borrowed last week? I need it. Come with me while I get dressed."

"I don't remember borrow—"

"Now," Linda said emphatically. Ignoring Tyler's quizzical look, she bulldozed Sadie out of the living room.

Sadie plopped down on Linda's bed. "You're not seriously planning to wear a sweatshirt, are you? What kind of bait is that?" She studied Linda critically. "Why don't you put in your contact lenses? I can't understand why you bought them if you never intend to wear them."

"Shh!" Linda whispered furiously. "He might hear you! I only bought those stupid things to get you to stop nagging me after that fiasco at the hotel. Just because I didn't wear my glasses that night didn't mean I wanted to get rid of them. And never mind the sweatshirt. Don't you have somewhere to go?"

Sadie was wearing black tights under silver spandex shorts, her Run For Life T-shirt peeking out from under a maroon windbreaker. A fitness buff who ran three miles a day, she'd planned on jogging before driving Linda to the restaurant. "Okay, I can take a hint. I'm leaving. I take it this means my services are no longer required. I assume you're letting Tyler take you to your car?"

"Yes," Linda said, flustered. "I mean no. Oh, just go, all right?"

Sadie's eyes grew serious. "Are you sure, honey? I can stay, if you don't want to be alone with him. Just say the word. I'll do whatever you say."

"I'll be fine." The mischievous twinkle reappeared in Sadie's eyes, and Linda peered at her with suspicion. "What is it?"

"Well, since you asked… He's got that look all over him. I recognized it immediately. I saw it on Frank's face, just before he popped the question. Maybe Tyler isn't the scumbag I thought he was. Maybe he aims to do the right thing."

"Right for who? Him? You? I don't want what you

want, remember?" Apparently what they'd talked about last night hadn't sunk in. Linda sighed. She knew it wasn't her friend's fault. Sadie had been watching over her for so long, she didn't know how to stop. "Go for your jog. The sooner I deal with Tyler, the sooner all this will be behind me." Hadn't Sadie said that a person had to confront her demons before she could move on?

"Uh-huh." With a wink Sadie stood up, then left the room. "Catch you later!" Linda heard her say to Tyler, in a singsong voice.

The front door clicked shut and Linda let out a breath of relief. But her relief was short-lived. The task of dealing with Tyler still lay ahead. What if Sadie was right? What if he'd come here to propose? It wasn't as if marriage hadn't crossed his mind. "If I agreed to marry you," he'd said last night on the beach.

It's a conspiracy, she thought, pulling her denim skirt from her closet. The whole world was plotting to get her to the altar. She deliberated between a bulky wool sweater and an oversize pullover. Why were all her clothes so *big*? She considered borrowing something of Sadie's. That low-cut cashmere sweater would be a little tight across the chest, but so what? It would look great with the denim skirt. She was halfway out the door to Sadie's room, when she stopped in her tracks. What on earth was she doing? The idea was to send Tyler away, not lure him in, as Sadie had suggested. She chose the bulky sweater.

As she dressed, she tried to plan what she'd say to him. She had to make it clear that she wanted nothing from him. But the fact remained that he was the father.

What if he insisted on being in his child's life? Could she deny him? More importantly, could she deny her child? Both she and Tyler knew what it was like growing up without a father.

A wave of anxiety spilled through her. What if he sued for custody? What if that was the reason he wanted to test the baby's paternity? He could be planning to use the evidence in court.

Her head was spinning. Recalling Sara's words about remaining rational, she breathed in deeply, forcing herself to calm down. The idea of Tyler suing for custody was preposterous. What court would grant custody to a man who lived with constant danger?

She and Tyler would go out for breakfast and they would talk. Calmly. Rationally. She was sure they could reach an agreement, but if they failed, if he so much as hinted at custody, she'd fight him tooth and nail.

An image came to mind, and in spite of her anxiety she smiled. She pictured the two of them donning boxing gloves, prancing around each other in the ring. "Shake hands and come out fighting," she imagined the referee saying. Maybe she and Tyler would do it in reverse. Maybe they'd emerge from the ring as friends.

Why not? The more she thought about being friends, the more it made sense. If he insisted on being in his child's life, it would be easier on everyone if they weren't foes. She could handle friendship. Friendship between a man and a woman was perfectly acceptable.

She pulled the sweater off and tossed it onto the bed, choosing to wear a cream-colored jersey instead. It didn't plunge the way Sadie's cashmere sweater did, but it was soft and feminine. Her choice had nothing to do with his inviting smile or compelling eyes, she told herself. It had nothing to do with the way her skin had tingled under his gaze.

Tyler was studying the photographs on the mantel when she joined him in the living room. "Is she always like that?" he asked, glancing up.

In spite of her resolve to remain calm, she couldn't just stand there listening to someone put down her best friend. "Sadie means well," she said tightly. "She would go to the ends of the earth for me."

"No, I mean, does she always have that much energy? It tires me out just watching her. But I like her. She has spunk."

Oh. He was only trying to make conversation. No sense biting his head off just because she was terrible at small talk. "Sadie is Sadie. We make a good team. We balance each other. She's messy and disorganized, I'm a neatness freak. She's artistic, I'm practical. She's extroverted, I'm—" She stopped abruptly.

"Levelheaded," he filled in for her. "That was the first thing I thought about you when we met."

Levelheaded? That was supposed to be a compliment? That was what he'd found attractive about her? He was making fun of her, she decided. She'd been anything but levelheaded in that skimpy skirt and halter top, and now he was throwing her trampy behavior back in her face. "You don't have to be insulting," she said, bristling.

He put down the photos. "Just for one minute, can you stop thinking of me as the enemy? Let's pretend I'm just a guy and you're just a girl, and we're going out on a date. Simple. No complications. Do you think you can handle that?"

"I don't date."

He sighed. "Let me rephrase that. Think of us as two friends going out to share a meal, and since it was my idea, I'll treat."

She couldn't argue with his logic. Wasn't friendship the objective? "All right, but I insist on paying my own way."

"You're too late," he said. "I stopped at the market near my apartment and picked up a few things. We're dining alfresco. How does Douglas Park sound? It's just west of Douglas Street, right? Not too far from here."

Apparently, his idea of breakfast differed from hers. Who went on a picnic at eight o'clock in the morning? He'd parked his car just outside the building and, after stopping to collect what he'd bought, they set off for the park.

She peeked inside the bags in his arms as they strolled through the streets. "Looks like you thought of everything—cheeses, spreads, bagels, orange juice, even disposable picnic supplies. You haven't left anything out."

"No coffee, though. Not even decaf. It can't be good for the baby. I didn't want to drink it in front of you, knowing you shouldn't have any."

"That was considerate," she said with sincerity. Still, she was sure he was up to something. What if Sadie was right? What if he was planning to propose?

The park was surprisingly busy at this early hour. From the picnic area, she could see the basketball and tennis courts, which were quickly filling up. In the playground a few yards away, children were either playing in the sandbox or on swings, their voices resounding with delight.

An unfamiliar contentment took hold of her. Maybe there's something to be said for breakfast in the park, she thought. The sun was shining; the air was unseasonably warm. It was a beautiful, fogless San Francisco morning, a rare treat at this time of year. After they'd chosen a picnic table under a sweet-scented eucalyptus tree, Tyler put down the bags, and she began to empty them.

He was at her side immediately. "Here, let me do that."

"No, you carried these all the way here. The least I can do is set the table." She was conscious of his stare as she methodically folded the napkins in half, then in half again. "There now," she said, after inserting the plastic flatware into the pockets she'd created. She stood back and examined her work. "Isn't this nice?" Why was he looking at her like that? Just because this was a picnic didn't mean they had to be slobs. Besides, the sun was shining and it was a beautiful day. That alone was cause for celebration.

"Very elegant," he said, surprising her. "It's missing something, though." He picked up one of the bags and pulled out three red roses. "One for you, one for me and one for the baby," he explained, placing them into a large paper cup.

Her heart skipped a beat. Here it is, she thought. Here's where he's going to ask me to marry him. Here's where we're going to get into an argument.

He poured them each some juice. "*Santé,*" he said, raising his cup. "To your health."

She sighed with relief. Maybe Sadie was wrong. Maybe all Tyler wanted was to be friends. She felt herself relax. He had a comfortable way about him that made even small talk seem easy, and the next two hours seemed to pass in an instant. He made jokes; she laughed. And when she laughed, he smiled. They were both careful to avoid topics like their previous lives, exerting extra caution when it came to Walter. She talked about her job, though in generic terms, and about Sadie. He talked about his job in even more generic terms.

She lifted her face to the sunshine, basking in its warmth. She'd have to get out like this more often, she decided. Lately her stress level had risen at least a dozen notches. For one thing, the IRS was breathing down her neck—not that she or Walter had done anything wrong. She kept the books in impeccable order, and everything in them was on the up-and-up. But even more disturbing than being audited by the IRS was what was happening at work. On more than one occasion, people she could only describe as thugs had shown up unannounced, demanding to see Walter. No doubt they were trying to bully him into making illegal deals. Not that she was worried that he would comply. He wasn't that kind of man. But the whole thing had everyone at the office on edge.

Then, of course, there was the pregnancy. That alone had raised her stress level to record heights. Not to mention Sadie. In less than a week, she was getting married, leaving Linda to fend for herself.

Tyler began to clear the table. Interpreting this as a cue that their outing was over, her good mood suddenly vanished. What did you expect? she asked herself. He probably has a thousand things he'd rather do than spend an entire day with someone like me. She remembered Conrad's date from Sara's party. Weren't identical twins supposed to have the same preferences?

"Is this the sort of thing you usually do on a date?" she blurted. She felt her face redden. Now why had she gone and said that? She wasn't interested in him that way.

"I thought you said this wasn't a date," he said, a sly smile curling his lips.

She would have to learn to stop blushing. "I didn't mean to imply that it was. Dating hardly seems appropriate, given the situation."

He cocked his head. "All right then, if this isn't a date, what is it?"

"Two friends simply enjoying each other's company."

He looked amused. "Is that what we are? Friends?"

"Those were your words," she reminded him. "'Two friends going out to share a meal.' Given the situation—"

"You already said that."

This conversation was making her dizzy. "I already said what?"

"Situation. Why do you refer to the pregnancy as the situation?"

"Isn't that how you regard it?"

"No. A situation sounds like a problem. And it's not. I mean, yeah, it could be. But I have a solution."

She felt her chest constrict. Here it comes, she thought. Sadie was right, after all.

"I want you to marry me."

Bingo. I'll give him this much, Linda thought. He's bent on doing the right thing. But the problem was that, for him, the right thing seemed to change from moment to moment. "I wish I could promise you more than just now," he'd said that first night. "But it wouldn't be right."

Granted, his sudden turnabout was because of the baby. Babies did that. They had the power to change your perspective on a number of things. But not on the subject of husbands. The last thing she wanted in her life was a man telling her what to do.

She knew he was waiting for an answer. But what could she say without going into her past? Pensive, she looked over at the playground. A young mother was pushing a baby in a stroller, trying unsuccessfully to keep up with a boy of around three. "Johnny, you come back here this instant!" the woman yelled, but undaunted, the boy darted ahead.

The mother looked frantic. The boy was headed straight for the swing set, where he'd surely be knocked down by either an empty chair let loose after someone had jumped, or by the legs of a child, kicking for momentum.

Apparently Tyler had also spotted the danger. He jumped to his feet and raced toward the playground. "Whoa there, tiger," he said as he swept the boy up, out of harm's way. He carried him back to his mother.

"Johnny, how many times have I warned you not to run ahead!" The woman took her son from Tyler's arms and held him tightly. "Thank goodness," she said into his hair. She shifted her son onto her hip and extended a hand to Tyler. "Hi, I'm Claudia Patterson. I can't thank you enough for your quick thinking. You are…?"

"Tyler Carlton," he answered. "Detective Carlton," he clarified, then smiled. "All in the line of duty, ma'am."

All in the line of duty, my foot, Linda thought, watching them. Couldn't he think of a better line? And why was that woman still holding his hand?

"A real live 'tectiv?" Johnny asked, his eyes wide. His face turned solemn. "Mommy, what's a 'tectiv?"

"He's a policeman," Claudia explained. "His job is to catch the bad guys and protect us." She gave Tyler a dazzling smile. "You can't possibly imagine how grateful I am."

Even from where Linda sat, she could tell that Claudia had more on her mind than gratitude. She deliberated what to do. She couldn't just sit there and not join them. That would be rude, wouldn't it? But she didn't want to suddenly appear at his side. That would be admitting she was jealous, which she most certainly was not.

"That's what I want to be, too!" Johnny exclaimed. "Can I be a 'tectiv when I'm all growed, Mommy?"

"I bet you're one of the fastest kids in the whole park," Tyler said, tousling his hair, "and in this business you have to be fast. There's just one thing," he added, pretending to be very serious. "You have to do a lot of looking around. That means looking where you're going. How else will you find the bad guys? And you have to be very, very careful. Like just now. You weren't very careful when you ran away from your mother. Do you know what I'm saying?"

The boy grinned. "Yeah. I better listen to my mom or else she won't take me to the park no more."

Tyler laughed. "I think he got the message," he said to the boy's mother. "He's one smart kid."

"Smart, but a handful. Never gives me a moment's rest. It's not easy raising two kids on your own. What about you?" she asked demurely. "You're good with children. Do you have any?"

Linda rolled her eyes. The woman was so obvious,

she could be neon. She wasn't asking if he had kids; she was asking if he had a wife.

"Not yet," he answered, motioning to Linda. "But I have one on the way."

Hearing his words, Linda felt a strange mix of smugness and relief. So there, you hussy, she thought, then realized she was being uncharitable. The woman was just trying to be friendly. And even if she had set her sights on Tyler, so what? It's not as if I care, Linda thought.

Pushing the stroller, the woman walked away, her son by her side. Linda waved at them. There was no reason she couldn't be gracious.

"Claudia was right," she said when Tyler had returned. "You're good with kids."

He sat down next to her at the table. "You sound surprised."

"Of course I'm surprised. I don't know you, Tyler. And that's why I can't marry you."

It was the truth. Even if she were inclined to get married, which she was not, how could she marry a man who was practically a stranger? Everything she knew about him was based on what she'd read in the papers and what she'd learned from his sister Sara. It was all hearsay. She couldn't take into account the night they'd spent at the hotel. They'd both pretended to be other people; all they'd learned about each other was bogus.

"Look at me, Linda." He cupped her chin with his hand. "Do you believe in fate? A wise man once said, 'God doesn't play dice.'"

"Wise is an understatement. Einstein was a genius. But I don't understand what—"

"Don't you see? We were meant to meet that night. The baby is proof. Every child comes into this world for a reason."

She stood up and began filling an empty paper bag with the trash from breakfast. "That might be true, but it has nothing to do with marriage. If every person is born for a reason, it follows that every child in this world has a right to be here. I believe that every baby is legitimate, which means we don't have to get married."

"We do if we want him to have a father."

She stopped what she was doing and looked down at him. "If you want to be a factor in his life, I won't stop you. You can see him as much as you want."

"I can't see him as much as I want unless I'm living with him. I want more for my child. I want what I never had." His tone took on a note of urgency. "I won't lie to you. It's more than that. When it comes to the subject of legitimacy, it's one thing to tell me what you believe, but it's another convincing the rest of the world. I want my kid to have my name."

"He will. I'll put it on the birth certificate." She wanted to assure him that everything would be all right, that their child would never feel the loneliness Tyler had suffered. She reached out to touch him, but shyness stopped her.

He crushed a paper cup with his fist and threw it onto the table. "That's not good enough. I want my child raised in a home with two parents. I'm not talking about common law, either. I want that piece of paper. What sort of role model would I be to my son if I didn't marry his mother? I want to be there for him, physically, morally and legally." His eyes darkened, and he seemed to disappear somewhere deep inside. "I know my mother did the best she could, but I also know that something was missing. It was as if her heart had been ripped from her body. Sara, Kathleen, Conrad…we all felt it, and we all suffered because of it. Walter was responsible, and I swear, if it takes me the rest of my life, I'll make him pay."

Linda recoiled, frightened by his anger. He wasn't just determined; he was obsessed. Suddenly, she felt foolish. What did she think he would do? He wasn't one of those thugs she'd seen at the office; he was a cop.

She regarded him closely, and saw the vulnerability in his eyes. In spite of her shyness, she touched the side of his face. "We don't even know each other," she said softly. "How can we get married?"

Either her touch or her tone must have mollified him, because all at once his anger dissolved. He took her hand and eased her back onto the bench.

His expression stilled. "I can wait, if I have to, but I think you're wrong. All we need to know we learned that night at the hotel. We haven't changed. We're still the same people we were two months ago."

She stared at him incredulously. "How can you say that? You're not Thomas and I'm not Lyla. We're not the same people at all."

"Granted, I lied about who I was, but only because I wanted to remain anonymous for as long as possible. In my line of work, some things are better kept secret, at least until we know who and what we're dealing with. San Francisco isn't such a big place. Your turning out to be Lyla is proof of that."

"But we were each just playing a role," she protested. She knew she was talking more about herself than she was about him, but the fact remained that they weren't who they'd claimed to be.

"You're still the same beautiful, shy but gutsy woman I made love to. Lyla or Linda, a name is just a tag. It doesn't change who you really are. We were drawn together then, just as we are now. You can't deny that there's something between us."

Gutsy? *Beautiful?* Who was he talking about? "There's nothing between us," she insisted. But even to her own ears, her protest sounded weak.

He broke into a wicked grin. "Are you sure?" He lowered his head, and her pulse went haywire. He was going to kiss her, and she felt powerless to resist.

Then, just like that, he withdrew. She looked up at him, unsure if she felt hurt or relieved. What had just happened? Had she done something wrong?

"I don't want you to do anything you don't want to," he said soberly. "I'm not happy, but I'm willing to wait as long it takes."

Her confusion deepened. Was he talking about marriage or sex? But how could he mean sex, when they'd already made love? Unless, she reasoned, he'd finally accepted that they'd been two different people that night. In a sense, the next time would be their first time.

Not that there'd be a next time, she reminded herself.

Nevertheless, she was moved. If he was willing to wait—for sex or for marriage—he believed she was worth waiting for. She heard her mother's voice in her head, warning her not to trust him. She forced the voice away.

Sitting so close to him on the bench, she felt a vaguely sensuous quivering. His thigh grazed hers, sending an unwanted fluttering coursing through her body. She didn't want to feel this, didn't want to feel anything for him. Yet in spite of her reserve, she lifted her head to his, as though an invisible force was directing her. And still he held back. She parted her lips. He didn't flinch. She brought her hand behind his neck and slowly lowered his head to hers. His lips brushed alongside her cheek, sending an electric shock ricocheting down her spine.

"Linda," he murmured, speaking her name tentatively as if, sensing her reluctance, he was asking if she was sure. She wasn't sure of anything. All she was aware of was the heady scent of his aftershave and the feel of his lips on her skin as his breath mingled with hers.

He must have taken her silence as acquiescence, because he placed his hands around the small of her back, turning her to him, drawing her even closer. She melted into him easily, as though in his arms she knew she was safe. In his arms, she was protected.

And then it happened.

She stiffened.

Then she pulled away.

"Linda…"

"No, don't say it."

His voice was so soft she had to strain to hear. "Linda, what are you afraid of?"

She lowered her eyes. Then, with an honesty that surprised her, she looked up and met his gaze. "Everything," she whispered.

Chapter Five

He thought his heart would dissolve.

He wanted to take her back into his arms and hold her tightly but, believing he would only frighten her more, he resisted the urge.

"I would never hurt you," he said softly.

"You don't understand. There are things about me you don't know. Things in my past." She stared straight ahead, gazing toward the playground. "And that's where I want them to remain."

"Linda, look at me," he prodded gently. "You don't have to keep everything bottled inside. Talk to me. Let me help."

She let out a small laugh. "You're saying I should trust you. Now that's almost funny, coming from you."

He winced. "I wish we could turn back the clock and start over, but we can't. We have to move forward. We have another life to consider. We have our baby. If it were just about us, we could forget about that night and go our separate ways, but it's not."

Could he? he wondered. If she weren't pregnant, could he just walk away?

She sighed. "Sorry. I didn't mean to snap at you. It's just that trust isn't something I do easily. I don't feel…safe." Her voice took on a hard edge. "My mother was murdered. There, I said it. Are you satisfied?"

He knew he should appear shocked, but in truth, he already knew about her mother. He'd read about the murder in Robert Jackson's report, back in July.

He also knew how difficult it must have been for Linda to say the words aloud. The least he could do was match her honesty. "I know," he said.

He pictured the photos attached to the file. That night in the lounge of the hotel, he'd thought that Linda looked familiar, but he'd attributed the familiarity to his fantasies. "You're the woman of my dreams," he'd told her after they'd made love. Last night, he would have cringed at the memory of the words, but this morning… Hell, he didn't know how he felt.

Sitting next to her at the picnic table, he braced himself for the attack. Even though he'd read the report before he'd met her, he was sure she would accuse him of spying.

"Yes, I suppose you do know," she said, surprising him. "It's your job." When she spoke again, her voice sounded hollow, as though coming from a distance. "I was seventeen. I was out with…friends. When I got home, there were police cars everywhere. Someone had broken into the house. A robbery, they called it. As if we had anything worth stealing. His name was Timothy Sands, and he was much older than the other boys, but I guess you know that, too."

"You went to live with your sister," Tyler filled in. "When she and her husband were killed in a car crash, you left Montana to live with Sadie." No one should have to go through so much, he thought, a lump forming in his throat. He wanted to promise he'd never let anything happen to her again, but he refrained. He knew it was a promise he might not be able to keep. No one could.

Her expression was contrite. "I'd told you I was from Wisconsin. I've never even been there."

"Lyla from Wisconsin," he said, smiling sadly.

"You probably also know that I testified against Timothy at the trial, and that my testimony helped to convict him. I knew him from school. He hung around with…a friend of mine."

She didn't continue, and Tyler searched his memory. According to the file, she'd confided to someone— David Farber, he recalled, or was it Daniel?—about her mother's jewelry. Farber, in turn, had tipped off Sands. Tyler looked at Linda with confusion. Something didn't jibe. Only a moment ago, she'd told him that she and her mother hadn't owned anything worth stealing.

"Timothy was given a life sentence with no possibility of parole," she continued, her voice still sounding far away. "I thought that was the end of it, but four years ago, he was released on a technicality. I was terrified he'd come after me. There were phone calls…threats…" She took a moment to compose herself. "Walter hired someone to dig into Timothy's past. As a result, Timothy was tried and convicted for a similar crime. To this day, I'm convinced that Walter saved my life. But I guess you know that, too."

He tried to hide his surprise. He'd known about the second trial, but not about Walter's involvement. He now understood the reason for her unwavering loyalty. Gratitude went a long way. But it was more than just gratitude that tied her to Walter; it was blind devotion. How could the man who had helped put away her mother's murderer do any wrong?

Tyler suspected there was more to the story than what she'd told him. Certainly more than what was in the report. But he knew she'd never trust him with the truth as long as she held on to her delusions about Walter. How could she trust him when he was so intent on destroying the one man she believed in? He had to prove to her that he wasn't the bad guy in the story. It wouldn't be easy. She'd never believe anything he'd say against Walter.

But she might believe someone else. Someone officially assigned to the case.

He rose from the picnic table and took her hand. "Come on, let's go. I want to make a stop before I take you to your car. There's someone I want you to meet."

"Are you sure I can't get you anything?" Brooke asked. Tyler's cousin set the coffeepot onto the table.

"We ate at the park," Linda said, "but thank you." She gazed around the café. Through the glass door of the refrigerator she could see an assortment of cakes and pastries; on the shelf next to the espresso machine was a variety of teas. A half-dozen tables crowded the little bistro, giving it a European flavor. Right now, however, the other five tables were empty. She turned to Brooke, who had sat down next to her husband, Mark. "I'm surprised you're open on Sunday."

"We're open seven days a week," Brooke said with pride.

"We stay open on Sundays because of the competition," Mark offered, putting his arm around Brooke's shoulders. "This café is a recent addition. In another hour, the place will be crowded. No rest for the wicked, I always say. Brooke just about lives here."

Brooke waved at him dismissively. "Oh, don't listen to him. I don't work every day. I do like to come in on the weekend, though. It's our busiest time, and I enjoy talking to the customers. It also allows me to give the staff more time off. Dad will be here later, too." She smiled affectionately at her husband. "Mark comes in to help, whenever he's not out and about chasing criminals."

"The greatest drawback to marriage," Mark said, "is that sleeping late on your day off becomes a thing of the past."

Brooke playfully poked him in the ribs. "I didn't hear you complaining when I nudged you at six."

Linda glanced at her and then back at Mark. It took her a moment before she realized that they were teasing each other. It took her another moment before she realized what Brooke had meant. Good heavens, was everyone in this family so casual about sex?

Tyler laughed. "Wait till you have kids. I'm told this will seem like a holiday."

"What about you, Ty?" Mark asked, and Linda nearly choked. "What brings you here so early? Granted, it's nearly eleven, but it's still morning. Don't you always sleep until noon on your day off?"

Now that's a surprise, Linda thought. He'd shown up at her apartment at eight, hadn't he? But then she remembered the morning at the hotel. When she'd slipped out of bed, he hadn't even stirred.

"I wanted Linda to meet you," he said. "We left the party before she had a chance."

Brooke nodded. "Yes, we know. I'm glad you're feeling better, Linda. You gave us quite a scare."

A silence fell over the group. What? Linda thought. She looked at Mark and then back at Brooke. Did they know? But how? It couldn't have come from Sadie. Which left Sara. Good grief, if Sara was telling everyone who was family, the whole city would be buzzing with the news.

"Word travels fast," Brooke said, as though Linda had spoken out loud. "Mark's brother Nick was here earlier this morning." She smiled warmly. "Now that all this is out in the open, I'm sure we're going to be seeing a lot of you."

Nick? Wasn't he Tyler's partner? Linda shot Tylor a poisonous look. Apparently he'd been busy since he left her last night. He was the one who had spilled the beans, not Sara. Who else had he told?

Mark winked at Linda. "It sure took this guy long enough to find you. Nick told us that Tyler combed every bar in the city."

Tyler had looked for her? Now this was news. But she was more relieved than surprised. They weren't talking about the baby; they were talking about the night at the hotel. Her relief quickly vanished, and she felt herself blushing. She peered at Tyler. What exactly had he told his partner?

Tyler shifted in his chair. "Mark…" he warned.

But his friend was relentless. "You should have put me on the trail, Ty," he said, half joking, half serious. "It would have saved you a lot of time."

Linda's ears perked up. "Are you on the police force, too?"

"Nope, I'm strictly private."

"A private investigator?"

Mark laughed. "Yeah, but Tyler went after you all on his own. We wouldn't have even known about Lyla if Nick hadn't spilled the beans."

At the park, when Tyler had talked about his cousin, Brooke, he'd also mentioned his partner, Nick. He'd told her that Nick had an older brother, Mark, but she hadn't realized that this was the same Mark she'd read about in the newspapers. Mark Banning. The man who caught the gunman who'd tried to kill Brooke's father. The gunman, the papers had speculated, whom Walter had hired.

"Mark!" Brooke reprimanded. "Can't you see you're embarrassing them?"

"Remind me to speak to Nick," Tyler grumbled.

"Now don't be too hard on him," Brooke said. "It was my fault. You've been acting weird these past two months, and after you disappeared with Linda last night, I thought there might be a connection. When Nick came by for coffee this morning, I pried it out of him."

Tyler shrugged. "Water under the bridge."

"All's well that ends well," she said, brightening.

Mark chuckled. "When it comes to matters of the heart, my wife thinks she's Dear Miss Lonelyhearts. If it were up to her, everyone would be in a relationship."

Brooke rolled her eyes, but it was obvious she wasn't offended. "It seems to have done you a world of good," she pointed out.

"Yes, dear," Mark said, and the two of them laughed. He took his wife's hand, and she gave him an adoring look.

"Life sure plays funny tricks," Tyler said out of the blue. "If it hadn't been for the investigation, you and Brooke wouldn't be together now."

Mark shot him a warning glance. Tyler nodded, ever so slightly, and Mark seemed to relax in his chair.

An alarm went off in Linda's head. What was that about?

"Have you come up with anything new on the Parks case?" Tyler asked casually.

Too casually, as far as Linda was concerned. Why would he even ask that? If something had broken in the case, wouldn't he already be on top of it? Besides, she didn't know much about police procedure, but she didn't think they should be discussing the case in front of her. Wasn't he breaking some sort of code, like the Hippocratic oath?

"Off the record, of course," he qualified, as though privy to her thoughts.

"I'm not breaking any confidentiality when I say this," Mark said in a contrived-sounding voice. "Walter and his empire are in for a fall. The D.A. is close to pressing charges, and there's no doubt in my mind that he'll get a conviction." He turned to Linda. "You'll probably be subpoenaed, but there's no reason for you to worry. We know your hands are clean. But if there's anything you want to come forward with, now would be the time."

What was that supposed to mean? Was Mark implying that she could be accused of withholding evidence? She regarded him through narrowed eyes. She felt as if she were a suspect in a second-rate cop show. Tyler and Mark were playing good cop, bad cop, except she didn't know who was supposed to be who. One thing she was certain of, however. This meeting was a setup to get her to talk. Well, it wasn't working. Even if she were inclined to help them, which was unthinkable, what could she possibly say? Walter hadn't done anything wrong.

She sat back in her chair, anger stirring inside her. It was apparent why Tyler had brought her here. He thought he could scare her into defecting to his side.

Brooke jumped to her feet. "No shop talk on Sunday," she said, as though sensing Linda's discomfort. "Come on, Linda. Let me show you around the bookstore before it gets crowded. Do you like browsing through rare books? We just got in an entire case of first editions."

Glad to put an end to Tyler's obvious charade, Linda followed Brooke into the adjoining bookstore, and the next hour passed quickly and pleasurably. The two women perused unusual books while the men, Linda assumed, discussed the case.

Unless they were discussing *her*.

"I have something extraordinary to show you," Brooke said with pride. "I'll be right back."

Linda picked up a book of Emily Dickinson's poems and let her mind wander. She recalled the conversation in the café, particularly Mark's comment about Tyler combing the city, looking for her. If what he'd said was true, then Tyler hadn't known who she was at the hotel, after all. Which meant he hadn't sought her out specifically to obtain information.

She wasn't sure if Mark was totally on the up-and-up, but she'd warmed to Brooke immediately, finding no reason to distrust her, and Brooke had confirmed what Mark had said.

Linda was torn with conflicting emotions. Maybe she'd judged Tyler too quickly. Maybe he hadn't brought her here to scare her into talking. What if, knowing she'd never believe anything he'd say regarding Walter, he'd simply wanted to warn her that her life was about to undergo changes?

Changes she'd need to prepare for, changes that had nothing to do with the baby.

Although she didn't want to believe what Mark had said about the case, what if it were true? What if Walter was convicted? For the first time since this nasty business began, she had doubts. Not about Walter's innocence—of that, she was certain—but about the future. She wasn't just thinking about herself; she was worried about the baby. How would they live? She'd be the ex-accountant of a convicted embezzler. Fat chance of her finding work again in this city. As Tyler had said, San Francisco wasn't such a big place.

She forced herself to focus on more cheerful thoughts. She recalled how Tyler had related to the boy in the park, and a smile came to her lips. The boy's mother had been right when she'd said he had a way with kids.

Ah, yes, Claudia. It would also seem that Tyler wasn't the philanderer his twin brother was, or he would have been more receptive to the woman's obvious offer.

It was ironic, Linda thought. Here she was, terrified of guns, and she was seriously considering marrying a man who carried one.

She set down the book she'd been leafing through. Wait a minute. Seriously considering?

Well, why not? Even if Walter wasn't convicted, her future was uncertain. Where would she live if she had to give up her apartment? How could she raise the baby by herself? Not only that, she was terrified at the prospect of living alone. Tyler was a cop, which meant he could provide her with the protection she desperately craved.

Whether she liked it or not, seriously considering was what she was doing.

For some reason the expression, "Keep your friends close and your enemies closer," popped into her head. She dismissed it immediately. Tyler wasn't her enemy. He wanted to marry her, didn't he?

She wouldn't kid herself into thinking his proposal had to do with anything other than the baby and, to be honest, she preferred it that way. If he didn't expect more from her, he wouldn't be disappointed. But if she accepted his proposal—and that was a big if—it didn't mean she'd cross over to his side of the case. The marriage and Walter would have to remain two separate matters.

Of course, anything she might just happen to learn as Tyler's fiancée would be an added bonus. A disturbing thought occurred to her. He could very well be thinking along those same lines.

Smiling, Brooke returned with a book in her hand. "Look at this," she said excitedly. "A first edition of

Jane Eyre. This is one of my favorite novels. It's got everything—love, marriage, suspense and drama."

Linda knew the story well. Don't forget deceit, she thought.

Tyler hadn't missed the look on Linda's face when he'd brought up the case. How could he have been so naive? Had he really believed that talking to Mark would get her to see the truth?

This is what happens when you let a woman under your skin, he thought. It clouds your judgment.

"I like your cousin," she said as they drove to the restaurant to pick up her car. "She's a down-to-earth, genuinely caring person. She went out of her way to make me feel at home."

Was he hearing right? Linda had been as wired as a surveillance van. He gave her a quick glance. She was smiling brightly. Okay, so maybe she meant what she'd said. He couldn't deny that she and Brooke had clicked like old friends.

He had to loosen up. This whole business was turning him into a cynic. "She liked you, too. I imagine we'll be seeing a lot more of her and Mark." He let out a chuckle.

"What's so funny?"

"It's just that everywhere I turn, more relatives crop up. My Christmas list keeps growing and growing."

"But you must have known that your mother had a younger brother," she pointed out.

"Yes, but Derek—Brooke's father—disappeared before I was born. I only recently found out that I had a cousin. Mark, by the way, was instrumental in locating my uncle."

Tyler glanced at her again, but this time her face was blank. He tried to figure out what she was thinking. From her reaction earlier in the café, he'd assumed she hadn't known about Mark's role in the investigation. But how could she not have known? The newspapers had blown the P.I.'s cover to pieces. After Brooke had taken the bullet meant for Derek, the media had had a field day.

"It's a small world," Linda said. "It seems that lately everyone I meet is in some way connected to the Parks family."

"The Parks network, you mean." The Parks web, he thought grimly. We're the flies, and Walter is the spider.

"It's certainly complicated," she said evasively.

Did she know more than she was letting on? Hoping to draw her out, he proceeded with caution. "It can't be easy for Walter's children, not knowing what side of the fence to sit on." He was referring to Walter's legitimate children, not to him and Conrad. For him and his brother, the choice was clear.

"Yes, I imagine it would be. Though, of course, I wouldn't know. Some people might think that family problems are actually a blessing."

Now that was a strange comment, he thought. But then he recalled the photos on the mantle in her apartment. He'd figured they all belonged to Sadie, since Linda wasn't in any of them. Maybe the remark wasn't that strange, after all. Having family problems meant having a family. "This baby means a great deal to you," he said quietly.

She didn't answer right away. "Why didn't you tell them?"

"Tell who what?"

"Brooke and Mark. Nick. All of them. Why didn't you tell them I was pregnant?"

"Did you want me to?"

"I don't know. I guess it doesn't matter. They'll find out soon enough."

"I think we should wait until we decide what we're going to do." He wanted to say, "Until we decide on a wedding date," but he held back.

"All right," she said.

His heart jumped. "All right, what?"

"Blood test, DNA test, whatever. I don't know much about these things. I'll do whatever you want. You have a right to be sure."

Was this her way of accepting a proposal? "Linda, I don't want to have the baby tested. I know it's mine."

"But you said—"

"I know what I said, and I was wrong." He pulled into the parking lot of the restaurant and turned off the ignition. "Linda, hear me out. In the instant I first laid eyes on you, my whole world turned upside down. Call it fate, if you want. Or destiny. I know it sounds crazy, but these days nothing seems to make much sense. Yet there are two things I'm sure of. One, the baby is mine. Two, we should get married."

"Fate," she repeated flatly. "That's what Brooke said. She and Mark met in August, and now they're married. She said that sometimes it happens that way. Sometimes you know right from the start, even though you might not admit it."

He'd known right away, too, the first time he'd seen Linda, but if anyone had told him he could feel like that, he would have laughed. "Sounds like you and Brooke had an interesting conversation."

"But I'm not convinced," she continued. "I still think a couple needs to spend time together before making a commitment."

So it was back to that. So much for thinking she wanted to marry him. Well, if dating was what she wanted, dating was what she'd get. Except it had better be the condensed version. He wanted to get married before their child was born.

She unfastened her seat belt and reached for the door. "Um, I had a nice time. Thank you for breakfast."

He had to suppress a smile. She sounded like a schoolgirl. "Can I see you later? What about dinner?" he asked, not bothering to hide his eagerness. With amusement, he realized that he probably sounded as young as she did.

She hesitated. "I promised Sadie I'd help her pack."

"What about tomorrow? I can pick you up at noon, and we can go to lunch."

She looked horrified. "Come to the office? I don't think so. The atmosphere at work is tense enough."

She had a point. Meeting her at the office wasn't such a good idea, now that the DNA had hit the fan. "All right, meet me somewhere. Let's have dinner later, too. I want to spend time with you."

She gave him an apologetic smile. "I'm going to be tied up all this week helping Sadie. We have a ton of last-minute details to take care of, and then there's the rehearsal, not to mention the dinner for the out-of-town guests."

He shook his head. Dating had never seemed so difficult. "When is it?"

"The rehearsal dinner's on Friday. But—"

"No, I mean the wedding."

She peered at him with suspicion. "Saturday. Why?"

"What time?"

"The ceremony is at five, but the photographer arrives at four. Why?" she repeated.

"I'll pick you up at your apartment at three." He smiled at her slyly. "Unless, of course, you already have a date." Somehow he knew she didn't.

"No, but—"

"Then it's settled. I'll see you on Saturday."

Maybe, just maybe, seeing her best friend get married would trigger a response. Weddings were supposed to be contagious, weren't they? If so, he'd be right there beside her when she succumbed.

"Say cheese!"

Linda sat next to Tyler at the head table, watching couples whirl around the dance floor. A flash exploded in her face as the photographer snapped their picture. The guests at the other tables tinkled their glasses with their spoons, a sign for the bride and groom to kiss. The photographer focused his camera on the happy couple, who didn't disappoint the guests.

Linda thought back over the past week. It had been long and arduous with last-minute preparations and one catastrophe after another. Two members of the band had come down with chicken pox, and Sadie and Linda had had to scramble for another group. The tablecloths and napkins were not what Sadie had ordered, but after the caterer agreed to knock down the price, Sadie decided that pale yellow went well with her dusty-rose scheme after all. In the end, the whole affair was proceeding without a hitch.

The evening had begun at St. Francis Church and was now winding down at Windsor Hall, where the reception was being held. Overlooking the Bay, the banquet room was ornately decorated with flowers in a tradition of warmth and elegance. A silver candelabra glistened at each end of the head table, the other tables adorned with candled centerpieces. On the small stage a three-piece band played an eclectic mix of dance music as couples moved across the floor in the muted lighting.

Linda was filled with happiness for her friend. But something else filled her, as well, something unfamiliar, as she watched the blissful couple raise champagne glasses to each other's lips. It was unfamiliar because she'd never before felt this strange mixture of envy and poignancy.

"Care to dance?" Tyler asked, strikingly handsome in a formal suit and tie.

She imagined herself in his arms, moving to the rhythm, floating across the dance floor…stepping on his toes. "Uh, I don't think so," she mumbled, ashamed to admit she didn't know how.

Refusing to take no for an answer, he took her hand and eased her from her chair. The music was playing something foreign, and she looked up at him with doubt. "I don't know about this, Tyler. Why don't we get some punch instead?" She gestured to a table where frozen baby roses bobbed in a large crystal bowl.

"I don't trust anything that's been spiked with flowers," he joked, leading her to the dance floor. "Don't worry, it's easy. Before this dance is over, you'll be a real *milonguera*."

She looked at him warily. "A real what?"

He gently extended her arm. Clasping her hand, they moved across the floor in a rhythmic stroll. "A *milonguera* is a woman whose life revolves around the tango," he explained. "ONE, two, THREE, four. That's it. You're getting it. It's easy when you allow yourself to feel the beat. Slow and steady. Step when I do, only on the major beats."

Good grief, the tango? What next? Skydiving? One thing about Tyler, he was a man of surprises. "Where did you learn this?"

"Pay attention, Linda. Look to the right. Keep the weight over the balls of your feet, but don't stand on your toes—it'll tire you out. ONE, two, THREE, four. ONE, two, THREE, four. By the way, dancing isn't my only talent. There's a lot about me you don't know, and I intend to spend the rest of my life showing you."

Suddenly, he pivoted around and faced the other way. To her amazement she ended up in the same direction, moving gracefully along the ballroom floor. He was right. It was easy once you let yourself feel the music. She closed her eyes, imagining she was a jungle cat, slinky and beautiful.

He placed his arms around her waist, lowering her into a dip. She opened her eyes, and their gazes locked. A rainbow of butterflies fluttered in her stomach. Maybe it was the sexy tempo of the music, or maybe it was the way he was looking at her, but she knew that this time if he tried to kiss her, right there on the dance floor, she wouldn't pull away.

The music came to a halt, and he whirled her up to her feet. "Not bad for a beginner," he said, casting her a devilish grin.

She wanted to make a clever retort, but as usual, nothing came to mind. The music started up again, and he pulled her back into his arms. Saved by the bell, she thought. Or in this case, by the band.

The tempo of the music was leisurely, and Tyler pulled her closer. At least slow dancing doesn't require any special skill, she thought.

Saved by the band? Hardly. Locked in Tyler's embrace, she was acutely aware of the danger as they slowly swayed to the music, hardly moving at all. She felt his breath on her neck, his cheek grazing hers.

"Have I told you how lovely you look tonight?" he murmured in her ear.

Usually, she detested being part of a wedding party, not because she was forced to wear an outfit that inevitably made her feel like an ostrich, but because she didn't like the attention as she walked down the aisle. But tonight, as Sadie's maid of honor, she'd felt as if she'd been floating on air. A princess out for a stroll.

She'd balked when Sadie had chosen this design. Far from traditional, the satin gown plunged in the front and was practically backless. Okay, so it wasn't hideous. In fact, it was stunning. And seductive. But neither stunning nor seductive was exactly her style.

Suddenly the music stopped, and the lights brightened. "And now, ladies," the band leader announced, "the bride is going to throw the bouquet. We need all the single ladies out here. Come on down, don't be shy!"

Tyler practically threw her into the crowd.

She retreated to the back of the room.

"Are you ready, Sadie?" the musician spoke into the microphone. "Here we go. On the count of three…"

From the stage up front, Sadie caught her eye. Don't, Linda silently begged. Don't you dare.

"…three!"

But, of course, Sadie couldn't hear her, and even if she could, Linda knew it wouldn't make a difference. With a determined look her friend hurled the bouquet straight at Linda. It soared through the air, clear across the room. If Sadie's business ever failed, Linda thought, she could always become a quarterback for the 49ers.

Alone at the back of the room, she felt as if everyone was watching her. Watching and waiting, cheering her on. She froze. What to do? What to do? She couldn't just stand there and deliberately drop the darn thing.

Oh, what the heck. Why not go for it? It was just a dumb custom. Didn't mean a thing. She braced herself, extended her arms—here it comes!

Heidi, Sadie's seven-year-old niece, had made a mad dash down the sidelines, and before anyone could bat an eye ran right out in front of Linda. What to do? What to do? Heidi looked so adorable in her flower girl's dress; how could Linda disappoint her? Linda deliberately fumbled, and Heidi made the catch. The watching guests laughed and applauded.

Tyler returned to Linda's side, looking annoyed. "What's your problem?"

"Excuse me?" Standing on display at the back of the room had made her feel uncomfortable; she didn't need his attitude, as well.

The band broke into a lively polka. "Let's get out of here," Tyler said, raising his voice to be heard over the oompah-pahs coming from the stage. His hand on her elbow, he guided her out into the lobby, where it was quieter.

"I can't believe you're angry over a bunch of flowers."

He sighed. "It's not about the stupid flowers. It's about us. You. Me. The baby. I want to get married as soon as possible."

"What happened to your not pressuring me?" she asked, pulling her arm free. "Just a few days ago, you said you were willing to wait as long as it took. Now suddenly, you're singing a different tune. How am I supposed to trust you when you keeping changing your mind?"

"I haven't changed my mind about marriage. But I want to be a father to this child before he comes into the world."

She took a deep breath. "Well, then fine."

"Well, then fine, what? Why do I feel like I'm on a merry-go-round? Could you be a little more specific?"

"Well, then fine, I'll marry you."

He looked stunned, as if he couldn't figure out what had just happened. "Just like that you change *your* mind?"

She planted her hands on her hips. "Look, do you want to marry me or not?"

He leaned in close, and she dropped her arms. She studied his face. Was he going to kiss her? She couldn't be sure. She'd thought he was going to kiss her when he'd dipped her on the dance floor, but she'd been wrong.

The butterflies in her stomach returned, this time

with a vengeance. Go away, she implored. I don't want to feel this. Butterflies or not, she couldn't let her libido interfere with real life. She knew all too well what happened when you gave in to the fluttering.

He touched her cheek, his fingers against her skin sending shivers down her spine. "The last thing I want is to make love to a woman who isn't interested," he said quietly. "But eventually I want us to have a real marriage. You can deny it all you want, but there's something between us. I felt it that night at the hotel, and it's still there."

She stepped out of his reach. "I won't lie to you, Tyler. I said I'd marry you, but there's a condition. This has to be a marriage of convenience, or the whole thing is off."

He didn't speak for a long moment, as though thinking over what she was implying. Then he nodded and said quietly, "If I have to live this way, I will. I intend to be a father to my child, and that means under any condition. But I won't lie to you, either. I'm not pleased with the arrangement."

He might not be pleased, but for her the setup was ideal. She would have safety, financial security and her child. She thought of it as a career move.

This job, however, wouldn't include fringe benefits.

Chapter Six

"I still don't understand why we have to get married here."

Linda sat next to Tyler on the gray tweed couch in the minister's office. In the corner of the room, a tall Queen Anne clock ticked away the seconds, competing with the pounding in her chest. If just meeting the minister made her so anxious, what would the actual ceremony do?

The wedding was turning into a nightmare. For the past five days since she'd accepted Tyler's proposal, they'd been arguing about the details. Not only did he want a church ceremony, he wanted his family and friends to witness the event. She could just imagine herself in a chaste wedding gown, walking down the aisle while scrutinizing eyes burned into her, making her feel like an insect in a jar. He also wanted to hold a reception at a fancy restaurant or hall, which she insisted wasn't going to happen.

"I already told you, this is where all the Carlton and Parks weddings take place," he said with impatience. "I intend to assume my place in the family, once and for all."

"I don't want to turn the wedding into a circus. If you invite your whole family, half of San Francisco will show up."

"I can't not ask my family to come," he protested. "And what about Sadie? Don't you want your best friend to be your matron of honor?"

"Let me remind you, our marriage is just an arrangement. Think of it as a business deal. You wouldn't invite your family or friends to a merger, would you? In any case, you said you want to get married as soon as possible, and as soon as possible doesn't leave room for much planning. Do you have any idea how long it took to put Sadie's wedding together?"

She could tell she wasn't getting anywhere with her reasoning, but then she had a stroke of genius. "If you want family at the ceremony, we'll have to invite Walter. If you're so insistent on having a traditional wedding, who else do I have who can give me away?" That was a bluff. How could she ask Walter to walk down the aisle when she didn't have the courage to tell him she was marrying his son?

Apparently the bluff worked, because Tyler caved in. At least on that point. "Fine," he said with resignation. "We'll have a small wedding. But I still want us to get married in this church."

"Churches are for *real* weddings," she said, attempting one last stab as they waited for the minister.

But Tyler was adamant. "Walter took everything, and it's high time I reclaimed what's rightfully mine. I'm not talking about money, I'm talking about a sense of belonging. Getting married in this church is just one step toward that, but it's a step in the right direction. No one will ever force me to be an outsider again."

She could see there was no dissuading him. Like everything else, this was about Walter. Scowling, she stared straight ahead.

"Tyler Carlton?" A sprightly-looking older man had entered the office and was smiling jovially. "I'm sorry to have kept you waiting. I couldn't find my appointment book. I'm Reverend Bob Nelson, and you," he said, nodding at Linda, "must be the bride." He sat down in the armchair across from the couch. "Oh dear, now where are my glasses?" Chuckling, he pulled them down from the top of his head. "Ah, right where I left them."

Bright assessing eyes peered at her from behind his wire-framed glasses. He looks more like a mad scientist than a man of the church, Linda thought, regarding his bushy white hair with uncertainty.

He opened the book on his lap, his face alight with merriment. "Wedding dates are usually set well in advance. If parents want to get the date they want, they should probably book the wedding as soon as their children are born. Of course, these days more and more young couples insist on planning their own weddings. On the one hand, I like to encourage their independent spirit, but on the other hand, it's always sad when a tradition is lost. How does a July wedding sound? We still have a Sunday open."

Linda's mood sank even lower. If July was the earliest date available, they'd have ample time to plan the kind of wedding Tyler wanted. If just the thought of getting married in front of an audience made her want to dig a hole and go into hiding, what would she feel like pushing a stroller down the aisle?

Tyler cleared his throat. "Reverend, I think you misunderstood me on the phone. We need to get married as soon as possible."

"I see," the minister said.

He knows, Linda thought, her face flaming. Could Tyler possibly have been any less subtle?

"All right, then," the minister said, pushing his glasses up on his nose. "Let's take another look." He studied the ledger. "The earliest date I can give you is in two weeks, if you don't mind getting married on a weekday."

"Two weeks!" Linda blurted. She didn't want to wait until July, but two weeks was way too soon. Growing accustomed to the idea that she was going to have a baby was easy; acquiring a husband was another matter. "That doesn't give us much time to get to know each other." She groaned inwardly. How could she have said something so stupid?

Tyler regarded her with impatience. "Linda, we've already been over this. As soon as possible doesn't mean sometime in the distant future."

The minister raised an eyebrow. "Just how long have you known each other?"

"We met a week before last Saturday," Linda answered nervously.

"I see," the minister said again. "Tyler, you don't have a problem with that?"

Tyler looked at him blankly, and then understanding registered in his face. "The baby is mine," he said tightly. "What my fiancée means is that we just found out who we are. We actually met in August under, uh, special circumstances."

Why wait for the wedding? Linda thought, mortified. Why not dig a hole right here? She glared at Tyler, hoping that looks could kill. She had no doubt the minister knew what Tyler had meant by "unusual circumstances."

The minister was studying them intently. "I'm sure the two of you have given this a lot of thought. Just the same, the church offers premarital counseling. I'll sign you up for Tuesday."

"That sounds like a good idea," Linda said. "This way, Tyler and I will get to know each other before we have to live together."

Get to know each other before they have to live together? Had she actually said that? She was on a roll today.

"Thank you, Reverend," Tyler said, "but that won't be necessary. We don't need counseling. We've already made up our minds."

"I'm afraid you don't understand. These sessions are mandatory. It just so happens that I have an opening in next week's group. I don't like to meet with more than four couples at a time. If you decline, the next opening isn't until January."

Tyler looked aghast. "Did you say 'group'? As in group therapy?"

The minister smiled. "It's not as bad as it sounds. All the prospective husbands balk at first, but they soon come to appreciate the benefits. Some couples even form lasting friendships."

Linda nodded. "It's important for a couple to be friends."

"He means with other couples," Tyler said tersely.

She felt like a wire that was strung so tightly it was about to snap. "The next time you feel the need to correct me, I'd appreciate it if you wouldn't do it in public."

"I wasn't correcting you. I was pointing out—"

"You always do that," she accused. "You point things out as if I'm incapable of thinking for myself, and you do it in a way that's not too obvious, which is even worse. It's undermining and manipulative, not to mention patronizing. Like that fiasco with Mark, when we were at the bookstore. Did you think I wouldn't know what you were up to?" She turned to the minister. "Sign us up. It's apparent my fiancé needs counseling."

"The session begins promptly at seven—"

"*I* need counseling? Reverend, she can make a neat freak look like a slob. I've never met a woman so organized."

"What's wrong with being organized? You say the word as if it's blasphemy—oh, excuse me, Reverend, I didn't mean anything by that. That's another thing about him. He refuses to clean up his language."

Tyler rolled his eyes. "Which word do you find offensive? 'Organized' or 'freak'? Anyway, it's true. You're a neat freak. I swear, Reverend—sorry, I didn't mean swear, I meant promise—that with her, every little thing has to be just so. God forbid, pardon the expression, she sees a tiny wrinkle in one of her starchy blouses. It drives her crazy, and that in turn drives *me* crazy. And speaking about driving, do you know what it's like being in a car with her? She gives the term back-seat driver a new definition."

The minister opened his mouth to speak, but Linda beat him to the punch. "You'd be concerned, too," she said to him, "if you saw the way he drives. He thinks just because he's a cop, he can ignore the speed limit."

"Children, please!" the minister interrupted, and the room fell silent. The ticking from the Queen Anne clock was so loud, Linda felt sure it would explode.

The minister clicked his tongue. "As I started to say earlier, the group meets at seven Tuesday evening. In addition, the two of you will be required to go on retreat. This is where you'll talk to each other about your…issues, without a counselor to intervene or any distractions from the outside world. We have a special room set up right here in the church." He looked back down at the book, then raised his head and said, "The room is available next Thursday. Will it be difficult for either of you to take time off from work?"

Tyler frowned. "How much time?"

The minister smiled wryly. "I usually ask the couple to be prepared to spend a full morning or afternoon. But in your case, I must insist on the whole day."

Couples therapy, Tyler thought with disdain. Man bashing would have been a better description. Why was it that the counselors at these things were usually female? "Reverend Nelson must have a cruel streak," he grumbled. "First, he subjects us to couples therapy, and now this."

Linda frowned. "I hope you plan to take this retreat more seriously. Last week, you didn't open your mouth the whole time."

He stared at her in disbelief. "Did you really think I would air my dirty laundry in front of strangers?"

"The idea was to talk about our personal expectations. Not everything is about the Parks empire."

Agitated, Tyler paced the floor. "This place is like a cell. There isn't even a window. What if there's a fire? What if we have to go to the bathroom?"

"The door's not locked," Linda said with exasperation.

"What type of minister shuts off his parishioners from civilization? To think I gave up a full day's work for this farce. Have you seen the remote?"

"Will you please sit down? We need to resolve our differences."

He walked over to the TV and flipped the switch. Nothing. If they weren't allowed to watch TV, why didn't they just remove the damn thing? It wasn't cruel; it was downright sadistic. It was like leaving a pack of cigarettes in front of a person who had just given up smoking. Maybe there was a radio. Hell, he'd even settle for a game of solitaire.

"Tyler, will you please stop pacing? You're making me nervous."

"Everything makes you nervous," he mumbled.

"There, you see? That's exactly what Reverend Nelson was talking about. You're confrontational. Your attitude is one of the problems we need to resolve."

He leaned over and peered into her face. "Okay, I'll play along. But remember, this is a game for two. I'm not the only one here with issues."

"What are you doing?" she asked, flinching under his scrutiny.

"I'm looking for crow's feet. At couples therapy, when I told the group my age, you admitted you were older than me, but you wouldn't say how much."

"What difference does it make?" she asked huffily.

He knew he'd struck a nerve. "It makes no difference to me, but apparently it does to you. Why else would you lie on the marriage license?"

She glared at him. "And how, may I ask, do you know my age?"

"Robert Jackson's report, remember? It's a good thing the license clerk asked for proof of age. This marriage might not be normal, but it's going to be legal."

She stiffened visibly. "There's no need to take that tone. You seem to forget that getting married was your idea in the first place. So if I were you, I'd stop complaining. Unless you want to call the whole thing off, in which case, be my guest."

He sighed, then sank down next to her on the couch. He wished there were someplace else he could sit, like on the other side of the planet. "All right, you want to talk issues, let's talk issues. For starters, what about the living arrangements? I want us to live at my place."

"I told you, it doesn't make sense. Now that Sadie has moved out, I have an extra bedroom."

"You live in an expensive part of town. We won't be able to afford your place on just one salary."

She jutted out her chin. "I don't intend to give up my job."

"You might not have a choice," he reminded her.

Her mouth pulled into a thin line. She obviously

didn't want to enter into a discussion about Walter, which was fine with him. A retreat was one thing; mortal combat was another. But the wedding was next Thursday. They had to resolve their living arrangements before then. "My apartment isn't as large," he said, determined to have his way, "but it'll save us a lot of money."

She looked up at him with dark, beseeching eyes. "I don't care about the money. I care about safety."

Aw, hell. He hated when she got vulnerable on him. It gave her an unfair advantage. His chest tightened, and he took her hand. To his surprise, she didn't pull away. "It's pretty safe where I am downtown," he said, trying to sound reassuring. "I don't have the same fancy video surveillance you have, but there's always a patrol car cruising the streets. And don't forget," he added jauntily, "you're marrying a cop."

"To serve and protect," she said, managing a small smile. "Every cop's motto."

Excitement for their future mounted inside him. "As soon as we've saved enough, we'll make a down payment on a house. It won't be fancy, but it'll be in a safe, clean neighborhood. We'll have a yard in back, maybe a porch out front. I'll build a swing, maybe put in a barbecue. You can plant a garden. I've never had a green thumb, but I'll bet you're a natural."

She hesitated. "I won't deny it, a home like that sounds wonderful. It's the kind of place I used to dream about. The kind of place I used to tell my friends I'd live in when my father came home."

He felt his heart turn over. Maybe there was merit to this retreat business, after all. It looked as if she was finally opening up to him. He knew that to achieve intimacy, they needed to be candid. And intimacy was what he was aiming for—despite her protests against wanting a real marriage. "Tell me about your father," he prodded gently.

"It's no secret. I never knew him. He drove a truck for a living. My mother said that one day, soon after I was born, he set out on a trip across the country, and that was last she saw of him. I'd always hoped he'd return, but when I was fifteen, we heard that his truck had been hijacked and that he'd been killed."

"That must have been tough for you," Tyler said, giving her hand a gentle squeeze. Not only had she never known her father, now her mother and sister were gone, too. "You certainly haven't had an easy time."

She shrugged. "I managed. After I moved out here, I worked as a filing clerk at a leasing company and went to night school to become a CPA. After that, I heard that Parks Fine Jewelry needed an accountant. I arranged for an interview, and Walter hired me on the spot. Apparently, his previous accountant had mysteriously disappeared."

He nodded. "Yes, I know how you came to work for Walter. The report was detailed." Though not detailed enough, he thought, remembering his surprise when she'd told him about Walter's participation in getting Timothy Sands reincarcerated. "You're an amazing woman, Linda. You've accomplished so much. In spite of everything that happened, you didn't let life defeat you."

He pondered how far he could go with this, afraid that if he pushed too hard, she would retreat into herself. Yet how could he expect her to be open when he couldn't return the honesty? It wasn't that he didn't want to; on the contrary, she affected him in a way no one else ever had. In spite of their differences, he related to her on so many levels, particularly when it came to their parents. But he knew he had to hold back. Even though they'd each had a parent who'd been murdered, how could he talk about his past without pointing a finger at Walter? The best he could hope for was a vague kind of communication, something that didn't entail mentioning her boss.

"I can understand a lot of what you must be feeling," he said carefully. "I know what it's like to grow up without a father."

She gave him a small, bleak smile. "My mother always made it clear we were better off without him. She said he wasn't the domestic type, and that no man was."

"Not all men refuse to live up to their responsibilities," he said quietly.

She paused, as though deliberating her next words. "For what it's worth, Tyler, I think you're going to be a good father. You try to come across as hard-boiled, but inside you're a warm and caring person. Maybe a little wounded, but who isn't? You know what I think? I think your past has made you afraid of happiness. You're afraid that once you find it, it'll be snatched away. It's perfectly understandable, given the way you felt while growing up. But you're using Walter like a shield. We both know that he isn't the monster you make him out to be, but to admit that, you'd have to give up your armor."

So much for not mentioning Walter. Tyler didn't want to discuss him, but he saw no way around it. Walter was at the root of their problems. Linda looked up to him, as though he could make up for her growing up fatherless. "You regard Walter as your surrogate parent," he said uneasily.

She surprised him with a smile. "That's what I've been saying all along. I'm so happy you finally see it my way."

Oh, boy. "Linda, I'm going to ask you something and I want you to think carefully before you answer. Believe me when I say this, I'm not trying to upset you."

She looked at him expectantly, a worried expression creasing her brow. "Go ahead."

"Don't you ever question why Walter took you under his wing? He treats you better than he does his own children. You don't think that's strange?"

"No, I don't," she said, her voice taking on a defensive edge. "He's not close to his kids, and he's lonely. You're not the only one who despises him. Can you imagine how he feels? His own children plotting to see him behind bars! I give him what his own children won't—respect and affection. We've maintained an easygoing, nonjudgmental relationship in spite of everything that's happening."

"I'm not sold, but I'm going to let your explanation slide for now. But did you ever ask yourself why he hired you in the first place? You'd just become a CPA. Walter's business is enormously successful. Why would he hire someone so inexperienced?"

"What are you saying? That I'm incompetent?"

"I'm not saying that at all. All I'm saying is that you were like a clean slate. Did you ever think he hired you *because* you were inexperienced?"

"You mean naive," she said dryly. "Let me remind you, you're only twenty-four and you already have your gold shield. Do you think they gave it to you because you're inexperienced?"

"It's not the same thing," Tyler insisted. "Look, forget I said anything. I knew you'd react this way. I shouldn't have brought it up in the first place."

"You're right. You shouldn't have. And you're right about something else. This retreat is a farce. I knew you wouldn't take it seriously. I knew you'd use it as a means to deride Walter. This discussion is over."

She opened her purse and pulled out a paperback. But then she raised her gaze and said, "There's one final matter, however, that we need to resolve. The matter of where you'll be sleeping. If we're going to be living in your apartment, I assume the baby and I will be in the bedroom."

He felt an emptiness in the pit of his stomach. But it wasn't just because of her decision to remain abstinent. He'd accepted that there would be no sex—what choice did he have?—but he'd never considered that they'd be sleeping separately. He'd been looking forward to waking up next to her, seeing her face first thing in the morning. Now it seemed he was to be denied that, as well.

Not bad, Linda thought as she studied herself in the mirror on the bedroom door. The winter-white skirt of her chic designer suit fell just below her knees, accentuating the curve of her calves. Under the stylish collarless jacket, a gold camisole peeked out to match the buttons down the front. Feminine but functional, she decided, pleased with the effect.

"But it's your wedding," Sadie had protested when Linda had told her she was planning to wear the outfit she'd worn to the welcoming party. "You can't wear that dingy bag! You only get married once, hopefully. And I still don't understand why you don't want anyone at the ceremony, anyone meaning *me*. What's this world coming to when you can't even be there when your best friend gets married!"

"If this were going to be a real marriage," Linda had explained for the umpteenth time, "things would be different. I'd be wearing a flowing white gown with a twelve-mile train, and you'd be my matron of honor. But it's not going to be a real marriage, and I won't pretend otherwise. A traditional wedding would be a lie."

Explaining this to someone who had just returned from her honeymoon was an exercise in futility. Sadie had looked so forlorn that, in the end, Linda had agreed to go shopping with her for a suitable outfit. "But nothing traditional," she'd warned her friend.

So far, this whole day was going against tradition, she thought now as she put in her earrings. For one thing, she wasn't surrounded by a flock of bridesmaids trying to conceal her from the groom's gaze, as superstition dictated. Here she was about to get married, alone in her apartment, waiting for Tyler to come by and take her to the church. Not only that, she'd insisted that the ceremony be held late in the day so neither of them would have to miss work. I don't want a fuss, she'd told Sadie. And no fuss was what she was getting.

So why was she fussing over how she looked?

The saying, "Something old, something new, something borrowed, something blue," popped into her head.

Okay, so maybe she didn't want to go down the traditional route, but why tempt fate? She looked down at the shoes she'd bought for the welcoming party. They were two and a half months old; that made them old, right? Her outfit took care of something new. Sadie had lent her a gold beaded bag. That would take care of something borrowed. Now all she needed was something blue.

Something blue, something blue, she mumbled to herself while rummaging through her nightstand drawer. And then she saw the medallion. Suspended from a masculine gold chain, St. Michael's profile was set against a background of blue enamel. "The closest thing to my heart," Tyler had said the night he'd given it to her. At the time, she hadn't realized the signifi cance. St. Michael was the patron saint of policemen. She fastened the chain around her neck and tucked the medallion under her camisole.

Next to the spot where the necklace had lain was a small box. She picked it up. Why not? she thought, opening the carton and removing the lenses. No sense letting them sit around doing nothing.

Fifteen minutes later, she was still struggling with the lenses. How was she supposed to get them in when she couldn't see what she was doing? The buzzer rang, startling her, and when she blinked, the right lens slipped into the corner of her eye. "Oh, gross," she said aloud, then dashed into the hallway.

"You look wonderful," Tyler said moments later, his gaze never leaving her.

"So do you," she said, a flush of heat coursing through her veins. It was the same reaction she'd had when he'd shown up to take her to Sadie's wedding, looking devastatingly handsome in his suit and tie. She gathered her composure. "I can't go."

"It's a little late for second thoughts," he said, visibly disturbed.

"No, you don't understand. One of my lenses is stuck in my eye. I think we should go to the E.R."

He chuckled. "I don't think this exactly constitutes an emergency. Maybe I can help. Come into the kitchen. The light's better there."

In the kitchen, he pulled out a chair from the table and motioned for her to sit. He pulled out another chair and sat facing her. "Now don't move," he said, his fingers gently prying her right eye wide open. "Just one minute. Hold still."

His head was just inches from hers, and his musky aftershave created a heady elixir, sending her senses reeling. She stared straight ahead, trying not to blink.

"There it is. Okay, it's over." He grinned. "No one can accuse me of being inept with my hands. They don't call me Toolman Tyler for nothing."

He'd removed his hands from her face, but his gaze remained unwavering. "What's the matter?" she asked, suddenly alarmed. "Did it fall inside my head or something?"

He laughed. "No, it's in place now, right where it belongs. Can't you tell? You can see clearly, can't you?"

"Oh." So why was he still sitting there? Why was she?

He touched her face again, this time with so much tenderness she thought she would melt. "I wish…" he began, but then stopped abruptly. She knew what he was thinking, and for a brief moment she wished the same thing he did.

If only things were different…

"You're so beautiful," he whispered, his gaze locked on hers. "I can't believe you're going to be my wife."

She averted her eyes. "Tyler, please don't. You're making it difficult."

"Why do you always do that? Why do you look away whenever I compliment you?"

"I guess I'm not used to it," she said with honesty.

"You'd better learn to get used to it, because I intend to spend the rest of my life flattering you."

Something occurred to her that she hadn't thought of before. "Tyler, do you realize how old you'll be when I turn forty?" she asked, horrified.

"Over thirty? Is that too old for you? I guess you'll have to trade me in for a younger man."

"You're incorrigible," she said, smiling.

"Now, that's much better. You know, I'm beginning to think that maybe, just maybe, with a little communication and a truckload of humor, we might be able to make this work."

"I hope so." A silence fell over them, and she stood up. "Well, then," she said uncomfortably, "I guess it's showtime."

She took a look around, and a sadness overcame her. She'd spent so many hours in this room, burning the midnight oil, talking with Sadie. This place held good memories.

Several boxes were stacked along the kitchen walls. More boxes remained in the bedroom, waiting to be taped up and hauled to Tyler's apartment. They'd already moved some of her belongings, and they'd be returning daily until everything was moved, but from this night on she'd be staying at his place. Her lease wasn't up until the end of the year, but thankfully the landlord had allowed her out of the agreement. Sadie had taken only a few pieces of furniture to Frank's place; Linda would be putting what she didn't need into storage, selling it at some later date.

Sadie had been right when she'd called her a pack rat. It was a good thing Linda had the organization gene, or she would be living in chaos. It was amazing how much a person collected over the years. But not all of it was the kind of stuff that could be packed away in boxes. Excess baggage, Sadie had called it. It was time, Linda decided, to let some of it go.

Tyler pulled into the driveway outside his building, then came around to her side.

"Aren't you coming up?" Linda asked. "What about dinner?"

He planted a kiss on her nose. "'Fraid not, sweetheart. No time. Got a stakeout tonight. I'll change my clothes at the station. But don't worry, the freezer is full. Lots of microwave dinners in there, since I know you don't like to cook. I should be home by midnight."

She felt oddly disappointed. She would have thought that tonight, of all nights, he would have made an effort to be with her. Maybe theirs was just a marriage of convenience, but he might have shown a little consideration. Just because they'd decided not to have sex didn't mean they couldn't spend the evening together. "You only get married once," Sadie had said. Linda frowned, recalling how her friend had qualified the statement with a flippant "hopefully."

She unlocked the door to the apartment and turned off the alarm. At her insistence, Tyler had installed a keypad system. She sighed. It was better than nothing, but it wasn't the security she'd hoped for. What was the use of marrying a cop if he wasn't around to protect her?

She changed into jeans and a sweatshirt and set about making dinner. Tyler hadn't been kidding about the freezer—it was jam-packed with prepared dinners. She pulled out a chicken potpie. A bottle of chardonnay on the counter caught her eye, and for a moment she was tempted. If she weren't pregnant, she wouldn't have hesitated. Wasn't a wedding toast in order?

The evening passed with agonizing slowness. She tried to read, but couldn't concentrate. She turned on the TV, then clicked it off. She thought about calling Sadie, but decided against it. She couldn't keep running to her best friend every time she felt out of sorts. She was a big girl now, a married woman.

She went into the bedroom to unpack the boxes she and Tyler had brought over yesterday. Clicking her tongue, she picked up a pair of his socks from the floor. She hadn't said anything about the clutter in the living room—why on earth did a person need so many remotes?—but if the bedroom was going to be hers, he might have made an attempt to tidy it. As she was dusting the bureau, a silver gift bag caught her eye. A present from Sadie, she remembered. "Guaranteed to make your wedding night memorable," the card had read.

She pulled out the teeniest, flimsiest nightgown she'd ever seen. She examined it closely—what there was of it. Good grief, you could practically see right through it! Did women actually wear these things? It certainly wasn't practical. Her idea of sleepwear was a cotton nightgown in the summer, flannel pj's when it was cold.

Sadie was hopeless. Linda had been adamant about not wanting to wear something traditional to the wedding ceremony, so what did her friend go and do? She bought her something traditional for the wedding night. Traditional according to Sadie. Linda had always believed that the wedding night should be elegant and romantic, not something out of an X-rated movie. Not that there would have been a *real* wedding night, even if Tyler had stayed home.

She thought about the wedding. She hadn't wanted a fuss, and no fuss was what she'd gotten. At six o'clock, only one week after the retreat, Reverend Nelson had ushered them into the chapel, and by six-fifteen it was over. It's amazing how in just a short time an entire life could change. One minute, she'd been Miss Linda Mailer, single; the next minute, Mrs. Tyler Carlton, married. "Married," she repeated to herself, over and over. If you said it often enough, it seemed to lose its meaning.

"You don't regret doing it this way?" Tyler had asked when they'd pulled out of the parking lot behind the church. His voice had been tinged with disappointment. "The ceremony was so cold, so impersonal. It left me feeling empty."

"You know I hate fusses." But in truth, she'd felt let down, too. To be honest, it would have been a comfort for her to have had Sadie by her side. The matron of honor had been the minister's secretary; the best man, his bookkeeper. And, Linda had to admit, it might have been nice to have some sort of celebration dinner following the service. Getting married wasn't something you did every day.

"I never really believed that marriage could be just an arrangement," Tyler had commented on the way home, his gaze on the road ahead. "The ceremony really drove it home."

After that, he'd remained quiet, and she'd thought, What happened to "a little communication and a truckload of humor"?

"Told you so," she imagined her mother saying. Audrey Mailer's austere face rose in her mind. If my mother had been a little less rigid, a little more understanding, Linda wondered, would my father have stayed?

She didn't want Tyler to leave her. She didn't want to be alone. But her fear of being alone wasn't the only reason she wanted him to stay. He made her feel wanted. Made her feel beautiful. She'd liked the way he'd looked at her after helping with her contact lenses. She'd liked the way his eyes had gleamed when she'd said, "I do."

The nightgown felt soft and slinky in her hands. She fingered the delicate lace on the bodice, reminding herself that what she was planning had nothing to do with the way he made her feel.

What she was planning was a compromise—a compromise and an investment in her future. Call it a compromise, call it an investment, but any way she looked at it, tonight was her wedding night. What she was planning wasn't something she'd make a habit of, but once in a while wouldn't kill her.

She stripped off her clothing and slipped into the sexy garment. She glanced at herself in the mirror but, embarrassed at what she saw, she averted her gaze. This isn't you, she reminded herself. This is just a role.

She lay on the bed, waiting for his return. In minutes, she felt herself dozing. She dreamed she was standing outside her mother's house, watching as police cars arrived, listening to the sirens as they wailed in the night.

She jerked awake. Moments later, she heard Tyler's key in the lock, and she darted into the adjoining bathroom to freshen up. What she saw in the mirror shocked her, but she didn't turn her head away. Intrigued, she peered at the reflection. Was that really her?

Lyla.

She shook out her hair, smiled wickedly at her image and returned to the bedroom.

Chapter Seven

"Hi," Tyler said awkwardly, his back turned to her as he rummaged through a drawer in the dresser. He felt like a stranger in his own home. "I'll just be a minute. I suppose I should move some of my things to the living room, since that's where I'll be sleeping." He shut the drawer, turned around—and his mouth dropped open.

"What's the matter, baby?" Linda asked, smiling suggestively. "Cat got your tongue? That would be most regrettable," she added, licking her lips.

"Linda, are you feeling okay?" He didn't know what he'd expected when he'd come home, but he hadn't expected this. Why was she dressed in that tiny nightgown? Not that he was complaining. The way she looked made his pulse fly straight off the charts. He might be confused, but he certainly wasn't unhappy.

"Come to Mama," she purred. "No, stay there. Mama's going to come to you." She sashayed over to him, and he realized that the fabric of her gown wasn't flesh tone; it was transparent. He stood there staring, and she laughed.

She looked him over seductively. "Well, Detective, are you just going to stand there, or are you going to show me some action? Or maybe you should arrest me. I'm about to do something illicit."

So, she wanted to play. Hell, if fantasy was what she wanted, fantasy was what he'd give her. "What do you have in mind?" he asked, moving his fingers slowly across her breasts.

"Bad boy," she mock-scolded. "Keep that up, and I'll have to put you in handcuffs."

Whoa. Handcuffs? Was this the same woman who'd given him advance warning not to kiss her when the minister pronounced them married? "I don't like public displays of affection," she'd explained primly. Public? The minister, his secretary and his bookkeeper had been their entire audience.

An unsettling feeling began to stir inside him. "Linda," he said gently, "you don't have to do this."

"Do what?" she asked, feigning ignorance. "This?" She trickled her lips along his cheek. "Or this?" she asked, then teased his ear with her tongue. "How about this?" She wrapped her arms around his neck, pressing herself against him.

Her endeavors didn't go unnoticed. In spite of his misgivings, he felt himself growing hard against her stomach. He drew her into a full embrace, and she arched her back in response. But when he tried to ease her toward the bed, she refused to budge.

"Let's not be conventional," she said huskily. "I want to initiate the room properly. What I suggest," she murmured while nibbling on the corner of his mouth, "is that we start on the floor, then work our way to the bureau. After that, Detective, if you still have energy, we'll do the bed. I intend to convert this room into our little playroom."

Suddenly, her hands were everywhere at once—unbuttoning his shirt, unfastening his belt, unzipping his trousers. She reached inside, and he let out a gasp.

"We have all night, honey," he said, gently moving her hands aside. "Do you think we can take it just a little slower?"

And then, silence. The fire in her eyes died, and she backed away. When she finally spoke, her voice was cold. "Take it a little slower? Why? Isn't this what you want?"

"Linda, please. I'm sorry. I didn't mean—"

"You didn't mean what?" she lashed out. She turned her head away. "Oh, God. I feel like such a fool. Oh, God."

"Linda, no." He reached for her, but she jerked away. She pulled a bathrobe from the closet and then rushed out of the bedroom, slamming the door behind her.

Aw, hell, he thought, plopping down on the bed. He'd sure bungled that. Talk about being insensitive. He knew his words had hurt her, had realized it as soon as they were out of his mouth. Only, he wasn't sure why. All he'd done was suggest that they slow down, but she'd acted as if she'd been mortally wounded.

He couldn't figure her out. Dammit, he was a cop. He was supposed to be good at figuring things out. But

Linda was something else. She was an enigma he just couldn't solve.

One thing he did know, she felt something for him. She'd responded to him too many times for him to think otherwise. The problem was, she wouldn't follow through.

He didn't want to pressure her, but a man could dream, couldn't he? He'd believed it was just a matter of time before she gave in to her feelings, and she'd made him think that tonight was the night.

He changed out of his clothes, into a T-shirt and sweatpants. Normally he liked to sleep in his boxers, but under the circumstances it wasn't a good idea. He supposed he'd have to go shopping for pajamas.

He deliberated going into the living room. He didn't know what was wrong—all he knew was that somehow he had to fix it. He and Linda needed to talk. If they wanted their marriage to work, they'd need to work out their problems.

He opened the bedroom door to a dimly lit room. Her presence was everywhere. Her coat was on a hook by the front door. Her books now joined his in the bookcase. The Picasso from her bedroom hung on the wall by the window.

He remembered when he'd hung the print a few days ago. "A little to the left," she'd instructed. "No, that's too much. More to the right. A little higher. No, lower."

"I don't get it," he'd said, staring at the picture after she'd finally made up her mind. Two misshapen figures loomed down at him from the wall. He could have hung it upside down, and it would have made just as much sense.

"Things aren't always what they appear to be," she'd said in a cryptic voice.

He entered the living room. Curled up under a throw on the futon, she was watching TV. He felt a tug at his heartstrings. She was sniffling into a tissue.

"Care for some company?" he asked gently. When she didn't answer, he sat down beside her. "What are you watching?"

"*Shrek,*" she managed through her tears. "It's one of my f-favorite m-movies. I must have seen it a d-dozen times."

"It's one of my favorites, too. That's why I bought it. I think the animation is brilliant." He smiled. "I never would have thought you'd enjoy a movie about an ugly ogre who lives in a swamp, eats slime and makes candles from his ear wax."

"B-but this one…this one is s-so…s-sweet." She blew her nose daintily into a tissue.

Tyler shook his head. She was an enigma, all right. One minute, she was seducing him; the next minute, she was crying over a children's movie.

"It's very clever," he said, settling back on the couch. "I like the way they weave in the fairy tales. It's a fairy tale, too, in a way."

He didn't want to sit here and talk about fairy tales. He wanted to talk about what had happened in the bedroom. But afraid she would retreat into herself, he held back.

"It's not your typical fairy tale," she said, wiping the moisture from her face. "Fiona is one smart cookie, and tough, too. But not only that, she has a dark secret."

He was afraid to move, afraid to touch her. He remained next to her, wishing he had a magic wand that would make all their problems disappear. He knew she was hurting; he just didn't know how to help her. He felt her pain as acutely as if it were his own.

Maybe he could weave the subject into the conversation, the way the movie had woven in the fairy tales. But he'd have to be a little more subtle, he thought, recalling his contrived conversation with Mark at the café. She'd seen through that ploy right off the bat. "Fiona can only realize her true self once she finds true love," he said softly.

Suddenly, she looked up at him and asked, "Do you believe in happy endings?"

The question caught him off guard. "I believe in doing the right thing," he said.

She smiled sadly. "They're not always the same thing."

"No, not always, but if you don't try to do what's right, you'll never find happiness. How can a person be happy knowing he deliberately set out to do something wrong?"

"I guess some people have no conscience." She regarded him steadily. "What if you believe you're doing the right thing, but the right thing turns out to be wrong?"

"What do you mean?" he asked cautiously.

"You believe that Walter is guilty, and I believe he's innocent. We're each acting on our own belief. According to you, if either of us acted any differently, it would be wrong. How can we both be right?"

So, he thought, disappointed, she wasn't talking about what had happened in the bedroom. Funny how the conversation always returned to Walter. He sighed. "Sometimes a belief evolves erroneously. Sometimes we need to reevaluate the evidence."

His answer must have appeased her, because she nodded. "Spoken like a true lawman. But I know what you mean. I know how easily impressions can change." She hesitated. "When I first joined the company, I thought it would be the perfect place to work. It was so cold, so impersonal."

He grimaced. Those were the two words he'd used to describe their wedding. "Go on," he said tentatively. What was she getting at?

"Parks Fine Jewelry is a huge, successful business, and I thought I could lose myself in the work. The last thing I wanted was to form any attachments. But as time went by, I grew close to Walter. He was there for me when Timothy Sands was released from prison." She straightened the coverlet on her legs. "Here's the thing. Even if I turned out to be wrong—which won't happen—how could I turn my back on the man who saved my life? If Timothy hadn't gone back to prison, he would have come after me. No matter the circumstances, it would be wrong for me to turn against Walter after what he did for me."

"They say that the road to hell is paved with good intentions," Tyler said tightly, then immediately regretted his words. Here she was opening up to him, and he had to go and get judgmental.

Her eyes flashed with anger. Or was it hurt? He couldn't tell. She sat rigidly on the couch, not responding to his remark.

"I'm sorry," he said with sincerity. "I didn't mean to sound harsh." He tried another tack. "But how can you be so sure you're right? You don't have all the facts. You're a smart woman, Linda. I can't believe you'd base your convictions on blind faith alone. You know what I think? I think you've been doubting Walter all along, but you won't admit it."

"Let me remind you," she snapped, "that in this country, a person is innocent until proven guilty."

Dammit, why couldn't he learn to keep his mouth shut? He might just as well have accused her of being Walter's accomplice. When it came to her boss, she was closed-minded.

They watched the rest of the movie in silence. After the last scene, in which a whole horde of fairy-tale creatures came together to celebrate the marriage of Shrek and Fiona, Linda rose and said, "And on that happy ending, I think I'll call it a night. Do you need help making up your bed?"

"No, I'm fine. I'll get the linen from the closet. Good night, Linda."

The bedroom door closed behind her, and he aimed the remote at the TV. He clicked the off button, and the picture died.

And that's that, he thought. Happy endings were only for fairy tales.

"I want to do what's right," the woman said over the phone. "I have something that belongs to you. Ronald wanted you to have it, and I aim to give it to you."

"I don't understand. Who are you?" Not wanting to be overheard, Linda spoke in a hushed tone. Laughter wafted into her office through the open doorway. The day was winding to a close.

"I told you. The name's Charlene. Charlene Butler, Ronald Pritchard's girlfriend. He said he had something you'd be interested in, something to do with the business. But if you want it, come get it. I did my part. I called you."

"Isn't he dead?" Linda blurted. The only thing she knew of the man was that he'd disappeared more than five years ago, shortly before she'd started working for Walter. The papers had linked his disappearance to organized crime. Apparently he'd been involved in some serious gambling. It had been reported that he'd been shot and killed for not paying back what he owed.

"Of course he's dead," the woman said. "Why else would I be calling you? But like I said, I done my part. You want what's yours, you come by the Starlite Lounge. Be there at eight. I ain't calling again."

"Where is this place?" Linda asked, apprehension filling her.

"It's on Market Street, west of 6th."

Linda frowned. She knew the neighborhood. "I still don't understand—" She heard a click, then found herself listening to a dial tone.

She put down the phone, mulling over the strange conversation. What did Walter's previous accountant have to do with her? What could he possibly have wanted her to have? If it was related to the business, why hadn't Charlene contacted Walter instead?

Must have been a crank call, she decided. Since this whole thing started, she'd been getting one after another. She grimaced. She could just imagine herself traipsing out to Market and 6th. Not exactly one of San Francisco's finer districts.

She pushed the conversation from her mind. Unable to concentrate on work, she allowed her thoughts to drift to last night. Every time she recalled the scene in the bedroom, she felt like disappearing into thin air. She pictured herself the way she imagined Tyler had seen her. Cheap. Tawdry. She'd believed she was offering him what he wanted, but apparently she'd been wrong. Take it a little slower, he'd said. Every time she recalled those words, her face burned with humiliation.

"Linda?"

Startled, she looked up to see cool, brown eyes staring down at her. How long had Walter been standing at her desk? How long had she been lost in thought?

"Walter," she acknowledged, feeling flushed. He leaned his tall, athletic frame in close, glancing at the papers scattered on her desk. Noting the grim look on his leathery tanned face, she sighed deeply.

He knew. He knew about her marriage.

She hadn't really believed he wouldn't find out. It was inevitable. The Parks network, Tyler had called the family. He'd told her he was planning to tell Cade and Emily, but she hadn't thought he'd tell them so soon. Heavens, she hadn't even been married one full day! She was surprised that no one knew about the pregnancy. Or maybe everyone did, but they were too polite to mention it. She could just imagine them talking in whispers behind her back.

"I wanted to wish you all the best," Walter said. "With everything that's been happening around here, I know we haven't had much time to talk, but to tell you the truth, I'm a little hurt you didn't even mention you were seeing Tyler, let alone planning to marry him. One other thing troubles me, as well. I don't understand why you showed up at work today."

He means he doesn't understand why I haven't quit, she thought. "Walter, let me assure you that I'll never let my marriage interfere with my work," she said carefully. She wanted to add, "Or with us," but that wouldn't be the truth. How could it be? Tyler and Walter were blood enemies.

He gave her a quizzical look. "I meant, I'd thought you'd be off somewhere on a honeymoon."

"Oh. I thought—"

He held up his hand. "I know what you thought. But you were wrong. I have no intention of letting you go. You're a good girl. You're loyal and hardworking. I trust you, and these days, a little trust goes a long way. All I want is for you to be happy. I'd hate to see you get hurt." He hesitated, then turned to leave. "Good night, Linda. Enjoy your weekend. I'll see you Monday morning."

Coat in hand, he left her office. A few more goodbyes trickled in from the corridor, and then there was quiet. She swiveled in her chair to stare out the window. As touched as she was by Walter's concern, she couldn't help but wonder why he hadn't fired her. If I were in his shoes, she thought, *I* would fire me. "A little trust goes a long way," he'd said. How could he trust the woman who'd married his enemy?

Keep your friends close and your enemies closer.

Stop it, she ordered herself. This is all Tyler's doing. He's turned you into a paranoid mess.

She didn't want to believe that Walter was guilty. Didn't want to believe that someone who'd been so good to her could have committed those heinous crimes.

She had to learn the truth. Had to know which side of the fence to sit on, as Tyler had put it. The uncertainty was making her crazy, causing her to doubt everything anyone told her. If she didn't find out once and for all, she'd end up losing them both.

Maybe this Charlene character was on the level. Maybe she had information regarding Walter, information that could lead to the truth. Talking to her was worth a shot.

Linda had told Tyler she was planning to work late, and he'd said he'd be working, too. The stakeout last night had been unsuccessful, and he and Nick were going to try again. He'd said not to expect him home until midnight.

She had no reason to tell him she'd changed her plans.

After a quick dinner at the apartment, she rummaged through her closet, looking for something to wear. She couldn't show up at a place called the Starlite Lounge looking like a prude. If just the prospect of going alone to a bar made her feel uncomfortable, what would looking conspicuous do? You have to blend in, her mother always said. If no one notices you, you can't get hurt.

She brushed aside her oversize dresses and skirts with a sweep of her hand. Maybe Sadie was right. Maybe she needed a livelier wardrobe. Another thought came to her, this one making her smile. Soon, all these clothes would fit just fine. Not that she intended to wear them. Just because she was pregnant didn't mean she had to look frumpy. She laughed out loud. She was beginning to sound like Sadie.

Maybe this weekend she'd do a little shopping. But

what about the problem at hand? She needed something now. What could she wear that wouldn't make her stand out like a clothed woman on a nude beach?

Her gaze fell on the black leather skirt she'd worn the night she'd met Tyler. Why not? she thought. She'd wear the little halter top, too. That and some makeup, and she'd fit right in. Besides, it could be fun. Kind of like being in disguise. She felt a rush of excitement. Was this how Tyler felt when he went undercover? Okay, so she wasn't a cop, and Charlene seemed to know exactly who she was, but she was out to get information. Why not get in the spirit?

This time, she had no trouble putting in her lenses. That done, she applied her makeup and studied herself in the mirror. She smiled. Nancy Drew she wasn't.

She glanced at her watch. It was already after seven. I'd better get a move on, she thought, envisioning driving around and around, looking for a parking space. She had no intention of walking any great distance in that neighborhood. If she had to, she'd circle the block until she found a spot right out front. Eight o'clock, Charlene had said. Linda didn't want to be late and risk missing her. She grabbed her coat and headed for the door.

The parking fairy must have been in a good mood, because there was an empty spot just outside the lounge. In fact, the whole block was empty. This place sure is popular, Linda thought, grimacing. Well, if hardly anyone showed up, at least she wouldn't feel inconspicuous. Which meant she wouldn't have to remove her coat to display her skimpy outfit. Tugging the coat close to her body, she glanced at the neon sign above the door. Some of the letters had burned out, and the sign read, THE TAR T LOUNGE.

She was a half hour early. Now what was she supposed to do? If the inside of the lounge was as seedy as the outside, she was in deep trouble. No way would she sit in there, alone, for thirty minutes.

She decided to wait in the car. A man in a torn, scruffy coat teetered down the sidewalk, stopping to look at her through the passenger window. She averted her eyes. Oh, God. What was she doing here?

She counted to ten, then stole a glance out of the corner of her eye. Even though he was gone, her uneasiness hadn't abated. She couldn't just stay out here like a sitting duck. A cold fear swept through her. Sure, the doors were locked, but someone could smash a window, right? What if he had a gun? Well, that answered that. She was going in.

She drew in her breath and made a dash for the lounge. Inside, she couldn't see much. The only lighting came from the fluorescent lamp in the ceiling above the bar and from the lanterns on the small round tables. It didn't take her long to realize that they weren't lanterns; they were small lamps in the shape of topless hula dancers.

She headed straight for the back of the room and sat at a table. Her eyes now accustomed to the dimness, she could make out the tan Leatherette stools at the bar. A man in a dirty overcoat sat alone, drinking from a bottle. Next to the cash register behind the bar, a woman in a red bustier was reading a newspaper.

Linda fidgeted nervously in her chair. The wood frame creaked. The woman looked up, folded the paper and approached her. "Don't know why anyone reads that rag," she said. "First they say that Elvis came back from the dead, and now they say he's the father of quadruplets. Yeah, right. Quadruplets! What can I get you, sugar?"

"Um, nothing, thank you," Linda said, fascinated. The woman, who appeared to be in her mid-forties, looked like an aging dancehall girl straight out of a fifties' TV western. Her bleached blond hair was teased into a beehive; her makeup was so heavy she could have been wearing a mask.

"If you're going to sit here all night on your fanny, you're going to have to order something."

"Um, I'm waiting for someone."

"I just bet you are. Look, sugar, if you're not going to order something, you're going to have to take your business somewhere else."

Good Lord, did the woman think she was a prostitute? "A Coke," Linda answered, flustered. "Diet, in a tall glass with two cubes of ice. And a twist of lemon. No, make that a ginger ale. With two cubes of ice. But no lemon."

"Lady, you winding me up? I got no time for gags. I'm a busy person, in case you haven't noticed."

No time? The man at the bar was the only customer in the place. "I'm sorry. I won't take up any more of your time than necessary. Maybe you can help me. I'm waiting for a person named Charlene Butler. Would you happen to know her?"

To her surprise, the woman sat down next to her. "I'm Charlene Butler. You're early, Mailer."

"I'm sorry."

"Would you stop saying you're sorry?"

"Okay. Sorry."

Charlene rolled her eyes. "Look, why don't we get right to the point? Like I said on the phone, Ronald is dead. When I went through his papers, I found this." She pulled out a small crumpled envelope from the pocket of her tight black skirt and handed it to Linda. "It's got your name on it."

Something else was written on the envelope, as well. Scribbled under Linda's name were the words, "Upon my death." She looked back up at Charlene. "What's in it?"

Charlene looked insulted. "Do I look like the type who reads other people's mail? Besides, I don't want to know. Most likely, it has something to do with what's been in the papers, and I don't want to get involved. But I know Ronald wanted you to have this. I did what he wanted, and that's the end of it for me."

The man at the bar turned around on his stool and called, "Charlie! Get your fanny over here and bring me another beer!" With a shock, Linda realized that he was the same man who'd peered into her car.

"Hold your horses!" Charlene called back, hurrying over to the bar. "I'm coming!"

Linda tore open the envelope. She pulled out a yellowed piece of paper and examined it closely. Dated more than twenty-five years ago, it was a receipt made out to Parks Fine Jewelry for a safe-deposit box. She didn't recognize the name of the bank, yet a strange feeling passed through her, as if she'd come across this document before.

She chewed her lip, trying to remember. What was it about the receipt that seemed familiar? And then it came to her. Last August, when she'd been alone in Walter's home office reconciling his personal accounts, she'd come across another receipt dated twenty-five years ago. Only, that one had mentioned uncut diamonds and the name Van Damon. Thinking that the receipt had been misfiled, she'd tucked it in her purse, intending to file it properly at the office downtown. But she'd found no records there for Van Damon. She'd meant to ask Walter about it, but instead, she'd locked it away in her desk. She hadn't thought it important enough to probe further, but now, with the second receipt in hand, her curiosity was piqued. She knew that a lot of data had been archived. Maybe she'd been looking in the wrong place.

At the time, she hadn't questioned why she hadn't gone to Walter. Maybe Tyler was right. Maybe she'd been suspicious of her boss all along, but hadn't wanted to admit it.

The archives were located in the utility room across from her office. Although the room was kept locked, some of the employees, herself included, had a key. But hardly anyone ever went in there. If someone saw her searching through the dusty old boxes, he might become suspicious. She didn't want anyone asking questions.

No time like the present, she thought. Even though the jewelry store on the ground floor would be open until nine, she knew she'd be alone upstairs. She'd been the last to leave.

She placed the bank receipt into her purse. On her way to the entrance, she waved at Charlene. Charlene ignored her, but the man at the bar gave her a lewd smile. "It's a rough world out there, doll," he said as Linda passed by. "I'd hate to see you get hurt."

She gasped. Those were the very words that Walter had used.

Still feeling unnerved, she arrived at Union Square twenty minutes later. Most of the major department stores, as well as numerous art galleries, shops and cafés, were within walking distance from the square, and even though it was almost eight, the trendy district was bustling with shoppers.

She had a permit for the garage on Post Street, but she didn't like parking there at night. After working late, she never left the office without her pepper spray in hand. This must be my lucky day, she thought as she approached the jewelry store. Silently blessing the parking fairy, she pulled into a vacant spot just outside the store.

She considered taking the outdoor stairs up to the offices, just as she did every morning before the store opened. But she wanted to alert the security guard that she'd returned, so she decided to take the indoor stairwell at the back of the showroom.

"Evenin', Linda," the night guard said. "Thanks for the batch of cookies you left for me the other night. Loved the new recipe, and so did the missus." His smile faded, and he looked at her with disapproval. "Burning the midnight oil again, I see. How many times does that make it this month? They're working you too hard. After a full day, you shouldn't be stuck here in this place. You should be out having fun with your new husband. Congratulations, by the way. I hear he's a fine man."

Word certainly traveled fast. Why was she surprised?

The Parks network wasn't limited to family; it extended to Walter's employees.

"Thank you, George. Yes, Tyler is a fine man, and you're right, I work too hard. But you know how it goes. Every business has a busy season. Thanksgiving and Christmas are just around the corner."

But it wasn't the approaching holidays that had been taking up her time. Because of the upcoming audit, she'd been swamped with work. Even though she hated being alone upstairs—no one else ever stayed late, not even Walter, who disappeared every day at five with his secretary—she felt she had no choice. There were only so many hours in a day. She never would have had the nerve to stay alone if not for the night guard downstairs. He was just a panic button away.

She smiled at him, then said, "Fine evening to you, too, George. I have some paperwork to go over, but I'll be long gone before midnight." Truth was, she didn't know how long she'd be there. She wasn't even sure what she was looking for.

Something occurred to her as she climbed the stairs. What if she found something incriminating? Would she confront Walter?

She chided herself for being such a worrywart. She felt sure she wouldn't find anything, that her sleuthing would prove fruitless. She might have abandoned the whole scheme if not for the words on the envelope, *Upon my death.* Ronald had been gone more than five years. Why had Charlene waited until now to contact her?

At the top of the stairs she entered the code for the alarm, then opened the door and stepped into the corridor. She switched on the lights. The place always looks so different at night, she thought with a shudder. Her heart pounding, she went directly to her office.

She hung up her coat on the hook on her door. At her desk, she fired up her computer, then pulled out the receipt from her purse. She checked through the account database, but found no reference to the bank in question. She searched through the filing cabinet. There, too, she came up empty-handed.

She opened the drawer to her desk. The receipt for the uncut diamonds lay just where she'd left it, in an envelope tucked beneath her memo pad. She left her office and went to the utility room.

A bulb hanging from the ceiling provided the only light. She found the box for the year in question and began leafing through the files. Outside the room, a phone rang, and she froze. Afraid to let anyone know she was there alone, she never answered the phone at night. She held her breath until the service picked up, then continued with her search.

The archives contained no reference to either receipt. In fact, not one dossier, memo or any other paperwork had been filed for the entire month of July. She knew that the archives were by no means complete, but she found it odd that July was the only month missing from this particular box.

She glanced at the receipts again, thinking she might have misread them. But no, she hadn't been mistaken. Both were dated twenty-five years ago, one July 11, the other July 26. Disheartened, she placed the box back onto its shelf.

A beeping echoed in the corridor, and her pulse

jumped. The fax machine, she realized, and let out a nervous laugh. Giddy with relief and feeling a little foolish, she turned off the light and left the storeroom. She closed the door and locked it behind her. Once back in her office, she decided to look up Van Damon on the Internet. She groaned. The screen had come back with thousands of hits. She keyed in "diamonds." This time only one item popped up, and she clicked on the link. What she learned startled her. Van Damon was a Dutch warlord living in Africa. One of his many illegal activities included smuggling uncut diamonds into the States. She didn't want to believe that Walter was involved, but what other explanation could there be for the receipt?

She powered down the computer. The humming from the processor ceased, and an eerie silence fell over the room. Eerie not because it was nighttime, but because something felt different. Something felt wrong.

I'd hate to see you get hurt.

Nervously, she lifted her gaze, and a piercing scream sliced through the stillness.

The scream, she realized, was hers.

Chapter Eight

The room was spinning. She began shaking, her heart started racing and she broke into a cold sweat. She felt all the color drain from her face.

You...

Forcing herself to breathe slowly, she tried to recall the words she'd need to help her get past the anxiety.

...will not die. You will get through this, no matter how bad you feel.

Tyler rushed to her side. "Linda, are you all right?" His voice sounded muffled above the ringing in her ears. "I'm so sorry. I didn't mean to scare you."

She wanted to tell him not to worry, that this had happened before and it would soon pass. But her breath was coming in ragged hiccups, and she could hardly speak. "C-can't breathe," she finally managed. She leaned forward in her chair, gripping the armrests. "Ch-chest hurts."

It's not the situation that's bothering you. It's all in your thinking.

She hated feeling this way. It had been years since she'd had a relapse. Yet even though her mind was draped in haze, she was able to discern the difference between this panic attack and all the others before it. The other attacks had arisen from fear; this one, strangely, had sprouted from relief.

Stay in the present. There's no danger.

Tyler's face slowly came into focus. Standing next to her, he eased her head against him and gently stroked her forehead.

When she'd seen the shadow outside her office door, her first response had been to scream. Only after he'd called her name and she'd realized who he was did the attack take hold. It was a delayed reaction, but frightening nonetheless. Her heartbeat could attest to that.

You are strong. You are brave.

She closed her eyes and, leaning into him, gave in to his touch. He had a way about him that was gentle and healing. His hands, soft and rough at the same time, felt cool against her skin, like balm on sunburn. She was reminded of that night on the beach when dizziness had overtaken her and he'd held her until it had subsided. Except back then, she'd been feeling the symptoms of pregnancy; this was different. This is what happens when you're caught off guard, she thought, chiding herself for her weakness. Not only did she hate feeling helpless, she hated when anyone saw her this way.

The revolving room finally came to a stop, and her breathing returned to normal. Embarrassed, she pushed his hand away and forced herself to an upright position.

"What are you doing here?" Her question came out as an accusation.

"Better not make any sudden moves," he said in a worried voice.

"You sound like a cop," she said dryly. "Do I look like a suspect?"

He winced at her tone. "I meant, I wouldn't want you to pass out."

"Oh, you'd just love that," she retorted. "It would give you the opportunity to play Mr. Macho when you scoop me up in your arms. Let me remind you that it's your fault I felt this way to begin with. You scared me half to death!"

To her surprise, amusement crossed his face. "You're saying I came up here deliberately to scare you just so I could make you feel better afterward?" He narrowed his eyes. "Why are you so gussied up?"

"Leave my clothes out of this," she admonished. "What you did tonight was just a repeat performance. What about what happened at the welcoming party? It was because of you I fainted. You can't imagine the shock I felt when I saw you. You must have felt like a real hero, rescuing the damsel in distress in front of a full audience."

His eyes were bright with mirth. "Now you're saying I shouldn't have gone to a party that was being held in my honor? I should have realized that you—a woman I knew only as Lyla Sinclair—would be there, and knowing this, I should have declined?" A wry smile came to his lips. "You must be clairvoyant. How did you know what I was feeling when you fainted?"

"What?"

"You said I must have felt like a hero. How could you know how I felt? You were out cold."

"Don't twist my words, Tyler. You know what I meant."

"Now you're saying that *I'm* clairvoyant?"

"You know, you missed your true calling. You should have been a lawyer. All I'm saying is that I resent the way you use me to pump up your ego, especially since you're the one who gets me in these predicaments to begin with."

"It was your decision to work late, not mine." His expression stilled. "That man works you too hard."

"Leave Walter out of this. I'm talking about the pregnancy. If I weren't having a baby, I wouldn't be feeling queasy all the time, and you wouldn't be playing nursemaid."

"Now you're blaming morning sickness on me? All this time I thought nature was the culprit. As for your getting pregnant, I wasn't alone in the room when our child was conceived, or have you conveniently forgotten that, too?"

"No, I have not," she said in a huff. "All I meant was that you seem to relish my weakness."

He threw up his arms as if in surrender. "Fine. You win. If you want to play the martyr, go ahead. Only do it alone." He headed for the door.

"Tyler, wait."

He turned back to her and frowned. "Why? Is there something else you'd like to pin on me?"

"I'm, um, feeling better now."

"Glad to hear it," he said sarcastically. "Except now I feel like hell."

"Tyler?"

His frown deepened. "What?"

"I'm sorry."

He sighed audibly. "Must be hormones."

Must be, she silently concurred. Why else would she be acting this way? It seemed that whenever she was with him, all she wanted to do was pick a fight. Hormones or not, she had no right to keep haranguing him. "I do tend to relegate blame, don't I?" she said apologetically. "And about that macho thing—I don't mind, not really."

A slow grin spread across his face. "Nah, you're right. Sometimes I get a little carried away. Sometimes I forget I'm not a superhero."

She laughed at that, then quickly sobered. "It's an admirable trait, wanting to save the world. I shouldn't have snapped at you. It's just that lately almost everything seems to set me off. Maybe you're right. Maybe it's hormonal. I never used to be this way. Even as a child, I was complacent." A memory took hold, and a sadness filled her.

"What is it?" he asked, looking at her with concern.

"Just something I remembered. My mother used to park me in the corner and forget all about me—I was so quiet, you wouldn't even know I was in the room. I'd watch her as she went about her work in the kitchen. I wouldn't take my eyes off her, for fear of her disappearing."

"You miss her," he said simply.

Did she? She wasn't sure. "My mother was a stern woman, with unbending rules. She became even stricter when my sister ran off to get married. But I didn't complain. She was a single parent, raising me the best she could. I admit it wasn't easy living with her, but she was my mother. I loved her. I didn't realize how much until it was too late. I fell apart when she died. And then, losing my sister… For a long time after, I felt incapable of taking care of myself. Oh, I don't mean functionally. I went through the motions. I did what I had to do. I mean emotionally. But time is a great healer, and I became stronger. I just never got over being afraid. But I'm tired of letting fear control my life. I'm tired of depending on others to make me feel safe."

She stopped suddenly. Those last two statements had sounded like a declaration of independence, and that surprised her. When had self-reliance become so important?

Then something occurred to her. As safe and secure as she'd felt in Tyler's arms, it had been her own doing, her self-talk and forced composure, that had ended the panic attack. Not only that, she thought with a sense of accomplishment, it had been the shortest attack she'd ever experienced.

He nodded. "I can understand that. Fear is like a prison. No one chooses to live that way. Maybe becoming a parent has something to do with your new outlook. Prospective parenthood has certainly changed how I see the world." He chuckled. "Like my views on marriage, for instance. I used to be a confirmed bachelor."

Had prospective parenthood really changed his outlook? she wondered. Or was his revised perspective merely an extension of the way he'd always felt? His reason for marrying her, to give his child a father, was based on his childhood. He'd missed growing up without a dad. She supposed his wanting to be a parent was as good a reason as any to get married. Who was to say what made a marriage work? But what happened when one of the incentives no longer applied? She'd agreed to marry Tyler for a number of reasons. One, their baby should have a father. Two, it made sense financially. Three, she would feel safe. But suddenly the last reason no longer seemed paramount. Yes, she still was afraid, but she was no longer willing to live, as Tyler had put it, in a prison of fear.

Great. She'd just gotten married yesterday, and already she was having second thoughts.

"Truce?"

Jarred from her thoughts, she looked up at his expectant face. Well, why not? They were married, and she might as well make the best of it. No one said they couldn't be friends. Besides, her other two reasons were still valid. She forced her doubts aside and answered, "Truce."

He gave her a shy smile. "You know, I never answered your question. You asked me what I was doing here."

"What *are* you doing here?" she asked tentatively.

His smile grew wide. "I decided to drop by the office and take my wife out for a night on the town. After months on the trail, Nick and I finally made the bust, and I wanted to celebrate. The perp had the decency to make his drug deal early in the evening, so after we booked him, I came right over."

"How did you get upstairs?"

"George Hammond, the night security guard, is a retired cop. He used to work for the department. We talked for a few minutes about the force. Actually, he did most of the talking, about the old days. Then, after congratulating me on our marriage—said I had great taste, by the way—he let me come up through the back stairs. He unlocked the second-floor door by remote."

"Why did you go through the store in the first place? You could have taken the outside stairwell. There's a bell. I would have heard it."

"But would you have answered? I would have sounded like an idiot, yelling at the top of my lungs through that steel door. Besides, I wanted to surprise you. Note I said surprise you, not put you in a coma. Which is why I called out your name as soon as I stepped into the corridor."

She felt her ire stirring. "Obviously you didn't call out loud enough. And why on earth would you think I'd want to be surprised? I hate surprises—didn't you learn anything in couples therapy? And even if I were inclined to like surprises, which I don't, you knew I was alone. What were you thinking, creeping up on me like that?" Some truce. He'd broken it in less than a minute. Angrily, she turned her head away.

Her gaze fell on the receipts lying on her desk, and anxiety quickly replaced anger. She had to hide them before Tyler saw them. Fact was, when it came to Walter, Tyler was the enemy. He was working for the other side.

But what if he'd already noticed the receipts? What if he'd memorized what was written on them?

Calm down, she ordered herself. He hasn't seen them. He might be able to keep a poker face with strangers, but she was his wife. Albeit, she'd been his wife for only a day, but she knew his expressions. If he'd seen the receipt for the diamonds, the look on his face would have given him away. She hadn't known who Van Damon was, but she had no doubt that Tyler would have recognized the name immediately.

"Can you get me some water?" she asked, forcing her voice to remain steady. "The cooler's just down the corridor." As soon as he stepped out of the office, she tossed the receipts into her drawer. He returned just as she was dropping her desk key back into her purse. "I'm much better now," she said, after gulping down all the water at once. "Thank you. And I'm sorry. Again. Sometimes I overreact. I'll try to watch that."

He shrugged. "Hormones," he repeated.

She looked at him and smiled. "You mentioned a night on the town. A celebration for cracking the case. Why didn't you go out with Nick? I wouldn't have minded."

"Aw, hell, I can't lie to you. This doesn't have anything to do with the drug bust. I mean, yeah, it does, but only because we finished early. The whole time I was sitting in the car, waiting for them to make the deal, I kept thinking about our wedding. Maybe it wasn't the most memorable ceremony, but marriage is a still a big step. It deserves to be celebrated in some way."

It seemed she wasn't the only one who had regrets about the way they'd handled it. "What did you have in mind?" she asked, her curiosity piqued.

"I didn't have anything in mind, exactly. I just knew I wanted to make up for last night. I tried calling you, but there was no answer. Then I remembered that you said you never answer the phone when you work late, so I thought I'd take a chance and swing by. I saw your car out front. This weekend, I'm buying you a cell phone, by the way. Not a very romantic wedding present, but a definite necessity. You'll feel a lot safer knowing that 911 is just a speed button away."

He really was a sweetheart, she thought, her heart growing warm. "If you still want to go out with your shrew of a wife, I'm game. A night on the town could be fun. I feel fine now. It was just the shock that made me woozy." She suppressed a chuckle. Here they were, a married couple, and they sounded as if they were making a date.

His gaze roamed over her, then lingered on her legs. "I see you're already dressed for the occasion," he said, his eyes shining appreciatively. "You look nice, Linda. Just like the night we—" He stopped abruptly.

"What is it?" she asked, alarmed.

His voice grew quiet. "You still haven't told me why you're dressed like that."

"What's wrong with this outfit?" she asked, tugging at the hem of her skirt. "You didn't seem to have any objection the first time you saw me in it."

"And I don't have any objection now. But you were wearing different clothes when you left this morning."

She felt her face flush. "I never realized that having a husband meant having a clothes monitor. If you must know, I went home after work. I changed my clothes and went downtown to meet, uh, Charlie. But then I remembered something I had to do at work, and I drove straight back to the office." She'd nearly blurted "Charlene," but thankfully she'd remembered the nickname the man at the bar had used. Charlene wasn't an uncommon name, but why take a chance? Tyler would know plenty about Walter's previous accountant, including the first name of Ronald Pritchard's girlfriend.

He eyed her suspiciously. "Charlie?"

"Don't get all ruffled. Charlie's a woman."

"You've never mentioned anyone named Charlie, and you still haven't told me why you changed your clothes."

He was acting like a husband who'd come home early and found his wife in bed with his best friend. Did he really think she'd gone out to meet another man? Impatience and astonishment warred inside her. Impatience won. "Contrary to what you might believe, you don't know everything about me. We might be married, but we're still strangers. You don't know everyone I know. Take Charlie, for example. What is this, anyway?" she charged on. "The third degree? What are you, my keeper?"

"Why are you being so defensive? I'm not your keeper, but in case you've forgotten, we're married. We can't go around doing our own thing without advising each other of our plans."

"The way you advised me of *your* plans? What about the way you sneaked in here? You know what I think? You didn't want to surprise me, you wanted to catch me off guard." Involuntarily, she glanced at her desk drawer and then quickly averted her gaze. "Just because we're married, don't think I'm going to let any information regarding Walter fall into your hands. On the contrary, I'm going to be more careful than ever."

"I'm not spying," he said tartly. "I admit it would be nice having my wife on my side, but trust me, I'll get Walter with or without your help, and I won't have to stoop to his methods to do it."

She shook her head. "I want to believe you, really I do, but what else can I think? You didn't come here to surprise me—no one could be that thoughtless. Sneaking around like a prowler, you nearly gave me a heart attack! So what else should I believe? That you came after me in a jealous rage? I suppose it makes sense, after the way you grilled me about the way I'm dressed. Did you think you'd find me in the arms of a lover?"

He let out an ugly snort. "You? A lover? I don't think so."

All right, so maybe he hadn't come after her in a jealous rage, but he didn't have to be insulting. "What's that supposed to mean?"

"Nothing. Forget I said anything."

"No, tell me. I want to know."

He sighed. "Linda…"

"Don't Linda me! Why is it so impossible? Am I really that repulsive?"

"You're the most beautiful woman I've ever met," he said quietly.

"Yeah, right. I think you've seen *Shrek* too many times. Either that, or you've never bothered to update your lines. Or maybe you think that just because I slept with you once, I'd be spoiled forever for any other man. Well, I have news for you, superstud. Not every woman falls in love with every man she sleeps with."

Oh, God. Had she just said what she thought she'd said? What was the matter with her? For someone who'd never been able to think of a comeback, she'd certainly come a long way. Only now, she'd gone too far. After what she'd just blurted, he probably thought she'd been with dozens of men.

"Are you?" he asked.

"Am I what?"

"In love with me."

She felt her face turn crimson. "Love? Who said anything about love?" *I* did, she realized, then dropped her gaze.

He tilted her chin with his hand. "Linda, look at me."

"No."

He eased her up from her chair. "What are you going to do?" she asked, her heart beating wildly.

"I'm going to kiss you."

"This isn't a good idea," she said nervously.

"Then say the words," he murmured, his face dangerously close to hers. "Tell me not to. Tell me you didn't like it when I kissed you on the beach. Tell me you didn't like it the night we met."

The memory of that first night unfolded like a movie in slow motion. She saw herself wearing the outfit she had on now. Saw herself sitting at the table in the lounge with Sadie. Saw herself smiling at the handsome young man who'd approached them.

Saw herself kissing him, right out in the open, after Sadie had left.

After *Sandra* had left.

"I liked it," she answered, meeting his gaze. "I liked it a lot."

With an ardency that surprised him, she threw her arms around his neck and lowered his head to hers. "Oh, I liked it just fine," she said in a throaty voice.

Her sudden transformation sent his senses reeling. What had just happened? Why the sudden melt? She must have sensed his misgiving, because she pulled away and looked directly into his eyes. "I know we got off to a bad start," she said, smiling apologetically, "but that was because we didn't know what to expect. We got married so fast. We hardly knew each other—we still don't. We're still trying to find our way."

He supposed that made sense. Sort of. "About last night—"

"Shh," she said, placing her fingers on his lips. "I know I came on a little strong. I thought you'd like it, especially after the way I'd kept you at arm's length. It was all my fault. I didn't know the rules."

"There are no rules," he said gruffly. "It's just that you took me by surprise."

She smiled demurely. "Are you saying you don't like surprises, either?"

He slipped his arms around her waist. "I'm saying I want you to be sure."

"I'm sure," she whispered. "I've never been more sure of anything. I want you, Tyler. Now. Here."

He'd been an idiot last night. How could he have told her to slow down when he, himself, had been on the verge of losing control? Well, nothing would stop them now. He'd held back these feelings too long—feelings for her, feelings he'd never experienced with anyone else. "You're so beautiful," he murmured into her hair, pulling her closer. "So incredibly beautiful. In my wildest dreams, I never believed I'd hold a woman like you in my arms."

Raw emotion took over. With an urgency he couldn't contain, he thrust her against the wall, pressing his body against hers. His mouth crashed on hers, his tongue eagerly seeking the depths of her mouth. She clasped her hands around the back of his neck, her mouth clamped to his, igniting the need in him like a brush fire. Then suddenly, he was the one against the wall, her breasts pressed against his chest, and then they were rolling, bodies revolving as if in perpetual motion—his on hers, hers on his—along the wall.

"Do it," she said in a voice that nearly drove him over the edge. "We're alone. No one's coming."

A scene from an old crime movie flashed through his head. He imagined himself in the role of the tough hero, sweeping clear the top of her desk, scooping her up in his arms, then setting her down on her desk, climbing on top of her…

"Damn computer," he muttered, swiping his hand through his hair. It took up half the desktop.

She laughed. "Come here," she said, tugging at his arm as she lowered herself to the floor. "This is why carpets were invented."

She looked so innocent, the way she sat on her knees, beckoning to him with large, expectant eyes. Yet she was his temptress, tilting her head suggestively, her mouth curling up in that tantalizing way. He didn't have to be cajoled. She was incredible, and he couldn't take his eyes off her. Couldn't believe he was finally going to make love to her again. Couldn't believe they'd have night after night of that kind of bliss.

He knelt before her, too moved to speak. He slid his hands under her halter, and she let out a sigh of pleasure. She lay back, pulling his body on top of hers. She reached under his jacket, her right hand gripping his belt, her left hand on his holster.

Her hands stopped moving.

"Get up."

He stared at her, baffled.

"Get up," she repeated.

Jeez, not again. "What's the matter?" he asked, his pulse still hammering. He pulled to a sitting position, and she did the same. Suddenly he was alarmed. Had he hurt her? For God's sake, she was pregnant. What was he thinking? He had to learn to control himself.

"Take off your jacket," she ordered.

He felt a slow tug at his mouth. Ah. So that's how she wanted to play it. Tough. The one in control. This was a continuation from last night, but tonight he had no intention of botching it.

"You got it, lady," he said, pulling off the jacket. "Is there anything else you'd like me to remove?"

She stared at him, her face pale. "That," she said, motioning to his gun. "Take it off. Please."

He removed the holster and placed it on her desk. "There. Is that better?"

"No. I can still see it. Cover it with your jacket. I don't like guns."

"You're afraid of them," he said matter-of-factly. Now that was bright. Of course she was afraid. That wasn't lust shining in her eyes; it was fear, sheer and naked. "You're right to be scared," he said carefully. "Guns are dangerous, and in the wrong hands they're disastrous. But you're married to a cop. I live with guns, and now so do you." He eased her to her feet. "I want you to touch it," he said softly. "I want you to get to know it. I want you to know what it feels like."

She pushed away his hands. "I already know what it

feels like. I already touched it. At the hotel the next morning. You were still asleep. I saw it lying on the bureau, I touched it and then I ran off. I don't like guns," she repeated.

It was fine to have a healthy fear of guns, but she was bordering on hysteria. "It helps to talk about it," he prodded gently. "Didn't you say that you don't want fear to control your life? Linda, can you tell me what happened?"

"I just told you. I touched it, and it frightened me."

"That's not what I mean. What happened to make you so scared?"

"You know what happened," she whispered. "My mother was shot."

"Touch the gun," he said, determined to get her past this. "Don't worry, the safety lock is on, and I'll help you." He took her hand in his and placed it over the weapon. "That's not so bad, is it?"

"No," she said with uncertainty. "I guess not."

"I'm going to take my hand away. When I do, tell me what you feel."

She nodded slowly. "Okay, I'm ready."

He lifted his hand. "Well?"

"It feels the same as before. Cold. A chunk of metal."

"That's exactly what it is." He picked it up, and with a flip of his finger the magazine dropped out. He pulled back the slide on top of the gun and locked it. "Now it's not loaded," he said, putting his finger in the empty chamber. "I want you to hold it."

She took it from his hands. "It's heavy."

"It's a .40 caliber semiautomatic Beretta. You bet it's heavy."

"It could go off," she said nervously. "I could kill you."

"It's not loaded, remember?"

"But what if it was? Accidents happen."

"Statistically, the chance of dying from an accidental discharge of a firearm is one in two hundred thousand. You're almost thirty times as likely to die in a car accident."

She frowned. "That's a cheerful thought."

"Look, I'm no advocate for or against gun control. All I'm saying is that guns don't go off by themselves. As I said, you're smart to have a certain amount of fear, but remember, guns have no magical power. Tell you what. Tomorrow, I'll take you to the firing range, and we'll fire off a few rounds. You'll feel more comfortable after that."

"I don't know. I'll have to think about it." She put down the weapon. "I don't know how anyone can say he's comfortable with guns."

He could sense from her tone that she was still upset. "Linda, tell me what happened. All of it."

She spoke slowly, staring at the gun. "My mother told me not to go, but I went anyway. I was tired of listening to her go on and on about how boys were bad, how they only wanted one thing. All my life I'd done exactly what she'd told me to do, but that night I didn't listen. There was this boy, Daniel. Daniel Farber. I had a huge crush on him, but until that day, he'd acted as if I didn't exist. He asked me to go with him to a party, and I said yes. I couldn't believe he liked me."

"And then?" Tyler asked gently.

"My mother was supposed to be out—she worked at a cocktail lounge downtown—but that night she was home sick. After she went to bed, I sneaked out of the house. I waited for Daniel on my front porch. I didn't tell him that my mother was home. I was afraid he'd think I was a baby, if he knew I'd had to sneak out like that."

She stopped, and Tyler waited for her to continue. He could see how difficult it was for her to talk about what had happened, and he didn't want to push her. When she started to speak again, her voice was hard. "Daniel was friends with Timothy Sands, the boy who shot my mother. They ran in a rough crowd, the same crowd that was at the party. When Daniel and I arrived, I knew right away I'd made a mistake. Some kids were chugging beer and others were doing drugs. Some were taking turns going into the bathroom in twos and threes, doing God knows what. I told Daniel to take me home, but he laughed, called me a freak. I went upstairs. I thought if I stayed hidden, I'd be all right. Sooner or later, the party would break up, and Daniel or someone else would drive me home."

The creep probably came after her. Date rape, Tyler thought, and felt a surge of rage. So help me, he vowed, even after all this time, if I get within one foot of him... He didn't know what he'd do, but he knew it wouldn't be pretty.

"Nothing happened," she said, immediately putting his mind to rest. "But I decided I didn't want to wait around and take a chance. So I left. No one even noticed. I left and walked the four miles home."

"Thank God nothing happened," Tyler said, not bothering to hide his relief. In his relatively short career, he'd come across the same scenario time and again, except that the endings had been tragically different.

"Thank God?" she repeated, blinking. "When I got

home, there were police cars everywhere. My mother had been shot in cold blood, and for what? A handful of costume jewelry and a few measly dollars. Later, people kept telling me it wasn't my fault, but the fact remains, if I hadn't gone out that night, if I'd listened to her, she'd be alive today."

He gently pulled her to him and stroked her hair. "You couldn't have known what would happen. No one could. Sands is to blame, not you. He broke into the house. He shot your mother."

Suddenly agitated, she pulled away. "I knew what was going on, don't you see? At the party, while I was waiting upstairs in a bedroom, I overheard a boy's voice coming from the hallway. I went to the door and peeked out. He was bragging to a girl about a robbery that had taken place a few houses down from mine. He described how Timothy had orchestrated the whole thing, how he'd made sure no one was at home, how he'd broken in and gotten away with more than five hundred dollars. When the girl asked where Timothy was now, the boy laughed. I should have figured out what was happening, but I didn't want to admit that I'd been used. I felt so stupid. It was all a setup, my getting invited to that party." She looked down at her hands. "I was a nerd, and I dressed like I belonged in a convent. Timothy had heard about me from some kids at school. I'd told them that my father was a foreign correspondent, and that soon he'd be coming home for good. But that wasn't all. I'd said that he'd given my mother some expensive jewelry so she wouldn't forget him. How ridiculous was that? But they'd believed me, and Timothy, apparently, had believed them. He got Daniel to invite me to the party so the house would be empty. And it would have been, if my mother had gone to work."

"Timothy is locked away for life," Tyler said. "What happened to Daniel?"

"Even with my statement, there wasn't enough evidence for an arrest. He disappeared after Timothy's trial, and that was the last I heard of him." Tears flowed freely down her cheeks. "Daniel was the first boy who ever paid any attention to me. I'd never believed that someone could like me, and until that night I'd never disobeyed my mother. When she died, part of me died, too. Time went by, and men started asking me out, but I wasn't interested. Maybe I believed I was undeserving, I don't know. I just knew that something in me was missing." She smiled shyly through her tears. "You were the first, Tyler."

She was saying she'd been a virgin that night at the hotel. A thirty-year-old virgin. Yet as inexperienced as she'd been, she'd made him feel as if no other man had ever mattered. No other man? Hell, he'd been the only man, period. It was true that not all women felt pain the first time they made love, but dammit, how could he not have known that she was a virgin?

"Let's get out of here," he said, fearing his voice would catch in his throat.

The office was no place to consummate a marriage. Their first time together as man and wife had to be special. But he didn't know when that would be. It could be tonight or sometime in the future. All he knew was that he wanted her to want him as much as he wanted her, without false bravado, without pretense. As wonderful as their first night had been, it had been based on fantasy. He wanted honesty. He wanted the real thing.

Chapter Nine

Tyler was waiting for her in the parking garage when she arrived at the apartment. He pushed the button for the elevator, and silently they entered, the tension inside so thick she swore she could see it.

"I'm a little more tired than I thought," he'd said as they left her office. "Tonight's bust was a little tricky, and it's just catching up with me now. Do you mind if we postpone our night on the town for another time?"

She wasn't surprised that he'd wanted to go straight home. Who wanted to be around a wet blanket like her?

Why was the elevator moving so slowly? The apartment was only four floors up from the basement, but at this pace it might as well have been on Mars.

She couldn't believe the things she'd told him. Couldn't believe she'd spoken about her past at all. Maybe it was the cop in him, but Tyler had a way about him that got her to open up. She wasn't sure how that made her feel. On the one hand, she didn't want to trust him. As long as he was working against Walter, she'd have to watch what she said. On the other hand, she'd liked how she'd felt in his arms, in spite of her earlier resolution not to depend on anyone to make her feel safe. She'd found herself wanting to confide in him, wanting him to reassure her that nothing bad would ever happen to her again.

She had to admit, though, reassurance wasn't all she'd craved, and safety wasn't the only thing she'd desired in his embrace. She'd tried to convince herself that the stirrings she felt weren't real, that the way she was dressed had catapulted her into a kind of alter ego. Yeah, right. Who was she kidding? Her outfit had merely helped her shed her inhibitions. She would have wanted him even if she'd been wearing a pillowcase, and she wanted him now.

But Tyler had rebuffed her twice—in their bedroom and at the office. How many times could she take his rejection? He'd once said that he wanted a real marriage; obviously his definition differed from hers.

Granted, she was the one who'd broken the mood when she'd felt the gun under his jacket. But the way he'd practically whisked her out of her office, after she'd confided in him, had been nothing short of abrupt. Before they'd left, she'd gone to the ladies' room to splash cold water on her face, and when she'd emerged he was already at the exit in the corridor, holding her coat, anxious to leave.

The elevator passed the second floor. So slow... agonizingly slow. Not wanting to meet his gaze, she stole a glance out of the corner of her eye. He was watching the floor numbers flash overhead as the elevator continued its snail-like ascent.

She didn't know what she'd been thinking, coming on to him like that, not once, but twice. She'd never been the sort of person to make the first move. Make the first move? Come on, be honest, she reprimanded herself. Until she'd met Tyler, she'd never even considered having sex. Now, the problem was, she didn't know how to proceed. Was it her aggressive behavior that had turned him off? He hadn't complained that first night at the hotel. She didn't know what she was doing wrong; it wasn't as if she had much experience to fall back on.

The number four lit up, and she stole another glimpse at him. His gaze was still locked on the overhead display as though it contained the answers to all the secrets of the universe. The elevator finally came to a stop and the doors opened, and in continued silence they headed down the corridor.

He unlocked the door to their apartment, then turned to her with a shy smile. "I hope you're not angry about the change in plans. I think this is better, anyway. We could use some quiet time alone. It's true what you said in Reverend Nelson's office. We don't really know each other at all."

She couldn't argue with that, and she knew exactly what they could do to amend the situation. She'd give it one last try; after all, it took three strikes before you were out. But she'd learned a thing or two from her last two attempts. This time, she'd be less direct.

"Aren't you forgetting something?" she asked coyly.

"You first?" he asked, moving aside so she could enter.

"Always the gentleman. But no, I'm not talking about etiquette. It's customary for the groom to carry the bride over the threshold. You didn't get a chance to do it last night."

He hesitated, then gently gathered her up into his embrace. She wrapped her arms around his neck, and… nothing. He didn't even look at her as he set her down in the entryway.

"I didn't have time to eat tonight, and I'm famished," he said. "What about you? Are you hungry? What do you say we order a pizza?" He took their coats and hung them on the rack, then plopped down on the futon. He kicked off his shoes and leaned back, resting his feet on the coffee table.

Pizza? The last thing on her mind was pepperoni and cheese. She sat next to him, regarding him closely. She couldn't deny that he looked tired, and maybe he really was hungry, in which case a meal would revitalize him. He'd need all the energy he could get if they were to finish what they'd started at the office.

"Why order out when we have a full freezer?" she asked casually. Delivery was so slow, and she'd waited long enough, thank you very much. To be precise, thirty years for her first and only time, but who was counting? "I've already eaten, but I can nuke you something. It'll save us a lot of time."

You didn't get more subtle than that. Nevertheless, she resolved, if he rebuffed her again, she'd nuke him instead.

He kissed her on the forehead. "No, I don't want you

to bother. You're tired, too, and you've had a stressful evening. We have to think about the baby."

Since when was nuking a frozen dinner stressful? "Tyler, I'm perfectly fine," she insisted, frustration setting in. She was more than fine, and she wasn't the least bit tired. She felt like a revved up engine with no place to go.

Strike three, she thought miserably.

He took out his cell phone and was about to start dialing, when suddenly it buzzed in his hand. After speaking in that cryptic cop terminology, he disconnected, frowning. "So much for a quiet evening at home. That was the precinct. Gotta go, sweetheart. There's trouble with a case." He kissed her again, this time on the cheek. "Don't wait up for me. I don't know when I'll be back." He grabbed his coat and was gone in a flash.

What had just happened? She wasn't referring to his sudden exit; as a cop's wife, she knew she'd have to get used to his being on call. She was referring to the way he'd treated her, as if she were a porcelain doll. And what were those chaste kisses all about? He'd acted as if she'd shatter if he so much as touched her.

She entered the bedroom to change into her pajamas, catching her reflection in the mirror on the door. No wonder he doesn't want me, she thought. Her outfit had "one-night stand" written all over it, and their one-night stand was long over.

Her mother's voice entered her head. *Cheap. Tawdry.*

She stripped off her clothes in front of the mirror, then let out a small derisive laugh. He thinks I'm beautiful, she thought. He must be blind. She scrutinized her naked reflection. Okay, so maybe she wasn't that bad.

Her legs were long and shapely, her waist still trim even though she was almost three months pregnant. Her firm breasts were larger and fuller, but basically it was the same body.

Yet the closer she stared, the more she became convinced that something about her was different. Maybe it was because of the way she now wore her hair, bouncing freely down her neck, framing her heart-shaped face. She held the strands back with her hand, then let them fall loosely once again. No, that wasn't it. Maybe because of her contacts? No, that wasn't it, either. She couldn't figure it out, but something about her had definitely changed.

She turned away from the mirror and slipped into her flannel pajamas. Even though it wasn't even ten o'clock, after washing up in the bathroom she climbed into bed. In no time at all she felt herself drifting off to sleep, a strange dream filling her head with fairy-tale nonsense. She saw herself locked in a chamber at the top of a castle, like Rapunzel with long, flowing hair. "I can't get to you," a man in a soldier's uniform called out, and she immediately jolted awake.

"You must have felt like a real hero, rescuing the damsel in distress," she'd told Tyler, earlier that evening in her office.

A realization washed over her, and she groaned out loud. Afraid to come near her because she was so inexperienced, he was treating her like the proverbial virgin princess. But what about that night at the hotel? How could he have forgotten that?

She turned on the lamp on the nightstand and glanced at the clock. Four o'clock in the morning. She'd been asleep longer than she'd thought. She climbed out of bed and tiptoed to the door. Worried it might creak, she opened it slowly. In the dimness, without her contacts in place, she could barely make out the living room. Her eyes adjusted to the darkness, and her gaze rested on the futon where Tyler was sleeping soundly. At least, she thought it was him. It could just as easily have been the pillows. As quietly as possible, she darted back to the dresser and groped for her glasses. She returned to her post at the door, and what she saw made her heart flip over. Wearing only his shorts, he was lying spread-eagled on the futon, the linen heaped in a pile on the floor.

She didn't know why she found the sight so endearing. Maybe because he looked so young and vulnerable. She recalled when she'd run out of the hotel scared out of her mind. Now, the memory seemed almost ludicrous. He'd been asleep then, too. He hadn't been a threat that morning, and he wasn't one now.

She wanted to snuggle close to him, wanted to feel his arms around her. She realized then what had been different about her reflection in the mirror earlier that night. She'd seen the face of a woman in love.

Darn—no, make that *damn*—she didn't want to feel this way. She'd never wanted to fall in love. "I told you it would happen one day," she imagined her best friend saying. Well, Sadie would have a good laugh now. Except, Linda thought, if it was so funny, why wasn't she laughing?

The answer to that was obvious. How could she allow herself to love a man she didn't fully trust? As long as Walter remained between them, trust would remain elusive.

And what about how Tyler felt? She especially didn't want to be in love when the feeling wasn't mutual. Or was it? The way he'd held her and looked at her were all telltale signs that even she, a woman of little experience, could read. If he wasn't in love, he was on the edge.

He'd told her he wanted a real marriage, but for some reason he couldn't seem to reconcile Lyla with Linda. "Lyla or Linda," he'd said, "a name is a just a tag. It doesn't change who you really are." Obviously, he was confused. He might be falling in love; he just couldn't decide with whom.

She turned and went back to bed, leaving the door open behind her. She'd struck out three times, but this was just the first inning. She knew what she had to do. Subtle? She planned to give the word a whole new definition.

"What's that wonderful smell?" she asked, stretching luxuriously.

"Sleeping Beauty awakes," he said, looking her over with appreciation. Damn, even in her terry cloth robe, she was delectable. The amazing part was, she had no clue as to the effect she had on him. He returned his attention to the pan sizzling on the stove. "Hope you like pancakes," he said, skillfully tossing one into the air and catching it just as deftly.

"Apparently, the tango isn't your only secret talent. You certainly are a jack-of-all-trades. Can I do anything to help?"

He served her a generous helping. "Yes. You can eat. You have to keep up your strength. I have a full day planned for us. First, a visit to the wireless phone store.

Then, on to the shooting range. After that, I thought we'd go shopping. The apartment could use your feminine touch. And, of course, we'll need baby things, too." He regarded her carefully. "Unless you have any objections. We don't have to do anything, if you don't want to. We're married. We make the decisions together."

She sat down at the table. "I'm okay with all the shopping, but I'm not so sure about the shooting range."

"Tell you what," he said. "Once we get there, give me five minutes. After that, if you want to leave, I won't argue."

She cast him a dubious look, then sighed. "All right. Five minutes, but that's all."

He smiled to himself. His motives for helping her get over her fears weren't completely selfless. Inside that tangle of doubt and fear was a vibrant, courageous woman, and that woman was the one he wanted for his wife.

He served himself a stack of pancakes and sat down next to her. "Later, I thought we'd go out for dinner, and afterward, if you're up to it, maybe we can catch some blues at a club downtown."

"Dinner? What happened to lunch?"

"You're having it. In case you haven't noticed, it's already past noon."

She took a bite of the pancakes. "Mmm, these are good. I could get used to this."

"To serve and please. That's my motto."

She laughed. "That's 'To serve and protect,' but I don't mind the amendment."

Two hours and the purchase of one cell phone later— Does this come in different colors? Don't you have anything smaller? What do you mean we get charged for incoming calls?—they pulled into the parking lot outside the shooting range. Inside the building, he waved at a few familiar faces and reserved a lane.

"Before we shoot anything," he told her, "we need to play school."

"Ooh, that sounds like fun," she said, flirtatiously. "If I give you an apple, will you give me a bite?"

I'll give you a lot more than that, he wanted to say, but held back. There was something about a woman in tight jeans and knee-high boots that heated up his blood. Down boy, he ordered himself. You need to focus. Guns are serious business.

He led her to a row of rooms in back and unlocked a door. "These are the classrooms," he explained. "This place offers a full course in the handling of firearms."

She smiled brightly. "Okay, Teacher, ready when you are."

They entered the room and sat down at desks. "First things first," he said, picking up a small revolver from a side table. "This is a .22 caliber revolver. It's the perfect gun to start with. It's easy to handle. I'm sure you'll catch on right away."

"I have no doubt." She leaned back in her chair, crossed her legs, then uncrossed them again. "I have the best teacher in the entire school."

He wished she would stop doing that. How could he concentrate with her crossing and uncrossing her legs? "Rule number one," he said, forcing his attention back to the gun. "Always assume that the weapon is loaded." He opened the chamber and spun it around. "Empty, see?" He handed it to her. "Now it's your turn."

She took it hesitantly, then looked inside. Relief crossed her face. "Empty. Now what, Teacher?"

"Rule number one. Never point the gun at anything you don't want to destroy."

"Rule number two," she corrected, crossing her legs again. "Rule number one was always assume the gun is loaded."

"Good. You're paying attention." He wished that he could, dammit. He cleared his throat. "Rule number three. Keep your finger off the trigger until you've made the decision to shoot."

"We wouldn't want to fire prematurely," she said without batting an eyelash.

O-kay. "And lastly," he continued, choosing to ignore the remark, "always be aware of the target, especially what's around it." He then gave her a brief explanation on how the gun discharged.

"Five minutes," she said.

"Excuse me?" he repeated.

"Five minutes, you said. I believe they're up."

He put down the gun and sighed. "All right, you win. Let's go."

"Don't be silly, Teacher. I'm enjoying this. Now, where were we?"

Women. Did they all go to the same secret school to learn how to torment men, or was it a natural talent? He picked up the gun. After showing her how the mechanism was put together, he demonstrated how to load it, using blanks. "So what do you say?" he asked. "Care to fire off a few rounds? We don't have to, if you don't want to. We can leave right now."

"Just call me Annie Oakley."

For a brief moment he saw the old fear in her eyes, but she quickly recovered. He had to give her credit. She was determined to go through with this.

He handed her protective glasses and earplugs. "Safety gear," he explained as they headed toward the firing lane. "Gun blasts are pretty loud. You'll still be able to hear me, though, with these plugs in place."

"I understand the reason for the earplugs, but why the goggles?"

"Sometimes you get a backlash of sparks." He looked at her face for a reaction, but saw nothing. She was determined to prove how tough she was.

He attached a paper target to a wire and reeled it out in front. He loaded the gun, this time with live ammunition, then placed it beside the open window that looked out onto the range. "Stand with your right foot slightly ahead of your left. Place your weight on the balls of your feet."

"Like this?" she asked, leaning backward.

"The balls of your feet, not the heels." Standing behind her, he placed his hands on her waist and gently pushed her forward. "There you go."

"Do you do this for all your students?" she asked, looking back.

"You're the first person I ever taught," he admitted. "But maybe I should look into this as a second career. It seems to have some definite perks."

"Now what, Teacher?"

"Pick up the gun with your right hand. Pretend you're shaking hands with someone you want to impress. Keep your trigger finger extended straight along the side and lock your thumb down to tighten your grip. There. That's it."

"Is the safety lock on?" she asked, her voice becoming tremulous.

"Yup, safe and snug." He lifted her left hand and placed it in position next to her right hand. "See that switch? When you're ready, you'll flip it down to undo the lock. But before you do that, let's work on your aim." He gestured to the human outline on the target. "Keep your left thumb over your right, and hold the gun steady. Focus on the center ring."

"Is that supposed to be my attacker? Where's his nose? Couldn't they make something more realistic?"

He rolled his eyes. "This isn't art school, Linda." He explained how to align the gun with the target, and how to gently squeeze the trigger. "Ready?"

She took a deep breath, then exhaled. "Ready." She released the lock, took aim and fired. "Wow! Did you see that? It was like the Fourth of July! Did I get him?"

"No, but you weren't too far off."

She leaned out the window. "How far off? I don't see any holes in the target."

"Uh, about two feet away."

"Oh. That's not good, is it?"

"Here, let me help you." From behind, he placed his arms around her. He cupped his hands over hers, and together they raised the gun and took aim. "Steady now," he said, feeling a mite unbalanced himself. His chest pressing against her back, he could feel the rise and fall of her breath as she slowly squeezed the trigger.

"How did I do this time?" she asked, looking back at him over her shoulder.

"Better. You hit the target. But the idea is to shoot for the guy's chest, not his feet."

She turned around and gave him a coy look. "You'd better show me again. I don't think I understand exactly what I should be doing."

That makes two of us, he thought. Why couldn't he keep from touching her? "Let's try it again," he said, pretending to study the target. She faced forward, and once again he wrapped her in his arms.

"Tighter," she said. "I need all the support I can get."

So do I, he thought, taking in the scent of her hair. Standing near her in the close confines of the lane was scrambling his senses. He held her tighter. "Ready?"

"Ready when you are." She released the catch and fired, then put down the gun. "How did I do this time, Teacher?" she asked, still facing forward.

His hands dropped to her waist, his body still pressed against hers. "Much better."

"I think I have the general idea," she said, moving his hands slowly down to her hips. "You don't have to aim for me, but if you could hold me like this, it'll help keep me steady." She picked up the gun and aimed. This time, she was the one to ask, "Ready?"

Oh, he was ready, all right.

"Bull's-eye!" she sang out after the gun had exploded.

Bull's-eye? He peered at the outline. She'd nailed the poor guy right in the crotch. Tyler recoiled, as if he was the one who'd been shot. "Lesson's over. Time to go."

"Just when I was getting all worked up," she said, reluctantly handing him the gun.

Someone was getting all worked up, but it sure as hell wasn't her. "Are you saying you want to stay longer?"

"I thought I'd try something with a little more power. I'm just getting started."

This was the woman with the deadly fear of guns? "Wait here." He returned shortly with a larger revolver. "This is a .38 special. It's powerful enough to win a gunfight, but its kick is mild enough for even a woman to handle."

She raised a brow. "Even a woman?"

He shook his head. Give a female a weapon, and suddenly she's a feminist. "Wrong word choice," he muttered. "I meant, amateur."

"But not for long," she said smugly. "I'm a quick study, in case you didn't know."

She was amazing. Not only had she conquered her fear, she'd proved to be a reasonably good shot. He leaned against the wall and folded his arms across his chest. "I didn't know, but I'm learning, sweetheart. You'll find I'm a quick study, too."

"I'm a little tired," she said six rounds of ammunition later. "I'd like to skip the rest of the shopping, if that's okay. Why don't we go back to the apartment? I could use a short nap. It's too early for dinner, anyway."

"We can skip dinner," he said, suddenly worried. "I shouldn't have planned such a full day. I don't want you overdoing it."

"I'll be fine," she assured him. "Besides, you promised me a night out on the town."

He had to admit, he didn't want to cancel their dinner plans. He'd made reservations at a new Italian bistro downtown. It was small and cozy, the perfect prelude to intimacy. Even though he was filled with desire for her, he was determined to wait until the time was right before they consummated their marriage. Intimacy wasn't just about two bodies groping in the dark. It was about getting to know each other, about learning what made the other person happy.

But most important, it was about honesty. If they wanted their marriage to work, they'd have to talk frankly and openly about the issue that threatened to destroy it. They'd have to talk about Walter. A quiet dinner in a neutral setting would help set the stage.

"I made reservations for eight. Will that give you enough time?"

She smiled. "It's perfect. And Tyler? Thank you. I don't see myself ever packing a piece, as they say on TV, but at least now I won't break into a cold sweat every time I hear the word *gun*."

"No problem," he said, a warm feeling flowing through him. Step one in Operation Linda had been a success. Next, step two, an intimate dinner with his wife.

She brushed her lips along his cheek. He knew it was meant to be merely a simple affectionate gesture, but the feel of her mouth on his skin sent his pulse into overdrive.

Step two? His brain might still be in the planning stage, but the rest of his body was soaring ahead.

He was on the futon watching a video, when his cell phone buzzed. "Jeez, not again," he grumbled. These days, it seemed to be raining criminals. "Carlton," he grumbled into the phone, expecting to hear either Nick's or the captain's voice on the other end.

"Tyler, can you come in here, please? I seem to be having a small problem."

Linda? Calling him from the bedroom? Problem?

The baby. Something was wrong. He rushed into the bedroom. "What's the matter?" he asked, anxiety knotting inside him.

She was lying in bed on her side. Drawn up over her shoulder, the blanket was slightly bunched lower where her hands peeked out, as she played with the buttons on the cell phone. "I was testing the phone, and I was wondering what this little thingamajig is."

Relief flooded through him, and then irritation took over. "You called me from the bedroom for that? Jeez, Linda, I thought something had happened."

"Don't be ridiculous. If something had happened, I would have yelled for you." She rolled onto her back and sat up, the blanket dropping to reveal a generous expanse of cleavage. With one hand she clutched the fabric to keep it from falling lower; with her other hand she passed him the phone. "So, can you?"

"Can I what?" he asked, memory filling in what the blanket covered.

"Take a look at the phone, silly. Tyler, what is it? Why are you looking at me that way?"

Why was he looking at her that way? "You're… naked," he said, barely getting the words out of his mouth.

"Well, of course I am. I didn't want to put on my pj's. It's not nighttime, for heaven's sake."

He didn't understand the logic in that, but at the moment nothing would have made much sense. The temperature in the room had escalated to heat-wave proportions, and he suddenly had trouble breathing.

She pulled the blanket up to her chin. "I've embarrassed you. I'm sorry. But it's not as if I'm not covered up. Besides, you've seen me in the buff before. If something slips out from under the blanket, so what?"

If something slips out? Now why did she have to go and say that? He had visions of her body slipping out, bit by bit. First one long, graceful leg, then the curvaceous turn of a hip, followed by a creamy, white shoulder, culminating in the display of what he'd already been given a sneak preview. He'd told her earlier that sometimes he forgot he wasn't a superhero. At the moment, he'd trade in his shield for X-ray vision in a heartbeat.

"But if it makes you uncomfortable," she continued in a maddening matter-of-fact voice, "I'll put something on. Would you mind handing me my robe? It's on the armchair."

He supposed that after he gave her the robe, she'd ask him to turn around while she dressed. Holy Moses, hadn't she heard about the power of suggestion? How could anyone be so cruel?

Cruel—or wily? He grinned. "You don't want your robe," he stated, matching her businesslike tone.

"True, it is a little warm under the blanket—"

"And you don't have a problem with the cell phone."

"Well, actually, that little button—"

"No, the problem isn't with the phone," he said, setting it down on the nightstand, "although we do have a problem with communication."

"How so?" she asked, flashing innocent eyes.

"I don't understand why I'm fully dressed while you're in your birthday suit."

"I've been wondering the same thing," she said demurely. "That's why I called you in the first place. As a matter of fact, I think I'd much rather stay home this evening, unless, of course, you have any objections. We're married. We make all the decisions together."

"The clothing dilemma is easily remedied," he said, undoing the buttons on his shirt, "and all objections have been overruled." He glanced at the phone and then picked it up.

"I thought you said there was no problem," she said, looking at him quizzically.

He turned off the buzzer. "Not anymore."

So much for their quiet, intimate dinner in a neutral zone. His reasons for wanting it had suddenly fallen away. Or so he told himself.

He set the phone back down and then pulled off his shirt. He reached for the blanket. Tomorrow. Tomorrow, they'd deal with the rest of it.

Chapter Ten

How could he tell her what he felt? He wanted to look at her, study her, memorize every detail. The way her long shimmering hair splayed across the pillow like an exotic fan. The way her breasts gently rose and fell with every breath she took. The way her eyes bathed him with promise and desire.

He felt his throat constrict. He'd waited a long time to be with her like this again, and he had no intention of rushing.

Naked, he climbed into bed and lay on his side next to her, propping himself up on his elbow. "So beautiful," he whispered, caressing the curves of her body.

She rolled onto her side, facing him. He fingered the medallion lying in the valley between her breasts—the medallion he'd given her on the night they'd met—and his heart turned over. He'd wanted her to have something to remember him by, not knowing he'd be leaving her with something that would tie them together forever.

The baby was their first miracle. The second was that they were now husband and wife.

Brushing his lips against hers, he leaned in close. Weaving a wavy path with the tip of his tongue, he inched his mouth lower, stopping long enough to taste one nipple, and then the other, before continuing slowly down to her belly.

She stiffened, only slightly, but he sensed her unease and raised his head. "You can stop me anytime," he said gently. "I don't want you to feel uncomfortable in any way."

"No, I don't want you to stop. It's just that I never…I don't know the rules."

He grazed her fingers with his lips. "Just let yourself feel. There are no rules."

"No rules. That's what you said yesterday." She gave him a shy smile, then pulled his head to hers.

It was all the invitation he needed.

Several long kisses later, he carefully pulled away to plant his lips over her eyes, her chin, her throat. She felt as if she were melting. Slowly he continued his descent, exploring every inch of her along the way, as though memorizing her with his fingers and his mouth.

He raised his eyes and she met his gaze. Brushing his lips across the swell of her belly, he maneuvered her legs over his shoulders. After moistening his fingers with his mouth, he slipped them inside her, then lowered his head. A thrill ran through her.

She closed her eyes and sighed, but just when she was about to abandon herself to these new sensations, he stopped. Her breath came in gasps as he stroked her thighs with his tongue, teasing her gently. She let out an involuntary moan, and he quickly returned to the object of her pleasure, sucking gently while pressing his fingers inside her.

This was a new experience for her, but she felt just like she had that night at the hotel—no hesitation, no holding back. "You realize," she said throatily, "if you stop again, I'll have to kill you." She pushed down on his shoulders, pulling him closer still. Arching forward, she abandoned herself to him completely as a series of shuddering spasms took over her body.

When her breathing returned to normal, he rolled over to lie next to her, folding her into his embrace. She snuggled against him, flushed with the warmth of having been loved. "Not that I'm complaining," she murmured, "but I'm a little confused. I thought I was supposed to be seducing you."

"Sweetheart," he said, pulling her on top of him, "the night is still young. And like I said, there are no rules."

She grabbed his head with both hands and firmly planted her mouth on his. *Is this really me?* she wondered, amazed. *Can I be this way without the costumes, without the pretense? Why not?* She wasn't the same woman she'd been three months ago. Hell, she wasn't the same woman she'd been yesterday. She remembered her initial fear when she'd picked up the gun. It hadn't been easy, but she'd done it. She'd had to prove to him she could. Had to prove it to herself.

These days, it seemed she was proving a lot of things, not that making love with Tyler required much effort.

"Just the night?" she teased. "Don't you mean the entire weekend? I can tell you're a man who likes to take his time."

Not that she minded. She'd liked the way he'd adored her with his eyes, the way his languid tongue had caressed her, the way she'd responded with a powerful climax, and now she intended to return the favor. She lowered her head, but apparently he had other ideas. Gripping her waist, he pulled her to a kneeling position above him, the tip of his arousal pushing against her. He eased himself inside her, then withdrew and entered her again, then again and once more, leaving her gasping until finally he pulled her down against him, sheathing himself inside her.

They rocked in perfect unison, lazily and steadily. Heat spread throughout her body, and gradually she increased the pace. At the hotel he'd been on top of her, and she'd liked the feel of his weight. But she liked this, too, maybe even better. She liked being in control. From the look on his face, she could tell he liked it, too.

They moved together in an easy, steady rhythm. Her breasts, fuller and more tender because of the pregnancy, tingled under his careful touch. If he so much as breathed, she felt a throb inside her, and with each thrust he made, she felt herself quiver.

He sat up, and she wrapped her legs around him. She didn't mind relinquishing control. They were equal now, shoulder-to-shoulder, face-to-face. She met his gaze, and in his eyes she saw her own need. Under his frank regard, she felt her face glowing.

He lowered his lips to her throat, and she moaned. Or was the moan coming from him? She couldn't be sure. But it didn't matter. They were like one, moving together in a steady, fluid motion. When he nuzzled his mouth between her breasts, this time she was certain that the moan came from her.

Clutching his arms, she pushed against his feverish body, their pace increasing as his thrusts grew harder. He reached below to touch her at the same time that she reached down to touch him, their fingers probing, feeling the wetness.

"Don't stop," she murmured. He didn't. He moved with long, steady thrusts, faster and harder, hips moving, until finally he released his stream of passion, leaving them both breathless.

She snuggled close to him, and he wrapped her in his arms. "Off the scale," he said, grinning.

"You weren't so bad yourself, Teacher," she said, laughing. "If I'd known sex could be this good, I never would have taken up baking."

He reached over and caressed the slight swell of her abdomen. "I hope this is okay for the baby," he said, suddenly looking anxious.

"Physically, there's no problem. As for the rest, I'm sure our child has far better things to do than be a voyeur."

He looked at her with amusement. "Oh, yeah? Like what?"

"Like lie in there all curled up, thinking about how wonderful his or her life is going to be." She grew thoughtful. "Tyler, do you think babies get to choose their parents?"

"If that's true, I must have been asleep when I was given the choice. Either that, or I really messed up."

She traced little circles on his chest. "How can you say that? You loved your mother, didn't you? And the bottom line is, if you'd had different parents, you wouldn't be the person you are today."

He frowned. "And what's so special about that? I'm just an ordinary Joe trying to get by in the world."

"You're not ordinary, Tyler. You're a remarkable person. You have more integrity than anyone I've ever known, and you have the courage to act on your beliefs."

He let out a scornful laugh. "I think you're confusing courage with revenge."

"You can't fool me, Tyler Carlton. I see through your facade."

"Oh, yeah? And what facade is that?"

"You're not as broken as you think you are. If you were, you wouldn't have the capacity to make me so happy."

"You're one to talk about a facade. On the outside, you come across all business. But the truth is out, Mrs. Carlton—you're really a warm, caring person."

"And sexy," she reminded him, sliding her hand across his abdomen. "Or have you forgotten Lyla already? I think she's getting a little lonely."

"So demanding," he teased. "You're getting a little bossy in your new role of mistress of the domain."

Mistress of the domain. She liked the way that sounded. "Complaining already, my lord?" She moved her hands down to his groin and, immensely pleased with herself, felt him grow hard in her hands.

"Do I sound like I'm complaining?" He pulled her back on top of him. "Thomas at your command, my lady."

Linda was humming when she arrived at work Monday morning. She was sure everyone knew how she'd spent the weekend, sure it was written all over her face. But she didn't care. She was a woman in love, and she wanted the whole world to know.

She looked at the stack of papers on her desk and sighed. How could she focus on work when she couldn't stop thinking of him? How could she concentrate when every thought brought a shiver of pleasure?

Enough daydreaming, she told herself. Time to return to earth. She unlocked her desk and opened the drawer. And stared. Something was different. Something was wrong. Her memo pad was upside down, her tray of pens shoved to the back.

The receipts, she thought with panic.

They were gone.

"Do you have a moment, Linda?" Walter asked, suddenly at her side. Startled, she looked up at him. It was as if he'd materialized out of thin air.

Walter. Walter had keys to everything. "Of course," she said, trying to keep her voice from betraying her.

He closed the door behind him. "Are you almost done checking the records? The IRS is sending someone over on Wednesday. How do we stand?"

"There's nothing to worry about," she mumbled, feeling the blood rush to her cheeks. Damn blushing. Her face would always be a dead giveaway.

"Good." He paused. "You're a good girl, Linda. I can trust you."

She felt as if her face were on fire. Why did he always have to say that? He patted her on the shoulder and turned to leave. She drew in a breath. "Walter, wait." She couldn't just let him walk out. She had to know if he'd taken the receipts. "What can you tell me about Ronald Pritchard?" she asked, her heart pounding in her ears.

His looked at her with suspicion. "Why do you want to know?"

"There were a few entries in the ledgers I couldn't reconcile. I thought maybe the previous accountant might have filed information somewhere else, and that maybe you, uh, forgot to mention it." Now that was obvious, she thought, dismayed. She wished he would stop looking at her like that.

He shrugged. "What can I tell you? Ronald Pritchard was incompetent. He was a compulsive gambler who let his addiction control his life. I tried to help him. At first, I even paid off his debts. I tried to get him into therapy, but he wouldn't go. Even after I discovered he was involved in some sort of illegal operation to fund his habit, I kept him on. I didn't want to have him arrested. He'd had too many bad breaks in his life already. But five years ago, his debts got out of hand, and when I refused to cover them, he resorted to embezzling. I had to let him go."

"What sort of illegal operation?" she asked, trying to sound nonchalant.

"I don't suppose you've ever heard of Van Damon," Walter answered, just as matter-of-factly. "He's the infamous Dutch criminal who made his fortune in Africa by looting diamond mines. Apparently, Pritchard had been making deals with him behind my back, smuggling in uncut gems at a reduced price, then funneling them into the market. But Van Damon wasn't stupid. Why should he deal with small fry like Pritchard? After a while, he approached me, but, of course, I turned him down."

"I see," Linda stated. Why was Walter so willing to disclose this information?

"All this isn't classified," he said, as though reading her thoughts. "The reason I never mentioned it before is because it's ancient history, and I never thought it would come up again. But with the investigation under way, you probably should know everything. The more you're aware of, the better prepared you'll be if you're questioned." He gave her a twisted smile. "You and I both know I'm not guilty of those reprehensible crimes they're accusing me of, but if you find anything out of the ordinary in the records, I want you to come to me immediately. The authorities have it in for me—I wouldn't put it past them to embellish something that's not quite clear."

"If the truth is there, the authorities will find it," Linda said. She didn't know what else she could say without sounding suspicious.

"Will they? Some people resent the way I do things, professionally as well as personally."

"If you mean Tyler—"

He raised his hand as if to ward her off. "Let's not go there. I can tell you're happy, and I don't want to say anything to make you feel you have to choose between us. Right now, I'm talking about Robert Jackson, the prosecutor assigned to the case. He's tricky and ambitious. A conviction like this would cement his career."

"Surely you don't think he'd do anything illegal," Linda said.

"Sadly, yes," Walter answered. "Just because you work on the side of the law doesn't mean you live there. I know what I'm talking about. How do you think I got Timothy Sands arrested? Everyone has a price, Linda. It's a tough lesson to learn, but the sooner you learn it, the better off you'll be. Less disappointment that way. Fewer expectations shattered."

She felt slightly woozy. "What are you saying? That you bribed the authorities?"

"I'm saying that I did what I had to do to secure your safety. He murdered your mother. What difference does it make how he got thrown back in jail? He's where he belongs."

After Walter left her office, Linda sat back in her chair, thinking. Walter had taken a risk by going outside the law to ensure her safety. Was going outside the law so wrong when it was done in the name of justice? Somehow, she knew how Tyler would answer. He would say yes. And yet, shouldn't justice prevail? Wasn't that what Tyler believed in above all else?

Ethics aside, she couldn't ignore the fact that Walter had taken a risk for her, and immediately she was filled with guilt for thinking he had broken into her desk. But if he hadn't taken the receipts, who else could have done it?

She felt a sinking in the pit of her stomach. What about Tyler? If he believed that justice must prevail above all else, surely he wouldn't let a little indiscretion like stealing from her desk stand in his way.

She thought back to Friday night. What if he'd seen

her shove the receipts into the drawer? What if the look on her face had set off an alarm? Before leaving, she'd gone to the washroom to freshen up. She hadn't taken her purse with her. He could have easily looked inside and scooped out her keys.

Walter had said he didn't want her to feel as though she had to choose between him and Tyler, but wasn't that exactly what she had to do? Who had taken the receipts? Tyler, because he needed evidence, or Walter, because he had something to hide?

Because of what Walter had done for her, she wanted to give him the benefit of the doubt. And yet, with all her heart, she wanted to believe in Tyler.

If anyone had answers, it would be the one person, outside of Walter, who knew what the receipts meant. But Ronald was dead, and the dead couldn't speak.

An idea came to her. Tyler was working tonight. He'd never have to know what she was up to. It was time she had another talk with Charlene Butler.

Tyler sat at his desk in the precinct, trying to catch up on the mounting pile of paperwork that filled his inbox. He couldn't concentrate. The memory of the weekend was still fresh in his mind, and he was impatiently waiting for the day to end so he and his bride could resume where they'd left off. The problem was, tonight he was staking out an illegal gambling parlor and he didn't know when he'd be home. For the first time in his life, a regular nine-to-five job began to look appealing.

Something else occupied his thoughts, as well. Knowing that Mark would be at the bookstore today,

Tyler had stopped by on the way to the precinct to talk to him about a case. He leaned back in his chair, as the events of that morning unfolded in his mind...

"I have news," Brooke had chimed in, after joining him and Mark in the café. "I'm so happy, I could shout it to the world."

Mark took his wife's hand and said, "Derek got an interesting tidbit of information in the mail."

Tyler's curiosity was immediately piqued. A few months ago, Brooke's father, Derek Moss, had come forward with his stunning story, claiming he'd seen Walter throw Jeremy's body overboard on that ill-fated cruise twenty-five years ago. But Tyler knew that Derek's testimony wasn't enough to warrant an arrest; the prosecution needed more evidence. Tyler held his breath, waiting for Mark to speak again.

"Seems that Walter wasn't the only one who did a little philandering," Mark said. He immediately added, "Sorry, bud. That was callous of me."

Tyler shrugged. "You don't need to mince words. Fact is, Walter and my mother were involved. I'm evidence of that. Go on," he urged.

"No, let me tell him," Brooke said, her eyes gleaming with excitement. "Apparently, Walter's wife, Anna, was briefly involved with my father. They'd met on the cruise ship. But that's not all. Nine months later, Anna gave birth to a son, Benton. Anna gave him my father's real last name, Ross."

Tyler shot straight up in his chair. "Are you saying it's possible that Anna was with Derek when the murder took place?" One witness could be dismissed in court under the clever examination of a good lawyer, but two… "Where is this Benton guy? Can we get in touch with Anna? When did—"

"Slow down, bud," Mark said. "Derek's already talked to the D.A. You should know, however, that Jackson doesn't think anything will develop from this. But I wouldn't worry. We'll soon have Walter behind bars, regardless."

"Nothing will develop from this!" Brooke exclaimed. "Maybe not as far as the case is concerned, but you seem to have forgotten one small detail. I have a brother. I want something to develop, all right. I want to find Benton. All my life I believed I was an only child, and now I find out differently. No one can possibly understand how I feel. I can't wait to meet him."

Not understand how she felt? If anyone could empathize, Tyler was that person. He was in a similar situation, except that Brooke seemed to be handling the discovery of her father's philandering, as her husband had put it, a lot better than Tyler had handled the news that his mother had cheated.

Then again, Brooke's father hadn't been murdered.

But an attempt *had* been made on Derek's life. Tyler remembered the bullet Brooke had unwittingly taken for her father, and admiration for her climbed ten notches. In spite of everything that had happened, she saw only the plus side. She'd gained a brother in the process. And she'd found love.

It seemed that Brooke's situation was more like his than he'd originally believed, he thought now, sitting at his desk. He, too, had found love from all this. If not for Walter, he wouldn't have moved to San Francisco, and he wouldn't have met Linda.

Love. He repeated the word in his mind, as if it was a sacred oath. *Was* he in love? He wasn't sure. He did know, however, that he'd never felt this way before. Linda had reached a place in him he hadn't even known existed, as though she could see into his soul.

Oh, he was in love, all right, but the discovery didn't please him. Friendship—mixed with respect and a healthy dose of lust—was one thing, but love was something else. Love meant sharing everything in your heart, something he was loath to do. Linda had her own heartache to deal with; she didn't need his, as well.

But that wasn't the only reason he didn't want to love her. He thought about his parents. They were proof that love didn't last.

Soon after Tyler had moved to San Francisco, he'd met with Robert Jackson to review Walter's case, which had only recently been reopened. The prosecutor had shown him Jeremy's old correspondence, hoping that Tyler would find something the investigation might have missed. Much of the correspondence, however, had nothing to do with the case. It consisted of letters that Jeremy had received from Marla, Tyler's mother, written while in her last year at college before she and Jeremy were married. Reading them, Tyler had learned that his mother and the man he'd believed to be his father had once been very much in love.

Anger filled him. If they'd been so much in love, how could they have let it slip away? He might not have learned anything new regarding the case, but reading the letters had reinforced what he'd always suspected. Love was something anyone with half a brain should avoid. Look at the misery it had brought his mother.

One love letter in particular came to mind. It had described how over the summer vacation Jeremy and Marla used to watch the sunset, planning their life together, sharing secrets as they sat hand in hand in the gazebo. Something stirred in Tyler's memory, but it was something he couldn't pin down.

His thoughts returned to the investigation. One letter from Jeremy had described a box of files that contained details regarding Walter's smuggling activities. The letter had been addressed to the FBI, but because of Jeremy's untimely death, it had never been completed or sent. Its existence had raised a question. Jeremy had recently formed an alliance with Walter; if he'd become suspicious of his new partner, why had he gone on the cruise? The question had never been answered. But the question wasn't what was nagging at Tyler now. It was something on the edge of his consciousness, something he couldn't quite define.

After the accident, the Carlton estate had been searched, but nothing had been found. The letter to the FBI had stated that the box of files was in Jeremy's home office; Jeremy must have moved it just before the cruise. Either he'd feared it would fall into the wrong hands if something were to happen to him, or he'd believed that Walter planned to have the property searched while they were out at sea.

Once again, the love letter from Marla to Jeremy rose in his mind. He recalled the police report that had detailed the search of the old property. Feeling as if he'd been socked in the gut, he realized what had been eluding him. Nowhere in that report had he read anything about a gazebo.

* * *

Last week, Charlene had told her to come by at eight, so Linda figured that eight would be the best time to show up tonight. Not wanting to sit alone in the lounge any longer than she had to, Linda remained at the office until the last possible moment. This time, she didn't go home first to change her clothes. Funny, the threat of feeling inconspicuous no longer concerned her, but never would she deliberately choose to sit alone in a place whose sign read THE TAR T LOUNGE.

As before, the street in front of the lounge was empty. She pulled over to the curb, then entered the shabby establishment. The same seedy-looking man she'd seen last week was drinking at the bar.

"Look who's back," he said, giving her a lewd smile. "Did you miss me?"

Ignoring him, Linda headed to the cash register, where Charlene was reading the paper. "Hi," she said pleasantly. "I hope you don't mind my coming back."

Charlene looked up. "It's a free country. Can I get you something?"

"No, I just came back to ask you a few questions."

"Talk's cheap, sugar. I told you last week, you can't just sit around taking up space. The boss don't like it."

"Well, the boss isn't here now," Linda stated with more bravado then she felt. She pulled out a twenty and slid it across the bar. "Maybe this will help." Good grief, had she actually handed over a bribe?

Charlene pushed back the bill. "I think it's time you stopped watching those old gangster movies. Go to the table in the back and I'll be there in a minute." She glanced at the man at the end of the bar, then lowered her voice. "In case you haven't figured it out, Max over there is the owner of this firetrap. He don't like me schmoozing with the customers, and I don't need to give him an excuse for canning me."

Linda headed for the same table she'd sat at before, and Charlene arrived a few moments later, carrying two glasses. She sat next to Linda and said, "I brought us a couple of Cokes. Max don't like me drinking on the job, and I can tell you're a teetotaler. I told him I'm on break, but you better make it fast."

"I'll get right to the point. I need to find out more about Ronald."

Charlene shrugged. "What's to tell? A quarter of a century gone down the toilet. Twenty-five years I gave that man. I got nothing more to say. I don't need more trouble."

Linda took a sip of her Coke, studying Charlene over the rim of the glass. "You sound bitter."

"Bitter? Damn right I'm bitter. You'd be bitter, too, if you'd wasted the best years of your life, and all because of that low-life piece of garbage."

Linda had figured Charlene to be in her mid-forties, but the harsh lines on the woman's face made her look older. She had the appearance of someone who'd led a hard life. Linda regarded her with curiosity. "If you were so unhappy with Ronald, why didn't you leave him?"

Charlene let out an ugly snort. "Who said anything about Ronald? I'm talking about Walter Parks, the man you work for."

Linda's mouth dropped open. "Walter! What do you mean?"

"I don't mean nothing," Charlene quickly added. "Forget I said anything. I told you, I got enough trouble."

Having lived with fear so long, it was something Linda recognized easily. "You're afraid," she said softly. "But keeping quiet won't make the feeling go away. Unless you face it straight on, it'll stay with you forever."

"You're talking about Timothy Sands, the man who killed your mother."

Linda gasped. "H-how did you know?"

"You work for Walter, don't you? Ronald made it a point to learn everything he could about him. After he went into hiding, he was like an animal stalking its prey, waiting for the right time to pounce." She looked down at her hands. "'Course he never got the chance. He died last week of the cancer, just like his old man done ten years ago."

"Last week! I thought he died five years ago."

"Twenty-five years," Charlene said as though Linda hadn't spoken. "Until five years ago, we lived together. Any day now, he'd say whenever I brought up marriage. Any day he'd get his break. I knew he was a gambler when I met him, but he was doing all right. He was a lucky man, he liked to say. And he had a nice, cushy job. It was real respectable, working for that fancy jewelry store. But he was always waiting for the big break. Said a woman like me deserved the best. Said I deserved to live in style."

"Why didn't you get married?" Linda asked. "What happened?"

"What happened?" Charlene repeated, spitting out the words. "The break never came, that's what happened. And then he was gone. No phone call, no note. Nothing. When the cops came pounding at the door, I couldn't tell them anything, even if I'd wanted to. For months, I didn't hear from him. Like everyone else, I believed the papers. Thought he was dead. Then, just like that, he showed up on my doorstep. Said he still loved me, but he had to stay in hiding. He'd changed his identity—got all new papers, driver's license and everything. But he said we couldn't live together. Said it was too dangerous. So we had to sneak around."

"I guess you know from the media that Walter will probably be indicted," Linda interjected. "You'll be subpoenaed to testify."

Charlene smiled wryly. "I don't think so, sugar. What would they want with me? They questioned me five years ago, and as far as the world knows, I haven't had anything to do with Ronald since. The man I was seeing wasn't my Ronald anymore, and I got the death certificate to prove it." She peered at Linda. "Even if you go to the cops, you got no proof."

Linda thought about the receipt for the safe-deposit box, which was now missing. Even if she still had it in her possession, it proved nothing. "How long do you think it'll take before they realize that the name on the death certificate is wrong?" she asked after a long moment. "Someone, somewhere, has seen the two of you together. Sooner or later, they'll figure out that the man who died last week was Ronald." She covered Charlene's hands with her own. "You wouldn't have called me unless you wanted it all to come out in the open. You did it for Ronald. You did it because you loved him."

Charlene's laugh was scornful. "Loved him? The

man was a coward through and through. He was always afraid. Afraid that Walter would come after him. I wanted a real home. You know, a little house, a couple of kids. I wanted marriage." Her demeanor suddenly softened, and she sighed. "Yeah, I loved him, in spite of everything, in spite of all his empty promises."

"Tell me," Linda gently prodded. "Tell me everything."

Charlene took in a breath before continuing. "Ronald had a gambling problem, and because of that, he was just the person Walter needed. Walter covered his debts and kept him out of the hands of the mob—in return for Ronald's soul, I always say. Walter was doing dirty business with some creep named Van Damon, and he made Ronald keep a separate set of accounting books. I'm not proud of what I'm going to tell you, but remember, I didn't learn all the details until recently, when Ronald found out he was dying."

She picked up her glass and took a long swallow. "Five years ago, Ronald got into a hell-load of debt, and Walter wouldn't cover it. Ronald needed money real bad, so he resorted to blackmail. He told Walter he'd go to the police about the smuggling if Walter didn't give him the money. Let me tell you, Walter was mad. So mad that he put out a contract on Ronald. Ronald went underground, and I didn't hear from him for months. Like everyone else, I thought the mob had got him. But then there he was, on my doorstep."

"It must have been so hard on you," Linda said, her heart going out to the older woman. "But why didn't he go to the police?"

"He couldn't go to the cops without incriminating himself. Don't forget, he was the one who'd kept the second set of books. He'd be arrested as an accomplice. His blackmail attempt had been a bluff, a stupid scheme that cost us our future." Charlene put down her glass. "Before he went to Walter with his scheme, he stole the books and locked them in a safe-deposit box. Extra insurance, he said. When he got sick, he got even more paranoid and moved the books again. He was afraid that Walter would get his hands on the evidence. He said that Walter had ways of finding things out. Said he had connections in high places."

Her mouth quivered, and a tear rolled down her cheek. "Just look at me, blubbering like a baby." She wiped her cheeks with the back of her hand. "In the end, it wasn't Walter that got him. It was the cancer. His father died young, and so did his brothers. That last night at the county hospital, he said he wanted to set things right. Said he was sorry about everything, and that he wanted Walter to pay for what he'd done. He vowed that if he couldn't bring Walter down while he was alive, he'd do it after his death. He said I should get in touch with you, that you'd know what to do. Then he told me to search through his belongings back at the apartment and take anything I wanted. I went through everything, even his old papers. That's when I found the envelope with your name on it."

Ronald must have addressed the envelope before he decided to move the books from the safe-deposit box, Linda figured. "Where are the books now?"

"He told me he'd hidden them somewhere on the old Carlton estate. He said it would be the last place Walter would look, since it had already been searched twenty-five years ago, and now it was abandoned."

The newspapers had been full of details about the massive, run-down property. Linda didn't recall the exact address, but she remembered that it wasn't far from an antique store Sadie had once dragged her to. "Where on the estate?"

"I don't know. He was rambling in the end. I could barely make out a thing. He was talking about artichokes, can you believe? And garages, too, for some reason. Nothing he said made sense. I don't know any more than what I've told you. He died before he could tell me anything else."

Max slammed his bottle down onto the bar and both women looked up. "Break's over," Charlene said. She rose from her chair and scooted back to the bar.

Even though Linda felt sorry for Charlene, she didn't entirely trust what the woman had told her. What if Ronald had been lying? What if Walter had no idea that these books even existed? Maybe Walter's story was true. Maybe Ronald had been conducting a little business on the side. Ronald could have kept a record for himself—making it look as if the transactions were his boss's. Extra insurance, he'd told Charlene. Linda had to find those ledgers and examine them—with an accountant's eye—before the prosecution did. Even if what Walter had told her was the truth, he wouldn't stand a chance once the authorities got hold of the books.

Innocent until proven guilty. She had to give him a chance to explain. She owed him that much.

She couldn't afford to wait. Once the police spoke to Charlene, they'd be crawling all over the place like ants at a picnic. Tyler was working tonight, but his schedule changed from day to day. She didn't know when she would get another opportunity.

She'd learned from the media that the old Carlton estate was currently the object of a nasty court case. The heirs of its last owner were haggling over the proprietorship, and at present it was untenanted. She wouldn't have to worry about being seen if she went there to snoop, but where would she look first? Where on the property could the books be?

She turned off her cell phone. Tyler had told her he wouldn't be home until late, but this way, if he tried to call her, he wouldn't even have to know she'd left the office. She dropped the twenty-dollar bill onto the table and, ignoring Max again, waved at Charlene and headed for the door.

Feeling shaky, she started the car, then set off for Half Moon Bay. She couldn't believe she was doing this. In the moonlight, as she drove south along the coast, she barely glanced at the open land and farms whizzing by. She passed several roadside vegetable stands, her headlights briefly sweeping over them. But one sign in particular, lit up by a lone light on a pole, caught her attention. U-pick: Eggplant, Zucchini, Artichokes, it advertised. Something about it played on the edge of her mind.

Artichokes. Maybe Ronald hadn't been so incoherent after all.

It wasn't a garage he'd been rambling about, either, she realized. It was the carriage house, which, according to what she'd read, Jeremy Carlton had converted into a home office.

She wasn't superstitious, but the last thing she felt

like doing was traipsing around a spooky old estate, going through a dead man's office.

There's nothing to be afraid of, she reasoned. The property was abandoned. Had been for years. It wasn't as if Jeremy's—or Ronald's—ghost would suddenly manifest, demanding retribution. It wasn't as if anyone would be there at all.

Chapter Eleven

Linda pulled into the long driveway, the car's high beams illuminating the tall iron gates that barred the entrance to the property. The only other light came from the pale half-moon, casting an eerie glow across the Keep Out! sign. She ignored the warning and stepped out of the car. Crunching leaves and twigs under her low-heeled pumps, she plodded through a tangle of overgrown weeds,

She jiggled on the padlock, then peered through the gap between the gates. Behind the ivy-covered barriers, the old mansion jutted into the dimly lit sky like a medieval castle. She felt as if she'd been dropped into a gothic novel. Imagining dark foreboding walls, secret passages and torture chambers, she nearly bolted, but then, as if she could suck in courage along with air, she drew in a slow, labored breath. I didn't come all this way to be chased off by my imagination, she thought with resolve. When she turned the handle on the pedestrian door beside the gates, a loud metallic sound from the other side rattled into the silence. The clanking of chains, she realized. The door was as securely locked as the gates.

She had to get over to the other side—but how? The gates had to be at least twelve feet high, and although the adjacent wrought-iron fencing was several feet shorter, it was strung at the top with rows of barbed wire, rendering it as daunting.

A sudden snapping erupted, amplified like a shot in the night, and she jumped. Stay calm, she ordered herself. The place is abandoned. It was probably just an animal.

Was that supposed to be reassuring?

She glanced around furtively. Nothing moved. Except for a light breeze and the gurgling of a stream somewhere on the property, the night was as silent as a tomb.

Moments later, after reminding herself to breathe, she decided she couldn't leave her car where she'd parked it just outside the gates. All she needed was for someone to drive by and report it as "suspicious." She could just imagine the scene that would follow later at the police station, after Detective Tyler Carlton was called in to collect his trespassing wife. She climbed back into the car and drove a short distance until she found what she wanted. After pulling into a narrow service road, she parked next to a clump of overhanging trees that would hide her car from the main road.

She retrieved her flashlight from the glove compartment, then looked down at her purse. Large and gray and ugly, it was too cumbersome to be toting anywhere, never mind on a half-baked excursion through the underbrush. She let out a nervous giggle. What had possessed her to buy it in the first place? She tossed it onto the back seat. After removing the car key from its ring, she locked the door behind her, then attached the key to the heavy gold chain around her neck.

She gave the medallion a squeeze for good luck. St. Michael was the patron saint of policemen; maybe the protection would extend to amateur sleuths.

Shining the flashlight in front of her, she trekked along the edge of the fence, surveying the borders of the property. Chain links had replaced the wrought iron, but the fence was still topped with strings of barbed wire. About ten yards from where she'd parked, a large oak tree leaned into the yard. She stopped and stared, an idea taking hold.

No, she thought emphatically. I won't do it. I'm afraid of heights. What *aren't* you afraid of? a voice in her head tormented.

Dammit, she swore under her breath, suddenly reversing her decision. If climbing a tree was what it took to help Walter, then climb a tree she would.

Grateful she hadn't gone home to change her outfit, as she'd done the last time she'd met with Charlene, she silently blessed her practical leather pumps. After securing the flashlight under her belt, she maneuvered through the overgrown brush toward the tree. To her disappointment—and relief—the lowest branch was too high to mount.

You're not giving up now, are you? the little voice

taunted. A strategy began to gel. She could climb the links in the fence to propel herself into the tree, then climb a branch or two higher and hoist herself over the top of the wires and down the other side.

Easy as pie, she thought—easy as baking cookies, she giddily amended—as she mounted the fence. She grabbed hold of the branch and pulled herself into the tree. Now for the hard part. You can look, but not down, she told herself, as though recounting from a list of instructions. Maybe when all this is over, she'd write a book. She could call it *A Woman's Guide to Breaking into Private Property without Breaking Her Neck.*

The breeze filtered through the top boughs, and she squeezed her eyes shut, a line from an old nursery song popping into her head. *When the wind blows, the cradle will fall.* She began singing to the deaf air, then stopped abruptly. I must be crazy, she thought. Here I am facing death from a tree, and I'm singing nursery tunes.

She opened her eyes and looked at the branch above, immediately noticing a torn white cloth. Evidently, someone else had had the same idea. Hooked to a twig, the material could very well have been ripped from a person's shirt.

Ronald's?

Well, would you look at that, she mused, staring at her legs after she'd hoisted her body higher into the tree. Her rumpled black skirt had been pushed up way above her knees, exposing her thighs for all the world to see.

"So what?" she asked aloud. "Who's going to look? Owls?"

She peered into the yard. Now what? Apparently she

hadn't thought this through. Crouching on the bough, she clutched the next higher branch with one hand, retrieving her flashlight with the other. She aimed the light on the ground on the other side of fence. It was earth, she realized. Not concrete or brick. She could jump.

Or not. The drop was only seven or eight feet, but it might as well have been a hundred, and even if she did land safely, how was she supposed to get back up? She wasn't an acrobat, for heaven's sake. And she was pregnant. What if something happened to the baby? She remained motionless in the tree, chastising herself. How could she have been so thoughtless?

Well, that settled it. She'd climb back down, wait for another opportunity and come back with a ladder and wire clippers. But when she looked down again, she felt paralyzed. It was as if the tree had wrapped its boughs around her arms and legs.

Now what? she asked herself again, trying to hold back panic. Her phone, she remembered, relief flooding through her. She'd call for help. So what if she was branded That Loony Woman Who Got Stuck in a Tree? It wasn't as if she had another option.

But her phone was in her purse.

And her purse was in the car.

She gritted her teeth. You can do this, she said to herself, over and over as if reciting a mantra. She reached for a lower bough—

...will fall. The cradle will fall. The cradle...

—and slipped. As if in slow motion she tumbled down, and like Alice plunging into Wonderland, her descent seemed to go on and on. Finally, with a splat, she landed in a soft patch of mud on the other side of the fence.

She suppressed a few choice words. Grumbling to herself, she picked up her flashlight and trudged ahead. Except for a sore derriere, a few scratches along her legs and a shredded pair of panty hose, she was fine. "At least I'm in camouflage," she muttered, thinking of soldiers with mud-smeared faces. Except it wasn't her face that had been soaked with the sticky mud; it was her bottom.

Approximately twenty yards into the property, she came across the imposing four-story redbrick mansion, which, she knew, had been in the Carlton family for generations before it was sold for payment of back taxes. To the right was the old carriage house, which Jeremy had used as a garage for his vintage cars, and later, after he'd sold the collection, as his home office.

It was then she saw the gate to the woods. The lock on the latch had been broken off and was lying on the soft earthy ground. This time, she didn't hold back her language. If she'd known about the gate, all she'd had to do was lift the handle to gain entrance into the yard.

She headed toward the carriage house, carefully picking her way through the weedy terrain. The outer doors to the home office opened easily, but she quickly realized that they were merely a front. The original entrance had been kept up for decorative purposes only. Inside was a heavy oak door, and, like the iron gates in the driveway, it was padlocked.

She walked to the side of the large one-story building. The metal bars in the large window had been pried aside, the glass completely broken away. Ronald, she thought again. He'd probably used a crowbar, wearing thick gloves to avoid the shards of glass. Unlike her, he'd done his homework before attempting his break-in.

She climbed through the gaping hole, lowering herself safely to the floor. A rank smell assaulted her senses. In the direct line of the moonlight, something in the corner caught her attention. She approached it tentatively, keeping her flashlight pointed at the floor.

The carcass of a rat lay rotting in the corner.

Fighting revulsion, she swept the light across the walls and floor. Disappointment quickly replaced repugnance. Any evidence that this had been an office had been removed. The trip had been in vain.

She was about to hoist herself back onto the window ledge, when a noise outside arrested her. It was only the wind whistling in the trees, and she laughed out loud. But it was a nervous, giddy chortle. You don't believe in ghosts, she reminded herself.

She wasn't just thinking of Jeremy. This estate had history. Lineage. Here, in these decaying ruins, she could almost feel a presence, as though heritage itself were a living spirit. Four generations, she thought. What a blow it must have been to lose the property.

She tried to conjure up an image of what the carriage house might have looked like at the turn of the previous century. Horse stalls, complete with polished wood floors, concrete water troughs, cast-iron chutes and railings unfolded before her eyes. And horses, too, of course. Horses and finely crafted carriages.

Wait a minute. Would a place like this have an attic?

She pointed the flashlight at the ceiling, and was

looking for a trapdoor when another noise startled her. This time, it wasn't the wind; it was a car. Could someone see the flashlight from the road? Not wanting to take any chances, she switched it off.

Suddenly, the noise disappeared. It didn't gradually taper off, the way a car driving into the distance would sound, but ceased altogether. Whoever had been driving had cut the engine. The old Carlton estate was the only property off the road; whoever had been driving would be headed this way.

Choking back fear, she groped her way in the dark and climbed back out the window. Barely moments later, a brilliant light pierced the air just outside the fence. She stood perfectly still. The only sound above the stream and wind was the pounding of her heart.

She heard a click, and the latch lifted. She slipped behind the bushes just as the gate creaked open. Tyler. He was so close that she could practically reach out and touch him.

She waited until he'd tested the doors to the carriage house and walked around to the side—just as she'd done earlier—before she escaped through the open gate. She knew he'd hear her driving off, but unless he'd seen her parked car in the thicket, which she fervently prayed he hadn't, he'd have no idea who was racing off.

She took one last look around. Without her flashlight turned on, visibility was poor, but in the haze of the moon she could make out his outline as he walked from the carriage house to somewhere in the distance.

Hope surged inside her. He hadn't found the books. But where was he going?

She had no intention of sticking around to find out.

Right now, only one thought ran through her head. If he hadn't figured out where the books were hidden, she still had a chance to clear Walter's name.

But as she hurried to her car, something else began to plague her. Why was Tyler here? Had he been following her? She didn't know what upset her more—that she hadn't retrieved the books, which she felt certain were lying in the crawl space of the attic, or that Tyler had treated her like one of his suspects.

He'd thought he'd seen a light inside the carriage house, but when he'd aimed his flashlight into the window, he realized it had probably been just a trick of the moon. The place was empty.

He plodded through the weeds to the back of the property toward the gazebo, or rather, toward what remained of it. Boards had come loose, the roof was half gone and the paint had all but peeled away.

He questioned the wisdom of entering the structure. It looked as stable as a house of cards. But he knew the risk would be worth the reward. He couldn't imagine anything more rewarding than walking off with Jeremy's files.

He hadn't told anyone he was coming. This was something he had to do by himself. His personal vendetta, he'd coined it. It was one thing to get hold of the evidence that could put Walter away for good; uncovering it with his own hands would be like icing on a cake.

Cautiously, he climbed the three steps onto the wobbly floorboards, planks of splintered wood creaking beneath his feet. Halfway into the gazebo, he stopped. Was that a car? He stood perfectly still, straining to hear better. But all he heard was the rushing of a stream.

Moonlight filtered in through the slats in the walls, casting shadows like jail bars across the crumbling floor. He shined his flashlight into every nook and cranny, but except for the rundown condition, nothing grabbed his attention. Discouraged, he sat down on the circular bench that lined the walls.

The bench, he suddenly realized, jumping back to his feet. Didn't this type of seating often double as storage? One by one he opened the compartments, only to be disappointed. They were all empty except for the chair at the back, which housed a child's broken doll. He picked it up, the word *zombie* coming to mind. Its eyes had been pushed back into its skull, its hair stringy and tangled.

He replaced the doll into its coffin and sat back down, trying to visualize what the gazebo might have looked like years ago. In his mind he saw a two-tiered pagoda with hand-turned railings and decorative corner pieces. It must have been the focal point of the landscape, he surmised. A place to reflect. According to Jeremy's letters, it had been a meeting place for him and his bride-to-be. But how long after their marriage had it remained a place of joy? Had Tyler's mother taken her two young daughters here to play? Had the doll belonged to one of his half sisters, a gift of love from her parents?

If only walls could talk. Tyler shook his head. These rotting old boards could hardly be called walls. The rickety structure barely even stood.

He felt overwhelmed with defeat. He'd been so sure

the files were hidden somewhere in the gazebo. But there was nothing here.

He pushed a button on his watch, and the face lit up. Ten o'clock. He still had another hour before meeting Nick. The dealer they'd busted the other night was a three-time loser who'd turned informant, and they were going after the main supplier tonight. Tyler figured it would all go down around one this morning. He sighed heavily. The night ahead would be long. Maybe tomorrow he'd take the day off. In any case, he planned on sleeping late.

A smile tugged at his lips. He'd need all the rest he could get, if the past weekend was any indication of what lay in store. Maybe he could convince Linda to play hooky with him, he thought, his anticipation mounting.

He instantly sobered. He wished he could convince her to stop working for that maniac altogether.

Disheartened, he stood up and crossed the gazebo to the stairs. Under his weight, the top step cracked and broke, causing him to trip. Swearing out loud, he broke his fall with the palms of his hand, scraping them on the splintered shards. The expletives stopped, and he sat on the floor, staring at the broken step. Then, as though possessed, he pried up the pieces of wooden board and ripped them from their bed.

Funny how things worked out. After meeting with Mark at the café, if he hadn't been reflecting on how he felt about Linda, his mind wouldn't have drifted to his mother and Jeremy, and he might never have made the connection to the gazebo.

Shoved into the hollow space above the concrete floor was a metal box. He picked it up and jimmied the lock.

It would be a long night, all right. Longer than he'd planned. After the drug bust, he planned to return to the precinct and go through every one of Jeremy's files.

Linda sat at her desk, staring out the window. Last night—and all the events that had led up to it—kept replaying in her mind. She didn't want to believe that Tyler had followed her, but what else could she think? How else could she explain his turning up at the estate?

Her thoughts drifted to Daniel Farber, the boy who'd used her to gain entrance into her house. Although he hadn't pulled the trigger, she'd blamed him as much as she'd blamed Timothy for her mother's death. And she'd blamed herself. If she hadn't been so gullible, her mother might still be alive. Never again, Linda had vowed, would she allow herself to play the patsy.

First they break you and then they leave you in pieces, her mother used to say.

What if Tyler had taken the receipts from her desk? He could have made the same connection she had. He could have decided it was time to pay the ex-accountant's girlfriend a visit. If I could figure it out, Linda thought, so could a cop.

Tyler had been at least twenty minutes behind her. What if he hadn't been following her? What if he'd figured out where she was going and set out to confront her?

She recalled the folder that was missing from the archives, the file that contained transactions for the month of July twenty-five years ago. What if Tyler had taken that, too?

Not knowing was making her crazy. If he had used

her, wasn't it likely he'd been using her all along? Why should she believe otherwise? Marriage might seem like an extreme measure to get what you want, but to someone blinded by obsession, it would be only a minor inconvenience, something that could easily be amended.

Was everything between them a lie?

Stop it, she ordered herself. Here she was, ready to convict him, and she had no concrete proof. How could Tyler have taken a file from the storeroom? He hadn't even known the archives existed.

The headache she'd been fighting all day seized her with a vengeance. She closed her eyes tightly, as though she could squeeze out the pain. All this speculation is too convoluted, she thought, rubbing her temples with her fingers. If the suspicion, the sneaking around, the constant what-ifs were what being a detective was about, Tyler could have it. Numbers, now that was a different story. If people could read each other as easily as they could read numbers, the world would be a simpler place.

She thought back to their weekend and, in spite of her headache, she felt a pleasant flush. But the weekend had been about more than just sex. Somehow, she'd recaptured something she'd felt the first time they'd met. She wasn't quite sure how to describe it, but it had something to do with loving and being loved for yourself. Something to do with honesty.

Honesty? It was a strange thought for someone who'd made herself out to be someone else. She wasn't just thinking about that night at the hotel. She recalled how she'd schemed to keep Tyler from finding out about her spying and was plagued with guilt.

Just what was all this about, anyway? When it came down to it, weren't they on the same side? They both wanted to get to the truth, didn't they?

When it came down to it, this was all about trust. She had to trust the stranger she'd come to love. She had to believe that he hadn't been using her.

She had to tell him about the books.

She hadn't spoken to him since yesterday afternoon and, not wanting to wake him, she hadn't called him earlier today. Last night, before she'd arrived home, he'd left a message telling her he'd be pulling an all-nighter. He'd also said, his voice sounding tight, that he'd tried to reach her but she hadn't answered her cell.

She picked up her desk phone and punched in her home number. After the fourth ring, the machine picked up. She tried reaching him on his cell and then at the precinct. Anxiety swept through her. Had something gone wrong last night with his case? But if anything had happened to him, wouldn't someone have contacted her?

A sudden commotion outside her office jarred her to the present moment. She heard the protests of Walter's secretary, Connie, then Tyler's official voice—the one he used whenever he talked about a case—and her feet sprouted wings. The next instant, she was in the hall-way, resisting the urge to throw herself into his arms. This was an office, she reminded herself. A little deco-rum was called for. But her heart was soaring. He was safe and he was here.

Wait a minute. *Why* was he here?

Behind him was Robert Jackson, whose face she recognized from the newspapers. She glanced at the prosecutor, then back at Tyler. And then she knew. Tyler had found the books and was here to arrest Walter. It was no wonder she hadn't been able to reach him. He'd been busy putting together the puzzle—the puzzle he wouldn't have solved without the pieces he'd stolen.

So much for honesty, she thought, disgusted more with herself than with him. So much for her believing that he wasn't using her. Once again, she'd allowed herself to play the patsy. "You found the files," she managed, her voice sounding tinny in her own ears.

"You knew about them?" he asked, confusion in his eyes.

"Don't play dumb with me," she said icily. "I know what you did. I must say, it didn't take you long to make the connection to Charlene Butler. Congratulations on a job well done."

"Charlene Butler? Ronald Pritchard's girlfriend? What does she have to do with all this?"

Linda had to hand it to him, he played a convincing role. But not convincing enough. "Okay, I'll play along. If the receipts didn't lead you to the files, then what did?"

"What are you talking about? What receipts?"

"You know what I'm talking about, so you can wipe that innocent look off your face." Before she could stop herself, words of condemnation began pouring out. "I should have trusted my suspicions, when I first found out who you were. You used me for information, and you've been using me all along. It was never about me or the baby. Right from the start, it was all about vengeance. Your obsession is like poison." She let out a derisive laugh. "Tell me something, Detective. You were never even assigned to the case—who did you have to bribe so you could make the collar? Well, you got what you wanted. And here's more good news. You won't have to pretend to be the happy husband any longer. I'm letting you off the hook."

"Linda, you're not making any sense," he said, his voice strained.

She bit down on her lip. Only moments ago, she'd held back from hugging him with relief, and here she was raving in public.

But suddenly she didn't care, and she didn't care that her tears were now flowing freely for the entire world to see. She didn't care about anything except getting as far away as possible from this stranger who called himself her husband.

She ran back to her office to get her coat and purse. Walter stood outside her door, his face devoid of all expression. "I'm sorry," she whispered through her tears.

"It's all right," he said in a tired voice. "You tried. You're a good girl, Linda."

The last thing she heard as she darted down the corridor was the resounding timbre of Tyler's voice.

You have the right to remain silent…

Chapter Twelve

Tyler stared at the empty space in the closet. She'd known about his commitment to the investigation right from the start. Why was she doing this? Why now?

He'd called her on her cell phone but, as usual, she hadn't answered. Then he'd tried to reach her at Sadie's, but no one had been home. It was just as well. In his state of mind, he'd probably say something irrational, something that would alienate her even more.

He kept turning the matter over in his mind, but he was too exhausted to think clearly. It was late Tuesday afternoon, and he hadn't had any sleep since Sunday. He decided to catch a few winks and then try calling her later. He kicked off his shoes and, not bothering to change out of his clothes, fell onto the bed.

But as drained as he was, sleep wouldn't come. What

was the matter with her? Why couldn't she understand how important it was for him to see Walter behind bars?

As important as it was for her to see Walter set free, his tired mind answered.

He covered his head with his pillow, as though trying to drown out the questions that troubled him. But it was no use. His mind kept replaying the afternoon's events. He'd never forget the shock he'd seen in her face. It was a look, he knew, he'd put there himself.

"Your obsession is like poison," she'd accused.

Too wired to sleep, he went into the living room and turned on the TV, hoping it would make him drowsy. He surfed through the channels, but all he found were reality shows. My life has too much reality as it is, he thought.

He noticed the jacket to *Shrek* on the coffee table. Recalling their wedding night, he felt a pang. Her reaction to the movie had been so sweet. "Do you believe in happy endings?" she'd asked, looking at him with sad eyes.

"I believe in doing the right thing," he'd answered with self-righteousness.

The right thing? He laughed with self-reproach. Making sure that Walter paid for his crimes was the right thing—nothing would convince him otherwise—but the way he'd gone about it was reprehensible. He knew what Walter meant to Linda. At the very least, he could have warned her it was coming. Not only that, he'd made the arrest on Walter's own turf, in front of his employees. Had it been necessary to throw it in her face? The arrest could have waited. Twenty-five years had passed since the murder. What difference would another few hours have made?

Something else disturbed him, too. Slapping the

handcuffs on Walter hadn't given him the satisfaction he'd anticipated. In fact, he'd felt just plain lousy. For months, he'd dreamed of that moment, about the sweet taste of revenge, but now he just felt empty.

He leaned back on the sofa and closed his eyes. Exhaustion finally won over, and he fell asleep. But his sleep was restless and filled with bad dreams. He woke up less than two hours later, feeling more unsettled than when he'd first arrived home.

He tried calling her again on her cell. Damn, he thought, slamming down the receiver. Why didn't she answer? He called Sadie, and this time he got lucky.

Lucky? Yeah, right. The words she spoke left him feeling numb. "She refuses to talk to you."

"Can't you convince her to come to the phone?" he pleaded. "You're her best friend."

"She needs time, Tyler. Don't rush her. Trusting doesn't come easy for her. You can understand that, can't you?"

If anyone could understand, he could, he thought after he'd hung up the phone. But how much time were they talking about? A week? A month? After the death of her mother, it had taken Linda thirteen years to come out of her shell.

Imagining a future without his child, he was filled with sadness. He pictured his son taking his first steps, then pictured him starting his first day at school. He saw his daughter scoring a soccer goal, then saw her graduating from college. He imagined his life without Linda, and anger against Walter surged again. He knew that as long he allowed his hatred to control him, Walter would have the upper hand, but he didn't care. He had nothing left.

He went to the kitchen, unable to remember the last time he'd eaten. He pulled open the freezer and stared at the packages. Deciding he wasn't hungry after all, he grabbed a beer from the refrigerator. After twisting off the cap, he raised the bottle as though making a toast. "Here's to you, old man. You won, after all."

Won? What was this, a game? A war?

He slammed down the bottle in disgust, fizz oozing over the counter. Walter hadn't defeated him; Tyler had defeated himself.

Linda was right. His obsession was like poison. It had destroyed everything he'd come to realize was important. His enemy was his own hatred, and the only war he fought was with himself.

"Just like old times," Linda said as they sat at Sadie's kitchen table. "Here we are talking about life over a plate of chocolate chip cookies."

"Almost like old times," Sadie corrected. "These cookies are store-bought."

"I don't know how you survive without me doing the baking," Linda said, pouring herself another glass of milk.

Sadie shook her head, as if to convey great hardship. "I'd put an apron on Frank, but it would clash with his uniform."

"So where's our gallant pilot off to now?"

"Australia. After that, he's taking a few days off, and I get him all to myself."

Married life agrees with her, Linda thought, observing the happy flush on her friend's face. But she wasn't surprised. Even though Sadie was a successful businesswoman, marriage and family had always been a priority. "Can I ask you something?"

"Sure. Anything."

"Frank spends so much time gallivanting to exotic places. Do you ever, uh, wonder about him?"

Sadie looked confused. "Are you talking about other women?"

"I'm sorry," Linda mumbled, feeling her color rising. "That was stupid of me."

To her surprise, Sadie laughed. "You know what they say. It doesn't matter where a man gets his appetite as long as he comes home for dinner."

Linda rolled her eyes. "Tell me you're kidding."

"Who, me? When do I kid?" Sadie frowned. "You want me to explain how I know I can trust Frank, but how do you explain a feeling? It would be like trying to explain life. It just is. All I know is that I love him, and he loves me. He'd never risk what we have by doing something stupid." She took a sip from her coffee. "I know the world is full of temptations, and let's face it, my Frank is a hunk, but he always comes home to get what he's missed—me. And speaking of going home, don't you think it's time you worked things out with Tyler?"

Stunned, Linda stared at her friend. And then it dawned on her. Sadie and Frank were still newlyweds. They'd want to be alone on his days off. "I'll go to a hotel," she murmured, feeling like a fifth wheel. "I've been in the way."

"You've misunderstood me. You're welcome to stay

as long as you want. You're my best friend and I love you, but as your best friend, I have to tell you what I think, or what kind of best friend would I be? I think it's time you and Tyler made up."

Linda couldn't believe what she was hearing. Sadie knew how angry she was with Tyler. "Are you saying I should go back to him? After what he did?"

"He's been calling twice a day for a week. All I'm saying is that you should talk to him."

From the way Sadie was looking at her, Linda could tell that her friend had something more to say. "What else, Sadie?"

Sadie put down her coffee mug. "Seeing how you asked…I don't understand what he did that was so wrong."

"So wrong! He broke into my desk and then followed me to the estate. He used me, and he's been using me all along. But what makes it even worse is that he led me to believe he wanted me. He's a liar, Sadie."

Sadie raised an eyebrow. "What about you? You set out to prove Walter innocent, but you didn't tell Tyler what you were up to. In my book, withholding information is the same as lying."

"How could I have told him?" Linda protested. "He would have used anything I found against Walter."

"Look, I'm not saying you were right or wrong. All I'm saying is that not everything is cut-and-dried. You accuse Tyler of being blinded by obsession, but how are you any different?"

"I didn't steal from him. You seem to be forgetting about the receipts. He took them from my desk."

"You don't know that," Sadie countered, "and you'll never know unless you talk to him. You know what else I think? I think you're looking for an excuse to end your marriage. You never wanted to be married in the first place, but then something happened. You fell in love. Someone finally broke through your armor, and now you're frightened. Trusting a man goes against everything your mother ever taught you. You're running, Linda. You're running because you're scared out of your mind."

"So you're excusing what he did," Linda said flatly.

"You're not listening, honey." Sadie reached for her hands. "People aren't perfect. They make mistakes. All I'm saying is that you should talk to your husband. Give him a chance to explain."

Even though everything Sadie was saying made sense, Linda was reluctant to see Tyler. He'd want them to continue as if nothing had happened. Sure, now that he'd put Walter in handcuffs, he'd believe that all their troubles were behind them. Easy for him to go on, but her trust had been shattered. "He used me," she repeated, her lips trembling. "How can I forget that? How do I get past it?"

"Is this really about Tyler?" Sadie asked gently. "Or Daniel?"

"It's about trust," Linda said, trying to push her mother's voice out of her head. *Not only are men controlling, they're undependable.* "Why can't you see that?"

"I see fine, honey. It's you I'm worried about. Day in, day out, women come to the salon looking for advice. I'm no shrink, but I've learned a thing or two. A lot of the time, it's not these women I hear complaining. It's their mothers I hear. It's as if the women are puppets, and their mothers are hovering above them, pulling their strings. When your mother died, all her talk against men became your gospel. Maybe it's time you stopped letting her pull your strings. Maybe it's time you buried her words, once and for all."

Sadie wasn't saying anything Linda hadn't told herself a million times before. But it was one thing to say the words, another to believe them. Yet she wanted to believe them, wanted to believe them with all her heart. Even though Sadie was concerned about her, nothing could mask the look in her eyes. It was a look Linda envied, the look of a woman in love.

The least she could do was talk to him, she decided. Maybe their marriage could never be more than an arrangement, but for the sake of their child they had to come to an understanding. For one thing, now that Walter was behind bars, Tyler would have to agree to let go of the case. As for her, she intended to resign from her job.

She'd given the matter a lot of thought. She was resigning not because she believed Walter was guilty—she'd let a jury decide that—but for the sake of her family. If her marriage was to have any chance at all, she couldn't continue to work for the man her husband detested. How could she expect Tyler to trust her if her loyalty was divided? It would be a constant reminder of his unhappy past.

But before she spoke with Tyler, she had to see Walter. She wasn't sure who would be running the business now that he'd been arrested, but it made no difference. She was going to hand in her resignation, and she wanted to tell him herself rather than have him hear it from someone else. It was the decent thing to do.

She pulled into the parking lot outside the detention center. The only evidence that it was a jail was the tall barbed-wired fence that circled the building. Recalling the fencing on the old Carlton estate, she grimaced. Her derriere still boasted the bruises from her fall.

After entering the institution through an electronic gate, she found herself in a large square lobby. She was instructed to remove her shoes and jewelry. After passing through a metal detector, she was given back her belongings. She was led to a rectangular room, where she sat in a small booth in front of a window, waiting for Walter.

The admittance procedure had been unnerving, but nothing could have prepared her for what she saw through the glass. Behind the barrier, two guards were escorting a hunched-over, haggard-looking man to the chair facing hers. She'd heard that sometimes shock turned a person's hair white overnight, but she'd never believed it. Suppressing a gasp, she stared at Walter's face. It seemed to have lost all its vigor, as though sagging with the weight of defeat. In spite of his sixty-plus years, the man she remembered had been youthful and vibrant, but now, as he sat facing her, his shoulders slouching forward, she saw only a tired, old man.

He motioned for her to pick up the phone. Her hands were shaking so badly she could barely manage. "How are you?" she asked, trying to keep her voice steady. The question was rhetorical. He looked terrible.

He attempted a small smile. "Don't worry about me. I'm fine."

She knew differently. When she'd called Sara yesterday to check on him, Sara told had her that his health had deteriorated and that he was having chest pains. "I don't understand why they're keeping you here," Linda said, not masking her worry. "What happened to bail?"

He gave her a sour look. "With my connections, you'd think my lawyers would have been able to swing it. But apparently the judge has problems with alleged murderers running loose in the streets."

In spite of the evidence that, according to Sara, had been found on the estate, Linda still refused to believe that Walter was guilty of embezzlement. As for the murder charge, that was ludicrous. Regardless of what the world believed, she'd always known her boss to be a kind, compassionate man.

"You could no more hurt a fly than harm another person," she offered gently.

His expression softened. "What are you doing here?" he asked in a tired voice. "This is no place for a girl like you."

She summoned her resolve. No matter what she still felt for him, she had to do what was right for her family. "I came here to tell you I'm resigning."

A sadness entered his eyes. "You're doing the right thing. Your first loyalty should be to your husband. To him and my grandchild."

She looked at him with astonishment. His telling her to side with her husband was not what she had expected.

Hearing him talk about his grandchild was another surprise. "You know about the baby. How did you find out?"

"Sara was here yesterday. I tricked her into telling me. You should have told me yourself," he chastised lightly.

The Parks network, she recalled Tyler saying. And now she was part of it. "I didn't know how you'd react. I know how you feel about Tyler."

"What's important is how *you* feel. About him and about yourself."

Even now, after she'd told him she was resigning, he was thinking of her happiness. Guilt coursed through her. If he was convicted, she would never forgive herself. She lowered her gaze. "There's another reason I came to see you. I came to apologize. If it hadn't been for me, you wouldn't be here now. I left an incriminating document in my desk. Tyler found it, and it led to his discovery of the evidence."

"Are you talking about that receipt for the safe-deposit box? Tyler didn't take it, Linda. I did."

She looked up again, her pulse hammering. "What about the receipt for the gems? What about the file from the archives?"

"You've been doing your homework. Yes, I took those, too."

Although she was relieved that Tyler hadn't been the one who'd broken into her desk, the last thing she wanted to hear was that the man she'd respected all these years was an embezzler. "But why?" she asked, afraid of what he might say. If he was innocent, why would he act as if he had something to hide?

He gave her a half smile. "You've always put me on a pedestal, Linda. You've always been too trusting."

She thought about how she'd hidden her actions from Tyler and nearly laughed out loud. Trusting? Her? Well, maybe where Walter was concerned, she conceded. Even now, she wanted to believe that he was innocent; even now, after he'd confessed to her that he was guilty.

But guilty of what? The last time she checked, taking papers from an employee's desk wasn't a capital crime.

He shouldn't have taken them, but she could understand why he'd done it. Worried that the prosecution would twist anything they might find against him, he might have torn through the office, looking for red herrings. She felt hurt that he hadn't trusted her enough to confide in her, but once again, she understood. She was married to his enemy. A definite conflict of interest, she thought wryly.

She met his gaze. "I didn't put you on a pedestal, I admired you. There's a difference. And yes, I trusted you. I still do. You've always been there for me, and I won't let you down now." She felt another pang of guilt. Quitting the firm could hardly be considered an act of faith.

To her shock, his laugh was scornful. "Let me down? You've been letting me down since day one. Let me tell you something, missy. If you hadn't told me you were quitting, I would have fired you. With me trying to run things from behind bars, this company will need an accountant with a lot more savvy, something you've never acquired."

His words startled her, but then she realized what he was doing, and her heart went out to him. This was his way of setting her free without guilt or regret. "You don't have to protect me, Walter. I'm not a little girl."

"In that case," he said dryly, "big girls deserve to be told the truth. What would you say if I told you I wasn't responsible for getting Sands reincarcerated? He managed that all on his own, but I saw it as a way to secure your loyalty."

Her breath caught in her throat. *He's doing this to release you,* she reminded herself. But even if what he said was true, she realized, it wouldn't matter. That segment of her life—Daniel, Timothy, her mother's death—was behind her, as was her career at Parks Fine Jewelry.

He must have been so lonely, she thought, regarding him with empathy. If anyone had known loneliness, she had. "You've been good to me, Walter. For whatever reason, you hired a young, inexperienced accountant and gave her a chance. You helped me rebuild my life, and for that I'm grateful. I only wish there was something I could do in return."

Maybe there *was* something. She was surprised she hadn't thought of it earlier. "Exactly what evidence was found?" she asked, her excitement mounting. If Tyler hadn't taken the receipts, how could he have made the connection to the books?

"Jeremy kept files," Walter growled. "Apparently he'd been plotting against me for a while, hoping to get me indicted for smuggling and embezzlement."

Three things occurred to her at once. One. The books hadn't been discovered. Tyler had found something else that night, something else to warrant the arrest. Two. Tyler might not have been tailing her. He could have been there of his own accord, following up on a tip regarding Jeremy's files. Three. Without the accounting ledgers to back up the evidence, how conclusive could Jeremy's files be?

Was Walter guilty? She didn't know. All she knew was that she had to give him one last chance. It was the least she could do for the man who'd given her a fresh start. "I know that your previous accountant tried to blackmail you with a second set of books. Tell me they don't exist. Tell me they were a bluff, a pack of lies fabricated by a vindictive imagination."

His mouth twisted into a cynical smile. "All this time, I thought Jeremy would be my nemesis. When his son—*my* son—first appeared in my office, I was sure the time had come. But it turns out it's going to be that bastard Pritchard who finally nails me on that embezzlement charge."

"Tell me about the books," she urged. Her voice fell to a whisper. "I don't know what to do."

Tell me you're innocent, she silently implored. If the books exist, tell me they're a fraud. Tell me to forget I ever heard of them.

He smiled at her sadly. "You're a good girl, Linda. You'll do the right thing."

His answer left her feeling vaguely uncomfortable. Was he telling her he was guilty of the embezzlement charge, or was he saying something else? What if he figured he had nothing to lose by telling her to go to the authorities? With or without her help, sooner or later the books would be discovered.

He knew she'd be subpoenaed. Was this a last attempt to secure her loyalty? An attempt to ensure she wouldn't denounce his integrity on the stand? He'd need all the character references he could get. She suspected that without her he might not have any.

Despite the warmth of her coat, she shivered. Was this about the embezzlement charge, or was this about murder?

Tyler sat on the futon, staring at the Picasso on the wall. Linda had told him that in this style of art, it was as if the painter took everything apart and then rebuilt it. Tyler sighed. He still didn't get it. If it ain't broke, don't fix it.

Things aren't always what they appear to be, he remembered Linda saying.

When he heard the key in the lock, his first thought was that she'd returned for more of her belongings. But when she entered and he saw the look in her eyes, hope ran through him. "We need to talk," she said, and his heart soared.

She hung up her coat, then went to the window and pulled up the shades. "Why is it so dark in here?" She gave him a hard stare. "You look terrible. Did you lose your razor? And when was the last time you ate?" She turned on her heel and headed toward the kitchen.

"Linda, slow down," he said. "You said we need to talk."

"After a nice home-cooked meal," she answered, sticking her head in the freezer. "A home-cooked frozen meal," she corrected. She turned to him and smiled. "Then later, how about some fresh-baked cookies? I can make up a batch in a jiffy." She stared at the pile of dishes in the sink. "After I get this cleaned up, that is."

"Sorry about the mess," he mumbled, trying to figure out a way he could sneak into the bedroom and pick up a week's worth of laundry from the floor without her noticing.

She assumed her schoolmarm pose. "It's you I'm worried about. A person can't live this way. It's not healthy." She spun around and turned on the faucet.

He placed his hands on her shoulders. "Linda, I'm sorry." He wasn't talking about dishes, and from the way her muscles relaxed under his touch, he could tell she understood.

She rinsed off a plate and put it into the dishwasher. "I'm the one who should be sorry," she said lightly, as though they were talking about the price of detergent and not their marriage. "I shouldn't have run away from you."

He shut off the water and turned her around. "No, you were right. I was obsessed. I let myself become blinded to everything else, including how you felt about Walter. If it takes me the rest of my life, I intend to make it up to you. If you'll let me."

"No, I was the one who was wrong. Seems I've been wrong about a lot of things. Living with fear will do that, I suppose. Makes it hard to trust people. Sometimes it makes you trust the wrong people. But I want you to know that's all over. I'm not afraid anymore. I'm a lot stronger than I thought I was." She gave him a tentative smile. "Not even the thought of living on my own frightens me."

His heart fell. She'd come to tell him she wasn't coming back. "I've always known you were strong," he said, trying to keep his voice from catching, "but you don't have to prove it by living on your own."

"You don't understand. I was afraid of everything, but more than anything, I was afraid of letting down my guard. Now the only one thing that frightens me is the thought of not being married to you."

He rested his hand on her cheek. "That's not going to happen."

"No, it's not," she answered, her eyes smiling softly. "But it took me a while to realize you weren't the big bad monster I'd made you out to be. I kept fighting you, pushing you away. I used Walter as the wedge, insisting that he was innocent. But he's guilty, Tyler, just as you always said he was."

"He manipulated you. It wasn't your fault."

"I allowed it to happen. I was so afraid."

"Of being alone?"

"Of falling in love in with you." She lowered her gaze. "I hope it's not too late. I hope you can forgive me."

"If anyone needs forgiving, it's me," he said. "I allowed my vendetta against Walter to control me, and somewhere along the way I lost sight of what was important. I love you, Linda. I've loved you since the first time I saw you." He smiled with the memory. "Your hair kept falling in your eyes, and you kept pushing it away. But then you looked at me, and it was that look that pushed me over the edge. I felt I knew you. Felt as if I'd finally come home." He smoothed away a few errant strands of her hair, and she looked up at him. "I want you to know," he continued, "now that Walter has been arrested, I'm taking myself off the case. Not that I was officially on it, and for good reason. Family members aren't exactly objective." He took her hands in his. "Case in point."

She shook her head. "You've come this far. You have to see it through. No matter how you look at it, what Walter did was wrong. You might have been seeking revenge, but you also wanted justice. How could you not? It's what you do, Tyler. Serve and protect, remember? It's part of who you are, who I fell in love with."

He sighed heavily. "All this is academic. Robert Jackson doesn't think there's enough evidence to get a conviction. He got a warrant to search his house but came up empty-handed."

"I'm not surprised. I remember back in August when he'd filed something into his safe. It struck me as odd that it was practically empty. Now I realize that he'd been disposing of evidence."

"He was thorough," Tyler added grimly.

"But not thorough enough." She gave him a self-satisfied grin. "Unless I'm mistaken, you have the evidence you need. Ronald Pritchard might have kept a second set of books."

"I know," Tyler answered. The question was, how did she? Not that anything she'd say would surprise him. Which was something he loved about her. He repressed a chuckle. Life with Linda might be a lot of things, but one thing he knew—it would never be dull.

Her mouth dropped open. "You know?"

"I know about Ronald Pritchard's blackmail threat.

His girlfriend let something slip years ago, and it was in the report. But the police believed it was just a bluff."

"There's one way to find out," Linda said excitedly. "Let's go to your family's old estate. Charlene Butler contacted me, and from what she said, I figured out that the books are in the attic of the carriage house. At least, I think they are. I didn't have time to go up there."

Understanding set in, and he laughed out loud. "So it was you I saw at the estate. I thought I'd seen something in the carriage house, but I'd chalked it up to my imagination."

"You're not angry?" she asked, her voice unsure.

"You never cease to amaze me," he said, gathering her in his arms. "If you ever decide to give up accounting, you can always become a P.I. We'll be like David and Maddie in that old show, *Moonlighting*. Or Scully and Mulder in *The X-Files*. Or—"

"Okay, I get the idea," she said, grinning. She gave him a mischievous look. "The thing is, I've never seen *The X-Files*. Who do I get to play, Scully or Mulder? Maybe you'd rather I just be Lyla?"

"Not that I minded Lyla," he said, pulling her closer, "but I'd rather be with the woman I married. Turns out she's a lot feistier than Lyla ever was."

"You mean Linda, that boring accountant?" she teased. Suddenly, she looked up at him, her eyes somber. "I did give up accounting, by the way. Well, maybe not forever, but I'm no longer working for Walter."

He knew how difficult it must have been for her to let go, and he felt his heart swell—with love, because she'd done it for him; with pride, because she'd done it for herself. "You did it for us," he said softly. "You did it for our future."

"So much has happened in such a short time," she said, the somber expression still in her eyes. "Do you think we've moved too fast?"

"Sometimes it happens that way. Sometimes you know right from the start."

She nodded. "Those were Sara's words."

"And they happen to be true. I love you, Linda. I loved you the first night we met, and I intend to spend the rest of my life proving it. The only evidence I have is the happiness I feel when I'm with you, the longing when we're apart."

Her eyes glistened. But then she pulled out of his embrace and gave him a tantalizing smile. "In that case, Detective, we should put off searching the carriage house. Right now, I think a more personal investigation is in order." She took his hand and led him toward their bedroom.

He returned her wicked grin. "I have to warn you, this investigation might go on all night."

"To serve and protect, that's still your motto, right?"

"To love and cherish," he amended. "For the rest of our lives."

"They're asking for you," the clerk announced outside the courtroom doors.

This was the moment Linda had been dreading. As Walter's accountant, she'd known she'd be subpoenaed. Now here she was, less than two weeks later, about to give her statement in a preliminary hearing that would determine whether the case would go to trial.

The D.A. had pressed for a speedy process, and it looked as though he would get his wish. The prosecution was claiming that Walter had been planning an off-shore pickup and that Jeremy had hoped to catch him in the act. Jeremy got what he wanted, but the price had been too high. He'd paid with his life.

The evidence was damning. Backing up the smuggling transactions alluded to in Jeremy's files, the other set of accounting books had been located exactly where Linda had said they'd be, in the attic of the old carriage house.

"Are you all right?" Tyler asked, concern in his voice.

For a moment, an old fear resurfaced. She recalled testifying against Timothy Sands, remembering the threats he'd made against her after he'd been sentenced. She quickly filed the memory away, along with all the other memories she'd once allowed to control her.

She looked up at Tyler, and he gave her hand a gentle squeeze. His eyes told her he was proud of her for her courage. His touch reassured her that his love was unwavering.

She squared her shoulders, and hand in hand they entered the courtroom. After the judge arrived, she was asked to take her place on the witness stand. One hand on the Bible, the other hand raised, she listened solemnly as the clerk swore her in. After she'd pledged to tell the truth, the clerk sat down, and a hush fell over the room.

She caressed the medallion around her neck. "The closest thing to my heart," Tyler had said when he'd given it to her that night at the hotel. It was now the closest thing to *her* heart. No, that's not so, she thought, smiling to herself. Tyler had that distinction. Tyler and their baby.

As if on cue, she felt a stirring inside her. She was only a little more than three months pregnant—too early to feel movement, she'd been told—but nothing could convince her that it wasn't the baby.

"Are you ready to proceed, Mrs. Carlton?" the judge asked.

She looked around the room, then rested her gaze on Tyler. "Yes, I'm ready," she answered with confidence.

It was the whole truth and nothing but the truth. She saw it reflected in her husband's loving eyes.

* * * * *

THE HOMECOMING

BY
GINA WILKINS

Gina Wilkins is a bestselling and award-winning author who has written more than sixty-five books. She credits her successful career in romance to her long, happy marriage and her three "extraordinary" children.

A lifelong resident of central Arkansas, Ms Wilkins sold her first book in 1987 and has been writing full-time since. She has appeared on several bestseller lists. She is a three-time recipient of the Maggie Award for Excellence, sponsored by Georgia Romance Writers, and has won several awards from the reviewers of *Romantic Times*.

For my brother-in-law, Mike Wilkinson.
Thanks for the travel info! Any errors are all mine.

Prologue

The bracelet in Jessica Parks's hand was undeniably pretty. Multicolored semiprecious stones were set in sterling silver, their facets catching the light and cheerily scattering it. But looking at the lovely bauble brought her no pleasure at all. Instead, she was filled with consternation at having found it in the pocket of the long black sweater jacket she wore over a white T-shirt and snug black pants.

She didn't recall putting the bracelet in her pocket. She remembered admiring it at a department store she had visited with her best friend, Caroline, but she had no recollection of slipping it into her jacket.

Swallowing hard, she turned to open a center drawer in her cherry dresser. Inside the velvet-lined drawer rested five small, easily pocketed items—six, once she added this bracelet. Ranging from a pair of gold earrings to a little cloisonné box shaped like a grand piano, the baubles had all shown up in her possession during the past year. Sometimes she found them in her pocket, sometimes in her purse, and one—a miniature crystal rose—she had found hidden in an art portfolio she had carried with her on a shopping and sketching outing. Sometimes she had been alone on those outings, other times with Caroline, but she never remembered taking anything.

Stashing the bracelet among the other things, she closed the drawer quickly, as if not seeing the purloined items would make them disappear. She knew she should do something with them—specifically, try to figure out a way to return them to their stores—but she just couldn't deal with that task yet.

The unremembered shoplifting incidents—for want of a better term—were disturbing enough, considering that she'd had a little habit of taking things as an angry and rebellious teenager. But she had always remembered those events, had been very deliberate about what she had taken and why. Most of her petty larcenies in the past had been aimed at her father, either from the jewelry stores he owned or from his office or study— and usually intended to provide cash for things she wanted to do that he had forbidden. But this was very different.

There were other episodes. Finding her keys locked in her car when she had been certain she'd carried them inside. Finding her wallet in the freezer and a melted container of ice cream in her art studio. Discovering cosmetics she didn't remember buying stashed neatly inside her makeup case.

More disturbing, on three occasions finding odd additions made to paintings in progress in her studio. Undoubtedly her own style of painting—but additions she simply didn't remember making.

Definitely not normal behavior. And it seemed to be getting worse, especially during the last few weeks as she had dealt with the tension of making secret plans in addition to her powerful and controlling father's arrest.

She should tell someone what was going on—a medical professional, at least—but she refused to give anyone evidence that she was becoming emotionally unstable. Especially not now, when she was so close to seeing the culmination of a plan she had been carefully putting together for what seemed like most of her twenty-six years.

She could handle this, she assured herself. Whether her odd behavior was due to stress or anxiety or simply artistic absentmindedness, she would get control of it through the force of sheer willpower. Perhaps she had inherited some of her mother's emotional instability, but it was combined with a streak of her father's ruthless determination.

She wasn't letting anything—or any*one*—stand in her way this time.

Chapter One

Sam Fields waited until Jessica's little red sports car was well out of sight before he broke into her cottage.

There was no need to follow her this time; he knew where she was going. She spent every Wednesday afternoon as a volunteer art teacher at a San Francisco school for emotionally disturbed teenagers. If she followed her usual routine, she would be gone for three hours, after which she would return and retreat to her art studio until late into the night. Something about her volunteer work always seemed to spark her creativity.

Just for curiosity, he walked into her studio after letting himself into her tidy, eclectically decorated cottage. Though he had never been inside the cottage before, he had no trouble finding the studio. The cottage wasn't big enough to get lost in, unlike the mansion just next door in which she had grown up.

He spent quite a while—too long, perhaps—studying the paintings sitting on easels and stacked against the walls. He had seen her work before, in local galleries, and he was always taken aback by the sheer power of it. It surprised him that such a delicate, almost fragile-looking young woman could create such bold, intellectually challenging works of art.

Had he guessed at her work judging solely by her appearance—a petite, fair-skinned blonde whose dimpled oval face was dominated by astonishingly blue eyes—he would have expected pretty watercolors or tidy still-life studies. Instead, her paintings were unpredictable and untamed, with strong hints of rebellion, anger and simmering sensuality.

His attention was drawn to three canvases propped in a corner, backs facing the room. None of them were finished, he noted when he flipped through them. It was as if she had reached a certain point with each and had stopped. Perhaps she had been unhappy with the way they were turning out.

As he studied them more closely, he could see that they were different, somehow, from her other works. Similar enough that he recognized the style, but more disturbing in content. Some additions seemed to have been slapped on in periods of extreme emotion, and others looked almost assembly line, as if painted by a computerized robot. Paintings that seemed to have begun with one theme had been abruptly altered, then abandoned.

Odd, he thought, putting everything back exactly as

he had found it. But then, he had come to expect odd behavior from Jessica Parks.

Methodically searching the little cottage in which she lived on her father's impressive Pacific Heights estate, he found little of interest until he reached her bedroom. A hardcover romantic suspense novel lay facedown on the nightstand, a bookmark showing it to be half-read. No photographs were displayed in the room, framed or otherwise.

Ignoring the frilly garments that might have intrigued him had he allowed himself to picture her in them, he rummaged through the vanity and dresser drawers. No diary or stashed letters, the two specific items he had been instructed to search for as a clue to her recent behavior. She must keep things like that well hidden, somewhere that would take a bit more effort to find. He found nothing at all of note until he opened a small drawer in the center of her dresser.

He looked thoughtfully at the disparate stash of baubles lying on the velvet lining. All were obviously new, some still bearing price tags. Picking up the stone-and-silver bracelet, he let it dangle from his fingers for a few long moments, his lips pursed thoughtfully. And then he replaced it with the other items, exactly the way he had found it.

A short while later, with plenty of time to spare before Jessica returned, he let himself out of the house, making sure the door locked behind him.

Jessica was being followed. And it wasn't the first time. She even recognized the guy. He was the same one who had been tailing her on and off for a couple of months.

He was wearing one of his disguises again—this time a scruffy, dirty brown wig pulled into a ponytail beneath a black knit cap. A pair of oversize dark glasses covered most of his face. He wore a grubby denim jacket over an untucked flannel shirt and faded jeans. She recognized him, just as she had made him in a tailored business suit, motorcycle garb, even a city sanitation worker's uniform once.

There was something about the way he moved that made him stand out to her, even in a crowd. Apparently he hadn't taken into account that she was an artist with a keen eye for details.

She didn't like to think of the number of times he might have spied on her without her seeing him. And she didn't want to know what sort of impressions he had formed of her while watching her—impressions he would have dutifully reported to the man she was certain had hired him.

Because it made her so nervous, she always seemed to do something stupid when she spotted him. Like the time she had knocked over a display of art supplies, causing such a mess in her favorite art store that she had been too embarrassed to go back since. Another time, she had dashed out of a department store without realizing she was still holding a silk T-shirt she'd been admiring when she saw him. The resulting clamor of alarms at the door had been humiliating.

She had babbled some explanation to the employee at the door about feeling light-headed and needing fresh air, then had bought the expensive T-shirt in three different colors just to prove she had intended to buy it all along. That purchase had cleaned out her checking account, resulting in several weeks of scrimping before the sale of two paintings had replenished the finances her father controlled with such a tight fist.

She wouldn't do anything stupid this time, she promised herself with a deep, steadying breath, but she would give her unwelcome shadow the slip. He couldn't be allowed to spy on the secret meeting she was to attend in less than an hour.

Making sure there was nothing in her hands—or her pockets—she glanced furtively around the pharmacy she had popped into for a refill of the medicine she took for occasional migraines. The man was now skulking on the other side of the store, examining a rack of over-the-counter pain relievers.

Wishing she could personally give him a reason to need an analgesic, she slipped through a narrow row of feminine hygiene products, then dashed out a side door and into a long, dim alleyway. She hoped by the time the guy realized she was no longer in the feminine products aisle, she would be too far away for him to find her again.

It was a heavily overcast afternoon, typical for San Francisco in early November. Gray clouds continued to deepen, throwing the alley into shadows that made it look more like early evening than midafternoon. She never even saw a man standing in the darkness of a recessed doorway until he stepped out in front of her.

Stumbling to a stop, she pressed a hand against her pounding heart. Her first thought was that it was the man she had escaped in the pharmacy, that he had somehow gotten ahead of her. But a second look showed her that this was a stranger. A very large and mean-looking stranger.

The man who had been following her was perhaps six feet tall and slim—this guy was a six-foot-five mountain.

"Excuse me," she said, making an effort to keep her voice brusque and her manner confident. "You're blocking my way."

"Am I now?" His face looked strange in the shadows, filled with deep hollows and sharp angles. His dark eyes swept her body with an insolence that set her teeth on edge.

"Yes." She took a step sideways, hoping he would let her pass now that he'd had fun scaring the spit out of her.

He moved in front of her again, taking a step closer at the same time. "Don't be in such a hurry."

Abruptly deciding she would rather take her chances with the man who had been following her than with this guy, Jessica turned on one heel to dart back in the other direction. Moving with a speed she wouldn't have expected from someone so large, the man grabbed her from behind.

After being mugged by a purse snatcher five years ago, she had taken several self-defense classes, but her diminutive size was most definitely a disadvantage in this situation. Still, she prepared herself for a fight, opening her mouth to scream like a banshee at the same time.

Before she could let out a sound, someone else appeared in the alley. Moving with a swiftness that made the bigger man seem to be stuck in slow motion, the newcomer grabbed Jessica's arm and shoved her roughly out of the way, his eyes never leaving the bigger man's face.

"You want a *real* fight?" the man who had followed Jessica into the pharmacy demanded, his entire body braced for battle.

This was the time to get out of here, Jessica decided, climbing to her feet with a wince. She had landed flat on her butt when her rescuer shoved her, and she was a bit sore, but not so badly hurt she couldn't run. Keeping an eye on the two men engaged in a snarling measuring match only a few feet away, she looked frantically around for her big red tote bag. She couldn't leave it behind. It held everything that was of particular importance to her just now.

On her knees, she leaned to look under a Dumpster. Spotting her canvas tote bag beneath the wheels, she dived forward to fish it out, snagging a handle and yanking it toward her. Cursing when the bag caught on something, she used both hands to pull, nearly tumbling over backward when it came loose.

Someone steadied her from behind. Clutching the bag to her chest, she scrambled around and to her feet, not sure whether she was relieved to see the man she had first spotted in the pharmacy. There was no sign now of the big guy who had accosted her. Apparently, he'd had no interest in fighting someone closer to his own size.

Holding both hands up in a gesture meant to reassure her, her rescuer asked, "Are you all right?"

She was already sidling away from him. "I'm fine."

"I'm sorry I made you fall. I didn't mean to push you so hard."

"Just stay away from me."

Though she couldn't see his eyes behind his dark glasses, she had the distinct impression they narrowed in response to her tone. "You're welcome," he muttered.

"I'm supposed to be grateful that you've been following me for weeks?" she snapped, hugging the bag more tightly.

That shut him up—but only for a moment. "I don't know what you're talking about."

"Right." She turned away. "And I suppose you aren't working for my father, either."

He didn't say a word as she walked away. At the end of the alley, she looked over her shoulder to say, "If I see you again, I'll call the police and charge you with stalking me."

She made her escape before he could reply, hoping he would admit defeat now that she had identified him. That was usually the pattern of the men her father hired to keep watch over her. The only reason she hadn't confronted this guy before was because he would only be replaced with someone she might not be able to identify so quickly.

Better the devil she sort of knew…

Sam Fields didn't give up quite so easily. Though it galled him that Jessica had spotted him often enough to know he had been tailing her—how the hell had she done that, anyway?—his irritation simply made him more determined to do a better job in the future.

He was confident that she didn't see him watch her meeting with Derek Ross that afternoon.

As he had predicted, she had rushed back to her place after their confrontation in the alleyway to change out of the clothes she'd soiled in her fall. Parked outside the estate walls where she couldn't see him, he had changed his own appearance while she'd freshened up.

He had ditched the cap and wig to reveal his own shaggy, dark blond hair, swapped his dark sunglasses for glasses with brown plastic rims and thick, clear lenses and shed his flannel shirt to reveal the long-sleeved Cal Tech T-shirt beneath. He replaced his ragged denim jacket with a V-neck sweater, and his dirty boots with a pair of brown loafers. He ran some pomade through his hair, slicking it back and making it look darker than his usual gold. That quickly, he changed from grubby street guy to young businessman on a day off.

When Jessica met Derek Ross at a dimly lit café in downtown San Francisco, Sam was in a nearby booth, his back turned to them. He was able to see them in a wall mirror, but he positioned himself so they couldn't see him in return.

Jessica wasn't making him this time, he promised himself.

He didn't know why he was being so persistent with this case. Yeah, sure, the money was good and his private investigation agency could certainly use the infusion of capital. But damn it, his client was in jail and the woman he was supposed to be watching was…well, Jessica Parks was a kook. Impulsive, unpredictable, temperamental. Always getting into trouble.

One expected artists to be that way, of course—at least from what Sam had observed over the years. But Jessica took eccentricity to new heights, according to her father. She had been getting into scrapes since she was a kid, enough that her family worried about her emotional stability. Apparently, her mother had been the same way, ending up committed to a mental institution for the past twenty-five years.

Maybe Jessica had inherited her mother's emotional problems, but Sam couldn't help wondering if the inclination for shoplifting he had been warned about had been passed down from her father. After all, Walter Parks was facing a preliminary hearing for a variety of charges, including gem smuggling, embezzlement—and murder.

While Parks fiercely maintained his innocence, claiming to have been set up by the enemies he had made during his climb to fortune and power, he insisted that his primary concern in hiring Sam had been Jessica's safety. He worried about his youngest child, with everything so chaotic and unsettled in their family, he had told Sam. Jessica didn't handle change and pressure well. She tended to respond by reverting to behavior that had plagued her in the past— shoplifting, sleepwalking, paranoia, even memory lapses.

Walter also expressed concern that his money made her a target for unscrupulous opportunists—as it had when she had been kidnapped eight years ago and held two weeks until Walter had paid a ransom. The kidnappers had never been captured, and Walter said it had been a miracle that Jessica wasn't harmed. He didn't want to tempt fate again, he insisted.

Walter seemed particularly disturbed by Jessica's recent friendship with Derek Ross, the brother-in-law of an old business partner of Walter's—the partner Walter was now accused of murdering. Walter had confided in Sam that Ross had once had a romantic interest in Jessica's beautiful, but unbalanced, mother. It worried him that Ross seemed to be cultivating an acquaintance with Jessica—what was the lying cheat up to now?

Jessica had long been obsessed with her mother, unable to accept that Anna Parks was too deeply disturbed to live without constant supervision. Of course, it was only natural that with her father ripped from his family and her siblings all very recently married, Jessica would focus on her long-absent mother, Walter had added plaintively.

Sam risked another glance at the mirror. Behind him in the café, Jessica and Ross were deep into a low-voiced conversation, neither touching the rapidly cooling cups of coffee in front of them. Sam would like to know what they were talking about. He didn't trust the way the older guy was looking at Jessica.

Sure, she was hot—as Sam had noticed way too many times, himself—but young enough to be Ross's daughter. Walter said Ross had once had a thing for Jessica's mother, whom Jessica was said to closely resemble. Surely the old guy wasn't turning his romantic attentions to this younger copy of his onetime love?

Repelled by the idea, Sam scowled into his own mug.

It was bad enough that *he* had to fight an unwelcome attraction to Jessica, and he was only twelve years her senior. Ross had to be more than twenty years older. Gross.

Wasn't any of Sam's business, of course—his job for now was simply to keep Jessica safe and out of trouble while her father was away. With his money, influence and crack legal team, Walter was justifiably confident about his chances of beating the twenty-five-year-old charges against him.

Still, Sam wondered whether he should quit. Walk away from the dysfunctional family and their money and let someone else take on their problems. Someone Jessica couldn't spot so easily, he added with a scowl of self-reproach.

Maybe it was time for him to take another assignment. Tailing a cheating spouse, perhaps, or gathering evidence on a sticky-fingered employee. If he was really lucky, he'd get an insurance fraud case or an interesting background check.

Anything had to be better than baby-sitting a beautiful young blonde who kept his head spinning with a combination of exasperation and unwanted attraction.

"I'm glad you could take the time to meet me today," Caroline Harper told Jessica Friday afternoon, the day after Jessica's meeting with Derek Ross. "I really needed this chance to talk."

Her friend's call had come at a very inconvenient time, when Jessica had been immersed in plans for the secret trip she would be taking soon. Since she had just seen Caroline last week for their shopping outing—

after which Jessica had found the bracelet in her pocket—she had been tempted to make an excuse not to meet at this popular coffee shop. But Caroline was pretty much Jessica's only friend, and she had sounded so blue when she'd called that Jessica hadn't been able to refuse.

"You know I'll always make time for you, Caroline. Haven't you done the same for me, too many times to count?"

Without answering, Caroline gazed down at the spoon she was slowly swirling in an oversize cup of hazelnut coffee. There were many times—such as this one—when Jessica found her friend's strikingly attractive face difficult to read.

On the surface, Jessica and Caroline were quite different. Jessica was five foot four on her tallest days, while Caroline was closer to five-ten. Jessica's figure was slight, but curvy; Caroline seemed to be made up of intriguing planes and angles. Both were blond, but while Jessica's shoulder-length hair was naturally silvery, Caroline's stylishly short cut was more golden, and straight out of a bottle.

They were different in other ways, too. Jessica constantly fought nerves and self-doubt; Caroline was the most implacable and confident person Jessica knew—outside the Parks family, anyway. To Jessica, who had been raised in wealth and privilege and knew how little true happiness either provided, money was simply a means to an end. Caroline was admittedly and unrepentantly materialistic.

After finishing the same art school three years earlier, they had gone separate directions careerwise—Jessica into painting and private showings, Caroline into the faster-paced and higher-paid world of advertising. Yet somehow they had remained friends.

It turned out that Caroline's problem on this afternoon was that her mother had been nagging her to fly home to Ohio for Christmas, which Caroline simply didn't want to do. She had just been back in July for her mother's birthday, she complained, and she had planned to ship her Christmas gifts next week, almost six weeks before the holiday so that they would arrive in plenty of time.

Family problems. Now there was something Jessica understood all too well. "You are her only daughter, after all."

Caroline groaned. "And she never lets me forget it. The only reason she wants me there is to parade me around in front of her friends. She's decided it will make her look bad to her acquaintances if I don't make the effort to come home for the holidays. She's whining and carrying on about her poor health—which is a crock—and her breaking heart—an even bigger crock—and telling me how unnatural and ungrateful I am. You know how it is when a mother gets into wounded-martyr mode."

Jessica's hands tightened a bit convulsively around her own coffee mug. "No, actually. I don't."

Caroline bit her lip. After a moment, she murmured, "Sorry. I wasn't thinking."

Jessica shrugged to indicate she wasn't letting the gaffe bother her. Caroline knew, of course, that Jessica's mother was institutionalized. But not even Caroline knew about Jessica's plan to bring her mother home.

Which only proved that Jessica could lie without flinching to anyone, even her best friend, when she felt it was necessary. When it came to her impending plans, she trusted no one—with the possible exception of Derek Ross.

Caroline sighed. "I'm sorry. I've been rattling on, and I know you've got a lot on your mind. So much has happened in your family. We should talk about how you're doing."

Jessica was very fond of Caroline, who could always be counted on for dry humor, witty observations and total acceptance of Jessica's personality quirks. Caroline was not, however, one who enjoyed deep, emotional discussions or introspective psychological dissections. So, Caroline's occasional questions about the latest soap-operatic developments in Jessica's family were probably prompted more by idle curiosity than genuine empathy.

Jessica could understand that. She was fully aware that her family had kept the tabloid gossips practically salivating during the past year. "I'm fine."

Caroline looked vaguely dissatisfied with the noncommittal response. "Come on, Jess, it helps to talk, sometimes—how do you really feel about what's happening?"

Jessica's mouth twisted. "Depends on what you're referring to. My father being in jail, charged with embezzlement and the murder of his onetime business partner? Or my oldest brother, Cade, a formerly conservative widower and single father, recently eloping with the daughter of the man my father is accused of murdering? Or maybe you're alluding to my only sister, Emily, marrying a European ruler and moving to his country to bear his child and to live as royalty."

Caroline shook her head. "Any of those things are enough to upset you."

But Jessica wasn't finished. "Don't forget that terrible time a few months ago when we thought my brother Rowan had died in a motorcycle accident, only to find out that he was living on a cattle ranch in Texas. Now *he's* gotten married to the mother of an adorable baby boy, leaving me the only single sibling—the one everyone thinks is emotionally unbalanced, by the way.

"And I haven't even mentioned my twenty-four-year-old half brothers, Tyler and Conrad Carlton, who just appeared out of the blue and announced that they were conceived during an affair my father had with the wife of the same man he is now accused of murdering. So they're Cade's half brothers and his wife's half brothers, which is really just too bizarre, when you think about it. I can't imagine why I would walk around these days feeling as if my head is going to spin right off my shoulders, can you?"

Caroline winced. "When you put it that way, my family annoyances don't seem half as bad. Yours sound like a daytime soap opera."

Jessica sighed gustily and shook her head. "Sorry. I didn't mean to unload on you. It's just that everything is so crazy right now."

"I understand. And it's enough to put anyone on edge. Maybe you should just hole up and rest awhile. You could paint, read, watch your favorite DVDs—at least until your father's out of jail."

Jessica had no intention of telling her friend that she planned to make good use of the time her father was away by slipping off, herself. But she couldn't resist commenting, "You make it sound as if there's no question that my father *will* be out of jail."

Caroline lifted one narrow, arched eyebrow. "Really, Jess, as often as you've complained about your father being controlling, distant and critical, you've never implied he could be capable of murder. Maybe he wouldn't be above a little creative accounting or a few shady business practices, but murder?"

Jessica would have given anything to look her friend in the eye and state with absolute confidence that she did not believe Walter Parks was capable of such a deed. But the truth was, she *couldn't* say that. Not after talking to Derek Ross. And not knowing what Walter had done to her mother.

"Jessica?" Caroline looked startled by her continued silence. "You don't think—"

"I don't know what I think," Jessica said wearily. "I told you, I'm too confused to think. For now, I'm just going to trust the courts to sort everything out and find the truth."

"He really does worry about you. As much as you complain about his overprotectiveness, it shows he cares. That's more than my long-absent father ever did for me."

Caroline didn't know, of course, exactly how closely guarded and totally controlled Jessica had been, and this wasn't the time to get into it. But Jessica increasingly doubted that love had anything to do with Walter's actions.

After a moment, Caroline sighed lightly and reached for her purse. "I've got to run. My calendar's full for the rest of the afternoon. Thanks for meeting me. I needed the break."

Jessica forced a smile and accompanied her friend to the cash register. A display of pretty, whimsical refrigerator magnets caught her attention, and she studied them while Caroline paid. Caroline had insisted on treating. And then Caroline turned to give her a quick hug and an air kiss aimed at her cheek. "See you later, kid. Don't do anything crazy, okay? Everything will work out."

Jessica was left to wonder what Caroline had meant by that "don't do anything crazy" crack. Maybe she was a little sensitive about such things, but the remark seemed particularly grating considering her mother's predicament.

Still replaying the conversation with Caroline, she stepped absently onto the sidewalk. Caroline was already gone, having headed in the opposite direction.

"'Don't do anything crazy,'" she muttered, tucking her ever-present tote bag beneath her arm and stepping onto the crosswalk. "I wonder how she would classify flying off to Switzerland to break my mother out of a mental institution. I wonder if she would consider that cr—"

A sudden squeal of brakes—much too close for comfort—drowned out her grumbling. Before Jessica even had a chance to look around, something hit her hard from behind and sent her flying.

Chapter Two

She landed hard on her hands and knees. Jolting pain shot up both her arms and her legs, and her palms felt as though they had just been shredded.

The smell of warm, oily asphalt assaulted her nostrils, making her grimace as she imagined what that fall had done to her good tan slacks. It was a frivolous thought, of course, considering that she had apparently come very close to being hit by a car, but she latched on to the mundane concern for her clothes—all in all, much better than remembering the shrill squeal of brakes and the sick certainty that she was about to be run down in the street.

Voices were raised around her, and a car door slammed as someone shouted, "Dude, she walked right out in front of me! I never even saw her."

Someone gripped her shoulders. "Are you okay?"

Shaking her head slightly as if to clear her addled thoughts, she looked up—straight into a pair of bright green eyes she knew much too well. "Damn it."

It was that guy again—the one who had been following her. The one who had rescued her from a menacing hulk in an alleyway—after putting her into the situation in the first place, she reminded herself defensively.

"Are you all right?"

She remembered his voice, too. For someone so irritating to have such a deliciously deep, rumbly voice was just entirely unfair. "I'm fine," she said curtly. "Now get away from me."

His eyes narrowed, but before he could snap back at her a young man with greasy hair and an unfortunate complexion stepped into her view. "You walked right in front of me, yo," he accused her. "I almost hit you. You know what that would have done to my insurance rates?"

The man who had knocked her out of the path of the car turned his irritation toward the young driver. "Do you know what it would have done to *her?*" he demanded. "You were driving too fast and you weren't paying attention. You could have killed her."

"Hey, it ain't my fault that she's too dumb to read the Don't Walk signs."

The man started to rise, but Jessica placed a hand on his arm. "It was *my* fault," she said loudly and clearly. "I was distracted and I made a stupid mistake. I'm so sorry I frightened you," she told the driver—who couldn't have been more than nineteen.

He started to retort, but then he seemed to pause and study her face for the first time. A flush began somewhere in the vicinity of his prominent Adam's apple and traveled up to his shaggy brown bangs. "Well—that's okay. I guess I'm glad you weren't hurt."

"Thank you." Ignoring her seemingly habitual rescuer, she held out a hand to the young man. She wasn't above using the fragile blue-eyed blonde bit when it was to her benefit—a trick she'd been told she'd inherited from her mother. "Would you mind?"

Blushing even more brightly, the teen helped her awkwardly to her feet. "Is there anything I can do for you?" he offered. "Can I give you a lift, maybe?"

"No, thank you." She gave him a warm smile that had his Adam's apple doing an Irish jig in his throat. "It's very kind of you to offer, but I'll be fine. We'd better move along now, we seem to be causing a scene. Goodbye."

He moved somewhat reluctantly to the ancient sedan he'd pulled haphazardly to the curb after the near collision. Jessica tucked her tote bag beneath her arm and limped to the other sidewalk, relieved that the gawking bystanders moved on when they decided that there would be no further entertainment from her.

It annoyed her greatly that Green Eyes stayed close to her side as she walked away. "You landed pretty hard," he said, an unnecessary reminder since her knees throbbed with every step. "Maybe you should let someone check you out?"

"I believe I've been checked out quite enough for one day, thank you." She was aware that it was a lame response, but it was the best she could come up with at the moment.

"You're limping."

"I'll get over it. Please go away."

"Look, I'm just trying to make sure you're okay. It isn't as if I expect undying gratitude or anything—even though I did push you out of the path of a car—but the least you could do is be civil."

"Civil?" She whirled then to glare at him. "I'm sorry, did I miss an etiquette lesson along the way? Something about being 'civil' to stalkers?"

His cheeks darkened, but unlike the teenager's, this flush was due more to anger than embarrassment. Jade flames snapped in his eyes when he spoke. "I am not a stalker."

"I know exactly what you are," she answered him evenly, holding his gaze and hoping she gave him no sign that she was just a teensy bit intimidated by the way his handsome face hardened when he was mad. Made him look sort of dangerous—a word she hadn't applied to him before. "When you report this incident to my father—as I'm sure you will—tell him that I would rather be hit by a bus than to see your face again. Have I made myself clear?"

"Very." He pushed the single word out from between clenched teeth. And then he turned without another word and disappeared into the crowd—which was quite a trick, considering that there weren't that many people around at the moment.

Because rudeness didn't come naturally to her, Jessica was feeling rather guilty about the things she had said to the green-eyed man by the time she returned to the solitude of her own home. As had become her habit, she didn't even glance at the opulent stucco mansion she drove past on the way to her guest cottage in back.

She had been under some pressure from her siblings to move into the main house now that her father was in jail, but she much preferred her cozy cottage to the fifteen-room showplace in which she had been raised. She didn't want to have to deal with the minimal staff still residing in the mansion, preferring the privacy of her own rooms. Nor did she trust anyone on that staff—with the exception of housekeeper Brenda Wheeler, who was currently away on leave—not to report her every movement to her father.

As far as Jessica was concerned, her father had simply traded the high walls and massive iron gates of his estate for a less luxurious prison.

Once inside her cottage, she headed straight for a hot bath to soak away the aching reminders of her close encounter with the pavement, berating herself all the way for not handling the entire situation a bit differently.

"I should have pretended not to recognize him," she said aloud, stripping off her green cardigan. "Or maybe I should have been icily polite, thanking him for coming to my rescue yet again—the condescending-royalty-to-lowly-peasant routine. Made a comment about my father getting his money's worth from this minion—and maybe I should have offered him a nice tip for his trouble. That would have gotten his goat, without making me sound quite so—"

Her voice faded into shocked silence when her sweater fell to the bathroom floor and a whimsical refrigerator magnet rolled out of the big patch pocket on the left side.

Shaped like a colorful clown, the magnet seemed to laugh mockingly up at her as she stared down in disbelief. She specifically remembered studying that very magnet at the cash register earlier. She'd thought the twelve-dollar price tag was a bit steep for such a paltry trinket, but she hadn't particularly wanted it, anyway. She would have sworn she had put it back on the display rack, not in her pocket. She absolutely didn't remember stashing it there—

But then she had walked into the path of an oncoming car without noticing that, either, she reminded herself in despair.

She wrapped her arms tightly around her middle. Maybe she really was going crazy. Everyone kept telling her she was just like her mother—and everyone said her mother was unstable. Jessica had been trying to prove "everyone" wrong, based on a few letters from her mother that had seemed so sensible and sane—but maybe she had allowed herself to be misled by her lifelong longing for the mother she'd never had the chance to know.

Maybe Anna Parks really was crazy—and maybe she had passed that trait to her youngest daughter.

Dashing a scraped hand across her damp eyes, Jessica lifted her chin, sniffed defiantly and promised herself that very soon, she would have the answer to at least one of her questions. When she looked directly into her mother's eyes, she would know the truth.

"So she would rather be hit by a bus than to see my face again." Sam Fields glared at Jessica's cottage from his parking space in a nearby wooded area. The woods partially concealed the groundskeepers' gate at the back of the mansion, a gate which was kept locked, but to which Sam had been given access by the estate's owner.

The spot where he had been instructed to park was where the groundskeeper kept his truck when he was working on the meticulously landscaped property. There had been little grounds maintenance during the past month since Walter's arrest, leaving Sam free to make use of the space, which turned out to be a convenient position for spying on the cottage. Because that phrase bothered him, he mentally corrected it—it was a convenient position for keeping guard over the cottage, he thought, somewhat more satisfied with the way that sounded.

Though he was too far away to see into her windows, he knew Jessica was still there—her car hadn't moved since she had returned from the luncheon that had almost ended in tragedy more than two hours earlier.

He had made sure she'd gotten home safely, and he had been watching her place ever since, though for what purpose he couldn't quite say. She was certainly safe enough here on the Parks estate, with its walls and gates and vigilant staff—who had, very likely, been instructed to ignore him if they saw him. He had better things to do than to baby-sit an eccentric young woman whose father—his employer—could very well be a murderer, for all Sam knew.

He was beginning to suspect why Walter Parks had felt his youngest child needed a baby-sitter—face it, the woman was an accident waiting to happen—but damned if Sam intended to keep rescuing her from one misadventure after another while Walter awaited his trial.

He really should quit. Walk away, refund a part of the retainer he'd already spent, forget all about Walter Parks and his kooky daughter. Problem was, he wasn't sure it was going to be all that easy to accomplish the latter.

What was it about Jessica Parks that was keeping him on this case? It couldn't be just her beauty. As a divorce-burned, fiercely confirmed bachelor, he knew better than to let himself be captured by a pretty face, at least for more than a brief fling.

Had to be that annoyingly soft heart of his, the one he had spent years trying to harden. He had always been a sucker for a lost or wounded stray, and something about Jessica definitely brought those images to mind. There was something in her eyes…something in the depth of emotion he saw in her paintings…something that made him wonder if he was losing his grip on reality, too, damn it.

Her father was in jail, facing a lifetime sentence. Her siblings all seemed to be too busy with their own hectic affairs to make much time for the little sister who had always been regarded as a bit of a problem in the family. Perhaps they all thought she was safe enough in her cottage on the Parks estate—maybe they even thought she was content there. He knew better, on both counts.

Walter hadn't expressed undue concern about any of his other offspring, but they seemed to be doing fine on their own, as far as Sam could determine. The only other daughter, Emily, had recently married European royalty, so her welfare was certainly guaranteed. Emily's twin brother, Cade, was overwhelmed with responsibilities since Walter's arrest—in addition to raising his five-year-old daughter, and his recent marriage to the daughter of Walter's late ex-partner. The younger brother, the one just ahead of Jessica in birth order, was also a newlywed who had shown little connection to his family, on the whole.

Two other brothers had recently surfaced, twin boys born out of an affair between Walter Parks and his late partner's wife almost twenty-five years ago. Their mother had died recently, and they seemed determined to make Walter Parks pay for the shabby way he had treated her in the past. They, of course, barely knew Jessica and certainly had no emotional ties to her.

He didn't doubt that Jessica felt lonely and isolated now—which Walter had cited as the reason for her renewed obsession with her crazy mother. An obsession that was apparently leading her into an odd alliance with her mother's ex-lover, a man Walter had described as "dangerously unpredictable."

Between that development and her propensity for walking into secluded alleys and oncoming traffic, it certainly seemed as though Jessica needed a bodyguard. Walter said he had tried on numerous occasions to obtain one for her, but she had refused, making him feel it necessary to hire someone to watch out for her on the sly. At least until he was released from jail to take the job back, himself.

"I've been a lousy father, Fields," he had admitted with a candor some might have found disarming. "I didn't pay nearly enough attention to my children when they were growing up, leaving them to be raised by a housekeeper while I devoted all my time to my business.

And now the repercussions of my success have brought this shame to the family. I'm trying to do all I can to make it up to them, in the best way I know how. In Jessica's case, that means keeping her safe and protected from her own fragile nature until I'm in a position to get the best help for her."

Since Parks had made a big deal of being a model prisoner, casting himself in the role of long-suffering martyr whose only purpose was to accomplish as much good as possible while waiting for the justice system to discover his innocence, Sam had reserved judgment about the old reprobate's sincerity. Apparently the D.A. had some strongly incriminating evidence that would be brought out in the preliminary hearing later this month—not to mention a couple of rumored surprise witnesses.

But as far as Jessica needing to be looked after— well, that seemed to be something no one could accuse Parks of exaggerating by much.

Still, none of this was Sam's problem. After all, Jessica recognized him now, which made his job even more difficult, if not impossible. She had said herself that she would rather be mowed down by a bus than see him again.

Some guys might have considered that a pretty strong hint.

Yet every time he thought about quitting, he found himself remembering the moment he had watched Jessica step off a sidewalk and into mortal danger. His heart had leaped into his throat as he had thrown himself at her, not at all sure he would be able to reach her in time, or to keep himself from being flattened with her.

If he had quit last week, as he had been so strongly tempted to do, would she even now be lying in the city morgue?

The image that question brought to his mind almost made him shudder.

"What's this I hear about you refusing to spend Thanksgiving with any of your siblings?" Walter Parks demanded Saturday morning, the day after Jessica's near accident. He made no attempt to mask his annoyance or his disapproval with her holiday plans—or lack thereof.

Jessica sighed heavily into the telephone handset. "Even from jail you're trying to run my life?"

"Don't expect me to be here much longer," he snapped. "My lawyers will have me out of here by the end of the month—and then you and I are going to sit down and talk."

"You sound awfully confident for a man facing as many charges as you are."

He harrumphed, dismissing those charges just as easily as he had always dismissed anything that inconvenienced him—including his children, Jessica thought bitterly. Especially his youngest daughter, the one who had always openly challenged him the most. The one who looked and acted so much like the problematic wife he had banished from his life twenty-five years ago.

"Maybe I'll pay a steep fine, but they aren't going to put me away for making a little extra profit here and there. Everyone knows how the world of cutthroat business operates."

"And the…other charges?" She couldn't seem to make herself say the word *murder*.

"They have nothing," Walter said flatly. "Their so-called witness will be exposed for the lying weasel he is. As I said, I'll be out by the end of the month. In the meantime, I'm doing the best I can to take care of my affairs—and my family—from this cell."

"I assume by taking care of family, you're referring to having me followed everywhere I go?"

"If I *were*," he replied cagily, "it would be for your own good. With me here and you living there on the estate by yourself, you're much too easy a target. You think no one would consider taking advantage of our situation to snatch my youngest child for ransom? Again?" he added, heavily stressing the word.

She was instantly transported eight years back in time, to the two nightmarish weeks she had spent locked in a tiny room while her kidnappers negotiated a ransom with her father. Miraculously, she had been released unharmed, but it had been a long time before she had recovered from the ordeal—not that she had ever fully recuperated.

For more than a year afterward she had been subdued and withdrawn, abandoning the secret plans she had been so close to completing, willing to let her father take charge "for her own sake." A week after her return, Walter had confronted her with a letter from her mother that he had found hidden among her possessions, and he demanded to know how long she had been in contact with Anna. When she sullenly admitted that she had located and contacted her mother a year earlier, he had gone off on a tirade about how unstable and unreliable Anna was, and how Jessica was just like her.

Acting foolishly had almost gotten her killed, he reminded her—which she most certainly would have been if he hadn't sacrificed and paid the exorbitant ransom for her.

After that he had placed even tighter controls on her, restricting her money to absolute necessities, having her watched almost constantly, forbidding her to have any further contact with the mother who was such a horrible influence over her even from so far away. For just over a year, she had gone along, drifting aimlessly until she had impulsively entered art school.

Her obsession with the past and her concerns about her own problems had interfered with her studies, and she hadn't really concentrated on her art. Her teachers had insisted that she had more talent than she allowed them to see, but her heart wasn't really in the process then. Her work had been competent, but not inspired, just enough for her to get by in her classes.

It was her budding friendship with classmate Caroline Harper that had helped her restore some of her faith in herself. After graduation, she had even defied her father to move out of the estate and into a trendy loft apartment, making her living as a displays designer for a high-end department store.

She had enjoyed that brief period of freedom—until the mugging that had dealt her a sharp setback, reminding her too vividly of her kidnapping ordeal. She had allowed Walter to talk her into moving back to the estate, but into the guest cottage this time. Only then had she really begun to concentrate on her art, finding in it an outlet for all of her pent-up emotions.

Eventually, she'd found the courage to contact her mother in secret again, and in time she began to rebuild her precarious faith in Anna, even as her trust in her father started eroding once more. She had even reached a point where she had wondered if he had been behind that traumatizing kidnapping, and maybe even the purse-snatching incident three years later—just to keep her under his control.

For nearly five years she had wondered if he would really go that far, or if she was simply allowing paranoia to get the best of her. She still hadn't convinced herself he wouldn't resort to any coldhearted measure if he felt it necessary. Walter had always taken great pride in his willingness to do whatever it took to serve his own best interests—and those of his children, he had always added belatedly.

Pushing the old fears and self-doubts out of her mind, Jessica lifted her chin and spoke fiercely. "I can take care of myself."

"Not from what I've been hearing," her father answered, his tone familiarly cutting.

She cringed. Heaven only knew what Walter had been told by the green-eyed shadow he refused to acknowledge hiring. Did he know she had walked in front of a car? Her knees still throbbed from their hard contact with the pavement, as did her scabbed palms.

And then her breath caught as something even more unnerving occurred to her. Could Walter possibly know about the shoplifted items that kept showing up in her possession?

She was stressed, she assured herself. Not unstable. Lots of people became distracted under extreme stress, and she was definitely dealing with that condition. She would not let her father shake her self-confidence—or her resolve—again. After all, what could he possibly do to her now?

Before she could try to defend herself, he changed the subject. "Why won't you join your brothers or sister for Thanksgiving?"

"I'm not in a particularly festive or thankful mood this year. Besides, they're all busy with their new lives. I'll be fine by myself."

"I should have refused to give Brenda this time off. At least you'd have her to keep you company."

"Absolutely not. Brenda deserved a long holiday. I hope she has a wonderful time on her European cruise. It was my idea, after all."

"So I assumed," he grumbled.

She didn't tell him, of course, that she had wanted his longtime housekeeper, and the woman who had served as her surrogate mother, out of the way for the next few weeks. As much as she loved Brenda Wheeler, Jessica didn't want to risk any interference with her perilous plans, even from someone who truly did have only her best interests at heart.

"So maybe you'll come see me on Thanksgiving— since you don't have any other obligations."

"Come see you? In prison?" She was startled that he had even suggested it.

"We're allowed visitors, you know." He sounded peevish now. "Not that you've ever taken advantage of it. I'd like to see you, Jessie. I miss my family."

"I, um, really don't want to see you there," she said awkwardly. "It's too…painful for me."

Which was only partly true. She didn't want to see him at all for the time being—not until after she had accomplished her mission.

He wasn't satisfied by her lame response, but she gave him little chance to argue. Muttering a barely coherent excuse, she hastily disconnected the call.

Chapter Three

"Monica, this is fantastic. I can't believe how much you've developed your talent in such a short time."

Jessica gazed in satisfaction at the oil painting propped on an easel in front of her, her hands on her hips as she studied the bold, cleverly layered colors. "The power of this painting is almost palpable. It's as though I can almost feel waves of energy radiating from it."

The spiky-haired, multipierced Monica rolled her black-lined brown eyes. "You do get kinda carried away sometimes."

Jessica chuckled. "Art is supposed to carry you away. Good art, anyway. And yours is better than merely good."

Though she shrugged and muttered gruffly, the teenager couldn't entirely hide her pleasure with the compliments. Jessica doubted that Monica had heard many compliments during her short life. Because Jessica could identify with that, and with Monica's need to seek attention in ways that were sometimes self-destructive, she wanted very badly to be a positive influence in the girl's life.

Jessica had been lucky enough to have Brenda Wheeler, a loving and vigilant housekeeper, on her side. Monica had no one except the overworked staff and volunteers at this facility for troubled teenagers. Which was why Jessica was hesitant to tell her she was going out of town. "I'd like you to keep working on your paintings for the next few weeks. I won't be here for the next couple of Wednesdays, but I'll get back as quickly as I can to see what you've done and teach you some new techniques, okay?"

The girl's square, acne-spotted face hardened. "You're quitting?"

"I'm not quitting my volunteer work here," Jessica replied firmly. "I simply have to take a couple of weeks off for family business."

"Holiday stuff, I bet," a painfully thin boy said from nearby, where he was working on a clay sculpture that Jessica privately thought more closely resembled an aardvark than the Corvette he had proclaimed it to be. "Next week's Thanksgiving. Folks with normal families get real busy between Thanksgiving and Christmas. Unlike us defectives," he added with a wry look at Monica, "who'd rather spend the holidays in a smelly alley than with the weirdos we got for relatives."

He had no idea, of course, how painful his words were to Jessica. Her relatives weren't exactly weirdos— at least, her siblings were all sane enough—but she

could hardly call hers a "normal" family. Not considering where her parents were at the moment, one in jail,
the other in a mental institution.

"I'll be back," she assured them and the other four
scruffy teenagers working with various degrees of enthusiasm on projects in the classroom-turned-studio. "I
promise."

She hoped that by the next time she saw them, there
would be some major changes in her own life. Maybe
then she could concentrate more fully on helping them
make much-needed changes in their own.

Monica was clearly not happy about Jessica's plans
to miss a couple of Wednesdays, but she would not
openly admit that she had come to depend upon and
enjoy these informal art classes. Jessica hoped her plans
didn't interfere with the girl's therapy, which was pro-
gressing very slowly, but she couldn't let herself be distracted even by that important consideration.

She had come too far with her plans to take any
chance of being thwarted again, for any reason.

"Yo, Fields. Where the hell you been for the past
month?"

Sam turned slightly on his bar stool to acknowledge
the stocky, bristle-haired, recently retired cop who slid
onto the next stool. It was Wednesday evening, and Sam
had left Jessica safely tucked into her bungalow, where
he had seen the studio lights burning ever since she had
returned from her volunteer gig. It felt good to have a
free evening without having to worry about Miss Walking Disaster.

"Hey, Ed. What's going on?"

"I asked first. Where you been?" As he spoke, Ed motioned to the bartender and pointed to Sam's beer to indicate he would have the same.

"Busy."

"Work busy or play busy?"

Sam chuckled wryly. "Definitely work."

"Too bad. I thought maybe you'd gotten involved with a rich, gorgeous blonde and left all this behind."

Sam's eyebrows shot up. "What have you heard?"

Lifting his foaming mug to his lips, Ed paused. "I was just joking. Why? *Is* there a rich, gorgeous blonde?"

Shaking his head impatiently at his own uncharacteristic quickness to jump to conclusions, Sam replied, "Many of them. I just haven't found one willing to put up with me yet. In fact," he added with a slight smile, "the last one I talked to informed me she would rather walk in front of a bus than to see my face again."

That made his old friend laugh. "Ain't no surprise there. You do have a face that would scare a hungry grizzly back into his cave."

Automatically, Sam glanced at the mirror behind the bar. His own familiar face gazed back at him, a bit grimmer than usual, but still ordinary enough, in his opinion. His ex-wife had called him "good-looking—in an average Joe sort of way." He had never figured out if it was a compliment, but not being the vain type, he hadn't wasted much time worrying about it.

"So what are you working on now? Or can you tell me?"

Ed had always been curious about the small-time private investigation business Sam had started a couple of years ago after leaving the San Francisco police department. Still smarting from his ugly divorce—and still humiliated at having learned afterward that his cop-groupie ex-wife had slept with several of his co-workers—Sam had wanted a job that let him be his own boss, set his own hours and interact with other people as little as necessary.

Money hadn't been an issue. Sam's needs had always been simple, and he figured meals into his expenses when he billed the rich clients who appreciated his prudence about their business. The interest from a trust fund left by his maternal grandparents gave him a little cushion, but he would likely never be rich. That wasn't one of his goals.

When clients wanted to look important, they took their security concerns to the high-profile investigation firms. When their concerns were more personal and private, discreet word of mouth led them to Sam. He made it clear from the outset that he didn't break the law—though he'd been known to dip his toes into the shallow waters that marked the line—and he didn't talk, not even to the point of listing previous clients on his professional résumé.

So Ed's asking about his latest case came more from wistfulness than expectation; he knew Sam wouldn't give him any juicy details. "Can't discuss it, except to say that I'm sort of a bodyguard at the moment."

Ed grumbled into his beer. "You can trust me, you know."

"With my life," Sam replied without hesitation. And then added, "But not with the details of my assignments. You know that."

"Yeah, I know," Ed conceded with a slight sigh. "That was one of your problems on the job. You wouldn't even share your files with your fellow officers."

Sam shrugged. "What can I say? I've never been a team player."

"Just like your old man."

Sam winced. He never cared to be compared to his father, a longtime beat cop with a fondness for whiskey and women, and who had died ten years ago when a speeding drunk had mowed him down in front of his favorite bar at midnight. He'd had enough of those comparisons from his embittered mother, who had passed away three years ago still mourning the man she had divorced by law but had never banished completely from her heart.

"You know, this retirement life is pretty damn boring," Ed muttered, staring morosely at his own aging reflection. "When a man's used to having somewhere to go and something to do every day, it ain't easy getting out of bed when there's no reason to do so."

Ed's wife had died last year, and Sam imagined that the older man was at loose ends now that mandatory retirement had taken away the job he'd loved. "You should find something new to occupy your time," he offered awkwardly. "Volunteer work, maybe," he added, remembering Jessica Parks's regular stint at the behavioral facility.

Ed grunted. "Not so easy working for nothing when you're used to drawing a paycheck. Maybe for folks that retire with plenty of money, but a cop's pension doesn't exactly encourage philanthropy. Actually, I was thinking about finding a new job. Maybe some part-time work."

Sam nodded. Ed was only in his midsixties, and in good shape, considering. There was no reason he couldn't find work, assuming a prospective employer would overlook the age thing. "What are you interested in?"

Running a stubby fingertip around the top of his beer mug, Ed cleared his throat. "Thought maybe I could find a small investigation agency that could benefit from the experience of an ex-cop. I'm pretty handy with a computer, you know. Got plenty of experience sitting stakeout."

Oh, hell. Looked as though this friendly exchange had suddenly turned into a job interview. Sam squirmed on his stool, trying to decide what to say. Truth was, there were times he could use some help, as badly as he hated to admit it. And there was no one he trusted more than Ed Armstrong. But he would hate to risk a long-time friendship if a professional collaboration didn't work out.

"Maybe we can talk about it over dinner," he said after a moment. "But you have to remember, I've got a very small operation. There are times when I'm lucky to get paid, much less support anyone else."

"I've got my retirement check to tide me through the lean times. I need the work more than the money. And I've always thought I'd like to try my hand at what you do—me and every other cop on the force," Ed added wryly. "I've had a few friends in the business, and I know it ain't like TV. Mostly routine stuff. But it would be something more productive to do than watch my toe-nails grow. And, damn it, Sam, I need that."

Sam nodded again. It was a plus that Ed wasn't expecting nonstop drama and excitement. There were probably several tasks he could do that would help Sam out immensely. While the thought of being responsible for anyone else weighed heavily on him, he guessed if he had to work with anyone, Ed wouldn't be so bad.

"We'll talk," he promised again, trying to ignore the worry that hiring an employee was the first step toward the life of responsibility and obligation that he had escaped two years ago.

Satisfied that he had made his case, Ed obligingly changed the subject to the football playoffs while they finished their beers.

Jessica's nerves were stretched almost to the breaking point during the remainder of that week. She stayed in her cottage much of the time, finalizing her travel plans by computer, trying to burn off energy through her painting.

Her phone rang more often than usual. Caroline called several times, as did Cade and Emily. Perhaps her friend and siblings sensed that Jessica was keeping something from them. Something that made them uneasy—as she so often did. Jessica did her best to convince all of them that she was fine, simply busy with several new painting projects for an anticipated showing in February.

She hated lying to them, but she didn't trust any of them not to interfere if they found out what she was scheming. Caroline and Emily would be concerned about her, and so would Cade, in his rather bossy and overly responsible manner. She couldn't risk having any of them try to stop her. Or worse, say something to her father.

On the rare occasions when she had to go out, she kept looking warily over her shoulder, trying to spot the man who had been following her. She saw no signs of him, which meant either that he had given up or he had gotten more skilled at hiding from her. She wanted to believe the former, but she had a sinking suspicion that the latter was true. Something in the man's hard jaw and intense green eyes made her doubt that he was the type to give up easily.

That thought led her to an all new attack of anxiety. What if Walter had simply replaced one paid shadow with another one? How did she know there wasn't someone new watching her every move?

Sitting in a coffee shop in the financial district after going by her bank to make a withdrawal—one she hoped her father or brother wouldn't learn about too soon—she eyed the other customers, trying to decide if any of them looked particularly interested in her. Her gaze lingered on the back of a blond man in one corner, but then she relaxed when he turned his head and she saw immediately that it was not the one who had been following her.

Maybe he really had gone away. And maybe her father had decided to forget about having her followed for the time being.

And maybe pigs would fly, she thought with a frown.

"Excuse me, miss?"

Jumping slightly, she turned to look up at the older man standing by the tiny table-for-two where she sat with her latte and newspaper. Ex-military, she would bet, judging from the brush-cut hair and stiff bearing. Older than she would expect for someone hired by her father, but she wasn't ruling him out.

"Yes?" she asked, her tone cool.

"I think you dropped this." He held out a black leather glove. "It was on the floor behind your chair."

Automatically, she checked the pocket of her leather jacket. She dug out a single glove that matched the one he held. "Yes, it is mine," she said, her voice a bit warmer now. "Thank you."

He smiled, then nodded toward the mug in front of her. "Do you mind if I ask what you're having? That looks pretty good on a damp, cool afternoon like this."

"It's a mocha latte. And it is good."

"Maybe I'll try one, then. Have a nice day."

Automatically murmuring a response to the clichéd phrase, Jessica watched him walk away. He never glanced at her again as she finished her latte then gathered her things to leave, making sure she had both gloves this time. Apparently she had let her paranoia run away with her again. This was what her father always did to her, making her constantly question herself and everyone around her.

She hoped before long she would finally have some answers to those lifelong doubts.

She almost got away from him.

Sam didn't know what made him assign Ed to watch Jessica overnight Wednesday, since she rarely left her cottage after 10:00 p.m. or before 8:00 a.m. Something about the increasing secretiveness of her actions—and something about the furtive bank visit Ed had witnessed while tailing her—nagged at him.

Even as he asked Ed to keep an eye on her place from midnight to 7:00 a.m. while Sam got some rest, he wondered just how long he intended to keep this up.

Walter's hearing was scheduled to begin a week from next Monday—the last week in November. Sam's assignment had been to keep an eye on Jessica until then, after which Walter seemed confident he would be free to watch her himself. Even had Sam been more convinced of Walter's chances of walking away from that trial a free man, he wasn't sure he wanted to spend the next two weeks shadowing Jessica, especially this twenty-four hour surveillance he had initiated.

Damn, but he wished it was his commitment to his job—even eagerness for a paycheck—that had him watching out for her, and not an itchy feeling combined with an ever-present awareness of the vulnerability hidden beneath the bravado she had shown to him.

His cell phone rang just as he poured his first cup of coffee Thursday morning. He had already showered and dressed, and thought he had time for breakfast and the newspaper before relieving Ed on Jessica-watch. He'd been wrong.

"She's on the move," Ed reported. "I assume you want me to follow her?"

Startled, Sam looked at his watch. Not even 6:00 a.m. yet. "Where's she headed?"

"Not sure yet. Her car just pulled out of the driveway."

"Stay close enough not to lose her, but far enough back to keep her from spotting you. Remember, she isn't easy to fool."

He was already on the run to his own car, a bad feeling gripping him.

Jessica's heart was pounding so hard she could feel it banging against the wall of her chest. After all the years, all the careful planning, all the lies and anxiety, she was finally going through with the plan she had been making for so very long.

The last time she'd tried this, she had ended up locked in a room that was little more than a closet, certain she was going to die. Eight years later, the trauma of that ordeal still held her in its grasp, but she refused to give in to the fear. She wasn't eighteen and naive anymore, she reminded herself. This time she would be on her guard.

She took a winding route to the Oakland airport— just in case. There wasn't a lot of traffic, though the morning commute had begun. She'd left earlier than necessary to catch her flight, but she wanted to arrive in plenty of time. She'd been too anxious to wait any longer, anyway. She kept looking nervously up at the rearview mirror, but no vehicle in particular caught her attention.

She could have departed from the San Francisco airport, but she didn't want anyone finding her tracks too quickly. To further conceal her plans, she had carried the tickets and her passport in her tote bag everywhere she had gone lately, along with a few letters from her mother. She hadn't let that bag out of her sight for a moment, nor had she allowed the slightest hint of her intentions to escape her when she had talked to Caroline or her siblings.

She'd had to buy the tickets in her own name, of course, considering the state of airport security, but by the time anyone figured out she was gone, she hoped it would be too late to stop her. She could only hope Green Eyes hadn't been on the job this early.

She was prepared to fight him—or anyone else who tried to get in her way this time.

"Sam—she's headed for the airport."

Using the hands-free function of his cell phone, Sam tightened his grip on his steering wheel as he replied, "I'm almost there, Ed. Don't lose her. I'll get back to you."

Disconnecting that call, he placed another. "Got anything yet?" he asked without bothering to identify himself when a woman's voice answered.

"Jessica Parks is booked on the 11:00 a.m. flight to Chicago," Angie Sawyer replied, her rich voice still morning gravelly. "She should land in Chicago at around three this afternoon, our time."

"Why the hell is she going to Chicago?"

"From Chicago, she's headed for Zurich. From Zurich, she's taking a flight to Geneva. Barring delays, it's a trip of about seventeen hours total—and it's nine hours later in Geneva than it is here. Major jet lag ahead."

"Angie, you are a miracle worker," Sam told his old friend with utter sincerity. "I don't know how you do it."

"Let's just leave it at that, shall we?"

Because he suspected there were things about her methods he would be better off not knowing, he merely said, "I owe you."

"Big-time," she agreed. "Is the sun even up yet?"

"I know how you feel about morning, and I promise I'll make it up to you. Now tell me I've got seats on those flights, and I'll be your slave forever."

"You've got seats—and you don't want to know what they're costing you. Hope you've got your passport."

"Yeah, I've got it," he said in relief after scrambling in the glove compartment while trying to drive one-handed at breakneck speed. It would be another miracle if he made it to the airport in one piece, or without being stopped by a patrol car.

As for the expenses—Walter Parks would be picking those up. At least Sam sincerely hoped the old man would find a way to pay the debts he was racking up from jail.

He had little doubt Parks would order him to stay on Jessica's trail, though he wasn't sure what he was supposed to do once he caught up with her. Would Parks want him serving strictly as her bodyguard, or would he expect Sam to somehow try to interfere with her unexpected actions?

Sam had made some dicey business decisions before, but jumping on a plane to Switzerland on such short notice and without a specific plan in mind probably took the cake. Maybe he was taking his bodyguard responsibilities too far this time. Yet the thought of pretty, accident-prone Jessica Parks heading off to Europe on her own for heaven only knew what purpose made his head hurt. Damn it.

Angie seemed to read his mind—a talent he wouldn't put beyond her, since she was rather spooky in her ability to provide him with whatever information he needed on a moment's notice. "You've made last-minute unscheduled trips before, but this might be a record."

"I think you're right." Fortunately he kept a packed bag in his trunk, in addition to the passport in his glove compartment. In his line of work, it was always good to be prepared.

Chapter Four

Sam connected with his client while he was waiting to board, staying well in the background of milling travelers to keep Jessica from spotting him. It was an indication of Walter's wealth and influence that Sam had no difficulty having him summoned to a telephone; he'd simply said it was a family emergency.

"She's leaving the country," he said with little preamble. "She's booked on a flight to Switzerland."

Walter swore roughly through the phone lines. "Stop her."

"It's too late for that. The plane is already boarding."

"Damn it. Ahh—"

Because that sounded suspiciously like a grunt of pain, Sam frowned. "Parks?"

"I'm all right. Stress like this always gives me heartburn. Get on the plane with her, Fields. I don't care how you manage it. I'll pay your fare."

"Already arranged—but what exactly do you want me to do?"

"Keep her safe. And if there's any way on earth you can stop her from meeting with her mother in Lausanne, do it. I'll try to pull some strings from here, but there's only so much I can do under the present circumstances."

"Just why *are* you so opposed to Jessica meeting with her mother?"

"Haven't you been paying attention, Fields? Anna is dangerously unstable—so sick that she's been committed for most of Jessica's life. And Jessica, I'm sorry to say, is very much like her mother. I'm afraid that Anna and her ex-lover will have too much influence over Jessica, feed her a bunch of wild tales that Jessica might very well believe. That's just the sort of thing that could tip my daughter over the edge herself."

"Insanity is not contagious."

What might have been a growl rumbled in Sam's ear. "But it is hereditary. Why do you think I've watched my daughter so closely? You've said yourself that her behavior is erratic. Not to mention the danger of a wealthy, sheltered young woman traveling such a long way alone. The last time she tried to take off like this, she was kidnapped. It was a miracle she wasn't killed."

Sam had never particularly liked this guy—and he sure wouldn't go as far as to say he trusted him—but securing a high-profile client like Walter Parks had been a real coup for Sam's fledgling investigation business. Parks had directed a couple of other jobs his way, which had helped keep him afloat for the past year. Watching out for his daughter during Walter's incarceration had seemed like a simple enough task for a more-than-satisfactory fee.

The most difficult part of the job at the beginning had been Sam's unwelcome attraction to the young woman he was supposed to be objectively shadowing.

"Look, Fields." Walter sounded suspiciously cagey now. "I still have access to a couple of bank accounts the feds haven't frozen yet. I can have a sizable chunk of money transferred into your name with one phone call. All you have to do is keep Jessica safe. The best way would be to keep her away from her crazy mother. Try to get her safely back home and turn her over to her brothers. I'll make the arrangements for her care after that."

Sam suspected he knew exactly what sort of "care" Walter planned to arrange for his youngest daughter. The same sort of care he'd provided her mother for the past twenty-five years, most likely.

Every instinct he possessed was sounding an alarm as this call progressed. Something was seriously wrong, and he had a gut feeling it all originated with the man at the other end of the phone lines. The man who was about to be tried for several serious crimes—including murder.

"I'll take care of Jessica," he said into the phone. "You transfer the money. I'm going to need it. Last-minute trips to Switzerland are a bit out of my usual budget."

"Done." Walter seemed to have no doubt that the promise of payment had just bought him another unquestioningly loyal lackey. "Now, I have to go. I've got some calls to make. You stick close to my girl, and there will be a nice bonus for you if you get her home before midnight tonight."

Sam disconnected the call feeling as though he needed to go wash his hands. Walter Parks could well be the sort of man who would do anything for money, and maybe he thought Sam would, too. But he was wrong.

Sitting seven rows behind Jessica on the plane, Sam watched the back of her head, confident that she hadn't yet spotted him. It was inevitable that she would eventually, of course, if they were going to be traveling together for the next seventeen-plus hours, but he wanted to put the confrontation off for as long as possible.

There hadn't been time to don a disguise—not that he could have flown in disguise, anyway, in this new era of paranoid airport security. He had to settle for a baseball cap pulled low over his dark gold hair and a pair of tinted glasses with mirrored lenses to conceal his eyes.

Lacking anything better to do, he spent a while wondering what it was about him that she had spotted even in disguise. The way he walked, maybe? Something about the way he carried himself?

He'd have to practice walking and standing differently when he was undercover. He'd always been pretty good at it with everyone else, but Jessica had a particularly sharp eye, apparently.

He noticed that she drew a bit of attention from other men on the flight, men who didn't mind passing the time admiring a pretty young blonde. Most of them had the courtesy to be discreet about it, but there were a couple who ogled her with a boldness that made Sam's fists itch.

It wasn't a territorial thing, he assured himself. He had no intention of following up on his own unwanted attraction to Jessica Parks. But as her bodyguard, it was his responsibility to make sure she didn't have to fend off unwelcome advances during her long trip.

At least, that was what he told himself even as he glared at one particularly aggressive guy—a salesman, Sam would guess—who kept leaning across the aisle to make comments to Jessica. She appeared to be responding politely, but with little encouragement.

Sam could have told her that outright rudeness was the only way to get through to jerks like that, but rudeness didn't seem to be an intrinsic part of her nature. Even though she had tried her best to get rid of Sam with angry, cutting remarks, he remembered with a wry half smile.

The woman in the seat beside him apparently interpreted that smile as a signal that he was in the mood for conversation. She made a comment about the bad weather they were flying into, hoping aloud that it wouldn't interfere with her connecting flight to Boston, where she was going to spend the next week celebrating Thanksgiving with her family. Sam responded congenially, but he made no effort to keep the small talk flowing.

A brunette in her midthirties, she had a pleasant face and a musical voice, pretty dark eyes and a figure that was attractive even with the twenty extra pounds she carried. The kind of woman Sam might have flirted with had his concentration not been so focused on his job.

He hadn't looked for anything more than a pleasant evening with a woman since his divorce. Janice had stung him so badly that he couldn't even imagine putting himself into a situation like that again.

Hell, he hadn't really wanted to get married in the first place, but Janice had convinced him it was a good idea— and at first, everything had been just fine. He'd rather liked coming home to a warm meal and a warmer welcome. She'd been a bit of a fanatic about keeping a clean house.

It was only after he'd come home unexpectedly one afternoon to find her in bed with another cop that Sam had realized she was always prepared for company.

Shaking his head impatiently, he plucked a flight magazine from the back pocket of the seat in front of him and buried his face in it. He didn't really care about the articles, but anything beat sitting there thinking about the humiliating end of his short-lived marriage. He didn't know why he was thinking of that today, anyway.

He had a job to do. And not a clue about how he was supposed to do it.

Jessica had planned for every contingency, or so she had believed. The one thing she hadn't been able to predict was the weather.

She had known when she left Oakland that an early snowstorm was predicted in the Midwest. There had been warnings of delays in air travel, but she had taken a chance and left, anyway, afraid that if she didn't go today, she never would. Maybe she would be on the way to Zurich by the time the storm interfered with flights in and out of O'Hare.

But by the time the plane landed in Chicago, the pilot was already preparing them for the possibility that they probably wouldn't be leaving anytime soon. They had to circle for quite a while, so that it was almost four in the afternoon before they were cleared to land.

They were warned that the airport would soon be closed to both incoming and departing flights. Temperatures were expected to warm by the next morning, but because of the heavy snowfall here and also hitting the East Coast, they could expect delays of up to twenty-four hours, the pilot informed them sympathetically.

Groaning, Jessica thought that she wouldn't have put it past Walter to somehow arrange for this storm. Anything to keep her from finally getting to her mother.

"Bummer, isn't it?" The persistently flirtatious man across the aisle caught her eye with a commiserating grimace. "I don't know about you, but an overnight delay will put a serious crimp in my plans."

"Yes, mine, too." She laced her fingers tightly in her lap, trying to reassure herself that everything would still work out. After all, it would take a while for anyone to notice that she was gone.

She had plugged automatic timers into the lamps and the television in her cottage so that it appeared she was staying at home today. She'd dropped hints to her friends and family that she planned to concentrate on her art for a few days, and might not immediately return phone messages. They knew she sometimes holed up in her studio for days at a time, so that behavior wouldn't seem unusual to them now.

Even if her father's hired snoop was still on the job,

he wouldn't necessarily know she wasn't home, she mused. Green Eyes would very likely spend the entire day watching lights go on and off in her cottage windows, a prospect that she found quite satisfying. By the time anyone realized she wasn't home, and by the time they tracked her movements to the Oakland airport, she hoped to already be in Switzerland, her mission well under way.

"It would be a shame to spend all that time bored and at loose ends in the airport, don't you think?" the pushy wannabe Lothario persisted. "Maybe you and I could find something to do to entertain ourselves until the storm clears, hmm?"

"Fortunately, I brought a couple of good books," Jessica replied. "That's all the entertainment I want."

She deliberately turned her shoulder to him. Some men were incredibly slow to take a hint.

For some reason, she found herself picturing a green-eyed man with tumbled dark gold hair and a lazy smile. Even as she thought again that it was terribly unfair for anyone in league with her father to look that darned good, she was greatly relieved that she wouldn't have to deal with him again for the foreseeable future.

Something told her he wouldn't be nearly as easy to brush off as the man across the aisle from her.

The general pandemonium at O'Hare made it easy for Sam to keep an eye on Jessica without her spotting him. He watched as she joined a crowd of frantic travelers trying to persuade airport officials to let their flights take off despite the dangerous conditions, but she conceded more quickly than most, seeming to accept the inevitable delay with gloomy resignation.

Staying well behind her, he followed her to a bank of windows, where she perched on a vinyl bench and watched the snow fall. She clutched her ever-present red tote bag in her arms, and her face was as clouded as the sky outside.

He couldn't help wondering what she was thinking, and what had brought her to this place in this manner. Why had she felt it necessary to sneak away as she had? Why hadn't she been able to turn to her siblings for advice, if not to her father? Did she really feel so alone?

Damn, but she looked pretty sitting there framed in a frosted window, her fair hair reflecting the bright fluorescent lights above her, her big blue eyes dominating her oval face. Maybe if he were a few years younger, and not working for her father, and hadn't been burned by his faithless ex-wife...

"And maybe if frogs had wings," he muttered in disgust, shaking his head. A couple of elderly women standing near him gave him a wary glance and sidled away, obviously unnerved by his grim expression and the fact that he was talking nonsense to himself.

His attention was drawn quickly back to Jessica, and his frown deepened when he saw the pushy guy from the plane—the one Sam had dubbed "Not So Good Time Charley"—edging closer to Jessica's bench. That guy just didn't know when he was crossing the line, Sam thought irritably. And apparently Jessica wasn't doing a very good job of getting the message to him that she wasn't interested in an airport dalliance to pass the time.

As much as she would resent it, maybe it was time for Sam to interfere.

He relaxed against the wall again when the guy spoke to Jessica and she said something in return that had ol' Charley hurrying away with a scowl that indicated he had been firmly rebuffed. So maybe Jessica was better able to take care of herself than Sam had expected. Anyone who looked like that must have had plenty of unwelcome advances in her time. Apparently she had learned to deal with them harshly enough when necessary.

Relieved that he wouldn't have to reveal himself yet, he went back to watching her.

With each passing moment Jessica spent at the airport, she could almost feel her father closing in on her. Paranoid, of course, with him being in jail in San Francisco, but she had learned from hard experience that Walter had a knack for getting his way, despite the obstacles.

Unlike the hundreds of other stranded travelers, she didn't while away the hours exploring the shops and attractions in the airport. She bought expensive airport food at around 6:00 p.m. because she was hungry, but she ate mechanically, barely tasting the meal. She stayed close to the gate where her plane was to depart, almost afraid that if she moved too far away it would leave without her.

She made no effort to find a hotel room for the night, as so many others had done. Maybe she was being superstitious, but she felt as though staying close was her best bet for getting back on track in her mission.

She claimed a spot on the carpeted floor with her

back against a wall and pulled a paperback suspense novel from her tote bag. She buried her face in the book, hoping the fast-paced story would make the time pass more quickly.

Every so often she felt a funny sensation, as though she were being watched. Each time she glanced up surreptitiously to look around, but she didn't notice anyone in particular.

A few bored men tried to catch her eye, maybe hoping the young blonde would want some company, but she made sure she didn't do anything that could be interpreted as encouragement. Using her book as both a diversion and a shield, she forced herself to be patient, when every muscle in her body twitched with the need to be on her way again.

She was more than a little unnerved when a couple of television crews appeared to do a story about the airport shutdown, but she made sure she didn't get anywhere within range of their cameras. Chances were that no one would recognize her in the background of a weather-related news story, but she took precautions, anyway. She was relieved when the crews left, having nothing new to report except that flights were expected to resume the next morning.

As night fell, weary would-be travelers began to look for places to sleep. Every bench and chair was taken, and people stretched out on the floors, using bags for pillows and coats for blankets. Conversation levels, which had been quite loud earlier, fell to a muted buzz. A few whining children and crying babies could be heard in the background, but Jessica was able to tune them out along with the other noises as she pillowed her head on one arm and lay on her side with her back to the wall.

She was glad now that she had dressed comfortably for the flight in a white-trimmed black hoodie and matching fleece pants with sneakers. The fabric wouldn't wrinkle, and it was a comfortable weight even in the drafty terminal.

She was almost afraid to doze, worried that she might miss an important announcement, but she hadn't slept well last night and her eyelids were growing heavy. Letting herself relax as much as possible under the circumstances, she assured herself that she couldn't possibly sleep through a stampede of travelers anxious to board their flights.

Just as she slipped into a restless sleep, she had that eerie feeling again that she was being watched. It wasn't strong enough to make her open her eyes—and besides, for some reason it didn't unnerve her this time. She felt almost as if someone was watching over her, keeping her safe. Smiling a little at her foolishness, she deliberately allowed her mind to go gray.

She woke with a start, her heart racing as if she had been running. It took her a moment to orient herself, and then she tried to relax. Though she couldn't remember the details of her dream, it had been a bad one.

Her restlessly dozing mind had taken her back to the last time she'd tried to leave the country, and the kidnapping that had followed. It was an old nightmare, and one she made every effort not to remember. At least she hadn't woken up screaming this time, she thought in relief, her cheeks burning in humiliation at the very thought.

"Are you okay? You were whimpering."

The concerned question, asked in a husky male voice, made her swallow a groan. Apparently she hadn't been entirely silent during her dream.

"I'm fine, thank you," she said, turning her head toward the man who had scooted next to her to ask. "It was just a bad—"

Her breath caught in her throat and her heart, which had just slowed to a normal pace, began to hammer against her chest again. She could only hope she was still dreaming, still caught in a nightmare from which she would shortly awaken. She didn't want to believe this man was really here with her in this airport so far from San Francisco. "You—"

"Calm down," he said, reaching out quickly to lay a hand on her shoulder. "You don't want to cause a scene at four in the morning. Security will have us both whisked out of this terminal before you finish the first scream."

There was no mistaking that voice. The same deep, rough-edged voice she'd heard several times back in San Francisco—and damn it, in a couple of unwelcome daydreams. She didn't have to guess at the color of the emerald-green eyes hidden behind a pair of lightly tinted glasses, or of the burnished gold hair partially concealed beneath a baseball cap bearing an Oakland Raiders logo.

It was only his very sobering warning about airport security that kept her from shrieking at him. The one thing she did not want to do was to call attention to herself now.

Pushing herself to a sitting position, she shoved her tumbled hair out of her face and hissed at him, "What are you doing here?"

"That's pretty obvious, isn't it? I followed you. We were on the same plane, actually—seven rows apart."

Chagrined that she hadn't noticed him in all the hours that had passed since she'd left that morning, she clenched her hands into fists in her lap. So much for her smugness at getting away unnoticed. All her careful planning, all her secrecy and caution…

"Please tell me you haven't called my father," she found herself almost begging. "Whatever he's paying you, I'll double it," she added recklessly.

She didn't have the money, of course, but she would get it somehow. Whatever it took. "Please…"

"Jessica, I've already called him."

She groaned and closed her eyes, her shoulders sagging. "When?"

"Just before we took off this morning."

"Why has it taken you this long to say anything?"

"Because all I was instructed to do was to watch you. To keep you safe."

"Safe." She said the word on a toneless laugh. "Right. That's all my father wants. For me to be 'safe.'"

"You think there's something more to it?"

She tilted her chin to glare at him. "Would you believe anything I said?"

He hesitated a moment before answering. "Maybe."

At least he hadn't patronized her with a reassuring lie.

"Never mind," she said gruffly, turning her head again. "You work for my father. He's bought your loyalty."

His fingers tightened just a little on her shoulder. "No one buys me."

Maybe there was just a bit too much emphasis in his words. Protesting too much because he knew she was right?

She tried to shrug off his hand. "What are you going to do now? Are you going to try to take me back to San Francisco? Because I swear I'll fight you even if airport security locks us both up."

His sudden smile in response to her fierce whisper would have made her breath catch—had she been able to breathe since she had looked up and recognized him. "As intriguing as that sounds, I don't want to fight you, Jessica. I think it's time for us to talk."

Clutching her tote bag to her chest like a shield, she eyed him suspiciously. "Is it money you want? Because I need what I have with me now, but I swear I'll get you whatever you want if you'll—"

His smile vanished abruptly as he interrupted her. "Damn it, why do you Parkses think everything comes down to cash? I don't want your money. I want some answers."

"I don't understand. Are you working for my father or aren't you?"

"I am. Or I have been."

She didn't know whether to find any encouragement in those words. Clutching her tote more tightly, she asked, "What do you want from me?"

"I told you. I just want to talk."

Looking around the terminal crowded with bodies, both prone and upright, she asked, "Here?"

He followed her glance, then shrugged. "There's a restaurant on the other side of the terminal. The kitchen's closed, but they're letting people sit at the tables and talk. Let's see if we can find a couple of seats there."

She glanced toward the desk, where a weary-looking airline employee was talking on the phone.

"Don't worry, you won't miss any announcements," he reassured her. "The plane won't be taking off for a few hours yet."

She still didn't quite trust him, but she could see no other choice except to go with him. But if he tried anything…anything at all…she would give him the fight of his life, she vowed.

Chapter Five

They found a small table in a back corner of the airport restaurant. Sam even managed to obtain a couple of canned sodas from a vending machine. He handed one to Jessica as he took his seat across from her, and she opened it with the look of someone who craved caffeine.

It was a bit louder in here, since no one was even pretending to sleep. Everyone looked disheveled, tired and a bit grumpy, but at least no one was paying attention to the somber couple in the back corner.

Reminding himself not to be sucked into Jessica's paranoia, Sam ignored everyone else and focused on her pale—but still stunning—face. "Okay, talk."

She lifted one delicately arched eyebrow. "About…?"

"About where you're going. Why you felt the need

to sneak out of your house before dawn. Why your father is so determined to keep you from going."

What might have been bitterness darkened her blue eyes. "Haven't you heard? My father feels the need to protect me from myself. I'm crazy."

Annoyed for some reason, he snapped, "Don't give me that. No one has ever accused you of being crazy."

"Unstable, then. Emotionally fragile."

He couldn't argue with either of those assessments, since that was exactly the way her father had described her. Whether Sam believed it…well, that remained to be seen, and had everything to do with why he had finally decided to approach her after she'd awakened from her bad dream.

"Is that the way you see yourself?" he asked, instead.

She glared at him. "Of course not—even though my father has tried hard enough to convince me otherwise."

"And why would he do that?"

"Isn't it obvious? My father thrives on complete and total control. He wasn't always able to control my other siblings, so he made sure to keep his thumb on me."

"Why you, in particular?"

She ran a fingertip around the top of her soda can, avoiding his eyes as she answered. "I once heard my father tell someone that every time he looks at me he sees my mother looking back at him. It wasn't a compliment."

"Isn't it natural that he would worry about you?" Sam suggested tentatively. "After all, you are his youngest child—and your mother does have problems, apparently…"

Her eyes lifted to his, and the expression in them made his words fade to silence.

"Are you close to your parents, Mr.—I'm sorry, you have me at a disadvantage."

"Sam Fields."

She nodded. She didn't bother to lie that it was nice to meet him, he thought ruefully.

"Are you close to your parents?" she repeated.

"My parents are both dead. But no, we weren't a particularly close family. They divorced when I was just a kid. My father spent the rest of his life pretending his family didn't exist most of the time, and my mother spent the rest of hers trying to keep me from turning into him—with little success, according to her."

That caught her off guard. She studied his face for a long moment before saying, "So you know what it's like to be negatively compared to a parent. It hurts, doesn't it?"

"Yeah," he said, rather surprised at his own candor. "It hurts."

"When you were little—before your parents' marriage fell apart—did they ever tell you they loved you?"

It was hard to remember that far back, partially because he had spent so many years trying not to do so. "Yeah, I guess," he said, wondering how she had managed to turn the conversation to his childhood. "But—"

"My father never said those words to me," Jessica said flatly. "Not once. I don't know if he ever said them to my brothers or sister, but I doubt it. The only person who ever said she loved me was our housekeeper, Brenda Wheeler."

He squirmed in his seat with typically masculine discomfort at the nature of this conversation. "I'm sorry," he said, feeling incredibly awkward. "But—"

"I used to fantasize about my mother," she went on

as if she hadn't heard him. "I told myself she would come back someday and she would be the perfect mother. She would tell me she loved me and she was proud of me and that I was everything she had ever wanted in a daughter. And there would be laughter in our household, and warmth. And maybe she would even make my father happy again, so he would love me, too," she added in a near whisper.

Because he didn't know what to say to that, Sam kept quiet, watching the emotions play across her face. Fighting a totally inappropriate urge to reach out to her, just to hold her hand—a gesture he knew she would reject instantly.

"You wonder why I'm telling you these things," she said perceptively. "You think I'm making a play for your sympathy—and maybe you're right. I'm trying to make you understand how badly I want to see my mother. It's something I've wanted all my life."

"I can understand that. Hell, I'd feel the same way. But what if—"

"What if I get there and find out she really *is* crazy?" Jessica supplied when he hesitated.

He nodded, relieved that she had spelled it out so he didn't have to.

She shrugged and spoke in a tone that was obviously intended to sound nonchalant, but wasn't quite. "I'm aware that's a possibility. I can deal with it. I just have to know for certain."

"And how will you know for certain? Sometimes people who aren't…well, quite right can sound pretty persuasive."

"I'll know," Jessica repeated stubbornly. "Once I see her, talk to her, look into her eyes—I'll know. Besides, I have letters from her. Very lucid, believable letters. I think she's been kept locked up by my father for all these years just because she was an inconvenience to him."

"That's a pretty strong charge. And an unlikely one," he added gently. "Inconvenient relatives aren't just locked away these days without cause."

"Now *you're* the one who is being naive. With enough money, any nuisance can be made to disappear."

He didn't like being called naive. But he couldn't really disagree with her cynicism, either. Money did have a way of making unpleasant situations go away, he thought wryly. Wasn't that the very reason that Walter Parks was so confident he would serve little, if any, time for whatever crimes he'd been accused of?

But the Parks money didn't explain all of Jessica's behavior that Sam had observed during the past few weeks. "What about Derek Ross?"

She blinked a couple of times, but recovered quickly. "What about him?"

He figured if Jessica was willing to lay her cards on the table he should reciprocate—to a point. Besides, he needed to hear her side of the story before he formed his opinions. "Your father said Ross was once involved with your mother and now he's resurfaced to seek revenge against your family. He said Ross is dangerous, and he worries that he's using you in whatever scheme he's hatching."

"So that's the story Dad will use in the courtroom," Jessica murmured. "That Derek is demented and obsessed with revenge, so his testimony can't be trusted."

Sam lifted an eyebrow. "Ross is going to testify against your father?"

"So I'm told."

"Concerning the embezzlement charges?"

Jessica held his gaze steadily. "Concerning the murder charges."

"You think your father is guilty of killing his business partner twenty-five years ago?"

She framed her reply with care. "I think my father is capable of just about anything, Mr. Fields. And if you think that's paranoia, then you really don't know him very well."

The good news was that Sam Fields, if that was his real name, hadn't yet tried to haul her back to San Francisco.

The bad news was that he was there at all.

Jessica had a nagging suspicion that she was wasting her breath trying to make him understand why this trip was so very important to her. He probably couldn't care less as long as he got paid for following her around.

But still, he was listening. Even if he was doing so only to relieve the boredom of sitting in an airport, as long as they were talking she had a chance of getting through to him. And he had admitted that he knew what it was like to be unfairly criticized by a parent, which gave them a small point of reference—assuming he'd told the truth, of course.

"Well, Mr. Fields?" she prodded when he didn't immediately respond to her comment. "Don't you believe my father is capable of anything? Or would admitting it make you equally as bad, since you're willing to take his money?"

Okay, maybe digging at him wasn't the best way to bring him over to her side, she thought with a slight wince. Sometimes words just seemed to leap straight from her mind to her mouth without much interference in between, a trait that had gotten her in trouble too many times to count.

His eyes narrowed, and she had the sudden feeling that the temperature in the room had just risen a couple of degrees. She remembered those angry green flames in his eyes; she seemed to have a knack for igniting them.

For a moment, she thought he would tell her again that he wasn't for sale. But maybe he realized, as she did, that it was going to take more than words to convince her.

"Tell me what your mother said in her letters. And what Derek Ross has been telling you when you've met with him during the past few weeks," he ordered instead of responding to her question about her father.

"My mother told me that my father has kept her committed in Switzerland against her will."

"That's what you would expect her to say, whether she needed to be there or not."

"Perhaps. But she swears she was never diagnosed with the problems he claims. My father tells everyone that she was bipolar to the point of dysfunction, an alcoholic, suicidally depressed, completely out of control. He considered her a danger to herself and to her children, and that—combined with the lack of privacy for wealthy, prominent families in California—was why he sent her to Switzerland. He said that no medication has been effective for her in the long term and that she has never been deemed ready for release. According to Dad, she's had the best doctors available, but her condition is incurable."

"And Derek Ross?"

"Also according to my father, Derek is an example of how seriously disturbed my mother was. Derek is several years younger than my mother—he was barely twenty-two when he had an affair with her. Dad's explanation is that she found an equally troubled young man and seduced him by convincing him that she was being emotionally abused by her cold, evil husband. I don't think Dad knew about Derek when he sent Mother away, but he found out recently—when Derek surfaced along with rumors that he knows something incriminating about Dad's old partner's death."

Sam was beginning to look impatient. "All you're telling me is your father's side of the story. What have your mother and Ross told you?"

"Exactly what my father claims they would say," she replied flatly. "Mother admits she had problems with alcohol and depression, but she said she was never a danger to anyone, especially the children she loved. Derek told me that he met her when he was only twenty-two and fell desperately in love with her. Though he spared me the details, I got the impression the affair was very brief—maybe little more than a one-night stand. But he swears she was entirely sane, and that my father sent her away because she was a danger to him."

"What kind of danger?"

Jessica drew a deep breath. "Derek claims to have watched my father dispose of Jeremy Carlton's body. He said he told my mother about it just before she was sent away. She already had her suspicions, since she was on the yacht the night Carlton disappeared, and she heard my father and Carlton arguing violently."

Sam's expression held the skepticism Jessica had expected. "Why didn't Ross go to the police?"

"He was twenty-two. My father was already a very powerful man. After my mother disappeared, Derek was afraid the same thing would happen to him. He wasn't told what had happened to her, only that she was sent away. He didn't even know if she was still alive. He didn't think anyone would believe his story, especially if they found out he'd slept with Walter Parks's notoriously unstable wife. He left town and changed his name, living with his guilt and his memories until earlier this year, when Jeremy's sons—really my father's illegitimate children from his affair with Jeremy's wife—tracked him down while they were investigating their father's twenty-five-year-old death.

"He married not long after he left town," she added. "He had a daughter he raised alone after his wife died. He didn't want to risk the life he had built for her until his conscience gave him no other choice."

"And he told you all of this because...?"

"Why would he lie?"

"Maybe because he really is unbalanced. Face it, Jessica, it isn't exactly normal for a twenty-two-year-old man who supposedly witnessed a murder to simply skip town and change his name."

"Once again—he didn't think anyone would believe him. And he was afraid my father would hire someone to get rid of him."

"So he says. Maybe he's resurfaced for other reasons."

"Such as—?"

"Revenge. Money. If the Carltons are really out to hang your father in revenge for their father's murder and their mother's untimely death, they could have offered him a hefty bribe in return for his testimony."

Jessica shook her head. "He isn't like that."

In her opinion, Derek Ross was a nice guy—though admittedly somewhat weak to have given in to fear rather than do the right thing. The fact that he had married very quickly after he had moved away indicated that his emotions had been volatile twenty-five years ago. Still, he adored his daughter and wanted now to make amends with his past.

He fully supported Jessica in her quest to bring her mother home, though he'd said there was little he could do to help her, since he had to stay in San Francisco until the upcoming hearings. Even after meeting with him several times, Jessica had felt there were things he wasn't telling her, but still she instinctively trusted him—to a point. Maybe revenge was a part of his motive in testifying, but she didn't believe he was after money.

It annoyed her that Sam's gaze seemed to have become a bit pitying—as if he had no doubt that she was being too trusting. She lifted her chin defiantly. "I know what I'm doing, Mr. Fields. I'm going to see my mother. And there's nothing you can do to stop me."

He studied her face for so long that it was all she could do not to squirm beneath his scrutiny. She managed to hold her ground, keeping her eyes locked with his.

"Your father's going to try to stop you," he said after what felt like an eternity.

"Yes." She had no doubt of that.

Sam propped his elbows on the table and tented his fingers in front of his face, still studying her over them. "According to him, the Carltons are an embittered family who have had it in for him for some time. He swore to me that he's been set up and that his lawyers will make that very clear in court. He doesn't expect the prosecutors to have enough solid evidence to go to trial."

"Yes, that's what he's told me, as well," she replied steadily. "I hope he can prove his innocence in Jeremy Carlton's death. The thought that my father might have murdered someone is hardly comforting. Maybe Derek was wrong about what he thought he saw. After all, it was nighttime—and he'd been drinking—and he was very young."

She had looked for every hole in Derek Ross's story since she had first heard it. As many problems as she'd had with her father over the years, she didn't want to believe he was capable of murder.

"Whatever happened with Jeremy Carlton, I have to know for certain whether my father had my mother locked away because she was an inconvenience to him. I have to know if he's been telling the truth about her mental state—if he has, I want to find out what can be done to help her now."

Sam nodded. "That sounds reasonable."

She held her breath, waiting for him to enlighten her about what his next step would be. Was it too much to hope that he would concede her right to live her own life and go back to San Francisco without her?

She was taken completely aback when he said simply, "I'll go with you."

Jessica stared at Sam as if she couldn't quite believe she'd heard him correctly. "You'll do *what?*"

He lifted one shoulder in a slight shrug. "I'll go with you," he repeated. "I've already got tickets on your flights. This way I can be sure you're safe while you do whatever you feel you need to do."

"No." She had started shaking her head even before he finished speaking. "You can't go with me."

He merely lifted an eyebrow as an invitation for her to explain her reasons for refusing his company.

"I don't know you," she said bluntly. "I don't trust you. I don't want you to go to Switzerland with me."

He didn't take offense at her objections, so his tone was mild when he replied, "I won't interfere with your plans, unless I believe you're in danger."

"You're offering to serve as my bodyguard."

"I already am your bodyguard," he reminded her with a faint smile. "I have been for a while. Your father believes it's necessary, and I tend to agree with him— at least for the duration of this journey."

It was obvious that she'd been trying her best to be

calm and persuasive during their talk, but now her face took on that mulish expression he had come to recognize so well. "I don't want a bodyguard. I don't want you."

It irritated him to realize that he was suddenly wondering what it would take to make her want him, and not as a bodyguard. Especially since he had wanted her from the first time he'd seen her. Which didn't mean he intended to do anything about it, of course.

An involvement with Jessica Parks—even if he managed to talk her into it—was a recipe for disaster if he'd ever seen one. And Sam Fields was all about self-preservation these days—or at least, that was what he'd been trying so hard to believe.

"You have a choice," he said, pushing those irrelevant thoughts to the back of his mind. "You can accept my services, or you can resign yourself to having me follow you around the way I have been. Without your consent."

"You're determined to go to Switzerland?"

He patted the chest pocket of the leather bomber jacket he'd worn over a white oxford cloth shirt and faded jeans—the clothes he'd had on when he'd received Ed's call that morning. "I have my ticket right here. I don't intend to waste it."

Sam had never been particularly drawn to pouty women, but he had to admit that the way Jessica's full lower lip protruded slightly with her discontented frown made something tighten in his abdomen. A man couldn't help but look at that lip and wonder how it would taste, he reasoned. There was no need to read any more than that into it.

"I suppose I don't really have a choice at all," she murmured after a while. "You've already messed everything up, anyway, by calling my father."

"There's not a lot he can do to interfere from a jail cell," he pointed out, though he couldn't help remembering Walter's comment that he would do what he could from his end to keep Jessica from seeing her mother.

Jessica's expression turned wry. "I wouldn't have put it past my father to have arranged this snowstorm."

He couldn't help smiling faintly. "I think that might be giving him a bit too much credit."

She pushed her tumbled blond hair out of her face and murmured wearily, "When it comes to my father, it never pays to underestimate him. Or to anger him," she added in what might have been a subtle warning.

Damned if he would let Jessica's paranoia get to him. He'd made his decision to protect her during this pilgrimage she had planned for so long, and he would follow through—whether Walter Parks approved or not.

He decided it was best not to question his reasons too closely. Suffice it to say, he decided, when Sam Fields took a job, he saw it through to the end.

The morning dawned cold but sunny. As soon as it was light, the airport crews began to work on the runways, clearing them for takeoffs and landings. A general air of expectancy ran through the restless crowd in the airport terminals, and everyone began to prepare for departure.

Jessica tried to freshen up in the crowded ladies'

room, jostling for space in front of the mirrors so she could wash her face and comb her hair. She applied just enough makeup to keep her from looking pale and wan from tension and lack of sleep. Relieved that her clothes were still relatively fresh-looking, she tucked her tote bag beneath her arm, draped her black down coat over one arm and left the rest room.

Sam waited practically in the doorway, his arms folded across his chest and his booted feet crossed as if he was prepared to wait all day if necessary. He must have made short work of his own rest room visit, she thought with a touch of resentment. He looked as though he hadn't quite trusted her not to try to slip away from him—though she couldn't imagine where he thought she'd have gone.

Even though she knew she was wasting her breath, she tried one more time to reason with him. "Surely you have something better to do than go with me to Switzerland."

He shrugged, the smile in his eyes telling her that he knew exactly what she was trying to do. "I don't have any other plans. You're my only client at the moment."

"I am not your client."

He only smiled and motioned toward the gate where their plane was scheduled to depart. "We'd better get started on the security checks again. I've heard we could be boarding within the hour."

She didn't know how he accomplished it, but Sam managed to get the seat next to hers on the plane to Zurich. Now that he wasn't trying to hide from her anymore, he seemed to find it amusing to stay right at her side, making it difficult for her to ignore him. She tried, anyway, responding to his comments in monosyllables, avoiding his eyes as much as possible.

As soon as she was in her seat, she buckled the belt and pointedly buried her face in her book again. Surely even this guy could take that hint.

She should have known better.

"Are you going to ignore me all the way to Switzerland?" His voice was a low growl in her left ear.

She didn't look up from her book. "I'm going to try."

He chuckled. "Not very friendly of you."

"One doesn't have to be particularly friendly to the hired help."

She'd hoped to annoy him enough that he would back off. Instead, he merely laughed again.

She really wished he would quit doing that. Something about his rumbly laughter did funny things to her insides—and she did *not* want to be attracted to this man.

He still worked for her father, despite his promise to see her safely to her mother, and she would do well to keep that thought in the front of her mind. She could not trust her father—nor could she trust anyone who worked for him.

The engines began to rev, filling the cockpit with noise and the curious tension that always accompanies takeoff. Jessica clutched the armrests, preparing herself to leave the safety of the ground. She hoped the ground crew had done their job well so that the plane wouldn't skid off the runway. She hoped there was no ice on the wings, or wherever else ice built up and caused planes to crash.

"Nervous flyer?"

She could lie about it, but since she was clinging to the armrests for dear life, she doubted he would believe her. "Yes."

"Want to hold my hand?"

She curled her fingers more tightly around the armrest. "No."

"The offer stands if you change your mind."

"That's very kind of you." She tried to infuse her tone with sarcasm, even though her voice wasn't as steady as she would have liked.

"Just doing my job, ma'am."

It was obviously a mocking referral to her crack about the "hired help." Scowling down at her lap, she told herself she was quickly learning to hate this guy. But as the plane shot down the runway, it was all she could do not to reach for his hand.

Chapter Six

In preparation for the long flight to Zurich, Sam had bought a couple of paperbacks at an airport newsstand. Jessica had made it clear that she wasn't in the mood to talk, so he pulled out one of the books and settled in to wait. He wouldn't be the guy who bugged her on this flight, he vowed, but he'd bet before they landed she would be ready for conversation.

He stifled a smile when she pulled out an MP3 player half an hour into the trip and slipped the headphones rather defiantly over her ears. Oh, yeah, the silence was getting to her. Without glancing at her, he turned a page in his book, which would have been good enough to hold his attention had Jessica not been sitting so temptingly close to him.

Another twenty minutes passed before he heard her

make a sound that might have been a quick, muffled chuckle. He glanced in her direction, lifting his eyebrows in question. "Did you say something?"

She made a little face, her tone gruff when she replied, "I'm just listening to my theme song."

Without asking for permission, he reached over and removed her headphones.

"Hey," she protested, reaching for them, but he evaded her hand, slipping the earpieces into place so that he could hear the song that had amused her.

Because he spent a lot of time in his car and usually had the radio on while he drove, he recognized the song immediately. Matchbox Twenty's "Unwell." The singer insisted he wasn't crazy, just a little "impaired."

Sam didn't find the song as wryly funny as Jessica had. He tugged the earpieces away and handed them back to her. "You aren't crazy."

"Trying to convince me or yourself?" She turned off the player and stuffed it back into her tote bag. "Has anyone ever told you that you're entirely too pushy?"

"Once or twice." But he was still thinking about her so-called "theme song." "Why do you keep making cracks about being crazy?"

Looking out the window beside her, she shrugged. "That's what everyone says."

"Who's everyone? Your family? Your friends? Your doctors?"

She gave him a look then. "I haven't seen a doctor since I was thirteen. That one diagnosed me as angry and rebellious, but not seriously disturbed. I think my father was hoping the shrink would recommend I be put away—it would have made life so much easier for him."

"According to you, he didn't wait for such advice before having your mother locked away."

"My mother had no one to fight for her. Her drinking and depression had isolated everyone who had once cared for her. I had Brenda."

"Brenda?"

"Our housekeeper. She said all along there was nothing wrong with me that love wouldn't cure. She would have fought anyone who tried to lock me up, and Dad knew it. Because he valued her housekeeping and child-care skills too much to risk losing her, he turned me over to her and pretty much ignored me until he found out when I was eighteen that I had been corresponding with my mother. You can bet he got involved with my life again then."

"How did you get into contact with your mother?"

"I broke into his office when he was away one weekend and found the address of the asylum where he'd placed her. He had it well hidden, but I was persistent. When my father found out about it, I told him I'd found it while I was rummaging through his office to steal money for cigarettes. I didn't smoke—never could stand the smell—but I didn't think he needed to know that."

"You got a kick out of defying your father, huh?"

"As often as possible." She looked out the window again. "I guess I believed then that negative attention was better than no attention at all. I lied, I stole, I ran away, I did anything I could to get my father just to see me."

Sam found that quiet statement especially poignant. He pictured Jessica as a lonely little girl, fantasizing about the mother she had never known, striving for attention from the father who saw her only as an uncomfortable reminder of the wife he had sent away. A little girl who felt loved only by a paid housekeeper, and who would rather be punished than ignored.

He scowled when he realized he was doing it again— letting sympathy interfere with the objectivity he was trying so hard to maintain.

As if she had suddenly realized that she was getting too chatty with someone she had already proclaimed she didn't trust, Jessica crossed her arms and leaned her head against the back of her slightly reclined seat. "I'm tired. I'm going to take a nap."

"Good idea. We've got a long trip ahead of us."

She didn't respond.

Sam leaned back against his own headrest, his face turned so that he could look at her. She really was beautiful. She had the most perfect skin. Like...he hated thinking in clichés, but porcelain was the best comparison he could come up with. Except that porcelain was cold and hard. He would bet Jessica's skin was warm, and very, very soft.

"You're looking at me," she complained without opening her eyes.

"Yes."

"Stop it."

"If you insist." He turned his head forward and closed his eyes. A nap didn't sound like such a bad idea to him, either.

* * *

Jessica returned to full consciousness in small steps. She became aware first of the steady hum of jet engines, and then the sounds of other passengers talking. The overhead vent blew a soft rush of cool air directly onto her right cheek. Her left cheek was comfortably cradled against...

Abruptly opening her eyes, she straightened so quickly she nearly threw herself against the window. She couldn't believe she had been sleeping with her cheek on Sam's shoulder. Nor did she believe that she had put herself there. She glared at him.

Flexing his right arm, he gave her a suspiciously innocent smile in return. "Nice nap?"

"I was sleeping just fine in my own seat."

"I was afraid your neck would get stiff. You're a pretty heavy sleeper, aren't you?"

"Only when I'm exhausted." She glanced at her watch. She'd been asleep a little more than an hour, which meant a good five hours remained of this flight. There was nothing of interest to look at through the window, and she was tired of her book. The in-flight movie was one she had seen and didn't particularly like.

She squirmed restlessly in her seat. As much as she told herself to be patient, she was still anxious to reach the conclusion of this seemingly endless journey.

"Would you like to stretch your legs?"

"I'm fine," she answered shortly. "Just bored."

"Want to talk?"

She sighed. "That's all I've done since you showed up in the airport. I've told you just about everything there is to know about me."

"Oh, I doubt that."

She tilted her chin to look at him. "Maybe I should ask *you* some questions."

"What do you want to know?"

For someone who had shown no compunction at butting his nose into her business, he seemed awfully wary about revealing anything about himself. "Is Sam Fields really your name?"

"Of course it's my name."

"How did you hook up with my father?"

"I've done a couple of jobs for him in the past. Security stuff. Background checks. Information on an employee who was stealing from one of the jewelry stores."

"So he figured he could count on you to spy on his daughter."

Sam sighed. "To watch out for his daughter," he corrected. "It made sense to me at the time. Seemed natural that with him in jail and your siblings somewhat scattered, he would worry about your safety. Especially since you've been targeted before by someone hoping to grab a chunk of his fortune."

Jessica scowled. Sam Fields knew entirely too much about her. "He told you I was kidnapped?"

"Yes." A new note of gentleness softened Sam's deep voice now. "He said it was a terrifying ordeal for you."

She made sure there was no emotion at all in her own voice. "Yes. It was."

"For your father, too. He admitted to me that he's been overprotective since. He implied that he's recently heard rumors that he or his family could be in danger again with everything in such a turmoil because of his arrest."

Jessica locked her fingers in her lap so tightly that her knuckles ached. Voicing her suspicions about that kidnapping would serve no purpose other than to reinforce Sam's belief that she was paranoid about her father.

"Considering that history, and your unwillingness to take precautions on your own behalf, it seemed only reasonable to me to serve as your bodyguard for a few weeks. Just until after the hearing."

"I'm sure he paid you very well for your services."

She knew it annoyed him whenever she mentioned money, but she couldn't resist the occasional dig. Besides, it seemed like a good idea to remind herself every once in a while that the sympathy and concern Sam displayed toward her had been bought and paid for.

"You said you called my father when you figured out my travel plans yesterday," she said when he refused to respond to her comment. "What did he say when you talked to him?"

"I consider my communications with my client to be privileged information."

Narrowing her eyes at him, she noted the irritated slant to his nicely shaped mouth. She figured he was paying her back for referring again to his status as her father's employee. "You had no right to discuss my private affairs with anyone else, including my father."

"I was just doing my job, ma'am."

Now she was the one getting irritated again. "Would you please just tell me what he said?" she asked testily.

After a moment during which he seemed to conduct a brief mental debate, Sam shrugged, the gesture making his shoulder brush against hers. "First he asked me to try to stop you."

That admission took her mind off her too vivid awareness of their brief physical contact. "And just how did he think you were going to do that?"

"I don't know. I told him it was too late for that, anyway."

Trying to rein in her temper, she asked, "What did he say then?"

"He told me to follow you. Keep you safe while he…"

"While he did what?" she asked when he hesitated.

"While he did what he could from there to prevent you from seeing your mother."

Jessica's fists clenched more tightly in her lap. "Damn him. Does he really think he can stop me?"

"I don't know how he intended to accomplish it now that you're already on your way. He just asked me to guard you."

She'd had about all she could take of Sam telling her that her father only wanted what was best for her. "Maybe it makes you feel better to believe it, Mr. Fields, but you're wasting your breath trying to convince me that my father only cares about my safety."

"Would you stop calling me 'Mr. Fields'? My name is Sam. And would your father really go to the trouble of hiring me if he wasn't concerned about your safety?"

"To watch me. Not to watch over me. He wants to know where I am and what I'm doing at all times so he can keep me from finding out the truth about my mother. And maybe the truth about him, as well."

"And what do you think you're going to find?"

She could hear no inflection at all in his voice. If he was skeptical, he hid it well, but he wasn't making an effort to assure her that he believed her, either.

"I think he split up our family to protect his own neck, and I think he's trying to do the same thing now. And I think—I think there's a very good chance that he's guilty of everything with which he has been charged. Including murder."

Sam was certainly having his own doubts about Walter's innocence, or lack thereof. It was those mounting questions that had him second-guessing his particular role in this family melodrama. "You think you're going to find all those answers in Switzerland?"

"Yes," Jessica replied with a rather defiant lift of her chin. "I do think I will. Derek said my mother knows the truth about my father."

"Then why hasn't she come forward before? Why hasn't she tried to get back to the States—and to her children?"

Jessica bit her lip. "I don't know. Derek implied there was something holding Mother in Switzerland. I think he started to tell me what it was, but then he stopped himself and told me that perhaps it would be best if I heard it from Mother. Maybe he was worried about my safety—or maybe he was concerned that I would let something slip and it would get back to my father."

"And what do *you* think is holding her there?" He was trying very hard not to form any judgments, but Jessica's story did seem to get more convoluted each time she added a few details.

"I don't know," she repeated, and the look she gave him told him she knew he was having his doubts about Derek Ross's veracity—and possibly her own. "I'll find out when I talk to her."

He stayed quiet for a while, thinking about the things she had said.

Jessica broke the silence, sounding almost reluctant to ask, "Do you think there's really anything my father can do from jail to stop me from seeing my mother?"

"As you've pointed out several times now, enough money can make a lot of things happen. But he hasn't had much time to make arrangements, and surely he's somewhat restricted by his current circumstances."

"If it hadn't been for that snowstorm, I would be there now," Jessica fretted. "Now he's had all this extra time to make trouble."

"I doubt that there was anything he could do—but if he has made trouble, I'll help you see your mother."

Her blue eyes were round with surprise when she turned her head to look at him. "You will?"

"Yes." Now that he'd committed himself, he would follow through.

She blinked, and he couldn't help noticing how long and silky her eyelashes were. Surprisingly dark for a blonde, and she didn't appear to be wearing much makeup. A little eye shadow, maybe. He suspected she'd put on a touch of blusher to hide the pallor her near sleepless night had left behind. But her mouth was un-painted, its soft curves naturally rosy and tempting.

Her voice pulled him out of his mental inventory of her very attractive features. "My father won't like that."

"Too bad. The only thing I agreed to do for your father was to keep you safe."

"If you do anything to cross him, he'll fire you. You'll be lucky to be paid for anything you've already done for him. Not only that, he would use whatever influence he has left to make sure you never get any other assignments. My father is a dangerous man when he's crossed, Sam."

At least she had used his first name that time. The satisfaction he felt at hearing it on her lips was probably stronger than it should have been. "I'm not afraid of your father."

He expected a melodramatically clichéd response— something along the lines of him being a fool. He was taken aback when her eyes filled, and she whispered, "I am."

Now *he* was the one thinking in clichés as he stared into her eyes. Brilliant blue skies seen through a wash of spring rain. Shimmering blue pools. And, oh, hell, he was sinking fast. "Jessica…"

Her chin lifted, her shoulders squared, and she swiped a hand against her cheeks to erase any trace of tears. Her movements were jerky when she unsnapped her seat belt and stood.

"Excuse me," she said, looking pointedly at his legs. He swung them to one side so she could step past him, and then he watched her as she walked with measured, rapid steps toward the nearest lavatory.

He wasn't the only man watching her, of course,

he noted—but he was the one who would be making the remainder of this journey with her, he reminded himself.

Jessica was furious with herself for giving in to that moment of weakness in front of Sam. She blamed stress, weariness, uncertainty—she blamed herself for once again looking foolish and unstable in front of him.

After splashing water on her face and stalling as long as she could by tying up the lavatory for too long, she returned to her seat with her head high.

"I wasn't crying," she said as she snapped her seat belt. "I'm just a little tense."

"You have every right to be."

"And don't humor me."

"I wouldn't dream of it."

Pulling her book out of her tote bag, she buried her face in it. There were other questions she would have liked to ask him—quite a few more, actually—but she thought she had better shut up for a while now. Before she made an even bigger fool of herself.

Sam gave Jessica plenty of time to collect herself before he tried to engage her in conversation again. They both read for a while, and he dozed, though he didn't think she was able to sleep. A meal was served by the rather bored-looking attendants. Sam ate most of his, but he noticed that Jessica only played with her own food.

"It really isn't that bad."

She looked down at her plate as if she wasn't even sure what she had been served. "No, the food's fine."

"You should try to eat. You don't want to be light-headed by the time we finally arrive in Zurich."

"I'm not very hungry."

"Suit yourself," he said, and turned his attention back to his dessert.

He noticed out of the corner of his eye that she lifted a few bites of food to her mouth then, more an automatic gesture than with any evidence of enjoyment. Satisfied that some of the color was coming back into her face, he finished his own meal, drained his glass of soda, then nodded for the attendant to take his used dishes.

The attendant lingered to flirt for a few minutes, and Sam responded in kind. He figured she was trying to make the routine flight pass more quickly, and he was perfectly willing to share a few laughs toward that end. It wasn't as if Jessica seemed to even notice his presence, so deeply lost was she in her thoughts.

After a couple of minutes, Jessica thrust her plate toward the attendant. "You can take these, too," she said a bit gruffly. "I'm finished with them."

Sam reached out quickly to pluck off the wrapped cookies Jessica had left on the plate.

The attendant smiled at him. "Saving them for a sweet attack later?"

"Something like that," he replied with a smile, though he intended to make sure Jessica ate them later. She would probably need a sugar boost before this trip was over.

"Friendly sort, isn't she?" Jessica muttered when the attendant moved on to chat with another passenger.

"She seems nice."

"Mmph."

He wasn't sure what that muttered syllable meant, but she didn't sound overly impressed with the chatty attendant. Had the circumstances been different, he might have thought she was a bit jealous of the woman's flirting with him. But Jessica didn't even want him on this trip; she certainly didn't want his full attention along the way. More likely her strained nerves were just making her overly sensitive to chatter from other people when she was trying to concentrate on her own problems.

Shortly after the remains of the meal were cleared away, Jessica reached down to her feet and pulled her bulging red tote bag into her lap. Sam was always fascinated when she dug into that bag; she seemed to carry a little bit of everything in it. This time she drew out a green leather-bound spiral journal, set it in her lap, then started digging again.

Whatever else she was looking for seemed to be eluding her. He heard her mutter a curse as she sorted through the bag's contents.

"Lose something?"

"I know I have several pens in this bag, but I can't find one."

Sam had stashed his battered leather jacket beneath his seat. He leaned over to reach into it, then offered her the pen he always carried in his inside pocket. "Use this one."

Setting her tote bag aside, she accepted it. "Thanks. I just want to write a note to myself before I forget."

She studied the white-tipped black rollerball pen for a moment. "Mont Blanc?"

"It's the only gift my ex-wife ever gave me that I kept for sentimental reasons—I used it to sign my divorce papers."

"That's pretty bitter," she said, opening her notebook.

"Not bitter—just slightly sour."

"Were you married long?" she asked, keeping her eyes on her scribbling.

"Thankfully, no."

"How long have you been divorced?"

"Two years."

He figured he owed her a few personal details, considering he'd rummaged through her underwear. Walter hadn't said what suspicious items, exactly, he'd wanted Sam to look for, but he had suggested that Sam would find stolen items and maybe worse. Sam had assumed he meant drugs.

Though he'd found none of the latter, except for a few innocuous prescription and over-the-counter medications, he had found that odd collection of small, tagged items hidden in a dresser drawer. He still wasn't quite sure of their significance, but he couldn't help thinking of Walter's warnings about her shoplifting predilection. The compulsion seemed to intensify under stress, Walter said, and Jessica herself claimed she'd been under a lot of stress lately.

He had to admit that Jessica made him question everything Walter had told him. She seemed to have good reason to resent her father's interference in her life. And other than being a bit scatterbrained—partially explained by the facts that she was an artist and totally obsessed with getting to her mother before Walter stopped her—Sam had seen no indication that Jessica had serious problems.

"So you're the type who writes memos to herself, hmm?"

Still writing, she nodded. "I tend to forget things if I don't jot them down."

"Ever considered getting a PDA? They have calendars and notepads and alarm clocks and all sorts of other useful features for people who tend to be forgetful. I carry a small one myself, in the same jacket pocket with my pen."

"I've been given three of them for various occasions. I managed to lose one, fry the circuits on another, and I never learned how to use the latest one. I'll stick with a purse calendar and a notebook for now. I like to keep things simple."

"Now why do I find that so hard to believe?"

"I can't imagine," she replied, closing her notebook a bit huffily. She slid both the notebook and his pen into her tote bag, her mouth still turned into a slight pout, as if she thought he'd been mocking her.

"Um—my pen?" he reminded her.

Her expression went from annoyed to mortified. Waves of red darkened her cheeks, and she scrambled almost frantically in the bag to retrieve the pen. "I'm so sorry," she said with a dismay that seemed out of proportion for such a minor lapse. "I wasn't paying attention to what I was doing. I really didn't intend to keep it."

Lifting a quizzical eyebrow in her direction, he accepted the pen and slipped it into the pocket of his white cotton shirt. "No problem. I'm the one who was distracting you."

"Still, it was a stupid thing to do."

"Jessica, it's okay," he said firmly, laying a hand over hers, which were now clasped so tightly in her lap it looked painful. "I do things like that all the time. Everyone does."

The tormented look in her eyes told him she hadn't found his words particularly reassuring. He tightened his hands over hers, and thought he felt them trembling slightly. "It's going to be okay," he repeated, and he was no longer talking about the pen.

Whatever demons Jessica Parks had been battling, she had been fighting them all by herself for entirely too long, in Sam's opinion. It was time for someone to step forward and help her with them.

Although he had never considered himself the unselfishly heroic type—and he would sure as hell bet that Jessica didn't see him that way—it seemed that it had fallen to him to offer his services. Certainly no one else was hurrying to give her a hand.

Chapter Seven

The hand Sam had placed over hers was warm. Gentle. Yet reassuringly strong. Jessica was very nearly tempted to turn her own hand over so that their palms were clasped. She resisted only because she had never been the type to cling to anyone else and she had no intention of starting now, certainly not with this man.

She reached up to push a lock of hair behind her ear as an excuse to draw away from him. Taking the hint, he pulled his hand to his own side of the armrest.

Jessica drew a deep breath. "I think we need to get a few things straight before we land in Switzerland."

"I'm listening."

"I've been doing some thinking during this flight. It's clear that I'm not going to be able to force you to go back to San Francisco and let me finish the rest of this trip on my own."

"Right on that point."

"Let me continue. It would do me no good to fight you or try to run away from you. It would cause delays I can't afford, and bring attention to us that I don't want. It occurred to me at one point that I'm being awfully trusting to take your word that you are who you say you are, and that I really will be safe with you in a foreign country. For all I really know, *you* could be leading me into danger, or planning some stunt to get your hands on my father's money."

He nodded somberly. "I can see where that might occur to you. I realize I'm a stranger to you. I could show you my driver's license, but those can be faked."

"Exactly. So all I have to go on is your word, and my own instincts."

"I can tell you my word is reliable. How are your instincts?"

"To be candid, they haven't been that great in the past. I've trusted some people I shouldn't have, and relied on others who let me down."

"Haven't we all," he muttered, and she wondered if he was referring to the ex-wife of whom he had spoken with such rancor. He seemed to shake off a bad memory before asking, "What are your instincts telling you about me?"

"That I can trust you."

He looked a bit surprised. Before he could say anything, she held up a finger to silence him and qualified, "To a point."

"And what point is that?"

"I won't try to stop you from tagging along with me to Lausanne—but I want you to keep in mind that this is *my* journey. I didn't hire you as a bodyguard, and I don't want you interfering with my actions 'for my own good.' Nor will I allow you to try to control me on directions from my father. I've spent the past three years planning this trip, and I will not let you—or anyone else—get in my way."

"You sound very stern. I can't help wondering how you would stop me if I *did* try anything. Considering that you're about half my size."

"I don't know exactly what I would do," she answered honestly. "I'm certain only that I will not be stopped this time. Dad can give it his best shot—making trouble, sending people to interfere. Even arranging another fake kidnapping. None of it will work."

"*Another* fake kidnapping?" Sam leaped on that word with a sharpness that made her regret her imprudent tongue.

She shrugged. "I'm just saying it doesn't matter what he tries, he can't stop me from seeing my mother this time."

"Jessica." He leaned very close to her so he could speak too quietly to be overheard by any of their fellow travelers. "Are you telling me that you think your father paid someone to kidnap you eight years ago?"

She kept her own voice steady, despite a jump of nerves she attributed as much to his physical closeness as his question. "It took me a long time—years—to come to that conclusion, but yes, I think that's exactly what he did."

"What evidence do you have to support that claim?"

She lifted her eyebrows. "Were you by any chance a lawyer before you went into your current line of work?"

"I was a cop."

Interesting. "Yet you're working for a man who's in prison on murder and embezzlement charges?"

He had the grace to look uncomfortable. "I told you, I've worked for him before. He has always been considered an upstanding member of the business community. A bit ruthless, of course, but that's true of most of the powerful tycoons. He never asked me to do anything to cross my own ethical boundaries."

Jessica couldn't help wondering whether Sam's 'ethical boundaries' came anywhere close to her own.

"Anyway, why do you think he arranged to have you kidnapped?"

"The timing, for one thing. I had only recently discovered my mother's whereabouts, and I had started a secret correspondence with her through a post-office box I rented near my school. I took all my graduation money and what little I'd been able to earn by working in one of the jewelry stores, and I bought a ticket to Switzerland. My father confronted me with the letters I had received from my mother only a few days after I was returned by the kidnappers."

"Maybe he came across the letters in the process of looking for clues to your kidnappers. Maybe he thought they were connected in some way to your disappearance."

"He said he got a ransom call the same night I was snatched on my way to the airport. He told me he found the letters while searching my wardrobe to find out what

I was wearing so he could give a description to the police if necessary. I don't think that was the truth. I think he'd found out about my travel plans and arranged to interfere in a way that would keep me from going and make sure I would be too frightened to try again."

"He told me you weren't injured during your ordeal."

"Not physically. But I was locked in a very small, very dim room for almost two weeks. I had no human contact, except for a man who delivered food and water without speaking to me. I was given a couple of old magazines and a battery-powered radio to help me pass the time, but the minutes crept by so slowly I honestly thought I would die in there—if my kidnappers didn't kill me first."

"Your kidnappers never threatened you? Never asked any questions about your family?"

"They never spoke to me," she repeated. "When I asked questions, I was ignored. Just as they ignored me when I cried and…and when I begged to go home," she admitted. She hated to remember the emotional state she had been reduced to at the end of the ordeal.

He didn't seem to notice the slight break in her voice. "How were you released?"

She actually appreciated that he didn't offer any sympathy. His matter-of-fact questioning, whether intentional or not, helped her keep her voice steady. "I was blindfolded, and I was led outside to a car. There were two men. The only one who spoke to me said something like, 'You're going home, kid.' I thought they might be taking me someplace to kill me and dispose of my body.

"To be honest," she added in a near whisper, "by that

point I didn't really care. Anything was better than spending another day in that room."

"Where were you dropped off?"

"At the front gate of the estate. The man who had spoken to me got out of the car, opened my door, removed my blindfold and told me to get out. As soon as I did, they drove away. I stared after the car for a minute, then turned and ran as fast as I could through the gates."

"The front gates were open?"

"Yes. They aren't usually, but they happened to be then. I burst through the front door crying. Brenda grabbed me in a hug so tight I thought I would break, but it felt wonderful. Then my sister and my brothers hugged me. Emily was crying," she added. "Cade was trying not to."

"And your father?"

"He hugged me, of course. Briefly." She remembered clinging to him when he stopped hugging. He had placed his hands on her shoulders to hold her a few inches away from him then. "He said he was glad I was home safely. And then he reminded me that it never would have happened if I hadn't been so foolish. He said people with our wealth don't have the luxury of heading off alone, without taking certain security precautions."

"In effect, blaming you for what happened to you."

"That was the way I interpreted it."

But Sam's attention was already turning back to the details. "The security cameras at the gates of your father's estate—were they there eight years ago?"

"Yes. They've been in place for as long as I can remember. He updates them every couple of years."

"Were you dropped off within range of those cameras?"

She thought back. "Yes. As I said, we were right at the front gates."

"Which were open."

"Yes."

"The vehicle you were in—did it have a license plate?"

"Yes. I remember thinking I should try to memorize the number as I watched it drive away, but it just seemed like too much effort then."

"Yet the kidnappers were never caught."

"My father said there was no way to track them down."

"Did the police have you give descriptions to an artist? Did they try to help you remember details of the car or the license plate?"

"I never spoke to the police."

She heard the questions in Sam's silence. "My father said he kept the police out of it because the kidnappers said they would kill me if he called them."

"For two weeks?"

She nodded.

"And what about after you were returned safely?"

"He said it was too late to find any leads. And he didn't want the media to find out about it. He said if it became general knowledge that he had been willing to pay a substantial ransom for my return, we would all be targeted by greedy felons."

Sam raised a hand to squeeze the bridge of his nose.

"It all sounded entirely reasonable at the time," she told him. "My father can be very convincing."

"Tell me about it."

She wondered if his disgruntled mutter meant that he had finally begun to question some of the things Walter had said to him.

"As I've said, it was some time later when I began to question whether he might have had some role in the kidnapping. We were raised never to question our father, though Rowan and I did our share of rebelling during our teens. I suppose I did more than my share. And I still felt guilty for being careless and getting kidnapped."

"It wasn't your fault."

She knew now that she had been guilty only of being young, naive and reckless. "I know."

"So after that you stopped trying to get to your mother."

"Yes. I was a mess, emotionally. I couldn't have dealt with the stress of planning another escape. Besides, I had no money. My father made certain of that. He gave me just enough to get by with a few luxuries, but not enough to finance a trip to Switzerland."

"Did you continue your correspondence with her?"

"He stopped that, too. He closed my post-office box and started monitoring my mail at home. I didn't even know she was still in Switzerland until I received another letter from her three years ago. It came to my cottage address, disguised as a credit card solicitation. I don't know how she arranged that—I assume she had some assistance. Since then my mother and I have been secretly writing again. I've heard from her maybe five times in the past three years. She can't risk writing very often."

Sam was quiet for a short while, apparently digesting everything she'd told him to that point. "I have just one more question," he said finally. "For now."

"What?"

"If you've had so much distrust of your father for so long, why do you continue to live on his estate? You're what, twenty-six?"

He probably knew exactly how old she was. Her cheeks burned with resentment when she answered. "I moved out for a while, after I recovered from the kidnapping. I got an apartment in San Francisco a few years ago. My father was opposed to it, but I was working for someone else by then, making enough to pay my rent. I'd been living there only a few months when I was mugged."

"Damn."

"Yeah. That time I *was* hurt. I fought back, you see, instead of just letting him take my purse."

"Not exactly a wise thing to do."

"I was just so angry—maybe I was tired of being a victim. But it was a stupid thing to do. The mugger didn't seem to want to fight me, but I jumped on his back, and he reacted by flinging me off. I fell with one leg under me, and it shattered. It was a while before I could return to work, and by that time I'd lost my job and my apartment. I moved into the cottage with my father's promise that he would stay out of my life, which I took with a grain of salt. While I was recuperating, I started painting. It was my success with my paintings that let me stash away enough money to fund this trip."

He nodded. "So you stayed on the estate to be safe and to save money."

He still didn't seem to understand, exactly, but his summation was close enough. "Right."

Their conversation was interrupted by an announcement that the plane was beginning to descend toward Zurich. Jessica felt her pulse rate speed up in response.

"I've never been out of the States before," she told Sam. "I think I'm a little nervous."

"I'll keep you safe."

She scowled at his automatic response. "I wasn't asking for your help. I was simply making a comment."

His sudden grin made her already accelerated pulse go into overdrive. "Sorry. I accidentally slipped into bodyguard mode for a minute."

She managed somehow to hang on to her stern expression. "Well, stop it."

"Yes, ma'am," he murmured.

She didn't buy his meek expression for a minute. The minute Sam felt it necessary, he would go straight back into what he called "bodyguard mode." While there was some sense of security in knowing that he was there to watch out for her, she was glumly aware that it wasn't helping her in her quest to become a more independent and self-sufficient woman.

Though it was only midafternoon Chicago time, it was nearly 10:00 p.m. in Zurich, and it would be nearly twelve hours before Jessica and Sam would be able to depart for Geneva. The delay in Chicago had really fouled up Jessica's travel plans, turning what should have been an eighteen-hour journey into a three-day ordeal.

"Look at it this way," Sam said when her frustration

and impatience nearly got the best of her. "You wanted an adventure."

"I want to see my mother," she corrected him, and hated the primness of her own voice.

He cocked an eyebrow at her. "And the thought of being in a foreign country, far away from your father, doesn't excite you at all?"

When he put it that way...

She looked around the crowded terminal, letting the exotic mixture of sights and sounds wash over her. She must have heard more than half a dozen languages being spoken just within hearing distance of where she and Sam stood. And, yes, it was a bit exciting for a woman who had been so strictly sheltered and restricted for all of her life.

"Of course," she said. "But it isn't as if there will be time for sight-seeing between now and takeoff tomorrow morning."

"Not sight-seeing, maybe—but how about a little fun?"

"Fun?" She hardly remembered the meaning of the word. "Like what?"

He took her arm. "Let's get checked in to a hotel for the evening, and then we'll see what we can find."

She hesitated, frowning at him.

Sam sighed. "Separate rooms. Large crowds," he added, sweeping an arm around the bustling terminal. "There's no reason to look at me as if I'm taking you to a dark alley to have my nefarious way with you."

She had, after all, agreed to let him accompany her. And she'd said she would trust him—to a point. "Do you think we can find something to eat? I'm starving."

He grinned. "Bet on it."

She really wished he would stop doing that, she thought, mesmerized once again by the high-voltage power of his full smile. She had seen its effect on the flight attendant, and she had no intention of allowing herself to be so easily charmed.

Okay, so Sam Fields was a handy guy to have around at times, Jessica couldn't help admitting, if only to herself.

They were sitting in a cheerfully noisy restaurant-bar with heaping plates of deliciously prepared food in front of them. Sam had found two rooms in a chain hotel near the airport and, after they had quickly showered and changed, had then brought her to this nice place at the edge of the Old Town. He had even managed to procure a tiny table by a window overlooking the River Limmat, so that they had an absolutely stunning view of lights reflecting on purply-black water while they ate.

And he had handled it all in what had sounded to Jessica like flawless German.

Now that she was fairly confident she wouldn't keel over from lack of food, she wanted some answers. "Okay, spill it," she said. "How did you do that?"

He swallowed a mouthful of beef and reached for his wineglass. "Do what?"

"You've been to Zurich before?"

"Yes."

"Really?" It seemed odd for a cop-turned-P.I. to be so well traveled.

He nodded. "You aren't the only one who bought an airline ticket with high school graduation money. I spent two years in Europe—most of the time in Switzerland, Austria and Germany. I waited tables, worked on a couple of dairy farms, schlepped bags at a couple of hotels—whatever I could find to keep me busy and provide a little money."

There were so many interesting things to see around them, but Jessica found her attention focused almost exclusively on her dining companion, who seemed to be the biggest curiosity at the moment. "You speak like a native."

"My mother was German. Dad met her when he was stationed at an air force base there in the midsixties. I spoke both English and German growing up—though mostly English, obviously. My mother was the one who wanted me to come to Europe. She wanted me to meet her family—which I did, though we didn't really hit it off, since all they could do was talk about how much they disliked my father. I didn't stay with them very long before I decided to move on and see other places, to their relief and my mother's disappointment."

"She never came back herself?"

"No. They pretty much disowned her when she married my father against their advice. I think she was hoping my grandfather—who had some money—would like me well enough to forgive her. Unfortunately for her, he much preferred her brother's kids."

"That's very sad, for all of you. But especially for your mother, that she was never reunited with her family."

"You should know what it's like to rebel against a controlling father. And she wasn't completely innocent in the feud. My mother was an angry, bitter, bluntly spoken woman who caused a lot of her own problems."

Jessica knew there were happy families out there somewhere, people who had enjoyed loving, healthy childhoods. She just didn't happen to know any of them. But then, she didn't know that many people—her father had seen to that.

Sam seemed to come to the decision that he was revealing too much about himself. He guided the conversation into a less personal area. "Of course, the German my mother spoke was significantly different from the Swiss German—or Schweizerdeutsch—that's spoken here. There's enough difference that they often show German subtitles on Swiss films shown in Germany."

"You seem to get by very well."

He shrugged. "I've always had an ear for languages."

"That must have been so cool—living and working here, I mean. Did you get homesick?"

"Not particularly. I had a blast here—but then it was time to go home."

"Where you became a cop."

"Eventually, after trying a couple of other things that didn't hold my attention." He shrugged again. "It was what my father wanted. I didn't have any particular aspirations, and I thought it would be a challenge, so I signed up for the police academy when I was twenty-five. Mother was furious, but I reminded her that I'd visited Germany for her. I'd been on the job just over three years when Dad died. That was ten years ago."

Making Sam thirty-eight now, Jessica calculated quickly. She would have guessed him to be several years younger, judging by appearance. "You've had quite a varied background."

"I get bored easily."

She wondered if he had gotten bored with his marriage. Fortunately, that was one impolite question that didn't leap straight from her mind to her mouth.

Her gaze drifted to the window, through which she could see fanciful spires and towers illuminated by bright lights shining up toward the inky skies. She knew there were fascinating things to see on the other side of that glass. Old churches and art galleries, winding, cobbled streets and ornate, gushing fountains.

She wanted to soak in the sights of the snow-topped Alps and Lake Zurich, and to stroll through the shops that lined the famous Bahnhofstrasse. She longed to spend whole days in the galleries admiring and studying the art. But that wasn't why she was here, she reminded herself.

"What do you see out there?" Sam's quiet question cut into her daydreaming.

"Switzerland," she replied with a sigh.

"You aren't like most of the rich young women I've known. Not that I've known that many, of course."

That comment brought her gaze back to him. "What do you mean?"

"You haven't traveled much. You talked about having to save money for this trip. You don't seem to go to a lot of parties and other social affairs."

Which he knew because he had been following her for weeks, she thought with a quick scowl. "I'm not a jet-setter, that's for sure. My father never liked traveling, and the older he's gotten, the less he does it. Needless to say, he didn't let me go off on my own, especially after my rebellious teen years, and my one attempt to escape.

"I don't like big gatherings because I get tired of people pointing and whispering about my family. Wondering when I'm going to flip out like the crazy mother I look just like. And now, of course, speculating about whether my father really killed his business partner."

She reached for her water goblet. "As for the money, my father provided us with a beautiful home, nice clothes and cars, excellent educations and any material possessions we wanted. But the cash flow was carefully controlled, and we were never left in any doubt that it was *his* money. We were totally dependent on him for everything we received."

Sam was quiet for a few moments, and then he asked, "Are you finished with your meal?"

She glanced down at her plate, rather surprised to see that it was almost empty. "Yes."

"It occurs to me that we've spent the entire day talking about your problems with your father—even touched on my family baggage. Why don't we give it a rest for a while?"

He motioned toward the far side of the room, where a wide doorway led into a bustling club. "Want to go listen to some music? Maybe dance a little?"

"Dance?"

"You do dance, don't you?"

"It's been a while, but yes, I dance."

"Then let's go."

There was a brief debate over the check, but Sam insisted on putting the meals on his credit card. "I'm sending the bill to your father's accountant."

"And if they refuse to pay you?"

"Then I'll steal your daddy's limo and sell it to a chop shop," he replied without missing a beat.

"Help me see my mother, and I'll get you the keys to Daddy's limo," she offered recklessly.

He grinned. "Deal."

Chapter Eight

Maybe it was because of the tension she had been under lately, but Sam hadn't seen Jessica smile much. Though he had observed her laughing a couple of times with her tall, blond friend, he had come to think of her as a rather serious young woman, intense, absent-minded, often angry.

Beautiful, but troubled, was the way he had thought of her. Definitely off-limits, even had she not been the daughter of his client. Even had she not been twelve years his junior. Even if he had been looking to get involved with anyone—which he was not.

Sometime during an hour of dancing with her on this spontaneous night in Zurich, he began to rethink quite a few of those earlier impressions.

She had a lovely smile, full and curving, lighting up

a face that was already stunning. Her laugh was a low gurgle that went straight to his abdomen.

She was rather awkward with him at first, skeptical of his reasons for asking her to dance, still not certain just how far she could trust him. The specter of her father had seemed to hover between them all day, but the swirling lights of the dance club soon dispelled that shadow.

Maybe it was the wine. Maybe the setting. Or maybe Jessica really needed a break from her scheming and worrying. Within minutes after joining the crowd, who appeared to be mostly young professionals, on the dance floor, he could see the tension leaving her shoulders. Her eyes were brighter, her cheeks lightly flushed...and she smiled. At him.

He kept his emotions firmly under control as they danced. This evening was for her, he reminded himself. He was doing his job—keeping her safe, fed and entertained.

The music was American pop, peppy and upbeat. Easy to dance to, not particularly challenging to listen to. Just what she needed tonight, he decided. He kept their dancing friendly, platonic, touching her only lightly. He made innocuous small talk, like the near stranger he was to her. He didn't want to remind her of how well he actually knew her, or how he had learned so many very personal details.

Between everything he had been told about her, and the things she had revealed herself, during their flight, there was little about Jessica Parks's background that he didn't know. But he still couldn't say that he knew *her*.

A slower number brought even more people onto the

floor, and Sam held Jessica a bit more tightly. Even as he blamed the crowd, he knew he'd simply been waiting for an excuse to get closer to her.

Their bodies brushed now, and even that light contact was enough to raise his temperature a couple of degrees. She smelled very faintly of flowers. The mere suggestion of scent made him fantasize about burying his face in her soft hair.

The simple black jersey top and slacks she wore had probably been chosen for comfort and carefree packing, but Sam couldn't help admiring the way the fabric skimmed her slender curves and moved with her as she danced. He would have thought she was too fair to wear black, but somehow it worked for her, making her hair look warmer, her eyes bluer.

"You know what's funny?"

Her quiet question brought his mind off her appearance—temporarily, at least. He held her an inch farther away so he could see her face. "What?"

She glanced at the other dancers around them. "It's almost as if we're in a club back home."

He smiled wryly, understanding what she meant. A significant number of the people around them were Americans, travelers here on business or vacation who, like Sam and Jessica, had looked for a comfortable and conveniently located spot to wind down for the evening.

"I should have taken you to one of the more locally patronized places," he mused. "The concierge at the hotel mentioned that there are a lot of new clubs in the fourth and fifth districts around Langstrasse. And I remember a couple of good jazz clubs on Niederdorfstrasse and Oberdorfstrasse. But I was told that the food was good here and the service very quick—"

"Exactly what I needed tonight," she assured him. "I'm really too tired for the more lively clubs."

Someone bumped into him from behind, murmuring an apology in German. Sam responded, but the incident had brought him closer to Jessica again. This time he didn't try to hold her away. She felt so good in his arms— and his willpower had been strained almost to the limit.

A crooning love song began, and their movements slowed to a gentle sway. In a gesture that seemed more wearily content than personal, Jessica rested her head against his shoulder. His pulse leaped, but he thought he did an adequate job of concealing the reaction.

Aware of how easily she could shy away from him— and conscious that only a few hours earlier she had been ready to go for his throat—he laid his cheek very lightly against her hair. Oh, man, it felt as silky as he had imagined.

He hadn't had to struggle with his own body this way since high school. As skittish as Jessica was around him, the first sign that he was reacting quite physically to her nearness would likely send her running.

"I shouldn't be doing this," she murmured, her voice almost too soft to hear above the music.

"Doing what? Dancing?"

"Mmm." The reply was a rather sleepy murmur. "I still don't completely trust you, you know."

Considering the state of his emotions at having her snuggled in his arms, he couldn't say her mistrust was entirely unfounded. "I know."

"I'd intended to keep you at a distance during this trip. I would tolerate your presence, but I would give you no encouragement. I planned to pretty much ignore you."

"Go right ahead," he offered, settling her a bit more snugly against his chest.

Her soft laugh sounded rueful. "I can hardly ignore you while I'm dancing with you."

"I can't tell you how many girls did just that during high school dances."

"Somehow I doubt you've ever been easy to ignore. I spotted you even when you were following me all over San Francisco."

He winced. "You don't have to remind me of that. I really am good at what I do, you know. Very few people have ever spotted me tailing them."

"Yes, well, I'd been expecting my father to have me followed ever since I started planning this trip. I was sure he would know somehow that I was up to something—he always knows. And that he would try to find out what it was so he could interfere. And besides, you're—"

She stopped suddenly, as if she'd almost said something she shouldn't. Which, of course, only made him more curious to know what it was. "I'm what?"

"Noticeable," she said after a moment.

The fact that he liked hearing her admit that—a lot, actually—was merely further evidence that dancing with her wasn't such a good idea.

"Sam?" she asked after a pause, as the slow number was coming to a close.

"Mmm?"

"Could we go back to the hotel now?"

He wouldn't have minded that request so much if he hadn't been fully aware that she was talking about going back to their separate rooms.

"Of course," he said, though it took him a moment to make himself release her. He waited until the very last note of the song had faded away before doing so.

After all, who knew when—or if—he would have the chance to hold her again?

Jessica couldn't believe she had dined and danced with Sam Fields. What had she been thinking?

Well, okay, she knew exactly what she'd been thinking. Sam was a very attractive man. He knew how to be charming and attentive. How to make a woman feel pretty, and flattered by his interest. And she had been so narrowly focused on her quest for answers about her past that she hadn't even dated in almost longer than she could remember.

She was a healthy young woman with a healthy interest in male companionship. Being held in Sam's strong arms had been more than just pleasant. She had been strongly tempted to snuggle close to him and find out exactly how that lean, sexy body felt pressed against her own. He had smelled of soap and a light, spicy aftershave, and she had wanted to bury her face in his neck for a more intimate exploration.

And she barely even knew the guy, she told herself with a bewildered laugh as she crawled into bed, leaving a dim light burning in a far corner of the hotel room. But she knew he danced like a dream. And when he smiled, his deep green eyes crinkled delightfully at the corners. And the shape of his mouth inspired fantasies she shouldn't be having about a man she didn't trust and didn't want to like.

She really *would* be crazy to let herself become infatuated with him, she thought, sinking more deeply into the pillows. Because that thought touched a bit too closely on her darkest fears, she pulled the covers over her head and tried to will herself instantly to sleep.

Sam wasn't particularly surprised to discover the next morning that Jessica had pulled back from him during the night. She had probably spent the hours they were apart reminding herself of his connection to the father she had been struggling so hard to get away from. The pleasant evening they had spent together had been an aberration she surely had no intention of repeating.

At least she looked as though she had gotten some sleep. He studied her face, pleased to see that the signs of strain and exhaustion from the long trip were gone. He still saw hints of tension in her eyes and the set of her shoulders, but he imagined that was the result of his presence and her excitement at being so close to finally seeing her mother.

He was glad she had managed to sleep. He had dozed only fitfully, all too aware that she lay in the room next to him. Remembering how she had felt in his arms. How well they had fit together even with an eight-inch difference in height.

"I don't know about you, but I'm about to get tired of airplane seats," he said as they snapped their seat belts.

"I could go a long time without another takeoff," she agreed, even as the jet's engines began to rev.

He watched her hands tighten in her lap. "Takeoff is the worst part for you?"

"Yes. Once we're in the air, I'm okay. Mostly."

He laid his hand palm up on the armrest. "Some people think it helps to hang on to someone during takeoff."

She glanced at his hand, then away. "I'll be fine."

He grinned and wiggled his fingers. "Just keep in mind that I'm here if you need me."

"Thank you. I'll do that."

"A word of advice? I know you're trying to put me off with that icy, regal tone, but I gotta tell you—it kind of has the opposite effect. Every time you talk to me like that, I just want to kiss you senseless."

She stared at him with widened eyes, looking as though she couldn't believe she had heard him correctly. By the time she recovered, the plane was in the air.

"I suppose you think that was a clever way to take my mind off my anxiety."

"Sure. Okay. If that's what you want to believe."

Eyeing him suspiciously, she pulled out her MP3 player and rather defiantly donned the headphones.

Still chuckling, he leaned back in his seat and looked out the window at the snowy mountains beneath them.

Jessica thought he'd been teasing. And yet, she realized that he had meant exactly what he'd said.

During the four-hour flight from Zurich to Geneva, Jessica might have said half a dozen words to him, and those only in response to questions he asked. She gave every appearance of having forgotten he was there—

which gave him the opportunity to watch her during the trip.

She kept the headphones on most of the time, but he would bet she wasn't really hearing the music. She held one of her books open in her lap, but her eyes didn't track the words and she never turned a page. Rather than looking more excited as they neared their destination, she seemed to grow more tense with each passing mile.

"How are you planning to get to Lausanne?" he asked as the plane began the descent toward the Geneva airport.

"I thought I would take a train."

He considered a moment, then shook his head. "Let's rent a car. It will give us more control."

"But…"

"Don't worry. I'll handle everything."

That made her eyes narrow. "I don't need you to handle anything."

"You might as well use me for something, since I'm here anyway."

She looked quickly away, but not before he spotted a faint wash of pink high on her cheekbones. Had she taken his words as a double entendre? Had she unwillingly thought of another couple of ways to put him to use? Or was that only wishful thinking on his part?

Driving in Switzerland was an adventure, but Sam remembered most of the tricks. Fortunately, the weather was good, and the roads were clear. The other drivers seemed to be sane and sober, for the most part—and being used to San Francisco drivers, he found that a pleasant change, he thought with a wry smile.

It was only a forty-five minute drive from Geneva to Lausanne, and the scenery was spectacular enough to break through Jessica's distraction. "It's so beautiful here," she breathed. "Like paradise."

"I would be more than happy to play Adam to your Eve," he offered, just to get a rise out of her.

He succeeded. She punched his arm.

"Ouch." Laughing, he took his left hand off the steering wheel to massage his right biceps.

"You deserved that."

"Sorry. Couldn't resist."

"Next time...try."

Still grinning, he placed both hands back on the wheel of the tiny rental car.

Jessica's attention had already turned to the scenery again as he carefully approached the city center of Lausanne. "You know what it sort of reminds me of?"

"San Francisco," he answered confidently. "Lausanne is actually referred to sometimes as the San Francisco of Switzerland. The way the city rises from Lac Léman, the steep streets, the vineyards that line the outskirts of the city, the mountains rising beyond—it's very reminiscent of home, isn't it?"

"In some ways. Yet in others, it's very European," she mused, staring wide-eyed at the cars, buses and buildings that she would never see back in California.

Noting the busy streets and filled parking lots, he asked, "Did you make hotel reservations?"

"Yes." She pulled her notebook from her tote bag and read the name of the hotel and its address. "Do you know where that is?"

Her pronunciation made him chuckle, but he managed to disguise it as a cough. "I can find it. Um—you didn't take French in high school, I take it?"

"No. I took Spanish. I'm actually almost fluent in Spanish," she added with a sigh. "Not that it's done me any good on this trip."

"Unlike Zurich, where you hear mostly German, Lausanne is in the French-speaking region. Fortunately, many locals know at least a few words of English."

"I noticed that you spoke French when you rented the car. You sounded pretty good at it. Did you pick that up when you were here before?"

"I took four years of French in high school because someone told me girls are turned on by hearing guys speak in French. I don't suppose it did anything for you when you heard me speaking it…?"

She glared at him.

"Guess not."

"A cop-turned-P.I. who traveled Europe and speaks three languages. I suppose I should be impressed."

"And yet I sense that you're not."

She made a show of yawning delicately behind her hand. "Not particularly."

"Not even if I told you I actually speak four languages with varying degrees of fluency?"

She gave him a suspicious look. "Do you really?"

By way of reply, he informed her—in Spanish—that he hoped there would be a parking garage at the hotel where she'd made reservations, since finding parking places in Lausanne was sometimes difficult.

"Hispanic grandmother?" Jessica asked a bit too politely.

"Hispanic girlfriend."

"Oh, of course."

"Her name was Carmen. She was a grad student whose parents had moved to San Francisco from Mexico City. I dated her for two years after I returned to the States. We had a very amicable split, leaving me with another language, an appreciation for salsa music and a good friend to this day. I'm her oldest son's godfather."

"One thing I can say about you—nothing about you is predictable."

"Good. I can't think of anything worse to be called."

Jessica sighed a bit wistfully. "That's the way most people think of me, you know."

"You? Predictable?" He scoffed, "Yeah, right."

"Surely you followed me around enough to know what a dull life I lead. I paint, have an occasional lunch with a friend, volunteer every Wednesday at a youth center. I rarely do anything daring or impulsive."

"How about this trip?"

"Daring—maybe. Impulsive—hardly. I've been planning it for years."

"Still, I thought you were considered the least predictable member of the Parks family."

"The least stable," she corrected him. "Even in that, I'm fairly predictable. Everyone expects me to have an occasional meltdown or do something rather bizarre— and right on cue, I do."

"Stop being so hard on yourself. You're a talented artist with a promising future. You've made a life and a career for yourself with little support from your family. And you're making a difference in the lives of those kids you work with every Wednesday. So just stop it, okay?"

She stared at him a moment, then said, "I'm not sure if you're complimenting me or yelling at me."

He turned the car into the convenient parking garage of the hotel. "Both."

"Then—thank you. And bite me."

His scowl changed to a laugh. "As tempting as that sounds…"

The look she shot him stopped the words, but his smile remained in place.

The hotel room was large and beautifully decorated. A sitting area at one side included a comfortable-looking, chintz-covered sofa, a low coffee table decorated with an arrangement of fresh flowers and two side chairs holding pretty porcelain-based lamps. Set into a bow window was a small, round wood table flanked by two straight-back chairs with flowered cushions. A carved headboard accented the big bed, and the ruffled, fluffy-looking bed coverings invited a weary traveler to rest.

The color scheme was a restful dark green with touches of burgundy and cream to keep the overall effect from being too dark. Even the artwork was unusually pleasing for a hotel room, good-quality prints of impressionist masterpieces.

But Jessica was too irritated to appreciate either the room or the breathtaking view from the big window.

Waiting only until the bellhop had deposited the bags, accepted her tip and slipped out the door, she whirled on Sam, who stood in the center of the room looking braced for a battle. "The only reason we didn't have this quarrel downstairs is because I didn't want to cause a scene and risk being thrown out of the hotel, but now I can say exactly what I want. If you think I'm going to share a hotel room with you, you're crazy."

"You heard the guy downstairs. He said it in both French and English. There are no more rooms here, and chances are slim that I'd find a room anywhere else in Lausanne this weekend with the jazz festival going on."

"That's your problem, not mine."

"Jessica, be reasonable. This is a big room. I'll sleep on the couch. We're only going to be here a night or two, until after your visit with your mother."

The reminder of her mother had her shaking her head again, this time more firmly. As far as she was concerned, having Sam move to another hotel was the ideal solution. She would be more likely to slip away from him that way, if necessary. "I'm not sharing a room with you."

He shrugged. "Then I guess I'll sleep in the car. Won't be the first time."

She pictured the tiny vehicle they had rented in Geneva. There was barely room for a man of Sam's size to sit up fully, much less stretch out to sleep. "You can't sleep in the car."

"Doesn't look as though I have a choice, does it?"

"You could find another hotel. With your knowledge of this area and your fluency in the language, I'm sure you'd have no problem."

"The problem would be that even if I could find another place to stay, I would be leaving you alone here. No bodyguard worth his salt would sleep in a separate hotel from his client."

"I told you, I don't want or need a bodyguard."

"And I told *you* that you have one, whether you like it or not. So—I'll sleep in the car."

"Darn it, Sam, you aren't going to make me feel guilty. I had a reservation here."

"True. There's no reason for you to feel guilty."

She sighed and resisted a childish impulse to stamp her foot. "You'll sleep on the couch. And if you snore, I'll throw a shoe at your head."

"I don't snore."

She decided she didn't want to talk anymore about their sleeping arrangements. They would deal with that when it became necessary.

She glanced at her watch. "It's past lunchtime. I'm hungry. And then I want to find my mother."

"We can do that. How about fresh fish from Lac Léman? It's a specialty around here, and I highly recommend it."

That quickly, he'd gone from implacable bodyguard mode to charming tour guide again. She pushed a hand through her hair and sighed lightly, wondering how her carefully laid plans had taken such strange twists in the past three days. "Fine. We'll eat fish."

He motioned toward the door. "Then let's go."

She had taken only one step toward the door when the telephone on the nightstand beside the bed suddenly rang.

Chapter Nine

Jessica looked quickly at Sam, who stood closer to the phone than she did.

His eyebrows rose. "You want me to answer?"

She almost said yes. She tried to convince herself it was because he was more fluent in the local languages, but she knew it was pure cowardice that made her so reluctant to reach for the phone.

Because she was determined to overcome the fears that had plagued her for so much of her life, she squared her shoulders and reached for the receiver. "I'll get it."

Sam nodded and moved back across the room, giving her some space but staying close by.

"Hello?"

Cade exploded into speech the moment he heard her

voice. "What the hell are you doing in Lausanne? And why didn't you tell anyone where you were going?"

"How did you find me?" she asked her eldest brother rather than answering his questions. "Did Dad tell you?"

Cade and Walter had barely spoken since Cade had defied their father to leave the prestigious law firm Walter had encouraged him to join, but Jessica wouldn't put it past her father to contact Cade if he thought there was an advantage to him in doing so.

"Yeah, he called," Cade admitted reluctantly. "He said you'd run off to Switzerland on some quest to see our mother. He wanted me to talk to you and convince you to come home, but it took this long just to track you down."

"Yes, well, I had a few unexpected delays on the trip. I've only just arrived in Lausanne."

"I can't believe you did this. Do you know how vulnerable you are alone over there? Hell, you've hardly ever left San Francisco. Anything could have happened to you already, and we wouldn't even have known had Dad not given me a warning of what you were up to."

"And just how did *he* know?" she challenged, wondering exactly what Cade had been told.

Cade hesitated. "He's had someone watching you," he admitted at last, sounding braced for a temper tantrum. "I don't blame you for hating that, but he said he was doing it for your own good. You know I don't trust his motives any more than you do, but with everything in the family so chaotic now, we all have to take extra precautions."

"Oh? Does that mean he's hired a bodyguard for you? Or for Rowan? Emily doesn't count, I guess, since she's got more bodyguards than shoes now that she's royalty."

Cade cleared his throat. "Rowan and I can take care of ourselves."

"And I can't, is that it?"

"The fact that you're there at all proves you need *someone* looking after you, and since we don't know if Dad's bodyguard is still on the job or not, I'm worried about you. You shouldn't be there alone."

Jessica glanced at Sam, but something made her keep quiet about his presence in the room with her. He had his back turned to her now, and he was looking out the window at the breathtaking scenery outside, but she had no doubt he heard every word she was saying.

Choosing her words carefully, she said, "You don't need to worry about me, Cade. I'm fine. I simply wanted a chance to see our mother. Surely you can understand that, even if you don't share the desire."

"I didn't say I don't understand—I just think your timing's bad, that's all. With Dad in so much trouble now, and every move we make being watched and analyzed, how's it going to look for you to bolt during the trial to visit our crazy mother? You've heard the recent rumors that Dad had her put away because she knew too much about his allegedly illegal activities."

"Allegedly illegal," she repeated with a bitter taste in her mouth. "Stop being such a lawyer, Cade. You and I both know there's a very good chance that his activities were more than *allegedly* illegal. And it may be that Mother knows more about them than he wants us to hear."

"I'm afraid you're going to be disappointed when you

see her. She hasn't seen you since you were a baby, and she was too lost in her depression and alcoholism and whatever other problems she suffered to take care of you then. You have no way of knowing if anything she'll tell you is true or a product of her troubled imagination."

"And maybe I'll find out that she isn't as crazy as we've been told she is."

There was sympathy in Cade's voice when he replied, "Don't set yourself up for heartbreak, Jess. Have you thought about how you'll handle it if the meeting is a total disaster? Are you going to be able to…well, you know. Get over it?"

"You mean am I going to have a total breakdown and end up locked in a padded room, myself? Gee, I don't know. I suppose it's a definite possibility."

"Damn it, that isn't what I meant, and you know it."

"Do I?" There was as much sadness as bitterness in her voice now, and she was well aware of it. She was so tired of fighting the doubts. Her family's. And her own.

"Come home, Jessie. Or if you have to do this, let me join you there. I'll go with you to see her."

"No. I don't want to wait now that I'm here. Besides, you have too much going on there. I can handle this. No matter what happens. And don't worry about my safety, either. I'm—" she glanced again at Sam, then finished "—I'm taking precautions."

"What kind of—"

"Goodbye, Cade. I'll call you when I have something to tell you." She could hear him still talking rapidly as she replaced the receiver in its cradle.

She kept her back to Sam after she hung up, hoping

she would have her expression under control by the time she turned to face him. She didn't want him to see how badly her conversation with Cade had shaken her.

She should have known he didn't have to see her face. He had proven himself to be uncannily perceptive when it came to her.

His hands fell on her shoulders before she even realized he had moved to stand behind her. The guy really should make some sort of noise when he walked, she thought grumpily.

"Are you okay?"

"I'm fine. I just don't like to quarrel with my brother."

"Have you thought of reminding him that you're twenty-six years old and you don't need his permission to do anything you want to do?"

"Sometimes that message is a little hard to get through to him. To any of them. Maybe if I'd started acting like an adult a little sooner…"

"So you had a couple of setbacks. Considering everything, you seem to be doing pretty well to me."

"Just your average head case," she quipped with a short laugh that didn't quite come off.

His hands tightened abruptly on her shoulders, not quite to the point of pain. "Damn it, Jessica, stop saying things like that. It isn't funny."

She stared straight ahead at the blank wall in front of her. "There are some people who would tell you it wasn't a joke. That it's simply the truth."

"They would be wrong."

"Some of them know me pretty well."

"Not if they think you're a 'head case,' they don't."

She crossed her arms tightly in front of her. "Maybe they've seen things you haven't. Sometimes I do things—well, you saw me walk in front of that car…"

"Jessica." He spoke right into her ear now, his head almost resting against hers, standing so close behind her she could feel the warmth of him. "Being occasionally absentminded or careless—especially in times of stress—is not abnormal. You should have seen me when my marriage ended. I had trouble remembering to eat or shave—all I could focus on was my anger."

She moistened her dry lips with the tip of her tongue. She had never talked about her fears with anyone, not even Emily or Caroline. Why was she suddenly tempted to spill all to a man who was barely more than a stranger to her?

"The difference is that your mother didn't spend your whole life in a mental institution," she said so quietly it was almost a whisper. "And you didn't grow up hearing yourself compared to her every day."

"My father was an alcoholic. He stayed sober on the job, but headed for the nearest bar as soon as his shift was over. He was addicted to booze and women, and from the day I entered the police academy, my mother predicted I would end up following in all his footsteps. I haven't, but don't think I haven't worried about the tendencies I might have inherited from him."

Just like the first time he'd shared a glimpse of his past with her, what he told her made her feel a bit closer to him. Made her want to believe that she had found someone who understood—at least a little—what it was like to live in fear of one's own genes.

"At least you have a choice not to start drinking. What if—"

"What if what?" he asked gently.

She drew a deep breath, then blurted it out. "What if I look into my mother's eyes today and realize that she really does have serious mental problems? How can I know for sure that I won't end up just like her? That I'm not already headed in that direction?"

He turned her to face him. His hands still on her shoulders, he held his face close to hers. "It doesn't matter if you find out your mother is a raving lunatic. *You are not crazy,* Jessica."

"But how do you know?"

"I know because I've looked into *your* eyes."

His right hand was against her cheek now. His palm was so warm against her skin, his touch so comforting. She felt her breath catch as she found herself suddenly lost in Sam's heated jade gaze.

It took an effort for her to form coherent words. "I— haven't told you everything."

He shrugged. "That doesn't surprise me. We've only spent a couple of days together. There are a lot of things we don't know about each other. But I do know that you're as sane as I am—for whatever that's worth."

She swallowed hard, warning herself to be cautious. Yes, there was a certain appeal in finding someone who seemed to understand her in a way few other people had. And, yes, it was easy to feel as though their mutual experiences with difficult and absent parents created a bond of sorts between them. And, okay, the guy had absolutely gorgeous eyes. But still…

His smile had faded now, to be replaced by an expression that was rather stern. His left hand still rested on her shoulder, and she felt his fingers tighten in a reflexive movement as he used his other hand to trace the line of her jaw. His gaze was focused on her mouth now, and she felt her lips tremble when she imagined what it would be like to kiss him.

"Sam?" she whispered.

He ran his thumb very lightly across her lower lip. "Mmm?"

"Maybe I am crazy, after all."

He frowned, and started to speak.

She rose on tiptoe and covered his mouth with her own, effectively muffling whatever he had intended to say.

And to think that Jessica had called herself "predictable." Had Sam not been so very preoccupied with kissing her, he might have laughed.

Her mouth was as delicious as he had imagined when he'd studied it so intently during the past few days. Her body felt as good in his arms as he remembered from dancing too briefly with her the night before.

He hadn't expected her to kiss him, but since he'd been wanting to kiss her almost from the first time he had seen her, he couldn't say he was sorry she had. He suspected that it was a bad idea, all in all—but he didn't have the willpower to push her away.

Though powerful, the kiss didn't last long. Just as she had been the one to instigate it, Jessica was the one who brought it to an end.

She lowered herself from her tiptoes and dropped the

hands she had splayed on his chest, her lips separating slowly from his. He didn't try to detain her, as much as he would have liked to keep her there longer.

Remembering what she'd said just before she kissed him, he gave her a smile that felt decidedly crooked. "If that was crazy, I'm all for it."

He hadn't been sure how she would react to the attempt at a joke. He was relieved when she laughed lightly. Pushing a hand through her hair, she half turned away. "It *was* crazy. But it was pleasant."

"Pleasant?" He frowned, not sure he liked that description.

"Oh, stuff your ego in your pocket and take me to lunch, Fields."

"Okay—but maybe later we can try for better than pleasant?"

"Don't hold your breath. That was a onetime thing— a thank-you for being so nice."

Following her out of the room, Sam resolved to be as "nice" as possible for the remainder of the day.

They dined in a lovely café in Ouchy, at the bottom of Lausanne's sharply rising terrain. Once a fishing village, Ouchy was now a prime spot for strolling along the waterfront and admiring the mountains rising to the north.

Jessica lingered over her meal, her gaze turning often to the windows. As lovely as it was in the winter, she would love to visit in the summertime. She could very easily fall in love with Switzerland.

Some impulse made her glance at Sam then, and she caught him smiling at her. There was a place deep inside her that always started to tingle whenever she saw that particular smile.

She could very easily fancy herself in love with him, too, if she wasn't extremely careful. She was vulnerable, he seemed sympathetic; she had felt isolated for too long, and he claimed to understand her. And there was no denying the physical attraction between them.

No matter what he really thought of her, she couldn't mistake the appreciation in the way he looked at her. And in the way he had held her and kissed her.

"I'd almost forgotten how much I like it here," he said, obviously making conversation to take her mind off her worries. "The Geneva-Lausanne area has always been my favorite. I've heard the snow is just getting perfect for the skiing season, even though it has been a bit warmer than usual here at lake level."

The weather. Okay, there was a safe topic. "I've noticed it's been quite mild since we arrived. I expected to have to bundle up more than I have."

"The temperatures depend on the elevation, of course. If you travel only ten kilometers northeast, you'll find yourself nearly six hundred meters higher than you are here. It's much cooler there, of course."

"I'm sure it's lovely there."

"Yes, it is. Would you like to chat about how good our food is now, or do you want to tell me why you're trying to stretch this meal out as long as you can?"

She made a face. "I guess it's pretty obvious that I've been stalling."

"Yeah. You've pushed that same last bite of fish around your plate for the past ten minutes."

She set her fork down. "You're right. We should go."

"It will be all right, Jessica. Whatever you find out about your mother, you can deal with it."

"I know. I'm just…nervous."

"Understandably so." He tossed his napkin on the table beside his plate. "The longer we sit here, the more nervous you're going to get."

She nodded, drew a deep breath and rose to her feet. Sam was right. She had come all this way, and now it was time to find out some long-overdue truths.

The asylum wasn't as easy to find as the hotel had been. Even though Jessica had the address, in a village about ten kilometers west of Lausanne, the asylum was extremely secluded, located well off the main tourist path.

Having asked around a little, Sam had discovered that this was a place where the wealthy stashed their embarrassments. The schizophrenic son, the severely neurotic daughter, the uncle who thought he was Bonaparte and the aunt who talked to her cats—and thought they talked back. Or, in Jessica's case, the depressed, alcoholic, bipolar mother.

The place looked much like one of the exclusive resorts in nearby Montreaux. The main building was large and impressive, accessed by a sweeping circular drive. The grounds behind the building were fenced, but landscaped to downplay the heavy security. In the summer, Sam imagined that the lawns would be very green and probably covered in flowers. Now they were prettily dusted with snow.

"Nice place."

Jessica's face wore little expression as she looked around. "Yes, well, I've learned from experience that even the most beautiful locations can still be prisons."

She was talking about her own home, of course. Another immaculately landscaped estate in which there had been little joy for her.

Sam parked in a space marked for visitors, then rounded the car to open Jessica's door for her. It was a sign of her trepidation that she waited for him to do so; usually, she opened her own door and was out of the car almost before he cut the engine.

Feeling how cold her fingers were when he helped her out of the car, he wrapped his warmer hand around hers. He didn't let go as he escorted her up the sweeping steps to the front entrance, nor did she try to pull away. She seemed to appreciate the gesture of support.

He tried not to read too much into her holding on to him. Chances were she'd have clung to anyone who offered encouragement at that moment.

A marble-floored entryway led to a massive front desk. No one would enter the building without stopping there first, Sam noted, spotting signs of security everywhere.

A very professional-looking woman with black eyes and severely cut black hair sat behind the desk typing something into a computer. She wore a telephone headset, and she swung the transmitter away from her mouth when she greeted them. "Bonjour."

Jessica glanced at Sam. Taking her sudden attack of muteness as a sign that she would like his help, he flashed the charming smile he reserved for ferocious receptionists and secretaries. "Bonjour. Parlez-vous anglais?"

She waggled a hand. "Un petit peu."

Because he figured Jessica would be more comfortable if the conversation were conducted in English, he switched, speaking clearly. "My name is Sam Fields. This is my friend, Jessica Parks. She's here to visit her mother."

One perfectly arched black eyebrow lifting, the woman studied Jessica. "Your mother?" she repeated in heavily inflected English.

Jessica nodded, visibly relieved to be able to speak. "Anna Parks. She's a patient here."

"You are expected?"

"No. I'm afraid this is a spur-of-the-moment visit."

The woman frowned. "Je ne comprends pas."

"I'm not expected."

"Then you are not on ze list."

"No. But I've come all the way from America. Surely something can be arranged. Maybe I could speak to her doctor and get permission to see her?"

"Anna Parks?"

Jessica let go of Sam's hand to rest both of hers on the massive desk. "Yes."

The woman typed something into the computer, then shook her head. "No visitors."

"What do you mean, no visitors?"

Both eyebrows lifting in response to Jessica's suddenly raised voice, the woman turned away from the computer screen. "No visitors."

Suspecting he detected Walter's involvement here, Sam stepped up again. "Pardon—Quel est votre nom?"

Looking at him suspiciously, she gave her name. "Chantal DuBois."

"Mademoiselle DuBois?"

"Oui."

Increasing the wattage of his smile, he leaned against the desk and looked directly into her eyes. Speaking in French, he explained Jessica's situation, laying it on a bit thickly as he described her lifelong desire to see her mother, her long journey, the exhausting delays along the way. "Is there nothing you can do to help us?"

Chantal's pale face took on the faintest pink tinge. "Perhaps I could make a call. I don't know why this no visitors restriction has been added this weekend. There are only two people on her list of regular visitors, outside her doctors, of course."

"Can you tell me who those approved visitors are?"

"I'm not really supposed to—"

Sam leaned a little closer to her. "I assure you I will keep your assistance in confidence, Chantal. This is very important to my friend. And to me."

Chantal cleared her throat and glanced back at the computer monitor. "Her friend, Madame Bressoux. And her son, Mr. Ross."

Sam frowned. "You mean, her friend's son?"

"No. Madame Parks's son." Chantal stopped suddenly, as if concerned that she had said too much. "I assumed you—I'll try to call Dr. Rouiller."

Jessica tugged at Sam's jacket sleeve when Chantal turned away. "Well? What did she say?"

"I think she might be a bit confused." He summed up his conversation with the receptionist.

Jessica was shaking her head before he finished

speaking. "She *must* be confused. Neither of my brothers have ever visited my mother here."

"She called him Mr. Ross," Sam reminded her.

"That's Derek's last name. He told me he's never visited her here." She swallowed visibly and shook her head again. "It must be a mistake."

"I'm sure you're right. Maybe she meant your mother is occasionally visited by a friend and the friend's son— whose first name could be Ross. I'll admit it's a coincidence, but certainly possible."

"I suppose… Still, I don't know who they could be."

"Your mother has lived here for twenty-five years. It's entirely probable that she has made a friend or two while she was here."

"Yes. I'm sure you're right." She hesitated a moment. "This new restriction against visitors. My father arranged that, didn't he?"

"Very likely. I suppose it's all he could do, since he couldn't physically stop you from coming here."

She tilted her chin, her eyes flashing. "He won't stop me from seeing her. If I have to fight my way in, I *will* see her."

"Anyone ever tell you you're incredibly sexy when you're so fierce?"

"Pig."

He chuckled, then turned back to the desk when Chantal said, "I'm sorry, but Dr. Rouiller is unavailable today. I cannot give permission to enter without his approval."

"I want to see my mother," Jessica insisted, slapping both hands on the reception desk. "I've come all this way and I'm not going home without seeing her."

"If we could speak to someone in charge?" Sam suggested. "Someone with authority to approve a visit?"

"That would be difficult today. There is no one available. Regular weekly visitation is tomorrow afternoon. If you could come back then?"

"Tomorrow?" Jessica repeated. She looked at him then. "But, Sam, we're so close."

"I know. You want to fight your way in. I understand. But maybe it's best if we wait until tomorrow, as she suggested. We have a better chance of getting in if we play along at first."

"I'm not going home without seeing my mother," Jessica said stubbornly.

"I know," he assured her. "One way or another, we'll get you in. Tomorrow."

Though he could see how much it cost her, she nodded reluctantly. "I seem to have no other choice."

Chapter Ten

Jessica's steps were dragging a bit when they returned to the car. Sam knew she had to be bitterly disappointed.

"You'll see her tomorrow," he promised again as she fastened her seat belt.

"He's doing everything he can to stop me."

"Yes. But there's only so much he can do to interfere from a California jail cell. And other than being here when he's not, you do have one other advantage."

"What's that?"

"Me."

She clasped her hands in her lap and remained silent. After a moment, Sam cleared his throat. "Jessica?"

Without looking at him, she responded, "What?"

"You do believe that I'm going to help you, don't you?"

There was another pause before she said, "So you keep telling me."

"You don't sound overly confident."

Slanting him a sideways glance, she murmured, "It has occurred to me that I don't really know what you were saying to that woman when you were speaking French."

It took an effort for him to hold on to his patience and disguise his irritation when he answered steadily, "I told you word for word what we said."

Again, she said nothing.

Setting his back teeth together, Sam leaned a bit closer to her. "If I were going to try to stop you from seeing your mother, you never would have gotten this far."

"I'd have gotten here. Just like I'm going to see her tomorrow. By whatever means necessary."

"I believe you. And I'm on your side, Jessica. I want you to start believing that."

Still looking disgruntled, she pushed her hair out of her face and looked out the window at the few other cars parked around them. "This trip is costing a fortune. It's just one delay after another."

"Since you've risked everything to get here, you might as well take advantage of your visit," he said, driving away from the asylum and aware that Jessica was looking wistfully back as they pulled away. "How would you like to see a real twelfth-century castle? The Château de Chillon sits in the middle of Lake Geneva. It's been restored, and it's filled with tapestries and other artifacts."

She looked at him with a faint spark of interest. "I've never been in a real castle before."

"Then we should definitely go. It's not as if we have anything else to do to kill time until tomorrow."

"I think I'd like that."

Jessica Parks hadn't played nearly enough in recent years—if ever, he decided. And since he had been accused on more than one occasion of playing a bit too much, he was just the man to remind her of how to have a little fun.

It was very late by the time Jessica walked back into her hotel room. All too aware of Sam following closely behind her, she shrugged out of her black down coat and laid it over the back of a chair.

The red sweater and black slacks she had worn for the planned visit with her mother still looked fresh, despite the busy day. Fortunately, her black boots were comfortable, since she and Sam had done a great deal of walking that afternoon.

When she had been forced to leave the asylum in such bitter disappointment, she never would have expected that she would end up enjoying the rest of the day so much. She hadn't come to Switzerland on vacation, but Sam had given her the full tourist treatment that afternoon and evening. Castles and galleries, shops and châteaus—he had shown her all of them, and she'd had a wonderful time.

She hadn't brought a camera with her on this trip, but she had stored dozens of photographs in her head. She was well aware that Sam would always be predominant in most of those mental pictures.

He had been the perfect companion. Knowledgeable

of the area and the languages, going out of his way to make sure she had a nice time. They had eaten local delicacies and listened to excellent jazz. They'd danced again. And most surprisingly to Jessica, they had laughed. *She* had laughed, more than she had in a long time.

Who would have believed it?

Sam locked the door behind him. The sound of the latch snapping home made her heart leap into her throat. She swallowed, trying not to gulp.

"Man, I'm beat." His voice was cheerfully impersonal as he headed toward the sofa. "I haven't done the tourist thing in years. This sofa looks inviting right now."

She smoothed her hands down her sides. "Maybe you should take the bed. You're really too tall for the sofa."

"I'll be fine. This is your room. You get the bed."

"But—"

"You'll take the bed."

It was the first time all day he had used that particular tone. The one that let her know she would be wasting her breath to argue. "And," he added, "you can take the first bathroom shift. Take your time, I'm going to sit and stretch my legs out for a bit."

Deciding to concede with dignity, she gathered her things and locked herself in the bathroom.

As Sam had suggested, she took her time changing into her most conservative yellow flannel pajamas, washing her face and brushing her teeth. It felt so strange to know Sam waited in the other room. That she would be crawling into bed with him only a few feet away.

Part of the purpose of this trip had been to prove herself a capable, independent woman. She had done a lot

of things she'd never done before. Traveled by herself—
at least for the first leg of the journey. Slept in an airport. Dined and danced in Zurich and Lausanne. Toured
an ancient castle and sensed the ghosts in the shadows.

Spending the night in a hotel room with a man—even
in separate beds—was another first for her, though there
was no need for Sam to know that.

Perhaps she had been a bit too focused on her family problems during the past few years. A little too obsessed with her plans. Somewhat too wary and
suspicious of the motives of every man she met. She had
dated occasionally. But there had been no serious relationships. Not even casual affairs. And now that lack of
experience made her worry that she was too suscepti-
ble to Sam's sexy smiles and flattering attentions.

The fact that he performed his duties with charm
and enthusiasm shouldn't blind her to the reality of the
situation.

She didn't meet Sam's eyes as she moved out of the
bathroom and straight toward the bed. "It's all yours."

He straightened from the sofa, where he had spread
an extra blanket and propped a pillow at one end. "That
was quick."

"Yes, well, I'm tired."

"Good night, then. Go ahead and turn out the lights,
if you want. I can find my way in the dark."

She never slept with all the lights off. Ever since her
kidnapping, when the nights had been much too long and
too dark, she'd slept with at least a night-light burning
somewhere nearby. Because she was making such an effort to prove herself an adult now, she rather defiantly

turned off the lights in the hotel room, hoping that at least a glimmer of light would seep through the draperies.

But the heavy fabrics did their job. The room was plunged into total darkness, without even a crack of light showing beneath the closed bathroom door. Jessica felt her breath catch in her throat. She sank into the pillows and pulled the covers to her chin, reminding herself that Sam was only a few feet away. And then hating herself because that reminder made her feel better immediately.

She heard the bathroom door open, but Sam had already turned out the lights in there. Evidently he had eyes like a cat, because she heard him move to the sofa without stumbling, which was more than she could have accomplished.

She listened to the sounds of him settling onto the sofa, and she knew his feet must be hanging off the end. She considered offering him the bed again, but he'd made it clear that he had no intention of taking it. She closed her eyes and released a long, silent breath, willing herself to sleep.

It didn't work. She could almost feel the minutes ticking slowly past as she lay there, staring blindly up at the ceiling and wishing for daylight. Her mind raced with thoughts she couldn't put away. Thoughts of her mother. Of her uncertain future. Of the man lying on the sofa on the other side of the room.

She jumped when Sam spoke. "Would you be more comfortable if I turn on a light in the bathroom?"

Automatically going on the defensive, she replied, "I don't need a light."

"I could tell you were uncomfortable when I suggested you turn off the lights. It's no big deal, you know. Lots of people sleep with night-lights."

"I just don't sleep well in strange surroundings. Maybe I'm a little too keyed up about tomorrow."

"Is it because I'm here that you can't sleep? Because I can still move down to the car...."

"No," she said a bit too quickly. "There's no need for you to leave."

She hoped he didn't interpret her quick rejection of the suggestion to mean she didn't want to be alone tonight—even though that was exactly what she did mean. "I'm just a little worried about tomorrow, that's all. Concerned about how hard they'll fight to keep me from seeing my mother. And of course, I'm a bit nervous about when I do see her, and what she'll be like. And I can't help thinking about what will happen when I go back to San Francisco—what's going to happen with Dad and all. It's only natural that I'd have a little trouble sleeping tonight. I'm sorry if I'm keeping you awake."

"I'd find it hard to sleep, too, if I were about to meet my mother for the first time."

She rolled to her right side, trying to get comfortable.

"Jessica?"

"Mmm?"

"About what you said in the car this afternoon. Your implication that you still weren't sure you could trust me to help you see your mother?"

She winced. "Um—yeah, about that. I was mad, of course, that I'd been turned away. And disappointed that I hadn't been able to see her. I guess I lashed out at you."

"Does that mean you trust me, after all?"

She bit her lower lip, wondering how she was supposed to answer that.

"Jessica?"

She didn't have to see his face to know he was frowning. "If I didn't trust you, would I be sleeping in the same room with you?"

"That does take a certain leap of faith. And don't think I'm not pleased that you trust me that much, at least. But it isn't really what I asked you."

"You want to know if I still think you're trying to stop me from seeing my mother."

"Right."

Maybe the darkness made it easier for her to be honest with him. "I can't figure out why you would suddenly be on my side when you were working for my father until two days ago. I don't know what's in it for you."

"You think there has to be something in it for me?"

Oddly enough, he sounded more curious than offended. "Yes," she said simply. "There's always an angle. I just haven't figured out what yours is, yet."

"He's really done a number on you, hasn't he? And I thought *I* was cynical."

She didn't have to ask who he was referring to. "I prefer to think of myself as realistic."

"Has it occurred to you that I might simply want to help you?"

"Why? You don't even know me."

"Maybe I'm getting to know you a little better than you think."

After a long stretch of silence, he laughed a little.

"That scares you, doesn't it? You don't want anyone to get to know you too well, do you?"

She moistened her lips. "Maybe there are things about me you wouldn't want to know."

"Back to that again, are we?" He sighed, then said in a deliberately weary voice, "You are not crazy."

"'I'm just a little unwell,'" she murmured, once again quoting her self-declared "theme song."

"Then maybe we're both crazy," he said roughly. "Because no matter how many arguments I give myself why I should stay away from you—your distrust of me being primary among them—I'd still give anything I have to be in that bed with you. And if that doesn't give you a clue about my reasons for being on your side in this, then you haven't been paying very close attention."

What was she supposed to say in response to *that?* She gnawed on her lower lip, telling herself that the same arguments applied for her. It really was a bad idea for her to even consider inviting him into her bed—but the images now flooding her mind were enough to melt her spine, much less her willpower.

She hadn't forgotten how good it had felt just to kiss him. She couldn't even imagine what it must be like to make love with him.

"Go to sleep, Jessica," he said, and this time his weariness sounded genuine. "We'll deal with our problems tomorrow, after we've had some rest."

At least Sam had taken her mind off her family problems, Jessica thought as she nestled more deeply into the bed coverings. Now all she could think about was him.

* * *

Jessica was surprised to open her eyes and realize that she had managed a full seven hours of sleep. The clock on the bedside table told her it was 7:30 a.m. She lifted her head to see if Sam was still sleeping.

The sofa was empty. The blanket he had used was folded neatly at one end, with the pillow resting on top of it. The bathroom door stood open, and she could see that the room was empty. Where on earth had he gone?

There were signs in the bathroom that Sam had showered before going out. Though she tended to be a heavy sleeper, she was still surprised she hadn't roused when Sam had dressed and left the room. He really could move very quietly when he chose to do so.

She showered quickly, dried her hair, applied makeup and dressed in a peacock-blue sweater and a fresh pair of black slacks. To cut down on baggage, she had packed several pairs of black slacks and mix-and-match tops.

Sam was waiting when she came out of the bathroom. Because his cheeks were still a bit cold-reddened when he turned away from the table in the window to greet her, she figured he hadn't been back for long.

"Good morning," he said. "You look nice."

Suddenly remembering the things he had said to her in the darkness last night, she tucked a strand of hair behind her ear in a self-conscious gesture. "Thank you. What are you doing?"

He stepped to one side to give her a better look at the table behind him. A tall white taper in a crystal holder sat in the center, next to a single white rose in a crystal bud vase. Two snowy linen placemats were set with white china plates and cups, silverware and linen napkins. A cut glass plate held an assortment of delicious-looking pastries, surrounded by plump strawberries, and a white carafe stood next to the plate.

She smiled. "This looks wonderful."

He lifted one shoulder, looking rather pleased with himself. "I remembered a good bakery that I used to visit here. I wasn't sure it was still in business, but it looked exactly the way I remembered it."

He leaned over to light the candle with a pocket lighter. "As for the rest of the things, I found a helpful hotel employee. She brought this stuff up for me. She left while your hair dryer was still running, which is probably why you didn't hear us moving around in here."

Sam seemed to have a knack for charming people into assisting him, she mused. She hoped that talent would come in handy when they went back to see her mother later.

"I can't believe you put all this together so quickly. I really didn't take all that long to get dressed."

He studied the table. "Something's missing—oh, wait. I know what it is."

With a flourish, he opened the draperies. Jessica caught her breath in delight. "It's snowing!"

Smiling as if he'd arranged that, too, he held her chair for her. "It started while I was at the bakery."

"Oh, it's beautiful." Sinking into her seat, she gazed out the bow window. "It's like having breakfast inside a snow globe."

"That's a pretty image. Not as pretty as the one I'm seeing, of course."

She glanced away from the window to find him smiling at her from across the tiny table. The candlelight flickered between them, and she could smell the scent of the perfect white rose. The sheer romance of the moment made her catch her breath.

It should have seemed heavily orchestrated on his part; instead, it just seemed incredibly sweet. Which probably said a great deal about the way she had come to feel about him.

"You're very good at this, aren't you?"

He lifted an eyebrow. "At what?"

She waved a hand at the table settings, encompassing the candle, the rose, even the snowy window in the motion. "Charmingly romantic gestures."

His sudden frown looked genuine enough. "I wasn't trying to make a gesture. I just thought you might like a nice breakfast before we head out today."

Now she'd hurt his feelings. Oddly enough, she hadn't realized that she could.

"And I appreciate your thoughtfulness," she assured him quickly. "Everything is perfect. I just noticed that things like this seem to come naturally to you."

He was smiling again, though rather ruefully. "My ex-wife would tell you that I don't have a thoughtful bone in my body. Candlelight breakfasts aren't something I do all the time. It was just an impulse this morning after I bought the pastries. Something about the snow, I guess. Or just being here, in this elegant setting. Besides—"

"Besides, what?"

His expression was disarmingly sheepish when he replied, "I like to do nice things for you. I'm not sure that's something you've had enough of in your life."

Her cheeks warmed as she looked quickly down at her plate. The reference to his ex-wife had caused a little pang in her chest, but that feeling dissolved suddenly into a pleasant heat.

Sam could deny all he wanted that he was good at being romantic, but as far as she was concerned, he was a genius at it. How else could he have slipped so easily beneath the defenses she had erected against him?

"You make me a little nervous sometimes," she murmured, knowing her words were an understatement.

"Good. Because you scare the hell out of me."

She looked at him then, but he gave her a crooked smile and shook his head. "Let's just enjoy our breakfast, shall we? Pass me your cup."

She did so, then watched as he poured from the carafe. "I thought you'd brought coffee."

"Hot Swiss chocolate," he corrected her. "What else would you have with these fine French pastries?"

"I suppose I shouldn't even think about calories during this meal?"

"Absolutely not." He handed her the steaming cup of chocolate. "Sometimes it feels really good to be bad."

She eyed him over the rim of the cup, wondering if he was referring to anything other than breakfast. She couldn't tell from his blandly innocent expression.

Whatever his meaning, he was certainly right, she discovered quickly enough. It did feel wonderful to be bad. Sitting there in that window with the snow falling outside, a handsome, attentive man across the table, flaky pastries melting on her tongue and rich chocolate sliding down her throat, she was able to forget everything that had been bothering her for so long.

Just for that brief interlude, she was someone else. She wasn't being gawked at because her notorious father was in prison and her mother in an institution, or because her sister had married a king. Or because she was a bit odd herself.

She saw none of those things in Sam's eyes when he smiled at her across the table. Instead, there was an unmistakable masculine appreciation. An interest in what she had to say. Even respect for her opinions.

At that moment, she was just Jessica. And being valued for no other reason was much more seductive than the candlelight and flowers. More intoxicating than the smoothest of compliments.

She didn't want the novelty to end too quickly. "How long do we have until the maids come to clean?"

"I put the Do Not Disturb sign on the doorknob. We have as long as we want." Leaning a bit closer to her, he held out a hand. "Try this strawberry. I know they're technically out of season, but these are delicious."

She was tempted to take a bite while he held the berry, but since that seemed a bit dangerous, she reached up, instead, to pluck it from his fingers. "Mmm," she said a moment later. "That really is good."

His gaze focused on her mouth. He sounded quite distracted when he murmured, "Yeah. They're…good."

She swallowed hard in response to the look in his eyes. "Um—Sam…"

Still looking at her mouth, he sighed. "I'm trying to

behave. You make it difficult sometimes. You're so damn beautiful. I just thought you should know."

Her cheeks were probably bright red now, from the way they felt. Her hands weren't quite steady when she gripped them in her lap beneath the table. "When you say things like that…"

"I know," he cut in ruefully. "It makes it hard for you to start trusting me, doesn't it?"

"No," she said, wrinkling her nose in a self-deprecating expression. "It makes me want to kiss you again."

"Well, damn."

She had to smile at that, though it was a shaky effort. "I just thought you should know."

He cleared his throat. "You're trying to torture me, is that it?"

"You probably deserve it. But, as it happens, I'm just being honest."

He stood abruptly. "If you're finished with your breakfast, we'd probably better get out of here soon."

Jessica jumped to her feet—and promptly stumbled. Sam reached out to catch her, reminding her forcibly of the times she had done something foolish when he'd been following her around San Francisco. It was hard to believe it had been only a few days since she had considered him her enemy rather than her ally.

She wasn't even sure when she had started believing he was on her side. As late as last night, she had still been battling doubts about his motives. Had it taken nothing more than a few held glances over pastries and chocolate to win her over?

"You okay?" he asked, his hands still resting on her shoulders.

"I—" She looked up into his eyes and promptly forgot what she'd been about to say.

Sam muttered something she didn't understand. Before she could ask him to repeat it, his mouth was on hers.

Chapter Eleven

Sam pulled her closer as he deepened the kiss. He wanted her, she thought with a catch in her throat. Judging from the evidence, he wanted her badly. Could anything be more seductive for a woman who had spent most of her life wondering if she was truly wanted by anyone?

Her name rumbled in his throat as he tilted his head to kiss her from a new angle.

She had come on this trip at least partly to prove herself an adult. To stop living like a frightened child and make her own decisions. Her own mistakes, if necessary.

Perhaps Sam would eventually fall under the latter heading, but for now she wanted to know what it was to feel like a woman. She suspected that he was just the man to teach her.

Gathering her courage, she nestled closer to him, savoring the feel of his hard body against her softer curves. She touched her tongue to his, enjoying the taste of him.

His groan rumbled deep in his chest, vibrating against her sensitized breasts. She couldn't resist rubbing herself lightly against him, which made him groan again, more deeply this time.

"Jessica," he said, lifting his mouth from hers with obvious reluctance. "We really should stop this now."

"Stop protecting me, Sam. I don't need you to take care of me—not in this, or in anything else. And if you tell me again that it's your job to do so, I'll…I'll…"

He smiled faintly and touched a fingertip to her kiss-swollen lower lip. "What will you do?"

"Something that will make you sorry," she said, wishing she were able to come up with a more clever response.

The way he smiled gave her hope that she had gotten through to him. She didn't need a conscience or a keeper—and she sure didn't need another father.

"I think I mentioned before that I think you're just as cute as hell when you get all fierce and growly," he murmured.

"And I remembered that I called you a pig when you said that."

"I believe you did. So, does that mean you want me to keep my distance from you?"

"Is that what you want to do?"

His eyes darkened suddenly. His voice was gruff when he replied, "You know better than that."

"So, which one of us are you really protecting? Me—or yourself?"

"Damned if I know right now."

She reached up to rest her hands on his chest, leaning slightly toward him. "A wise man once told me that sometimes it feels really good to be bad." Lifting her mouth invitingly toward his, she added, "Let's see just how good we can feel."

Her new life had begun three days ago when she boarded a plane in Oakland. She didn't know where her quest for change would ultimately lead her, but she was eager to continue the journey.

She could almost hear him mentally listing the reasons they should walk away. But then he gave her a crooked smile and pulled her closer. "A wise man, hmm?"

"I might have been exaggerating a little…"

"Let's just leave it at that. I kind of like the sound of it." He spoke against her lips, his own curved into a smile. She looped her arms around his neck again and pulled his mouth more tightly against hers.

This time they left no space between them. She felt every inch of him pressed against her. The ripple of muscles in the arms that held her, the warmth of flesh beneath the fabric of his shirt. The ridge of his erection beneath his jeans. She felt her own body go limp and pliant in reaction.

He twisted to lower her to the bed, following her down. His weight pressed her deeply into the thick bed coverings, and she instinctively bent her knees upward to cradle him between them.

Now that she had convinced him she knew what she wanted—and that she wanted *him*—he seemed intent on proceeding without further delay. He slid her sweater over her head, tossing his shirt on the floor on top of it. Jessica barely had time to admire his bare chest—the line of his collarbone, the gold hairs that arrowed down to his navel, the deep hollow of his throat—before he moved to the waistband of her slacks.

Funny how she didn't feel self-conscious when he slid the fabric down her legs to leave her clad only in a black bra and panties. Not even when those scraps of lace joined the other clothing on the carpet next to the bed. She was too eager to experience more.

And Sam gave her more. The feel of his mouth on her throat, her breasts, her stomach. His hands at her hips, on her thigh, between her legs. His hairy legs rubbing against her smooth ones.

She wanted to believe she would have thought of protection before they went too far for it to matter. But it was Sam who took care of that detail, swiftly and matter-of-factly, digging the packets out of his bag.

She wanted to believe she was able to conceal the fact that this was her first experience with lovemaking, but she suspected he knew. Maybe it was the tentativeness of her movements, or the sheer wonder in her expression, but something gave her away.

Though he joined them carefully, there was no pain. Only pleasure. And when he started to move inside her, the pleasure built until she thought she would explode with it. Moments later, it felt very much as though she had.

Her startled cry was still echoing in the room when Sam followed her over the edge. She thought she had never heard anything more thrilling than the sound of her own name uttered in his broken gasp.

* * *

Maybe it had been a mistake. And he would probably pay for it later. But whatever the price, it would be worth it as far as Sam was concerned.

It wasn't that he had forgotten all the reasons he should have maintained a careful distance from Jessica. It was just that he had reached a point where none of those obstacles seemed to be insurmountable.

He knew why he'd made love with Jessica. After all, he had been fascinated by her from the first time he'd seen her. He had wanted her from the first time their eyes met—even if hers had been filled with anger. And when she had clutched his shirt so fiercely and told him she wanted him, too—well, hell. He was no saint.

So where did they go from here? Sitting behind the wheel of their little rental car, he slanted her a sideways glance. She had been distracted ever since they'd left the hotel room, which was understandable.

He cleared his throat. Waiting for her to bring up the subject was making him antsy. "It's a momentous day, hmm?" he asked, keeping his tone light.

"Yes. I've been giving it a lot of thought."

So, she had been thinking about their lovemaking, wondering where it would lead. "I guess you're wondering what's going to happen next."

"Of course. I just hope there's not a big scene."

He squirmed uncomfortably in his seat. "Well, there's no reason there should be, is there?"

"Only if they try to stop me from seeing her again. I'm not taking no for an answer this time."

"Oh. You were talking about your visit with your mother."

"Of course. What else?"

"Yeah. What else?" He kept his eyes focused on the windshield. The light snowfall earlier had stopped, for the most part, leaving only a light dusting on the roads, causing no driving problems. Still, he clenched the steering wheel a bit more tightly.

"I've made a decision. If they try to turn me away this time, I'll call my father. I'll tell him I'm not coming home until I see her, so he might as well give his permission."

She wore that fierce expression again, but Sam wasn't quite as amused by it this time. She was finding a bit too much satisfaction in openly defying her father for the first time in so long. Something about that observation bothered him.

Apparently satisfied that she'd made her point, she settled into her seat again with that same distracted expression from earlier. Knowing now that it was her mother who claimed her thoughts and not him, Sam made the rest of the drive with a scowl on his face.

The parking lot at the asylum was just a little more crowded than it had been the day before. Apparently, not many people took advantage of the regular weekly visitation hours, Sam mused. But then, he supposed he should have expected that from an institution known as a convenient place to stash embarrassing relatives.

The same woman was at the reception desk. She wore the same harried expression as yesterday as she faced a tall, rather arrogantly handsome young man with thick black hair, narrowed hazel eyes and an angry expression.

He spoke in French, his tone making it clear that he was accustomed to having his way. "I don't care what your computer says, I will see my mother, is that clear? You can either unlock that door for me, or you will get Dr. Rouiller on the telephone. Now."

"I'm sorry, Mr. Ross, but I have my instructions—"

The young man—Sam guessed him to be no older than twenty-five—leaned forward. "You have thirty seconds before I call my attorneys. I don't think the management will appreciate the legal problems they're going to encounter if I'm not let through those doors immediately."

Chantal DuBois quailed visibly. "I'll make a call."

"Good." Straightening away from the desk, the man pushed his hands into the pockets of his camel-hair coat and glowered at her, looking fully prepared to remain there as long as necessary.

"What's going on?" Jessica asked Sam in a low voice.

"This man is being denied permission to see his mother. Sound familiar?"

The man looked at them now, obviously having overheard and understood. "Have you encountered problems with visitation, as well?" he asked in perfect, if very slightly accented, English.

"My friend was turned away when she tried to visit her mother yesterday. We're here to try again."

The other man glanced automatically at Jessica. And then he did a visible double take, his jaw seeming to drop slightly. His voice was a bit strangled when he asked her, "Who is your mother?"

"Her name is Anna Parks. Do you know her?"

"Mon Dieu." It was little more than a whisper.

"We're told she looks exactly like her mother," Sam said, closely watching the other man's face.

"The resemblance is…uncanny."

Biting her lip, Jessica glanced at Sam, who wondered if he had already taken a few mental steps ahead of her to reach an unnerving suspicion.

The other man spoke again, his gaze still focused intently on Jessica's face. "May I ask your name?"

"I'm Jessica Parks. Oh, and this is my friend Sam Fields."

The offhanded way in which she had used the word *friend* made it sound to Sam roughly equivalent to "some guy I barely know and have no particular ties to." Or was he maybe being a bit too touchy?

"My name is Benton Ross." The young man studied Jessica's expression as he spoke, as if trying to determine if she had ever heard the name before.

Jessica frowned. "Your name was mentioned yesterday, in connection with my mother."

"Monsieur Ross?"

All three of them turned toward the reception desk in response to the receptionist's voice, but it was Benton who spoke. "Yes?"

Looking only at him, Chantal continued. "I spoke to Dr. Rouiller. He instructed me to allow you to go in."

Nodding in satisfaction, Benton turned to Jessica. "I will escort you to your mother."

Chantal shook her head rapidly. "I received permission only for you, Monsieur Ross. No other visitors have been approved."

Sam translated quietly for Jessica while Benton turned back to the desk. For a man so young, he had a definite air of authority about him. Not to mention a hint of threat when he spoke with icy control, "These people will accompany me. Do not try to interfere with me again."

Sam figured there was no need to translate that time. Benton's meaning was clear enough.

Chantal didn't actually throw up her hands, but her desire to do so was written in her exasperated expression. It was obvious that she had no interest in another battle—which she must surely have known would follow if she tried to bar Jessica from seeing her mother. "Fine," she said. "Take them with you."

Sam thought he heard her add beneath her breath, "It isn't worth it."

Jessica felt more as if she were inside a luxury resort than an asylum. Though the reception area had been formal, the inside was light and airy. Lots of greenery and fresh flowers, water trickling from built-in fountains, windows overlooking the fenced, but beautifully maintained grounds. It wasn't exactly the way she had envisioned her mother living for the past twenty-five years, but she was glad to see that this prison was a beautiful one, at least.

She cast a surreptitious glance at the man escorting them through the winding hallways, being greeted with familiarity by the few people they passed along the way. Benton Ross. An exceptionally handsome man with an air of wealth and subtle power that was familiar to her. But it was Benton's black hair and strong features that reminded her most vividly of someone.

He could very easily pose as a younger version of Derek Ross. Her mother's long-ago lover, she thought with a sudden pang of premonition.

They paused outside a door embellished with a wreath of grapevine and dried flowers. Benton reached out to knock on the door, but Jessica caught his arm to stop him. "Before we go in, would you please tell me who you are?"

Benton hesitated, then gave a slight shake of his head. "I think that would best be left to Madame," he murmured, and tapped lightly on the door.

"Entre."

Hearing the voice—her mother's voice—made Jessica's throat tighten. Without thinking, she reached out to Sam. He caught her hand in his, giving it a reassuring squeeze. Jessica noticed Benton watching them closely, and she nodded to indicate that she was ready.

They entered a spacious suite done in yellows and greens and light woods, so that it was almost like stepping from winter into summer. The sitting room was small, but inviting, with a big window overlooking a courtyard filled with birds flocking around hanging feeders. A closed door on one side of the room probably led into the bedroom. There didn't seem to be a kitchen, so Jessica assumed meals were served in a common dining room.

There were framed photographs on a low wooden sideboard. Jessica recognized several as pictures she had sent of herself and her siblings and her niece Stacy, Anna's grandchild. The others were all photographs of Benton Ross, from childhood to present.

Only after she had taken that brief moment to study the room—building her courage in the process—did she turn to the woman standing beside a wooden rocking chair that she had probably been sitting in prior to their arrival.

Anna Parks had been known for her beauty. Neither time nor adversity had taken that away from her. Her up-swept blond hair was now streaked with gray, and there were a few lines on her face, but at fifty, she was still striking. Anna had been compared to Marilyn Monroe in her youth, whereas Jessica's curves were more delicate. Though age had added a few pounds, Anna was still a woman men would look twice at on the street.

Anna's blue eyes filled with tears as she gazed back at her daughter. "Jessica," she breathed. "You're here."

Jessica swallowed and managed a shy-feeling smile. "Hello, Mother."

"Oh, my baby." Anna was sobbing now, tears cascading down her cheeks. "You were only an infant when I saw you last. And now look at you. So beautiful."

Benton pulled a snowy handkerchief from his pocket and offered it to her. She accepted it with a teary smile and a murmured, "Thank you, darling."

Delicately wiping her eyes, Anna took a step toward Jessica, who hadn't moved. "You've met Benton?"

Jessica nodded slowly. "He's your son, isn't he?

Yours and Derek Ross's. Why didn't you tell me in your letters?"

"I thought it would be better to tell you in person."

"Does Derek know?"

"Yes. I wrote to him recently to inform him."

"Why didn't he tell me?"

"I asked him not to. I believe he has told his daughter, but I wanted to be the one to tell mine."

"Oh, my God." Jessica raised icy hands to her cheeks. "You had Derek Ross's child. I have another brother."

It seemed that half brothers were popping up out of the woodwork these days. She shook her head slowly at this further evidence of the dysfunctional and destructive nature of her parents' marriage. "You knew?" she asked Benton.

"I've seen your photographs. When I saw you downstairs, I knew who you must be."

"Please, let's all sit down," Anna said, looking flustered. "I'll try to explain."

She glanced at Sam, who had remained quietly in the background. "I don't believe we've been introduced…"

"My name is Sam Fields, Mrs. Parks."

"Please, call me Anna. You must be Jessica's boyfriend?"

"He's not my boyfriend," Jessica answered quickly. "He works for Dad."

Anna's eyes narrowed, her hardening expression giving the first evidence of her hatred for her husband. Jessica had known about that hostility from their letters, but now she got a glimpse of the full extent of the emotion.

Sam looked no more pleased by her words. He gave

her a look that contained both anger and a hint of hurt. "I *did* work for Walter Parks," he said evenly. "On a contract basis. I'm a private investigator he hired as a bodyguard for Jessica. Once she told me what she was trying to do, I decided to help her. I thought she had a right to see her mother, and that Walter had no right to try to interfere."

Anna didn't look particularly reassured. "You are no longer working for my husband?"

He met her eyes steadily. "No, I'm not."

Benton's face had taken on that threatening expression he had used with the receptionist earlier. "If I discover that you are working with him to hurt my mother, I will make you very sorry."

Jessica watched as Sam sighed and rubbed the back of his neck. "You suppose we could cut the melodrama?" he asked a bit wearily. "I'm not the bad guy here."

"He's right," Jessica said, regretting that she had overreacted to hearing her mother refer to Sam as her boyfriend. Once again, her unruly tongue had gotten her into trouble, and she'd taken Sam with her this time. "Sam was simply doing his job, taking care of me. And he has been very helpful in getting me this far."

"Please sit," Anna said again. "We must talk."

Once everyone was seated, Anna drew a deep breath, as if wondering where to start. She must have decided to start at the beginning.

"I was very young and vain when I met Walter," she said. "My life revolved around parties and discos, beauty pageants and the few acting roles that came my way. Walter romanced me with promises of wealth and popularity, and my father wanted the business alliance our marriage would form, so I allowed myself to be persuaded to marry him. My life changed almost as soon as the honeymoon began."

She went on to describe how Walter had begun to isolate her from her friends and even from her family. How he had assured her that he was only trying to protect her, but had basically confined her to their luxurious mansion, where she had spent too many hours alone.

"Sounds familiar," Jessica murmured, picturing her mother's life all too easily.

"It wasn't so bad once the twins and then Rowan came," Anna went on. "I adored my children. But Walter began to spend more time away, and I suspected there were other women. I was starved for adult companionship. I suffered from bouts of terrible depression that I tried to alleviate with alcohol and pills. That only made things worse, of course. Walter and I got into terrible fights. Twice I accidentally overdosed, and had to be rushed to the hospital. Walter began hinting to people that I was unstable and suicidal, which effectively kept my former friends away from me."

"Didn't you ever try to leave him?" Jessica asked.

Anna's shrug conveyed both regret and self-recrimination. "I was afraid of him," she said simply. "He was too powerful, and he would stop at nothing to have his way. He threatened to take my children away from me, so that I would never see them again. And he threatened to have me locked away. He would eventually go through with those threats, of course."

"Mrs. Parks, what happened the night Jeremy Carlton died?" Sam asked bluntly. "There's a rumor going around that you were sent away because you knew too much about Carlton's disappearance. Is that true?"

There was still distrust in Anna's gaze when she looked at Sam. Blaming herself for putting it there, Jessica spoke up. "I'd like to hear that, as well. Dad is in jail and Derek Ross is planning to testify that he saw Dad kill Carlton and throw his body off the side of a yacht. Dad's bookkeeper, Linda Carlton, is going to testify to shady business practices on Dad's part. Embezzlement, tax fraud—I'm not even sure about all the charges. The trial starts next Monday. I need to know if he's guilty of the charges against him."

Anna turned to Jessica, and their gazes held for several long moments. Jessica had told herself that she would be able to look into her mother's eyes and know for certain whether she was mentally and emotionally stable. She had been so certain that was all it would take. But now she wondered....

Anna certainly seemed rational enough, and her story was believable to anyone who knew Walter as well as Jessica did. But there were still several significant details that hadn't been explained—and the most obvious was sitting in a chair right next to Anna.

"We were on the yacht," Anna said. "Walter wanted to hold a big party for all his senior staff and business associates. His partner, Jeremy Carlton, was invited, of course, along with Jeremy's wife, Marla, and Marla's younger brother, Derek."

She explained that she had known Walter and Jeremy hadn't been getting along for some time. She had even overheard Walter threatening Jeremy in private, though they were cordial enough in public. She had also suspected that Walter was having an affair with Jeremy's wife—a suspicion that had turned out to be true, since twin boys, Tyler and Conrad, had been conceived from that affair.

"I knew it would be a miserable cruise, and I dreaded it. I turned to my usual solace," Anna added flatly. "I wasn't sober that evening, and my behavior was hardly exemplary. I flirted shamelessly with Derek, who was several years younger, and I made him fall for me. I seduced him to bolster my own battered ego. Later, I passed out cold."

Jessica glanced surreptitiously at Benton, who had said nothing since Anna began her story. She assumed that he had heard it before, since he showed no surprise at anything Anna revealed.

"It was while Derek was trying to revive me that he saw Walter throw Jeremy's body off the side of the yacht. Walter thought I was sleeping, and he believed everyone else had left the yacht. He wasn't worried about me being a witness—he was too confident that he could control me with threats about our children."

Jessica said, "Derek told me that he was too frightened to say anything about what he had seen. He had been drinking, and he was guilty of making love with Walter's wife. He didn't think anyone would believe him, and he was terrified that he would end up the same way as Jeremy if he tried to do anything."

Anna nodded in response to Jessica's comments. "He told me the same things later that night when he whispered to me what he had seen. He managed to smuggle me off the yacht and to his apartment, but then he didn't know what to do. He believed Walter would kill us both if he found out the truth. I believed the same. After all, Walter had gotten rid of Jeremy when his partner became an inconvenience. I suspect Jeremy had learned something about Walter's illegal business practices, and did not approve. And who were we to be believed against a man like Walter? His crazy wife? A callow boy in love?

"I convinced Derek to take me home and then leave town. And I was the one who suggested that he change his name and forget he'd ever met me or Walter."

Chapter Twelve

"Y ou disapprove, Mr. Fields," Anna remarked, seeming not to mind whatever she had read in his expression. "I don't blame you. What Derek and I did was wrong, and a man got away with murder because of it—at least for twenty-five years.

"Walter concocted a story of how Jeremy had gotten drunk and fallen overboard, and without witnesses, the authorities had to accept that story despite their suspicions to the contrary. His wealth and power probably kept them from looking as closely at the facts as they might have otherwise. He always liked to boast that with enough wealth and connections, a man was above the laws that governed ordinary people."

"What happened then?" Jessica asked.

"I could not bear to look at Walter from that night on,

or to have him touch me. I spiraled into such a deep depression that I couldn't even get out of bed. Walter had no trouble convincing anyone that I needed to be institutionalized. Maybe he was even right at the beginning. But there was no reason for him to send me this far, or to keep me here for so long. He chose to lock me up and forget about me, and to make sure everyone else forgot me, too. It was four weeks after the night Jeremy Carlton died that I was shipped here."

"How did he keep you here against your will?"

"With money, Mr. Fields. A great deal of money. This place is lovely, and the residents are treated well, but we have no freedom. No choice in our own affairs. Someone else's money ensures that we stay here quietly out of the way. Most of the residents have suffered emotional problems in the past, and some truly need to be here. The rest of us simply became an embarrassment to our families."

"You never tried to get away? Never tried to contact attorneys or doctors in the States who could testify that you shouldn't be locked away?"

"A month after I arrived, I realized I was pregnant. I was just beginning to emerge from the paralyzing depression and I wanted very much to return to my children. But Walter made sure I got the message that I would not be welcomed at home. That he had made sure my reputation was so badly damaged that no judge would award me custody of my children. He even conveyed vague threats against my safety if I tried to return against his will."

She caught her breath. "I knew then that I had lost

my babies, as a result of his corruptness and my own weakness. I could not risk having him find out about my pregnancy—which I knew had to be a result of my night with Derek Ross. Walter would have insisted that my baby be destroyed, or taken away from me forever. I would not allow that.

"I had made some friends here, most notably a young doctor, Georges Rouiller. Dr. Rouiller was new to the staff, and had little influence with the management, but he was able to help me find someone to raise my child. He was a little in love with me then, I think, even though he was married and he knew we could never be together," she added with a hint of the vanity she had alluded to before. "He has been my friend and my supporter ever since. It wasn't that difficult for us to conceal the pregnancy from Walter, since he never called to ask about my welfare after he deposited me here."

"You stayed for Benton," Jessica murmured, looking from her mother to her newly discovered brother.

"Yes," Anna whispered. "It wasn't that I loved him any more than the four children I had left behind. Nor that I didn't long to be with you and your sister and brothers, Jessica. But you were lost to me, and Benton was all I had left. I simply couldn't take the risk.

"I was thrilled when I received that first letter from you nine years ago. I was afraid, of course, for you and for myself if Walter found out, but I had to know that you were all well. It has broken my heart that your father has turned the others against me so badly that they have had no interest in contacting me. And I was so sorry about what happened to you when you tried to come to me."

Jessica shrugged, taking on that faux-tough expression Sam recognized so well now. "I survived."

Her gruff tone hurt Sam's heart, because he knew how Jessica had suffered during the past few years. It couldn't be easy to find out the mother she had risked so much to contact and to try to visit had made little effort on her own behalf to be reunited with her eldest children.

"I became rather obsessed with protecting Benton from Walter," Anna admitted. "I was so sure Walter would harm him, perhaps because of the guilt I carried for leaving my other children, and for letting Walter get away with so many terrible things. Georges brought Marie Bressoux to me. A few years older than I, she was a wealthy widow with no children of her own. Georges' maternal aunt, actually. We made an arrangement whereby Marie would raise Benton as her own, giving him the best education and upbringing. Once a month, she brought him to see me. We told him that I was his aunt because we didn't want to confuse him."

"I figured out the truth by the time I was ten," Benton said. "They didn't lie to me when I asked them to confirm my guess."

"Benton was a brilliant child," Anna said with glowing pride. "He skipped several grades in school and finished university by the time he was eighteen. For the past five years, he has been working in the banking industry in Geneva, and already he is a very influential man."

"Mother tends to boast when it comes to me," Benton said indulgently. "She and Maman—which is what I call Marie Bressoux—still get together once a month just to discuss how wonderful I am. It's no surprise that I have a very healthy ego."

"Were you angry when you found out the truth?"

Benton looked a bit surprised by Jessica's question. "Why would I be angry? I was raised with the unconditional love and incredible support of two very special women. My childhood was a happy one."

Sam rested a hand on Jessica's knee, resenting for her sake that she couldn't make the same claim. "You know your mother doesn't belong in this place," he said to Benton, hearing the accusation in his own voice. "Why haven't you tried to get her out?"

"He could have done so, perhaps," Anna acknowledged for him. "But I asked him to leave things be. He needed to concentrate on building his own future. Walter left me alone as long as all that was required from him was a monthly check to the institution. When I heard from my daughter that she and my other children were well, I was able to stop worrying about them so much. Benton visits me often, as does Marie. They make sure I have everything I desire. I always knew that someday it would be safe to go home again, probably when Walter was dead. But having him in prison will be just as satisfactory," she added.

Sam had to wonder how Jessica felt at hearing the loathing in Anna's tone when she spoke of her husband. "Are you saying you're ready to go home now?" he asked.

Anna nodded. "I have been contacted about whether I would be willing to serve as a witness in Walter's trial.

Though I was, and am still concerned that my testimony would be twisted as that of a vengeful and unstable scorned wife, I am willing to do so."

Jessica moistened her lips. "You're going to testify against him?"

Anna's voice softened. "I'm going to tell the truth, darling. It's something I should have done twenty-five years ago."

"For what it's worth, he has been trying to make some amends," Jessica murmured. "He's made overtures to a couple of us since his arrest, and he even tried to apologize to me for some of the things he's done, though he doesn't do apologies very well."

"I hope his words bring some peace to you. But he will never be able to make amends to me for taking me away from my babies and depriving me of their childhoods."

"How do you plan to get back to California?" Sam asked, subtly changing the topic.

"My daughter bought an airline ticket for me when she purchased her own. I sent word through Derck that we would arrange the details of my release once she arrived here."

"I assumed I would be smuggling her out on my own somehow," Jessica added. "I didn't know about Benton, of course. I trust you will help me get her out of here?"

Benton nodded in confirmation.

Sam looked at Jessica. "You knew all along that you intended to take your mother home with you."

"Yes. I kept it a secret from everyone but Derek because I didn't want my father to get a hint of our plans."

She hadn't given *him* a hint, either, Sam couldn't

help thinking. She hadn't trusted him enough to tell him all her plans.

"I have to go back to make things right," Anna said. "And I want to see my other children. I want Benton to meet his other siblings, including Derek's daughter. And I want him to meet his father. I've been a coward for too long, hidden away here without fighting back. But my family needs me now. It's time for me to go home."

Sam hadn't said three words since they'd left the institution just over an hour earlier. Sitting on the side of the neatly made bed in their hotel room, Jessica watched from beneath her lashes as he paced, his thoughts hidden behind a stern expression.

"Are you angry with me?"

"You mean because you didn't tell me you were planning to take your mother home with you? Because you didn't trust me with that little tidbit?"

"It wasn't just you…" she began lamely.

"Oh, right. You didn't trust your father, either. Nice of you to put me in the same category with him."

"Give me a break, Sam. Only a few days ago you were working for him."

"And since then I've been totally on your side. Damn it, Jessica, we made love this morning. Doesn't that mean anything to you?"

She blinked. She had gotten the distinct impression that Sam had been the one who'd been unnerved by how close they'd gotten that morning. He had given off unmistakable "nervous bachelor" vibes afterward, and she had told herself it didn't matter because she didn't have any long-term plans for them, anyway. She knew exactly what that morning had been about, and a happily-ever-after ending wasn't a part of it. "I, um—"

"Never mind. What time are you supposed to meet your brother for dinner?"

"We have another hour. You're invited, too, you know. Benton made that very clear."

Sam shook his head. "You should take this chance to get to know him better and to finalize your plans for springing your mother tomorrow. I'll entertain myself."

"Are you sure?"

"Yes." He turned to pace the other direction.

Perched on the very edge of the mattress with her fingers tucked beneath her, Jessica continued to watch him. "What did you think about my mother? About the things she told us?"

Reaching up to massage the back of his neck, he glanced her way. "Are you asking if I think she's sane?"

"Just your general impressions of her. Honestly."

He shrugged. "Honestly? I think she's more than a little self-centered, vain, overly dramatic and probably a bit paranoid. I doubt that she'll ever be named mother of the year, but she seems like a nice enough woman, on the whole. She's made some very poor decisions in the past, but she's had to pay more severely for them than she should have. And I think she's as sane as most people. There's no reason at all for her to remain locked up."

She had asked for his honest opinion, she reminded herself when she felt tempted to protest his somewhat unflattering assessment of her mother's character. And to be truthful, he was probably right on target with much of it. But at least he didn't think she was crazy.

"So what do you think will happen when you take her home?" he asked. "How are your other siblings going to feel about her showing up so belatedly to testify against your father?"

"Once they hear her story, I'm sure they'll accept her the same way I have."

"And Benton? How will they accept him?"

"The same way they have our other newly found brothers, I suppose. Pragmatically. And as for whatever happens in court, I'm sure as long as Mother tells the truth, justice will be done."

"You trust her to tell the truth? She hates your father, you know."

"I know. But I'll have to trust the attorneys and the jury to sort out truth from bitterness and anger."

He nodded. "If she's as honest about her own mistakes as she was with us today, there's no reason to doubt her story. And she seems determined enough to stick with it, no matter how unpleasant it becomes for her."

She was relieved to hear that. She had wondered if Anna would be able to bear up under the charges of insanity and revenge that Walter's attorneys would most likely throw at her.

"The tabloids are going to love finding out there's yet another illegitimate member of my family."

"Forget the tabloids. Something new will catch their interest soon enough. Besides, maybe the notoriety will help you sell more of your paintings."

"Cynical way to look at it, but maybe you're right."

"Hey, if you can't beat them, use them to your advantage." Sam glanced at his watch then. "I think I'll head on out and let you get dressed for your dinner. I'll let myself in with my key when I return. Don't worry if it's late. There are a few old haunts I might visit."

She lifted her chin. "Fine. Have a good time."

"Yeah. You, too."

She glared at the door after he closed it behind him on his way out. She would never understand that man and the way he changed from one moment to the next.

Maybe that was his intention. Maybe his ex-wife had hurt him so badly that he would never let anyone get too close to him again. A woman could break her heart trying—and Jessica had already spent too much of her life chasing after impossible dreams.

Jessica had left the bathroom light on and the bathroom door partially ajar when she went to bed that night because she didn't want to lie alone in the dark. Still, she doubted that Sam could see that she was awake when he tiptoed into the room sometime after midnight.

From where she lay on the pillows, she watched him lock the door behind himself, then move stealthily toward the sofa, stripping off his jacket on the way. "Did you have a good time?"

Her voice made him freeze. "Sorry. Did I wake you?"

"No. I wasn't asleep."

"Oh." Silhouetted against the light from the bathroom, he sat on the sofa and took off his shoes. "Did you have a nice dinner with your brother?"

"Yes, very nice. He's an interesting man."

"Yeah, I got that impression."

"You didn't like him?"

"I didn't say that."

She silently watched him remove his shirt.

"Good thing we're going home tomorrow," he murmured. "I'd have had to buy some clothes."

At the reminder that their time together was coming to an end, Jessica clutched the sheet more tightly to her chin. "What are you going to do when we get back? Do you have any more clients lined up?"

"A few."

He wasn't in a very talkative mood, apparently. She supposed he was tired from his evening of…whatever he had been doing for the hours he'd been gone. "So, did you have a good time tonight?"

"Shouldn't you be getting some sleep? You've got a big day ahead of you tomorrow."

She bit her lower lip and remained quiet while he went into the bathroom and closed the door behind him, plunging the room into darkness. She regretted the distance between them, but maybe it was better to end things sooner rather than later. He obviously regretted making love with her, and he was sending her the message that there would be nothing more between them once they returned to California.

She told herself that was fine with her. She had a lot going on in her life. She didn't need any more complications. She didn't need Sam Fields.

Whether she still wanted him—well, that was a different issue.

The bathroom door opened again. "You want me to leave this light on?"

"No, you can turn it off."

A moment later the light was gone. She heard him move, and she wondered again how he made his way so well in the dark.

A solid, painful-sounding thud made her wince even as Sam let out a string of muttered curses. She sat up and reached for the lamp beside the bed. The light showed Sam clad only in dark boxer shorts as he leaned over to massage the shin he'd cracked against the coffee table.

"Sorry," he said. "I'm okay."

"Are you sure you're all right?"

"It's just a bruise."

"It sounded as though you hit it pretty hard."

"I'm fine, Jessica. Go to sleep, okay?"

She looked at him, standing there so bare and so gorgeously male. "I'm not sure I can."

What might have been a groan escaped him. "I'm giving you fair warning. Turn off the light and go to sleep or I'm joining you in that bed. I'm not made out of stone, Jessica."

"Neither am I."

"It's probably not a good idea," he said, though he took a step toward the bed even as he spoke. "Everything in your life is so chaotic right now, it's got to be hard for you to think clearly."

"Are you saying I'm crazy?" she asked politely.

"God, no." He sounded appalled.

"Because you would probably be right. Maybe it's

unwise, but I don't care right now. I don't want you to sleep on that couch tonight."

He put one knee on the mattress beside her. "I don't think I'd get much sleep over there even if I tried."

Reaching up to pull him down to her, she smiled against his mouth. "I wouldn't bet on getting much sleep here, either."

He seemed to have no complaints.

Chapter Thirteen

Sam watched Switzerland slowly disappear below him as the airplane climbed above a bank of thick, white clouds. He sat in the window seat with Jessica on his right. Anna sat in the aisle seat.

He would have offered Jessica his hand during take-off, but it hadn't been necessary. She had clung, instead, to her mother. She'd barely looked away from her mother ever since Benton had delivered Anna to the Geneva airport two takeoffs ago.

Sam didn't know quite how Benton had arranged Anna's release, though he suspected money and the mysterious Dr. Rouiller were involved.

Benton had said he couldn't get away from work just now, but that he would come to San Francisco as soon as he could to meet his father and his other half siblings.

He had hugged his mother tightly at the airport and then asked Sam to take care of both Anna and Jessica—a request Jessica had gotten a bit chippy about, since she was so into taking care of herself these days.

Sam was trying hard not to mind that Jessica had practically forgotten his existence since Anna had joined them. It was only natural, he told himself, that she would be absorbed with her long-lost mother after longing for so many years to meet her. They had a lot to catch up on, and the way they were chattering, they were going to try to learn everything there was to know about each other during this flight. Sam might as well pull out a book or something.

Of course, it did seem as if a woman would pay just a little attention to the man who had spent most of the night making passionate love to her, he thought with a scowl.

She did try once or twice to include him in the conversation, but her efforts didn't get them very far. Anna seemed to have little interest in talking to him. Whether she still didn't trust him because he had worked for her husband, or whether she sensed undercurrents between him and her daughter that made her uncomfortable, Sam couldn't say, but her attitude was decidedly cool toward him. Jessica gave him an occasional, faintly apologetic look, but he merely shrugged to indicate that he understood. Mostly.

He wondered if this was the way all the Parks would treat him if he tried to socialize with them. Walter would have no use for him after this, of course, and he would be livid if he knew just how close Sam and Jessica had become on this trip he had futilely tried to prevent. Sam figured he'd be lucky not to end up like the late Jeremy Carlton.

But what about her siblings? How would they feel about the ex-cop-turned-P.I. who had basically stalked and then seduced their sister? At least, that was probably the way they would see it.

He didn't try to delude himself that he was their social equal. Blue collar all the way, that was his background. Father a beat cop and a drunk, mother a struggling immigrant. Half his own family hadn't wanted anything to do with him.

Even with the current scandal, the Parks moved among San Francisco's elite. Emily Parks had married a friggin' king. Sam doubted that he would be seen as a suitable match for the youngest Parks daughter.

Not that he was considering marriage, of course. He wasn't in any hurry to make that mistake again. He was just imagining what would happen if he were even to hint at such a union to members of Jessica's highbrow family.

Jessica finally turned to him when Anna dozed off halfway through the flight. "She's so excited she's worn herself out," Jessica murmured.

"Or maybe she's worn herself out talking," Sam replied with a smile that felt fake. "Guess the two of you had a lot to discuss."

"She wanted to hear everything about my brothers and sister and everything we've all been up to for the past twenty-five years. She's missed so much in our lives."

He had to concede the truth of that. "It was very cruel of your father to take her away from her children."

"He'll never be able to justify that to me," she replied with quiet intensity. "Never."

"There is no justification."

She touched his hand where it rested on the armrest. "Sam?"

Just that light contact had made his heart beat a little faster. Someone who didn't know him better might even think he was lovesick, he thought ruefully. "Yes?"

"Thank you for helping me bring my mother home."

"You're welcome."

She rested her cheek against his shoulder in a gesture that held so much trust it made his chest tighten. "I can't get over how much you sacrificed for me. Dad will never pay you for this, of course. And if he manages to get the word out, he could harm your reputation with your other clients."

"Well, um, I was paid in advance for coming on this trip," he admitted candidly. "Your father transferred some cash into my bank account with a couple of phone calls from jail. He can't get it back now, no matter how furious he gets."

She lifted her head. "Oh. I didn't realize…."

"As for my reputation, I think his is a bit more tarnished at the moment. I'm not too concerned about anything he might have to say to my potential clients."

"Well. Good." She smiled very brightly. "I'm glad you didn't really have anything to lose by switching allegiance."

He wouldn't say that, exactly. He'd been very close

to losing his heart. Good thing he hadn't let it go quite that far, he assured himself.

"So what's the plan when you get back to San Francisco? Are you taking your mother straight back to the estate?"

"Yes. I'll call Cade from the airport and tell him we're on our way. What about you?"

"I'll need to check in at my office, of course. I have a new associate who's been keeping things going in my absence, but I'm sure I'll have a stack of things to take care of."

"A new associate?"

"Mmm. You met him once, actually. In a coffee shop near your bank. He told me you recommended a mocha latte to him."

She grimaced as she obviously remembered the exchange. "I just knew there was something about him…and I thought I was being paranoid again," she added rather accusingly.

"Sorry. You'd gotten too good at spotting me. I had to send someone else."

He wasn't sure why he'd told her. Maybe to remind both of them just who he was and where he'd fit into her life before. Nowhere, actually.

"He's a nice guy," he added lamely. "His name is Ed and he's a retired cop. A widower who needed something to fill his days."

"So you hired him. That's very generous of you."

Sam shrugged. "I needed the help."

"Yes, of course. Watching me was taking up so much of your valuable time."

"Jessica—"

Anna stirred, and Jessica turned immediately back to her mother.

Sam subsided glumly against the window. Okay, that conversation hadn't gone very well.

It was going to be a very long trip home.

Jessica noticed that Sam had his cell phone to his ear almost the moment they stepped off the plane at the airport. She assumed he was calling his office. She placed a quick call to Cade, who seemed relieved that she was back safely and agreed to meet her at the estate in a couple of hours. She didn't tell him who she had with her. She then placed a quick call to Caroline, leaving a message on her machine that she was back in town and would see her soon.

Those were the only people who might have genuinely worried about her while she was away, she mused, ending the second call.

"It feels so strange to be surrounded by so many people," Anna murmured, looking rather dazedly around the crowded airport. "It's been so long…."

Jessica took her mother's arm. "I'm sure there will be a period of adjustment for you," she said sympathetically. "Twenty-five years is a long time to spend strictly in one environment."

Anna's smile was a bit shaky. "So I keep telling myself whenever I find myself almost wishing to be back in the security of my rooms."

Jessica remembered how disorienting it had been for her to be returned to her family and her regular routines after being held for only two weeks by her kidnappers. She could imagine how Anna felt now. "You look a little pale. Why don't I get you a bottled water or something?"

Anna nodded. "Yes, I think I could use that."

Jessica looked at Sam, who had put away his phone and returned to where she and Anna stood. "Would you mind helping my mother find a seat? I'm going to get her some water. She just needs a minute to get her bearings."

"Of course." Despite the rather cool way Anna had treated him, Sam was nothing but solicitous when he offered her his arm. "I see an empty bench right over there, Mrs. Parks. Let me help you."

With the air of a woman who simply couldn't resist an attractive man's attentions, Anna reached out to rest her fingertips lightly on his arm, her smile holding just a shade of regal condescension. Anna might have spent the past twenty-five years in seclusion, but there were certain things she remembered quite well, Jessica thought with wry amusement.

Moving toward a counter where soft drinks and bottled water were sold, she felt the weariness of the long trip making her steps drag a bit. It was almost 6:00 p.m. here in California, nine hours earlier than Switzerland. She'd been up since the crack of dawn, Swiss time, after a night of interrupted sleep. She could use a solid eight hours of unconsciousness.

Not that she was complaining about her lack of sleep last night, she thought with a reminiscent smile. But then that smile faded as she found herself wondering if she would ever spend another night in Sam's arms.

* * *

Anna Parks was a woman who was accustomed to being catered to, Sam couldn't help noticing. Maybe she had spent half her life in an institution, but she'd apparently been treated like royalty there, judging from the way she acted with him.

"There's a wet wipe in the outside pocket of my bag," she said, waving a hand toward the leather tote sitting some six inches from her on the bench. "I saved it from the plane. Perhaps you could get it for me so I can wipe my face?"

"Of course." His mouth twisting a bit, Sam fished out the packet and opened it for her, unfolding the wipe before offering it to her.

"Thank you." She touched the dampened, lemon-scented square of paper delicately to her throat and forehead.

"I know that was a long, hard journey for you," Sam said, trying to sound sympathetic.

Dropping both the towelette and the queenly manner, Anna frowned at him. "I am not an old woman, Mr. Fields."

No. She was only twelve years his senior, actually. The same difference as between himself and Jessica, Sam thought with a slight wince. "I'm sorry. I didn't mean to imply that you are."

She sighed a little, and turned to toss the wipe into a nearby trash can. "I'm afraid I haven't been very polite to you. It's hard to get past the fact that you worked for Walter."

"I understand. Your daughter felt the same way about

me at first." He wasn't entirely sure that Jessica had ever completely gotten over it, either. The closer they'd come to California, the more she'd seemed to pull back from him.

He couldn't help wondering if he was just another check mark on the list of things she had done to defy her father during the past few days.

"Are you in love with my daughter, Mr. Fields?"

Just where *was* Jessica, anyway? He glanced toward the counter toward which she'd been headed, but a crowd of Japanese tourists were milling between there and where he stood, blocking his view. "Um—"

"Feel free to tell me it's none of my business. I merely wanted to see your expression when I asked."

"It's none of your business. And your daughter is very much like you, Mrs. Parks. Both of you have a way of making my head spin."

She seemed to like that. "You have potential, Mr. Fields."

He smiled. "So do you, Mrs. Parks."

"Anna."

"Sam."

She nodded, then looked across the terminal. "It's taking Jessica a while. Is there a long line?"

The tour group had moved on now, and Sam stood to get a better view of the refreshments counter. He frowned when he didn't see Jessica there—or anywhere else in the vicinity.

"Maybe she went to the ladies' room," Anna suggested, looking in the same direction.

"Maybe." Although he would have expected her to

tell him where she was going, it was just like Jessica to pop out of sight without thinking that it would make him nervous.

Anna stood. "Why don't I go in and see? I'm sure she's just freshening up from the trip."

Sam supposed his urge to yell at Jessica was an over-reaction. He wasn't her bodyguard anymore; there was no need for him to be.

Ten minutes later, he had reason to regret giving up his responsibilities so soon.

Jessica was missing.

Jessica had been angry with her father before, but never to this extent. If she hadn't known how closely they were being watched by his guards, she would have thrown herself at him in a genuine effort to throttle him.

"How *dare* you have some goon snatch me from the airport!" she raged at him, strangled fury more than discretion keeping her voice low. "How dare you have me brought here against my will? What gives you the right to frighten me like that again? What kind of monster are you?"

Walter Parks looked more like a haggard old man than a monster at that moment, but that was beside the point as far as she was concerned. She wouldn't allow herself to be concerned with how much he had aged here, not when he was still acting like the same arrogant, overly controlling, heartless man she knew all too well.

Facing her from the other side of a table in the tiny visitation room—one Jessica suspected was usually reserved for attorneys and their clients—Walter held up a hand to silence her. "There's no need for melodrama, Jessica. I know you're angry with me, but it was the only way I could get you to come to me. I've asked you to visit me before, and you refused."

"So you had me kidnapped? How did you know I was at the airport, anyway?"

"I've had a man stationed at the airport for a couple of days. I asked someone to notify him as soon as you returned from your trip, and he took it from there."

She flashed to a mental picture of Sam talking on his cell phone so quickly after they'd stepped off the plane. Surely he hadn't—

Walter went on before she could complete that sickening thought. "I'm sorry you were frightened. I instructed my man to reassure you as soon as you recovered sufficiently to understand where he was bringing you."

"Oh, I knew who was behind it as soon as my head cleared while I was in the car on the way here. What was that he sprayed me with, anyway? My whole mind blanked out until I couldn't even form a coherent thought. I still have a vicious headache."

"I'm sorry. It was just a little something to make you dizzy and disoriented so my man could escort you out of the airport with the excuse that you were ill and needed fresh air. No one questioned him, since you looked so pale and sick. I've been assured that it leaves no lasting effects—other than the headache, I'm afraid."

"Yeah, I'm sure that means a lot to you," she muttered, rubbing her temples. "You bastard."

She had never in her life spoken to him that way, no matter how defiant she had been at times. And it felt good.

It was a measure of his control that he didn't lose his temper, though a wave of red darkened his throat in a sign of anger. "I simply wanted to talk to you, Jessica. I knew you wouldn't come on your own."

"And you've never been overly concerned with giving other people a choice about something you want, have you? I don't know why you want to talk to me, anyway. I've already been to Switzerland. It's certainly too late to stop me now."

"I know you were somehow able to get in to see your mother in the asylum. I want to know what she said to you while you were there. And I want to know how much she convinced you to believe."

Jessica lifted an eyebrow. "Is it possible your source didn't tell you everything?"

"What are you talking about?"

"I brought Mother home with me. And if you make any effort whatever to harm her, I'll see that you fry. Is that perfectly clear?"

The flush of anger receded, leaving Walter pasty pale. "You brought her back with you? That's impossible."

"Is it?"

"She couldn't be released from the institution. I have paperwork."

Her laugh was bitter. "Your 'paperwork' isn't worth the paper it's written on. Turns out Mother has some connections in Switzerland that are just as powerful as you are. She's merely been waiting for the right time to use them to secure her release."

Walter clutched at his chest. "You would do this to me? Your own father."

Her lip curled. "Now who's being melodramatic? Give it up, Dad. You gave it your best shot and you lost. I'm free of you now—and so is my mother."

"She'll destroy me with her lies."

"If you are destroyed, it was your own doing, not hers."

Walter shook his head sadly. "I have always loved you and tried to protect you, Jessica. I love all my children. But what you've done—I can't protect you anymore. You'll all have to live with the shame and the scandal. And you'll have to bear the heartache when your mother turns on you the way she did me. When she abandons you as she did before."

Jessica stood then, and leaned against the table, supporting herself on her hands. The guard in the corner had gone on alert, moving a bit closer to her, but she ignored him. "I don't want to hear you say anything more about her. Yes, she's flawed—as we all are. But she didn't deserve what you did to her. None of us did."

"I just hope you don't live to regret what you've done."

Straightening, Jessica continued to hold his gaze with her own. "You can't scare me anymore, Dad. I can deal with the repercussions of any mistakes I might make on my own. We all have to pay for our actions at some point. You're paying for yours now."

One hand still resting on his chest, Walter was silent for a long moment. When he spoke, there was defeat in his voice for the first time Jessica could remember. "I've lost any love you've felt for me, haven't I?"

Her eyes filled then, despite her efforts to hold back the tears. Her own voice shook. "You didn't lose my love, Dad. You threw it away a long time ago."

Swallowing a sob, she turned toward the door then. "I want to go home."

"My man will drive you. He's been instructed to take you wherever you want to go."

"Goodbye, Dad."

When the guard held the door for her, she walked out without looking back.

It was dark now, but the prison parking lot was so brightly illuminated it could have been noon. Sam spotted Jessica as she stepped out of the prison door, escorted by a rather hulking sort who followed respectfully behind her. Having run that far from his car, Sam slowed a bit to catch his breath—the first time he had taken a full breath since he'd realized Jessica was missing from the airport.

"Thank God," he said.

She must have heard him, even above the bustle of the people coming and going around them. She turned her head and met his eyes. It hurt his heart when her expression didn't change. There was no pleasure to see him in her eyes, no relief. Nothing except a dull, weary pain.

"What a surprise for you to show up here," she said tonelessly.

He resisted an impulse to catch her in his arms only because he suspected she would have pushed him away. She had to be on emotional overload, so he would try to put aside his own need to just touch her and assure himself she was safe. "Damn, I'm glad you're here. I hoped I wasn't wrong about my guess about where you'd been taken."

"Brilliant deduction." She sounded oddly mocking. "Where's my mother?"

"I stashed her at my place with my associate, Ed. He agreed to keep her safe until I brought you back to her. She was very upset when you disappeared, but I convinced her I would find you. Last I saw, she was being consoled by Ed, who looked thoroughly smitten with her."

"You must have been confident you knew where I was."

"As I said, I guessed that if Walter hadn't brought you here, he'd know where you were. I was going to choke it out of him if necessary."

"Mmm." Jessica glanced at the man who lurked behind her. Her voice was cold when she spoke. "You can go. Mr. Fields will take me to my mother."

The man hesitated until Sam gave him a dismissive scowl. And then he nodded and moved away.

Jessica's expression was no warmer when she turned back to Sam. "Where's your car?"

"This way." He reached out automatically to place a hand at her back. She moved immediately away from his touch, making him drop his hand to his side.

Either she was still in shock, or she was just mad at the world in general, Sam figured. He couldn't really blame her for either.

He didn't know what he had done specifically to annoy her, unless it was letting down his guard at the airport so that she was snatched away right out from under his nose. She couldn't be angrier about that than he was at himself.

He still couldn't think about the moment he had realized she was gone without breaking into a cold sweat.

He'd wanted to head straight to Walter Parks right then, but he'd had her semihysterical mother to deal with. He'd kept his composure while he'd taken care of her, but inside he'd been a mess.

If he had been wrong about Walter being behind Jessica's disappearance…

"What happened at the airport?" he asked when they were belted into his SUV.

She told him in as few words as possible about the hand that had suddenly appeared in front of her, and the noxious spray that had clouded her mind and made it so easy for the man to "assist" her to his car.

Belatedly putting two and two together, Sam cursed beneath his breath, his hands clenching on the steering wheel. "It was that guy? The one who followed you out to the parking lot?"

"Yes. Dad's 'man.'"

"Damn it, if I'd known what he did to you, I'd have bashed his face in."

"That isn't necessary."

Maybe not, but it would have made *him* feel better, Sam fumed. Since he couldn't beat up Walter for scaring the hell out of everyone with this stunt, it would have felt pretty damn good to take his frustration out on Walter's representative.

"How could he have known you were going to be there at that time?"

"Dad said someone notified him as soon as we landed."

"Who…?"

Something about the look she gave him then stopped his words in his throat. "Surely you don't think…?"

She turned her head to look out the window. Sam was forcibly reminded of the first time they had left the asylum, when she had all but accused him of scheming in French with Chantal to keep Jessica away from her mother.

He felt his temper rising, and considering what he had been through during that very long day, he wasn't entirely sure of his ability to keep it from boiling over. "I called my office. Ed doesn't know your father, and he didn't call him."

And rather than give her a chance to express further doubts about him, he slammed one fist against the steering wheel. "Damn it, I'm tired of trying to prove myself to you! Have I been nothing more to you than another reckless adventure aimed at hitting your father where it hurts most? Someone you can't really trust, but don't mind using, is that it? What more do you want me to do for you, Jessica?"

"Could you please just take me to my mother?" she whispered.

"Isn't that what I've been doing all along?" he responded bitterly.

She didn't answer.

Chapter Fourteen

An emotional reunion with her mother pretty much put an end to any chance at further conversation between Jessica and Sam. He stood quietly in the background while Jessica described the enforced meeting with Walter to her irate mother.

"I'll see that he pays for that," Anna said between clenched teeth.

"Just tell the truth about whatever happened, Mother," Jessica answered wearily. "He'll get whatever justice he deserves if everyone just tells the truth."

"My poor darling, you're dead on your feet." Anna looked at Sam. "Would you mind taking us home so we can get some rest?"

"Ed's going to drive you to the estate," Sam replied. "I have some things to catch up on here."

"Here" was his home—a small house furnished in what Jessica thought of as "modern bachelor" style. Top of the line electronics, and a minimum of furniture and decorations. She hadn't really had a chance to look around, but she had seen little of his personality in the one room she'd been in, the living room.

Anna smiled at Ed. "That's very kind of you."

The gruff-natured ex-cop cleared his throat and shifted self-consciously on his feet. "No trouble, ma'am."

Jessica knew they should be on their way. She had called Cade and explained the delay to him. Waiting until he had calmed down enough to listen to her again, she made him promise not to leave the estate until she arrived.

She would have to make arrangements to retrieve her car from the Oakland airport. And heaven only knew what had happened to her bags. She didn't know if Sam and Anna had waited long enough to retrieve luggage before going in search of her, but at the moment she just didn't care. She was so very tired.

Ed gestured toward the door, offering to escort them out. Jessica looked at Sam, trying to decide what to say.

He didn't give her much chance to say anything. "You know where to find me if you need me."

Thinking it sounded very much like a brush-off, she nodded. "Good night, Sam."

There was no emotion on his face, but his eyes were dark with them when he looked back at her, his hands stuck in the pockets of his jeans. "Goodbye, Jessica."

She had thought she was too tired to even feel hurt. She had been wrong.

* * *

It was the most unusual Thanksgiving dinner Jessica had ever experienced. Her mother was there, for the first time in Jessica's memory. And her brothers were both accompanied by new spouses this year. Emily was absent, tied by royal duties in her new husband's country, though she had called that morning and promised to be home for Christmas. Benton would also be arriving just before Christmas, giving him a chance to meet all his half siblings at one time.

Anna was thriving on being reunited with her family. Sitting at the head of the table like a queen bee, she beamed at them all. Initial awkwardness was fading as they all spent more time together.

After hearing Anna's story, her children had all agreed to forgive her for the weaknesses that had led to her initial separation from them. They acknowledged that she'd had little say over what had happened to her since. All too familiar with their father's dictatorial behavior, they knew what it was like to be fully controlled by him.

For her part, Anna was delighted to find that her eldest children were happy and well. She immediately fell in love with Cade's adorably blond, five-year-old daughter, Stacy, though it still seemed a bit odd to her to hear herself called grandmother. And, while it had startled her to discover that Cade's new bride, Sara, was the daughter of Jeremy and Marla Carlton, she was soon won over by her daughter-in-law's pleasant nature. Not to mention Sara's obvious adoration of Cade.

The least demonstrative of the Parks offspring, Rowan had accepted his mother's homecoming with his usual equanimity. He, too, was a father now, having married Louanne Brown, the single mother of a precious one-year-old son, Noah. Jessica was actually surprised at how readily Rowan was adapting to his new role as husband and father. Falling in love had given him a new peace within himself that pleased his siblings, since he seemed truly content for the first time in their memory.

No mention was made of the most notably missing member of the family, though he was obviously present in everyone's mind.

Jessica couldn't help looking around at one point and thinking that an outsider looking in at them now would think they were a normal family. She had a fleeting moment of regret for the twenty-five years of separation from their mother, and for the father to whom wealth and power had meant more than family and honor. But it would do her no good to dwell on the past or fret about the future. She should concentrate, instead, on the present.

Not that the present was entirely rosy. The preliminary hearing to determine whether Walter would be tried for all of the charges against him, including the murder of Jeremy Carlton, would begin Monday, and that wasn't going to be easy for any of them.

And then there was Sam. Letting the others carry on the lively conversations around the table, Jessica pushed a piece of turkey around her plate with her fork and let herself drift into memories....

"Darling, are you all right? You look so pensive."

She forced a smile in response to her mother's concerned question. "I'm just enjoying our Thanksgiving together."

She knew the others were surreptitiously studying her face. Her siblings didn't know quite what to make of her since her return from Switzerland. They were all surprised she'd had the nerve to try anything like that again, and that she had managed to pull it off successfully.

Now that they knew Anna wasn't crazy, they could stop worrying so much about Jessica. But that meant they had to make a few adjustments in their thinking about her.

She was also aware that she had changed during that trip. She was no longer Walter Parks's anxious, reclusive, withdrawn youngest child. She had gone to Switzerland to find her mother, but in the process she had reclaimed herself. She had broken away from her fears, her ultrasafe routines, her father's domination.

And, though no one knew but her, she had fallen in love. Even if that love had left heartache behind, it was still a rite of passage she wouldn't have taken back even if she could.

But as she looked at her brothers sitting so happily around the Thanksgiving table with their new families, she couldn't help wishing....

Sam ate Thanksgiving dinner sitting in his recliner in front of a football game on the TV. His meal consisted of a thick turkey and provolone sandwich on whole wheat bread, a bag of jalapeño-flavored potato chips and a beer. He had a bakery pumpkin pie in the refrigerator for later.

Thanksgiving had never been much of an event in his past. Since his mother hadn't grown up with the tradition, she hadn't been overly attached to observing it. His father had seen it only as a day of football and booze. He and Janice hadn't been married long enough to form their own Thanksgiving rituals. As far as Sam was concerned, it was just another day.

But he couldn't help thinking that it must be much more than that for Jessica, especially this year. He could easily picture her sitting at a table with her family, so grateful to have their mother back among them. She was probably having such a good time that no thought of him even crossed her mind.

His appetite suddenly gone, he set the last couple bites of his sandwich aside and tried to muster some enthusiasm for the game.

Jessica stood in front of a canvas in her studio, studied the single stroke of red paint across it, and then set her brush down with a sigh. It was Saturday afternoon, and she had been trying to paint for the past three hours, this one red line all she had to show for her efforts.

For some reason she couldn't stop thinking about Sam. How could she miss him this badly when he had been in her life such a short time?

You know where to find me if you need me.

The memory of his words made her shiver. She wouldn't go so far as to say that she needed him, now that she had declared herself an independent woman who no longer relied on anyone but herself. But she had to concede that she wanted him.

She should be accustomed by now to not having everything she wanted.

Wandering out of the studio a few minutes later, she

went into her bedroom. She had spent the first couple of nights since arriving from Switzerland in the main house with her mother, but then she had returned to her own cottage. Anna seemed to be comfortably ensconced in the mansion again, but Jessica would never again feel that it was her home. There were too many painful memories for her there. She would always enjoy visiting her mother at the mansion, if that was where she chose to stay, but Jessica needed to find a place that was hers alone.

On an impulse, she opened the drawer of her dresser where she had stashed the small items she'd found in her possession during the weeks before her trip. She took them out of the drawer and arranged them on her bed, studying each one thoughtfully.

A knock on her front door made her straighten her shoulders and draw a deep breath before she moved to answer it. She wasn't looking forward to this visit, if her caller was who she expected.

Caroline Harper stood on the doorstep wearing designer clothes and a slightly puzzled smile. "I'm here, just as you requested," she announced unnecessarily.

"So I see. Come in."

Studying Jessica from the corner of her eyes, Caroline entered the living room and tossed her purse on a table. "It's really good to see you, Jess. You look great. How's your mother?"

"She's adjusting very well, thank you." Though Jessica hadn't seen Caroline since she'd returned, they'd had one long telephone conversation, during which Jessica had caught Caroline up on everything that had happened. Leaving out a few pertinent details, of course, mostly related to Sam.

It was only after that talk that Jessica had begun to think about all the times she and Caroline had been together in the past few months. And about a few other things that had been nagging at her since she'd returned from Switzerland, making only two calls from the airport.

"So, why did you want to see me so badly today? It's not that I didn't want to see you, you know that, it's just that it's sort of a hectic time for me."

Jessica motioned toward her bedroom door. "I'd like to show you something. If you wouldn't mind...?"

"Okay. Sure." Looking even more bemused now, Caroline entered the bedroom with Jessica close behind her. Caroline stopped abruptly when she saw the objects spread out on the bedspread. "What—?"

"I thought I was going crazy, you know," Jessica said conversationally. She moved to stand by the bed, picking up the clown-shaped refrigerator magnet. "I was terrified that my father would have me locked away."

"I don't know what..."

Caroline's denial faded into silence when Jessica looked up at her. "Please don't lie to me, Caroline. Not this time."

"Damn it." Apparently unable to look into Jessica's eyes, Caroline half turned away. "He convinced me it was for your own good."

"You thought it was good for me to think I was going insane?" Jessica was proud that her voice still sounded detached, unemotional.

"He said you were getting out of control. That you

were planning some crazy trip to Switzerland to break your crazy mother out of the institution. He said he was having you watched, but that he worried you would get away from him. He thought if little things started happening to make you doubt yourself, you'd be too frightened to try anything, giving him time to get help for you."

"How many 'little things' did you arrange for me?"

"A few. He might have had some other people doing things, too. I don't know for sure."

"You altered my paintings?"

"Yes. I was afraid that was carrying things a little too far."

Jessica might have laughed bitterly at that had it not hurt so badly. "He paid you."

Caroline hesitated only a moment before nodding. "I needed the money. My credit cards were maxed out and I was having trouble making the payments. It isn't cheap living in the style to which I would like to become accustomed, you know," she added with a characteristic attempt at sarcastic humor. "Not that you would know about that, having grown up on this luxurious estate with everything you ever wanted."

When Jessica didn't respond in any way to that, Caroline shrugged a little and went on, "I believed him, you know. He seemed so sincere when he talked to me. He was the very image of the concerned father—the one I always wished I'd had for myself. I believed your mother was insane, I believed your father was being framed for those crimes, and I believed that you were in trouble and wouldn't let anyone help you."

Jessica wasn't particularly swayed by Caroline's arguments. She suspected the money had a lot to do with making her usually shrewd and cynical friend more gullible than usual when it came to Walter's lies.

"You notified my father that I was back in town, didn't you?" she asked quietly. "I called you almost as soon as I touched down, and when you got the message, you relayed it to my father so he could have me snatched from the airport."

"I didn't know that was what he was going to do, of course," Caroline replied defensively. "I just assumed he wanted to make sure you were safe, maybe get you straight into counseling. And I didn't know your mother was with you. You didn't say on the message."

"It's a good thing I didn't mention her. He might have arranged to have her taken, too, had he known. And I'm not entirely sure she would have been safely returned. She's too much of a threat to him."

"You really think he's guilty of murder."

Jessica stepped squarely into Caroline's view. "I know he is," she said steadily. "He removed all doubt when he ordered someone to use a noxious spray on me and kidnap me from that airport. And I know that you're guilty of conspiring with a murderer to betray someone who thought of you as her only close friend."

"Jessica, I'm sorry. I didn't mean—"

"Please leave now."

Caroline hesitated only a moment before turning for the door. Jessica followed, this time to lock the door behind her former friend for the final time.

Caroline paused just inside the doorway, looking

back with an expression in her eyes that might have been genuine regret. "You've always known what I really was. You always seemed to like me, anyway."

"I did. Yet I mistakenly believed that I could trust you, as well. I never wanted you to be perfect, Caroline, but I needed you to be on my side. It turns out the only side you were on was your own. I can't be friends with someone who's just like my father."

Her face going pale, Caroline started to speak, but then simply turned and left.

There were tears in Jessica's eyes when she locked the door. And a hole in her heart that grew bigger every time someone else who had mattered to her walked away from her.

Sitting at the back of the crowded courtroom, Sam watched as Linda Mailer Carlton, Walter Parks's former accountant, placed one hand on a Bible, raised the other, then swore to tell the truth. The room grew silent as she began to testify, nervously toying with a small medallion that hung from a chain around her neck as she did so.

The mounting evidence being presented against Walter Parks was damning. Smuggling, embezzlement, tax fraud, murder. It was becoming very clear that Jeremy Carlton had begun to suspect that his partner was involved in illegal activities and had decided to quietly gather evidence against him. The prosecution claimed that Walter had been planning an offshore pickup of smuggled gems, and that Jeremy had hoped to catch him in that act. Walter had killed him rather than risk paying for his actions.

There were witnesses, and recently uncovered papers and financial books to back up the prosecution's charges. Marla Carlton had told her children everything just before she died, including that her brother, Derek, knew the truth, if they could find him and convince him to talk.

The defense team had an increasingly difficult, if not impossible, task ahead of them.

Walter Parks had built an empire, but he had done so on the blood of a former friend, and the sacrifice of his honor and his family and now his freedom. Sam shook his head in disgust, wondering how anyone could think even an empire was worth that extremely high price.

Parks looked like death, Sam couldn't help thinking as he studied the man sitting at the front of the courtroom. He must have aged twenty years in the past month. His hair had gone white, his skin gray, and there was a defeated stoop to his shoulders that contrasted distinctly with his former arrogantly assured posture. Was it possible the old man had acknowledged himself just how much he had thrown away in his long quest for wealth and power?

Sam turned his gaze to Jessica, who sat near the front of the courtroom between her brothers. Anna was in a different place, of course, secluded as were the other witnesses. Jessica was pale, but composed, listening attentively to Linda Carlton's testimony with no expression showing on her face.

It was torture to sit in the same room with her. Sam didn't even know why he was here, really. He'd simply felt he had to attend, in case Jessica needed him—most unlikely, considering she had her family to turn to now. Must be habit making him still watch out for her.

Damn, but she had hurt him with her lack of trust in him. How could she have believed he was still working with Walter even after all they had shared in Switzerland? And how could he have let himself care enough that she could break his heart that easily, he added with a low grunt of self-recrimination that made the tabloid reporter next to him glance at him in curiosity.

He ran into Jessica in a hallway very late that afternoon. She had just stepped out of the ladies' room, and he'd been returning from a walk outside to stretch his legs when they came face-to-face, their eyes locking.

Jessica's smile was a bit tremulous. "I saw you in the back of the courtroom earlier."

He nodded, keeping his hands in his pockets in case they attempted to reach for her despite his best intentions. "I wanted to know that you were going to be okay."

She moistened her lips with the tip of her tongue, and he was proud of himself that he didn't groan aloud. "I'll be fine, Sam. But thank you for being concerned."

He merely nodded.

She looked down to dig into the red tote bag she carried over one shoulder. "I brought something for you," she said.

He lifted an eyebrow. "How did you know I would be here?"

"I didn't, for certain." She pulled something from the bag and extended her hand.

His frown deepened when he found himself holding a set of what appeared to be car keys. "What is this?"

"The keys to my father's limo. I promised them to you if you helped me get to my mother, remember?"

Shaking his head, he held them out to her. "I don't want the damn limo."

But she had stepped back, putting her hands behind her. "I don't renege on my promises. I told my brothers what we said, and they agreed that I made a bargain. The limo will be delivered to you. You can sell it or drive it or whatever you want to do with it."

"Damn it, Jessica, that was meant as a joke. I didn't do anything for you in expectation of being paid."

"I know that now," she whispered. "It's taken me a while to realize that you were the only one who *wasn't* after anything from me. And I repaid you with such terrible accusations. I'm so sorry, Sam."

He could feel his heart opening again, slowly and painfully, still aching from the last time he'd let her in. There was a plea in her eyes when she gazed up at him, and he wanted very badly to give in to it, and to his own simmering need.

"Jessica. We're ready to go back in."

Somewhat impatiently, she looked beyond Sam, speaking to someone behind him. "I'll be right there, Cade." She looked back at Sam then. "Can you ever forgive me for doubting you?"

He leaned closer to her. Her mouth lifted to his when she realized his intention.

Ignoring the crowds milling around them, Sam kissed her slowly, lingeringly. And then he drew away. "Goodbye, Jessica. Be happy."

He dropped the limo keys into her tote bag before he turned and walked away, leaving a little part of his soul behind with her.

Chapter Fifteen

Jessica hung a delicate crystal ball from a fragrant fir branch, then stepped back to admire the way the faceted glass reflected the glow of the tiny lights woven into the tree. It was a lovely Christmas tree, she thought. Decorated in crystal ornaments and silver ribbons and hundreds of white lights, it sparkled cheerily in the big bow window of the mansion's front parlor.

She and Anna had considered not putting up a tree this year, but as the holiday rapidly approached, they reconsidered the decision. It would be Anna's first Christmas with her grandchildren, and she wanted them to have special memories of the occasion, though Noah was too young to remember, of course. Still, he would enjoy the lights and the presents, and his cousin, Stacy, would have a few memories of this holiday as she grew older. That seemed important to Anna.

It was important to Jessica, too. During the past difficult month she had been forcibly reminded of how much her family meant to her when they had all needed so badly to cling to each other.

Walter Parks was dead.

He had suffered a heart attack only hours after the end of the preliminary hearing, at which the judge had found more than sufficient evidence to hold him over for trial. There'd been little doubt in anyone's mind, including Walter's, that a trial would end in convictions on all the charges. Justice had caught up with him, and he had been unable to withstand the shock and humiliation.

No one could have known he was so ill, Jessica had tried to assure herself. It wasn't as if he'd told anyone he'd been suffering chest pains. They had simply assumed it was stress and mortification that had caused him to look so gray and sick at the hearing.

Still, she would always live with a pang of guilt that her last words to him had been such cold and angry ones. No matter what he had done, or for what reasons, he had been her father. She had loved him once, if for no other reason.

She and her siblings had grieved the loss of the father they had never really had, but the tragedy had brought them closer together. They had vowed not to take each other for granted so much in the future.

"It's beautiful, Jessica," Anna said as she came into the room holding a big basket of white poinsettias. "Stacy will say it looks like a fairy-tale tree."

"That's exactly what she'll say." Jessica turned away from the tree to smile at her mother, who was arranging the flowers on the mantel. "The house looks beautiful, Mother. Even prettier than it did when Dad brought in professional decorators every year to deck it out to impress the neighbors."

Anna had briefly considered selling the house after Walter's death, but she had decided to delay that decision for a while. Though her few years here had not been happy ones, this was where her children had been raised. It was a beautiful showcase of a house—all it had ever needed to make it a real home was love.

Anna stepped back to admire her handiwork. "I enjoyed decorating for Christmas when the twins were little. Then Walter decided that doing our own decorating was beneath our social status, and he insisted on bringing in professionals who paid little attention to what I wanted. Christmas changed after that."

Her face clouded for a moment, but then she shook her head. "We've agreed not to dwell on the unhappy memories. I promise I won't bring them up again."

"It's okay if you need to talk about it sometime," Jessica assured her gently. "I'm always here to listen."

"I know, darling, and I thank you. But there's really very little left to say about my unhappy past. I would rather concentrate on the future. It's going to be such a lovely Christmas, with everyone together once again."

Jessica smiled, nodded and tried to ignore the little pang in her heart at the thought of spending another holiday with her blissful newlywed siblings.

Anna seemed to have become quite perceptive about

Jessica's feelings during the past month together. She moved to sit beside her daughter on the couch that faced the tree. "What's wrong, darling? Are you sad about your father not being with you this Christmas? You needn't feel that you can't express that regret to me, you know, no matter how I might still feel about him."

"I'm sorry he couldn't have been the kind of father who would have appreciated the time together, but I've accepted his loss. I've even come to realize that it was better this way. Prison would have been torturous for him. Maybe he deserved to spend more time there, but I can't help being relieved that he didn't have to."

"You have such a kind heart." Anna lifted a hand to touch Jessica's cheek. "I should try to be more like you."

A little embarrassed, Jessica only smiled.

That smile faded fast when Anna dropped her hand and asked, "Have you heard from Sam since the hearing?"

Jessica kept her eyes focused intently on the tree. "Um, Sam? No, why do you ask?"

"You think I didn't recognize what I saw in your eyes when you looked at him? I've been in love a few times, you know. Enough to identify the emotion when I see it in my own daughter's face."

"I don't—" But Jessica stopped before she could complete her denial. She wouldn't start out her new relationship with her mother by lying to her.

"I did fall in love with him," she admitted quietly. "But even if he had started to love me in return—which is a big if, since he was hurt very badly in a divorce and wasn't eager to get involved that seriously again—I blew it by not trusting him when I should have. I hurt him, Mother, when all he was trying to do was help me. He can't forgive me for that."

Anna took her hand, cradling it in both of hers. "Have you asked him to forgive you?"

"Yes." She remembered the way he had kissed her in the courthouse before he had walked away from her. There had been no mistaking that it was a kiss of goodbye.

Whatever chance she might have had of making Sam love her had died that night in his car when she had accused him of calling her father to have her kidnapped from the airport.

"It wasn't just my lack of trust in him," she added with a sad shake of her head. "He sat through the entire hearing, you know. He heard exactly what kind of man my father was. Between that and all the other emotional baggage our family carries, who could blame him for wanting to run?"

Anna seemed to take offense at that. "I don't see those old scandals deterring Sara from loving Cade."

"Of course not. Her family's part of it all."

"And what about Louanne? She has willingly brought her son into our family to live as one of us."

"By the time Noah's old enough to understand, this will all be ancient history as far as he's concerned."

"And Lazhar? How do you explain his continuing loyalty to Emily?"

"He's the king of a country very far away from this one. He certainly doesn't have to worry about salacious San Francisco gossip."

"And you think Sam *does* worry about that sort of thing?"

Jessica cleared her throat. "He has his business reputation to consider."

"Ah. Perhaps my impression of him was wrong. I thought he was a man who cared little about what other people thought of him—except for you, of course. A man to whom money wasn't particularly important."

"You don't understand, Mother."

Anna gave her a sad smile. "I have so many regrets about my life, my darling. So very many. But the one thing that hurts me most, and will always hurt me, is that I didn't fight harder to stay with the ones I loved. I was too afraid to take the risk."

"Look, it doesn't really matter why he walked away. The simple truth is that he didn't want me." Jessica choked a little then. "He didn't want me."

"Then he's an idiot," Anna said promptly, reaching out to take Jessica in her arms. "Any man who wouldn't want you is an idiot."

For the first time in her life, Jessica was able to cry on her mother's shoulder. Yet not even the comfort she found there completely eased the pain.

Sam called himself an idiot even as he approached the front door of the mansion. A huge wreath hung in the center of that door. Other decorations gave a cheerful holiday air to the formerly cold and formal-looking house. A huge Christmas tree was visible in one of the front windows, looking as if it was ready for a happy family to gather beneath it with their gifts.

Several cars parked in the circular driveway indicated that members of the family had gathered for this

Christmas Eve. Though darkness had already fallen, the front gates stood invitingly open, which had allowed Sam to drive through without difficulty. The security consultant in him cringed at the carelessness, but he couldn't help thinking of how much more welcoming the Parks estate seemed now than it had the first time he had seen it.

He stood for quite a while in front of that door, trying to decide whether to ring the bell or simply turn around and go. He could leave the prettily wrapped package he held on the doorstep. It had Jessica's name written on a little card, and even though he hadn't signed his name, she would know who had left the gift.

If she wanted to call him afterward, she knew how to reach him. If she didn't call…well, that would be a message in itself.

Because he could so easily imagine himself following through with that plan, and because it made him feel like a coward just to consider it, he made himself reach out and ring the bell. If he was lucky, a member of the housekeeping staff would answer and he could leave the gift with her. That way he wouldn't interrupt Jessica's holiday with her family, he rationalized.

He probably looked like a delivery guy in his battered brown leather jacket, oatmeal-colored pullover and old, faded jeans. Maybe he should have dressed up a little more, but he'd left his house on impulse and hadn't stopped to…

Of all the people there must be in that monstrously big house, it had to be Jessica who answered the door.

Sam figured he should have expected it, considering the way things had unfolded between them so far.

She looked stunned to see him. There was no other word to describe the look on her face when she recognized him. "Sam!"

"The, um, gates were open," he said, motioning vaguely behind him. "I hope it's okay that I just drove on in."

"Of course. We're expecting Derek and Benton to stop in this evening for a Christmas Eve visit with Mother. That's why the gates are... Why are you here?"

Damned if he could remember at the moment. Not when she was standing so close, looking so pretty in her snug red sweater and dark, low-riding jeans that showed just a sliver of flat tummy. Heeled boots gave an illusion of height, and silver hoops swung from her ears. She had cut her hair, he noted automatically. Still shoulder length, it was more layered now, a little shaggier. He liked it.

"Sam?"

"Yeah." She smelled like Christmas, he thought. Sort of a mixture of evergreen and gingerbread, hinting that she had been decorating and baking. A delicious combination. He blinked and held out the package he'd been holding. "I brought you a present."

He doubted she could have looked more wary if he'd said, "I brought you a box full of poisonous snakes." She looked at the box as if she expected it to explode. "A present?"

"Yeah. Look, maybe this was a bad idea. I didn't mean to interrupt your time with your family." He thrust the package at her and started to turn away.

"Sam, wait. Please don't go."

He froze in response to the note of pleading in her voice. She gave him a shy smile when he turned back to look at her again. "You aren't interrupting anything."

He swallowed and nodded.

"May I open this now?"

"Sure. If you want to."

She closed the front door behind her, giving them privacy in the cool night air. Little bells jingled merrily in the wreath with the motion. Stripping away the wrapping paper, she handed it to him to hold while she opened the box inside.

A moment later she looked back up at him, and this time there were tears streaming down her cheeks. "This is…perfect," she whispered.

Feeling incredibly awkward, he resisted an impulse to shuffle his feet. "It's just— It isn't— I just thought you might like it."

"I love it." The gift was a high quality snow globe, the thick glass orb supported by a wooden base. Inside the globe was a snowy landscape featuring an intricately detailed Swiss chalet with the Alps in the background. Jessica shook the globe lightly, making snow swirl around the scene. "It reminds me of that morning…."

"'Breakfast in a snow globe,'" he quoted her, knowing exactly which morning she referred to. "That's what it made me think of, too."

The expression in her eyes almost made his heart stop. "I came here thinking maybe I would ask if you would like to see me again sometime," he said roughly. "Have dinner, maybe, or see a movie. But now—"

"You've changed your mind?"

"Yeah. I don't want to date you, Jessica. My feelings for you are way beyond that. I know I'm not part of your social stratum—hell, I'm blue collar to my roots—and I know I'm too old for you, and I know I'm not the easiest guy in the world to get along with at times. If you need more time for me to convince you that we belong together, I'll try to be patient and court you the way you deserve to be courted. Just don't tell me there isn't a chance for us. Don't—"

"I love you, Sam."

The quiet interruption made his words jam in his throat. "You—"

"I don't care about any of those things you see as obstacles between us. I've loved you since our first dance in Zurich. I thought I had thrown it all away when I lashed out at you after seeing my father that night. I never thought of you as just a way to get back at my father, but I can see where you must have believed that when I behaved so unfairly toward you. I thought I'd hurt you too badly for you to ever forgive me."

"I thought you had, too," Sam admitted, regretting the pain he saw in her eyes in response to the admission. "I told myself it wasn't worth setting myself up to be hurt like that again. And that you were better off without me, anyway. But I couldn't stay away. You're all I can think about, all I care about. I need you back in my life."

Holding the snow globe in both hands, she moved closer to him and lifted her face toward his. He took her in his arms and crushed her mouth beneath his, neither noticing nor caring that the globe was digging into his chest.

* * *

Sam slid the red sweater over Jessica's head and tossed it carelessly to one side of the bedroom in her cottage. "Red underwear," he murmured with a smile, stroking her nipple through her lacy bra. "Have I ever mentioned that I really go for red underwear?"

"No, as a matter of fact—" His mouth covered hers, smothering her reply.

After he had kissed her until her head was spinning, he eased off her jeans, finding and approving of the tiny red panties beneath. He took his time removing the undergarments, kissing and caressing and teasing every inch of her until she was the one who started frantically stripping them away, longing desperately for the feel of his bare skin against hers.

And when there was nothing left between them but desire, she pushed him onto his back and proceeded to drive him as crazy with need as he had her. She might be rather new at this sort of thing, she thought as a groan tore from his throat, but she was a very fast learner.

He caught her hips in his hands, guiding her to him as she straddled him. She lowered her mouth to his, letting their tongues mate even as he thrust upward to join them. Switzerland hadn't been paradise, after all, Jessica mused with her last coherent thought. Paradise had turned out to be right here, in her very own home.

"I'm not sure I've told you that I love you."

Jessica smiled and stroked a finger down the center of Sam's chest, which was still rising and falling rather rapidly. "Oh, I think you've made it clear enough."

"I'll say it, anyway. I love you, Jessica."

She kissed his shoulder. "I love you, too."

Resting his cheek against her hair, he sighed deeply. Contentedly.

After several long, silent moments, he spoke again. "I'm sorry about your father."

She nestled more snugly into him. "I got your flowers. Thank you."

The card had said simply, "I'm sorry for your loss. Sam." She had wondered at the time what he would have thought if he'd known she was hurting as badly over losing him as she had been the father who'd been so estranged from her.

"I hope you know that he did love you, in his own warped way. He really did want me to keep you safe, even as he worked to stop you from having what you wanted so badly."

"I know. He just wasn't capable of loving his family more than he loved his power."

She told him then about Caroline, and the way Walter had used and twisted their friendship with his money and his lies. About the fear she had lived with that she was losing her mind.

"My God, I'm sorry, Jessica. So many people you cared about have hurt you and betrayed you. No wonder it's so hard for you to trust anyone now."

She lifted her head then to look at him. "I trust you with my life. And with all my heart. I never want you to doubt that again. Of all the good people I've known, you are the most honorable, Sam."

She watched in fascination as a flush worked its way

up from his throat to his cheeks. "Don't make me out to be some sort of hero," he said gruffly. "I'll only end up disappointing you if you do that. I'm a long way from perfect. I've got plenty of flaws."

"I've come to realize that everyone has flaws. It's what we accomplish despite them that matters. I don't expect you to be perfect, Sam. I know you'll hurt my feelings at times, and you'll make me furious at others. Just as I can guarantee that I'll do things to make you mad, since I seem to have a talent for that. But the one thing I believe implicitly is that you will never disappoint me."

"I promise that I will never intentionally betray your trust in me," he said a bit shakily. "I will love you and stand by you for the rest of my life, if you'll have me."

Her throat tightened. "Careful, Sam. That sounds a lot like a proposal. And I know how you feel about getting married again."

"No, you don't. I want nothing more than to marry you, Jessica Parks. I want a real marriage this time, based on love and trust and total commitment. I can learn to trust again if you can."

Her eyes had filled with pesky tears again, but her voice was steady. "I'll never betray your trust in me, either. You have my word on that—and I would die before I break that promise."

He stroked his fingertips along the line of her jaw. "What have I done to deserve you?"

"I'm the one who should be asking that. Why don't we just agree to spend the rest of our lives making the best of our good fortune?"

"Is that a yes?"

She smiled against his lips. "That is most definitely a yes."

She knew her family would be wondering what was keeping her away from them for so long, even though she had left word that she would be in her cottage. She knew they would be eager to meet Sam and would be delighted to hear about her engagement—especially Anna, who had decided that she approved of Sam when he had been so kind to her at the airport. But there was really no hurry, she decided as Sam twisted to slide her beneath him. They had the rest of their lives to let love heal the wounds of the past.

As she wrapped her arms around Sam's neck, she realized that there was no more powerful cure.

* * * * *

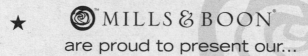